Into the Darkness

Crimson Worlds: Refugees I

Jay Allan

Crimson Worlds Series

Also By Jay Allan

www.crimsonworlds.com

Into the Darkness

Into the Darkness is a work of fiction. All names, characters, incidents, and locations are fictitious. Any resemblance to actual persons, living or dead, events or places is entirely coincidental.

ISBN: 978-0692354827

Chapter One

Excerpt from Admiral Compton's Final Communique to Augustus Garret:

You have seen the scanning reports, as I have. You know there is no other option. I know you, perhaps better than anyone else, and I understand how this will affect you. It is a crushing burden, and yet that doesn't matter. You have no choice, my old friend, and you know it as well as I. It is not just victory that hangs in the balance, not even the survival of the fleet. Nothing less than the continued existence of the human race rests upon your actions in the next few hours. If you allow this enemy force to get through the warp gate and into the X1 system, we will never stop them. They will destroy every planet in Occupied Space. When they are finished, there will be nothing but the unburied dead to mark that men had ever lived, silent graveyards where once prosperous worlds had been.

You have been more than a friend to me, Augustus...more than a brother. We have laughed, supported each other, gone to war together. I had no idea, when I left home for the Naval Academy all those years ago, that I would find a friend like you. We had quite a run together, Admiral Garret. It's been my great honor and pleasure to be at your side...to watch your back, as you have watched mine.

Though I know it is pointless, I will say this anyway. Do not blame yourself. You do not have a choice in this. Do your duty, as you always have, and then step boldly into the future. I am asking you to do this, to save mankind. Mourn the lost, as we always have, but think of me—and all those who serve with me—no differently than the thousands who have died in our many battles. Drink a toast to me and remember friendship fondly, shed a tear if you must...but do not spend the rest of your life tormenting yourself. It is my final request of you.

Go now. You will have to move ahead without me, my comrade, bear the burdens alone that we would have shared. I'm sorry I won't be there to help you face the next battle. Because we both know there will be another. There always is. And I know you will be ready, that you will stand again in the breach and do what you must. As you have done all your life.

There is one last thing I ask of you, Augustus. Look after Elizabeth for me. Try to ease her pain. I was going to ask you to tell her I love her, that I always have, but that would be selfish of me. I am gone to her, and I know I shall never see her again. I would have her forget me, move forward...to have a happy life, and not to wallow in misery over what can never be. It is my solace to imagine that happiness without me waits in her future.

You are the best, most honorable man I've ever known, Augustus Garret. Goodbye, my friend.

AS Midway
Deep in System X2
The Fleet: 242 ships, 48,371 crew

"You are clear to land in Bay B, Admiral Hurley." There was a strange sound to the launch bay coordinator's voice, not fear exactly, but something cold, almost dead.

"Acknowledged," Hurley replied. She knew, of course, what was happening. She'd seen the enemy ships on her own scanners, hundreds of them, more than the entire massed fleets of humanity could hope to defeat. She also knew what would happen next, what *had* to happen. Admiral Garret would detonate the massive bomb General Cain and Dr. Hofstader had found—and if the CEL scientist was as brilliant as everyone said, the warp gate leading back to X1, to human space, would be disrupted for several centuries, an impassable obstacle instead of an open pathway.

It was an ideal way to end the war, cutting off the massive First Imperium forces from human space without a fight. But there was one problem. *Midway*—and the rest of Compton's fleet, nearly half of humanity's combined naval strength—was on the opposite side of the system, light hours from the Sigma 4 gate. There was no way they could get back, not before the First Imperium forces were able to transit. And Hurley knew that was something Admiral Garret simply could not allow. No matter what the cost.

She understood the tone in the coordinator's voice. Word had to be spreading through the fleet. They were facing almost certain death, and everyone had to accept that in his or her own way. She was confident the Alliance spacers, at least, would stay at their posts and go down fighting. She knew damned well she would. Her fighters had been savaged in the combat, but they weren't done yet, not by a long shot. And as soon as they could refuel and rearm, she intended to lead them back into the fray.

"Bring us in, Commander." Hurley glanced over at her pilot. Commander Wilder had been under instructions from Admiral Garret to keep Hurley away from the worst of the fighting. Greta Hurley had no peers in the field of fighter-bomber tactics, and Garret knew she tended to put herself in the forefront of her squadrons. He'd been determined to keep his aggressive fighter commander from getting herself killed, and knowing how stubborn Hurley was, he'd figured a secret pact with her pilot seemed the likeliest way to achieve success. Wilder had made a noble effort, but in the end Hurley—and events—had prevailed, and Wilder had joined his commander in taking their fighter right into the maw of an enemy battleship—and delivering the killing blow to the behemoth.

"Yes, Admiral," the pilot replied. "Forty-five seconds to landing."

Hurley leaned back in her seat and took a deep breath. She had about 240 fighters left, less than half of what she had led into battle just the day before. But it was still a potent force. They might not have any real hope of survival, but she silently vowed that her people would sell their lives dearly to the enemy.

She looked through the forward cockpit, to the hulking form of *Midway* beyond. Compton's flagship was one of the greatest machines of war ever constructed by man, two kilometers of sleek hull, bristling with weapons. Until the First Imperium invasion, mankind had considered itself strong and technologically advanced, impressed, as men so easily were, by its own achievements. But now they were fighting an enemy thousands of years ahead of them. Courage and innovation had bridged that gap, at least in the battles on the Line, allowing the outmatched humans not only to stem the enemy tide, but to drive the First Imperium fleets back. But those victories had only stirred the enemy to bring forth its full strength, and now humanity was faced with the real power of their enemy. Against the massive array now approaching, even a battlewagon like *Midway* seemed weak and small.

The fighter moved steadily toward a large opening in *Midway's* hull. Hurley could see tiny shapes moving around the bay, technicians clad in environmental suits and small tractors carrying parts and supplies toward the fighters sitting in their cradles. A landing bay during a battle was a busy place. It took a lot of support to keep her birds in space and fighting.

She felt the deceleration as her ship slowed gradually. Landings could sometimes be a rough affair but not with a pilot like Commander Wilder at the controls. Hurley had been a great pilot herself, and a feared Ace who had racked up a still unmatched number of kills in the days before her advancing rank had, at least ostensibly, taken her out of the direct fighting. But she had to admit to herself, Wilder was even better than she had been. He worked the controls of the fighter like they were extensions of his own body. And now he dropped the craft onto the metal floor of the bay so softly, she could barely tell they had landed.

"Your ship is the last one, Admiral," the coordinator's voice said. "We're closing the bay doors, so if you wait a minute, we'll have the deck pressurized."

"Understood, Commander." She reached around and unhooked her harness, turning toward Wilder as she did. "That was a hell of a landing, Commander." She paused for an instant then added, "In fact, the entire battle was an example of magnificent piloting." Hurley lived and breathed fighter-bomber tactics, and her praise was highly sought after among her pilots and crews.

"Thank you, Admiral." She could hear the satisfaction in his voice at her words, but also a dark undercurrent. He had clearly come to the same grim conclusion she had. They were dead men and women, all of them. It was just a question of time—and how much damage they could inflict before they were wiped out.

She walked across the cramped cabin of the fighter bomber, heading toward the hatch as the other three crew members unhooked themselves and followed. She knelt down and waited.

"Landing bay pressurized," came the announcement a few seconds later. Hurley punched at the keys next to the small door, and the hatch slid open. She put her leg down, and her foot found the small ladder almost immediately. She climbed down to the deck and turned around, her eyes looking for the crew chief.

"Chief," she said as she spotted him, "I want these birds turned around in record time…and I do mean fucking record time, you understand me?" Hurley had a fearsome reputation among the maintenance crews. Most of them felt she asked for the impossible, yet they somehow managed to do what she commanded anyway. And it was hard to argue with a fighting admiral with Hurley's chops—especially when she'd just come back with barely half the birds she'd launched with a few hours before.

"The crews are ready, Admiral." Sam McGraw was old-school navy all the way, a chief petty officer who drove his staff relentlessly and who could stand up to any officer, even to a superior as terrifying as Greta Hurley. "They're already at work on the birds that landed ahead of you." He was waving his arm as he spoke, gesturing to a work party to get started on the admiral's ship. It was mildly inappropriate. Technically, he should have been at attention while addressing the admiral. But Hurley didn't give a shit about foolishness like that. No one had ever turned her fighters around like McGraw, and she wasn't about to give him shit for pushing his crews—or worrying about his job instead of kissing her three-star ass.

"Very well, Chief. I'll leave you to it." She saw a sudden difference in McGraw's expression, shock, tension. Then the non-com snapped to attention. She knew the veteran petty officer well enough to understand only one person on *Midway* could generate that kind of reaction from him.

"Well done out there, Greta."

She turned abruptly and snapped to attention herself. "Thank you, Admiral Compton." Greta Hurley was a force of nature, but Admiral Terrance Compton was like a god striding among mortals. Compton had nearly fifty years of service, having fought in both the Second and Third Frontier Wars. He'd been a hero of the rebellions, steadfastly refusing orders to bombard civilian targets, and somehow maintaining control of the fleet through the entire crisis. His victories were too numerous to be easily counted. He was the other half of the legend of Augustus Garret, the only naval officer who could match his lifelong friend's prowess.

"I take it you understand the current situation, Admiral?" Compton's voice was serious, but it lacked the grim resignation she'd heard in everyone else's.

"Yes, sir," she replied.

"Well, I've got a plan, Greta, and I need your help to pull it off."

"Of course, sir. Whatever you need, my people will see it done." She felt the power of Compton's legend, of his extraordinary charisma. She didn't expect to live more than a few more hours, but there was adrenalin flowing, excitement about fighting again for this man. She could face death in battle, as long as she didn't have to look into Compton's eyes knowing she had failed him. Thoughts of doom and imminent death faded away, replaced by a surge of determination.

"Our position isn't hopeless, Greta, no matter what everyone in the fleet seems to think. And this isn't a suicide mission for your people either, so you remember that. It's dangerous as hell, but I expect most of you to come back. In fact, I demand it." Compton's voice was firm, resolute.

"Yes, sir." She had a pretty good idea of the tactical situation, and she didn't see a way out. But she found some part of herself believing him, even as the rational side of her mind clung to its hopelessness.

She looked at the man standing in front of her. He was rock solid, not the slightest doubt or weakness apparent. Whatever Terrance Compton, the man, believed, the undefeated fleet admiral was firmly in control right now. She had a significant reputation herself, but now she drew strength from the man standing in front of her, feeding off his iron will.

Perhaps it's part of the legend, she thought. *The man is simply incapable of giving up.*

*   *   *

"Admiral, we're picking up massive energy readings from the X1 warp gate. Really off the charts…I can't even get a steady fix." Max Harmon was Compton's tactical officer. Indeed, he'd also served Garret in the same capacity when Compton had been wounded, and he had the singular distinction of being declared the best tactical officer in the fleet by *both* of mankind's legendary naval commanders.

Compton looked over at Harmon, but he didn't reply. There was no reason. They both knew what had happened. Garret had detonated the device. If Dr. Hofstader's calculations were correct—and Compton had no doubt they were—the X1 warp gate was now scrambled by a massive amount of captive energy that would only very slowly leak out. It would be centuries before a ship could transit to Sigma 4—and the human domains beyond. *And if it didn't work, if Hofstader was wrong, every human being will be dead in two years,* he thought.

"Alright, Max," he said, changing the subject. There was

nothing to be gained by dwelling on the fact that they were now officially cut off from home. "Transmit navigational instructions to the fleet." Compton sat in the command chair on *Midway*'s flag bridge, as he had throughout the war. "We're going to take it hard on the way in, but that can't be helped. Ships are authorized to defend themselves the best they can and engage any enemy within range, but *nothing* is more important than following the nav plan *exactly*. We're not going to be able to help any ship that falls out of the formation. This is timed to the second as it is."

"Yes, sir."

Compton sat back and listened to Harmon relaying his orders. He appeared confident, almost unconcerned, but it was 100% bullshit. He was nervous as hell, heartbroken at being cut off from human space, scared about what would happen in the next few hours. But he was Fleet Admiral Terrance Compton, and his people needed the legend now, not the man. If they were going to survive, he had to have their absolute best, and he wouldn't get that from despondent spacers resigned to death. He needed for them to have hope, to believe they had a chance. Because he had come up with a way to give them that chance.

"All vessels confirm receipt of nav data, sir."

"Very well," Compton replied. He stared at the tactical display. "Get me Captain Kato."

Harmon leaned over his station for a few seconds. Then he turned back toward Compton. "On your line, sir."

"Are your people ready, Captain?" There was a noticeable delay. Kato was on *Akagi*, about a light second from *Midway*.

"Yes, Admiral. We are ready." There was deep resignation in Kato's voice, and Compton felt his stomach clench. Kato was a talented commander and an honorable man. *Just the kind who'd sacrifice himself if he thought he was saving the fleet.*

"Aki, this is not a suicide mission. You are to engage the enemy until the designated moment…and then your people are to board the shuttles and abandon ship. And let me be absolutely clear…*you personally* are included in my definition of 'your people.' Is that understood?"

Kato's ship was badly damaged, and she had no chance to keep up with the fleet. Compton had ordered *Akagi*—and the other fifteen vessels too shot up to maintain full thrust—to form a line protecting the flank of the main force. They were to hold off the enemy as long as possible. But Compton had been clear. The ships were on their last mission, but the skeleton crews remaining onboard were not. He had ordered them to flee, and to link up with the rest of the fleet. The plans were clear, but Compton was still afraid of unauthorized heroics. It was easier for his spacers to throw their lives away when they believed they were as good as dead anyway. But he was still determined to get them out of this alive.

"Understood, sir."

"Remember that, Aki. Don't you dare get yourself killed. I need all the good people I can get now. Just do your best, and then bug out before it's too late.

"Yes, Admiral."

Compton flipped off the com. He hoped he'd gotten his message through. Aki Kato was one of the best officers in the fleet—and more importantly, he wasn't one of Compton's own. The fleet was an international force, and he knew if he managed to get them out of this he would have to deal with rivalries and old resentments. And he was doing nothing to help prevent that by having his own people in virtually every major command slot.

He wasn't making decisions based on national preferences, at least not consciously. But he couldn't help but trust his own people more than he did those from the other powers. Besides, the navy he and Garret had built was vastly superior to any of the others, and the officers who had developed under their tutelage and leadership were head and shoulders above their rivals. Compton had Alliance officers in key positions because they were the most skilled and reliable. But he knew it created bad feeling as well. A capable PRC officer he could trust was a precious commodity, one he could ill afford to lose.

He flipped on the com unit again, calling up Greta Hurley's fighter. She and her crews were waiting in the landing bays of a dozen ships, armed and ready to go.

"You all set, Greta?" he asked softly.

"Yes, Admiral. The strike force is ready to launch." Her voice was cold, hard. Compton wasn't sure he'd convinced her they had a chance, but he was certain she would do whatever was necessary to carry out his instructions.

"Very well. You may launch when ready. And Greta, remember…this is not a suicide mission." He was getting tired of reminding everyone of that fact. "I expect you to be at the designated rendezvous point spot on time. Understood?"

"Yes, Admiral. Understood."

"Fortune go with you, Admiral Hurley."

"And with you, sir."

She cut the line, and a few seconds later, Compton felt *Midway* shake softly—the first of the fighters launching. He looked down at his display, watching the small blue dots assemble in formation. If everything went according to plan, those ships would launch their attack and then link up with the fleet. They'd have to match vector and velocity perfectly, and the slightest inaccuracy would prove fatal. But they'd have a chance, at least. And that was all Compton could give them now.

He stood up abruptly. "Max, it's time. Give the fleet order. All personnel to the tanks now. Maneuvers begin in twelve minutes."

And if everything goes perfectly, we just might make it out of this system.

*   *   *

"All weapons ready." Kato was in *Akagi's* command chair. His ship was wounded, mortally so considering the situation. Even if Compton's wild plan was successful, the PRC flagship was far too damaged to escape. But she still had fight left in her, and Captain Aki Kato was about to demonstrate that fact to the ships of the First Imperium.

"All weapons stations report ready, Captain." Yoshi Tanaka

sat at the tactical station on the otherwise nearly empty bridge. *Akagi* normally had twelve officers and two guards in her control center, but Kato had cut his crew to the bone, evacuating all but the most essential personnel. That left Tanaka and the communications officer the only others there.

His face was twisted into an angry scowl as he stared at the display, watching the enemy move closer. Kato was a veteran of the Third Frontier War, and he'd fought hard in that conflict. He'd lost good friends too. But that war had paled next to the savagery of this one, and nothing matched the intensity of his hatred for the First Imperium. The soulless robots were brutal and relentless in a way no human enemy could be. And the sacrifices this war had demanded made the devastating losses of the Third Frontier War seem light by comparison.

It only made it worse that he knew his enemies did not feel fear. They didn't even hate their human enemies, at least not in the way mankind understood the emotion. Their attempts at genocide were logical from their perspective, and not driven by rage or prejudice. They were merely following orders in the truest sense. But Kato hated them—he hated them with all the passions his human emotions could generate. He wanted to kill them, to see them in pain, to watch them overcome with fear as he ignored their pleas for mercy. And the fact that he knew his enemy would never feel the pain or fear he wanted to inflict only drove Kato's anger. He didn't know if he believed any of his people would survive, but he was damned sure they were going to dish out some damage.

"All ships are to fire when ready," he said, his voice dripping with venom. He stared across the almost silent bridge as the comm officer relayed his order to the thin line of vessels under his command. Sixteen damaged ships was a poor force to stand against the massive array of First Imperium power now approaching, but no one expected his forlorn hope to stop the enemy or even damage them significantly. All they had to do was buy a little time, and if they could manage it, even a few minutes, they could increase the escape margin for their comrades—and for themselves if they were able to evacuate in time.

His eyes were fixed on the tactical display. The first enemy line, about fifty ships strong, was almost within missile range. Many of the vessels were damaged from the earlier fighting, and some, Kato hoped, were low on ordnance. Behind the initial wave there were others, over a thousand ships in all, including twenty of the massive new design that was already being called the Colossus. The whole fleet had twenty times the firepower needed to destroy every one of Compton's ships, but Kato wasn't worried about the massive waves of strength relentlessly approaching. His target was the first line, and in that fight, he knew his people could inflict a toll before they bugged out.

"All missile launchers…fire. One volley, continuous launches." He spoke softly, firmly, never taking his eyes off his display. *Akagi* shook as she flushed the missiles from her external racks. Normally, it took at least fifteen minutes to clear the superstructure from the hull to allow the internal launchers to fire. But Kato had already given his orders, and a few seconds after the missiles launched, the racks that had held them in place were jettisoned immediately, without the careful effort to direct the huge chunks of metal away from the ships. It was a dangerous procedure, and *Akagi* shook several times as discarded hunks of hyper-steel slammed into her hull. But Kato knew time was his most precious resource, and a concentrated missile volley had the best chance of overwhelming the enemy's defenses and scoring some kills.

"Racks cleared, Captain." Tanaka was staring at his screens as he reported. "We have some hull breeches, lost atmosphere in several sectors, but nothing vital. And no casualties reported."

Kato sighed softly. *That's one advantage of having 80% of the crew gone…fewer people around to get sucked out into space when their compartment is ripped open.* Dropping the racks so quickly had been a big risk, but it was looking like a gamble that had paid off. At least for *Akagi*.

"Admiral, *Orleans* reports extensive damage from disengaging external racks. She is streaming air and fluids, sir."

"Captain Amies is to evacuate immediately." The stricken ship was no longer capable of contributing seriously to the fight.

And that meant Kato couldn't justify risking even its skeleton crew.

He stared straight ahead, watching the cloud of missiles on his display accelerating toward the enemy. "Let's close to laser range, Commander. The task force is to accelerate at 5g."

Time to finish this.

*   *   *

"All squadrons, this is the highest precision operation we have ever attempted." Hurley's voice was like ice. She didn't have Compton's confidence that any of her people would make it through, but that didn't matter. Live or die, she would do it following the admiral's orders. And Compton had been clear. Besides, if they were fated to die, it meant something to her that they die well, hurting the enemy and helping give their comrades a chance to escape.

"We will be commencing our assault in one minute. You will each make a single attack run at your assigned enemy vessel, and then you will execute the exact navigation plan locked into your onboard computers. You will not delay, not for any reason. I don't care if you think one more run with lasers will take out a Leviathan…you will follow my orders to the letter. Admiral Compton's orders."

Her eyes were on the chronometer. It read forty seconds, thirty-nine, thirty-eight…

"There is no room for hesitation, no margin for error. We have to reach the rendezvous point on time, and align our velocity and vectors with our specific landing platforms. Then we will have to land rapidly, again with no room for delay or mistakes."

Twenty-four, twenty-three, twenty-two…

"I expect not only the best from all of you…I expect perfection. And so does Admiral Compton. It's time to do this, people, and do it right. And then we get the hell out of here so we can fight another day. Good luck to all of you."

She cut the line and looked over at Wilder. The pilot was also staring at the chronometer, waiting for it to count down to zero. "Alright, John. You ready for this?"

The pilot nodded slowly. "Yes, Admiral. I'm ready."

Hurley turned toward the rest of the crew. "Boys?"

The others nodded. "Yes, sir," they said almost simultaneously—and unconvincingly.

Hurley took a deep breath as she watched the display worked its way through the single digits...to zero.

She leaned back as Wilder hit the thrust and the pressure of nine gees slammed into her. She could hardly move, but she managed to glance down at her screen. The entire formation, 243 small blue dots, moved ahead in perfect order. She felt a rush of pride. Her force included craft from most of the superpowers, crews with different training doctrines and capabilities. There were former enemies fighting together, men and women who had struggled against each other in the great battles of the Third Frontier War. But she had forged them into a single cohesive unit, and she'd done it in just two years. And she was damned proud of every one of them.

Many of her people were already dead. Indeed, almost two-thirds of her strength was gone in the battles of the last few days. More would die soon, she knew, but the fighter wings had done their part and more. They had given all they had to give to defeat mankind's enemy.

"Captain Kato's ships have fired their missiles, Admiral." Kip Janz was the fighter's main gunner, but now he was manning the small scanning station. He was struggling to hold his head up over the scope, to push back against the massive forces bearing down on them all. "It looks like they somehow launched everything in one continuous volley." Janz' tone was thick with confusion, but Hurley understood immediately.

He blew off his racks. Hopefully, he didn't sustain too much damage.

"We'll be at Point Zeta in thirty seconds, Admiral." Wilder's voice was as strained as everyone else's. No one, not even the hardest veteran, could take nine gees without it affecting everything they did. "Cutting thrust in three...two...one..."

Hurley felt the crushing pressure disappear, replaced by the weightlessness of free fall. She looked down at her display, watching the icons align as thirty squadrons cut thrust simultaneously, maintaining almost perfect order. Then her eyes glanced toward the top of the screen, where a line of large red ovals marked the enemy vessels.

Her birds were already entering firing range, but not a shot came from any of her fighters. Every one of them was loaded with double-shotted plasma torpedoes, and the plan was simple—fly through everything the enemy could throw at them and close to point blank range before firing. She knew they wouldn't all make it through, but the enemy ships in the first line had been badly shot up, and with any luck, the defensive fire would be light. The First Imperium didn't have any fighters, and their defensive tactics had been thrown together to meet the threat posed by the small craft of the human fleets. Her birds were coming in fast, and that would minimize the time they spent in the hot zone. But they were also heading directly for their targets, and at almost 0.04c, they weren't going to be able to maneuver or alter their vectors quickly. In space combat, high velocity reduced the variability of a target's future location, in many cases making it easier to target them.

"We've got enemy missiles on the screen, Admiral." Janz' turned toward Hurley. "It looks like a heavy volley, but not as bad as it could be."

Hurley could tell from Janz' tone the enemy response was considerably weaker than he'd expected. "Man your guns, Lieutenant. It's time to take out some missiles."

"Yes, Admiral," he replied sharply.

Hurley could hear a loud hum as the fighter's anti-missile lasers powered up. The tiny ship had four of the small point defense weapons. They had an effective range of about 5,000 kilometers, almost nothing relative to the vast distances in space combat. But the missiles approaching weren't the enemy's big antimatter fueled, multi-gigaton ship killers either. They were barely firecrackers by comparison—20 to 50 megatons. They had to get close to take out one of her birds. A detonation within 300 meters would destroy a fighter outright. One half a kilometer away would probably give her entire crew a lethal dose of radiation. But any farther out, and the damage, if any, would be light.

She sat quietly and watched her tiny ship's crew go about their tasks. She didn't need to interfere. They were the best. She'd trained them, she'd led them. Now she would let them do their jobs.

"Missiles entering interception range in four minutes."

Hurley nodded, but she didn't reply. She just sat and waited. And wondered how the rest of the fleet was doing. Compton's plan had seemed crazy to her at first, but the more she thought about it, the more she came to believe he just might pull it off. It didn't pay to bet against Terrance Compton.

Getting through the warp gate didn't mean getting away, but it was a step in the direction. Once the fleet transited, Compton intended to drop a spread of mines just on the other side and blast toward one of the system's exit gates. The enemy fleet would follow, but its sheer size would slow its transit—and the minefield would disorder it further. With any luck, Compton would gain on the enemy, increasing the gap between the two forces. And he would need every kilometer he could get.

Compton had scouting data on X4, and the location of several potential exit gates. But whatever system lay beyond was a total mystery—and each successive transit would be a gamble. Would they manage to find an exit gate in each before the enemy caught them? Or would one of the systems prove to be a dead end, with no escape?

"Missiles entering range in one minute."

Hurley had great confidence in her people, but she knew this was a more than just a difficult mission. She tried not to think of it as a suicide run, as much because she knew that's what Compton wanted, and not because she particularly expected to survive. Her birds were moving at a high velocity, and that made the job easier for the enemy missiles. Her ships couldn't quickly alter their vectors, which meant the incoming warheads had a small area to target.

"Commencing interception."

Hurley heard the high pitched whine of the lasers firing, one shot after another in rapid succession. She'd always hated this part of an assault, pushing through the enemy's long-ranged interdiction, powerless, waiting to see if her ship would get picked off by a well-placed—or lucky—shot. Her fighters' weapons were deadly, but they were shorter ranged, especially if she wanted to do serious damage. And she damned sure wanted that. So there was no choice but to take what the enemy threw at her people, and hope for the best.

Survival wasn't pure chance, of course, and a gunner's skill was crucial in increasing the odds of a fighter closing to its own firing range. And Kip Janz was one of the best.

She glanced down at the screen, monitoring the status of the incoming volley. Janz and the ship's AI had taken out seven enemy missiles. That didn't mean all of those would have closed to deadly range, but still, she was glad they were vaporized. Anything that got within the 5,000 kilometer window had to be considered a serious threat.

She saw the warning lights go on—a detonation about two klicks away. Close, but not close enough to cause major damage. Still, there was a good chance she and her people would need a course of anti-rad treatments when they got back. If they got back.

The enemy missiles were mostly gone from the screen. Her birds were nearly through—and that much closer to releasing their own deadly attack. But Hurley's eyes were fixed on a dozen flashing icons. Twelve of her fighters hadn't been as fortunate, their gunners not as skilled as Janz, and now they were bits of plasma and debris. She found it hard to look at a scanner displaying that kind of data, at the generic symbols that represented real ships, real crews. A dozen flashing circles meant sixty of her people were dead, their ships destroyed before they even had the chance to fire. It was cold, impersonal. She wondered how the Marines and other ground troops fared, so often seeing their comrades killed right in front of them. *Is it easier that way?*

Or more difficult?

"We're through the missile barrage, Admiral," Janz said firmly. "Beginning final approach."

Hurley looked over at Wilder. "The ship is yours, Commander." Wilder and Janz had stepped aside during the last attack run, allowing their admiral to take the shot—a dead on hit that had finished off the ailing Leviathan. She'd appreciated the gesture, and she'd enjoyed the hell out of killing the First Imperium ship, but she didn't intend to make a habit out of it. She'd accepted the stars Garret had given her, and she was resolved to behave accordingly and not act like some gung-ho pilot. Most of the time, at least.

Technically, Hurley didn't have a job on her ship, at least not one involved in its operation. Her fighter's purpose was to carry her wherever she had to be to command the strike force. Much to the frustration of Admiral Garret's plans, it had proven impossible to keep her back from the fight, so now it was not only a moving headquarters—it was another ship in the line, one more attacker determined to plant a double plasma torpedo into the guts of a First Imperium vessel.

"Prepare for high-gee maneuvers," Wilder said.

Hurley sat quietly, looking at the display. She knew just where Wilder was going. The closest ship was a Gargoyle. Half a dozen fighters had already made runs at it, and three had scored solid hits. The ship was still there, but there wasn't much left of it, and there was no fire at all coming from it. But tucked in just behind was the target that had caught Wilder's eye. A Leviathan, also badly damaged, but still firing at the fighters buzzing past it like flies on a carcass.

"Heavy incoming fire," Janz said, staring at the scope as he did. The main First Imperium defensive weapon was similar to the Alliance's shotguns. Both systems were essentially large railguns, firing clouds of metallic projectiles into the paths of incoming fighters. The First Imperium version had been designed purely as an anti-missile platform, but it performed well enough against fighters to make the hair on Hurley's neck stand up.

The fighter pitched hard as Wilder hit the thrust. Hurley felt the force slam into her, an impact like five times her own weight. She focused on breathing deeply as the force increased…6g… 7g…8g. She held herself straight in her chair, angling her head slightly so she could see her screen. Her movement was slow, steady, disciplined. At 8g, she knew she could pull a muscle just moving wrong.

She could see the enemy vessel getting closer—and bigger—on the display. Another fighter streaked across, putting its payload right into the huge enemy vessel. The scanners were assessing damage, feeding a continuous report on the status of the enemy ship. There were a dozen great rents in the side of the vessel, and liquids and gasses were spewing out into space. On a human-crewed ship, men and women would be dying in those compartments, blown into space or frozen and suffocated in place. But she knew it was impossible to disable a First Imperium ship by killing its crew. The robots onboard were impervious to cold, to lack of oxygen. No, to kill a First Imperium vessel, you had to tear the thing apart, bit by bit.

Suddenly, the thrust was gone, and weightlessness replaced the crushing pressure. She took a deep breath, grateful for the ease of it. She glanced over at Wilder and then back to her screen. The range was counting down rapidly. They were moving at 5,000 kilometers per second, and the enemy was less than 50,000 klicks away. They were ten seconds out and on a collision course. She opened her mouth, but she didn't say anything. Wilder knew what he was doing.

Eight seconds. The pilot was totally focused, his head staring straight at the display, hands tight on the controls. Six seconds. The ship bucked slightly, as Wilder released the plasma torpedo.

Hurley stared straight ahead, watching the distance slip away. *We're going to hit that ship…*

Then 9g of pressure slammed into her like a sledgehammer, and Wilder hit the thrust barely four seconds from impact. A few seconds of thrust couldn't do much to alter the course of a fighter travelling at over 3% of lightspeed. But it didn't have to do much, just enough to swing the ship around the enemy vessel. And it did just that. Hurley looked down in disbelief at the scanners. The fighter had passed within 300 meters of the Leviathan before it continued on, putting 5,000 klicks a second between it and its stricken target.

Wilder's torpedoes had found their mark. It was a shot generally considered impossible, a degree of accuracy almost unimaginable considering the velocities and distances involved. But Wilder had dumped his doubleshotted payload right through one of the great rips in the Leviathan's hull. The enemy ship shuddered hard as the heavy weapon unleashed its power on its unarmored insides.

Hurley saw the data coming in, and she knew what was happening. The torpedo was gutting the interior of the ship, destroying everything in its path. But she knew one type of damage would prove to be its doom, and a few seconds later she was proven correct. The massive vessel disappeared in an explosion of unimaginable fury, as it lost containment on its antimatter stores and unleashed the fury of matter annihilation.

"Nice shot, John," Hurley said simply. Then she added, "Think you can cut it a little closer next time?"

"I'll try, Admiral," he said, an amused grin on his face.

Hurley looked down at her screen. The strike force had completed its attack. They'd hit the enemy line right on the heels of Kato's missiles, and they'd taken out half a dozen ships, including two Leviathans. And her people had only lost another twenty fighters. Normally she wouldn't draw comfort from another hundred of her people dead, but even at her most wildly optimistic, she had imagined several times that number.

The attack had been a massive success—and Kato's task force was just a few minutes out of laser range. With any luck, his ships would wipe out the enemy line before his people had to abandon their crippled vessels.

She smiled grimly, feeling a wave of satisfaction. *Compton wanted us to delay them. Well, I'd say wiping out their first line will cause a delay. The rest of the fleet is over an hour behind.*

Hurley just nodded and returned the smile. "OK, according to Admiral Compton's navigation, we should be close to the right course and speed to link up with the fleet." A hint of skepticism slipped into her tone. She'd never even heard of fighters landing on ships moving at this kind of velocity. She understood the physics, and as long as everything was perfectly aligned, it shouldn't be much different from a normal landing. Still, it was going to take a hell of a piloting job to pull it off, and she didn't kid herself that all her people were going to make it. And the ones who didn't would die. It was that simple.

Chapter Two

Unidentified Squadron Commander During Battle of X2:

Let's go you bastards...and hold those torpedoes until you can see the scratches on their hulls! Do you want to live forever?

AS Midway
System X2, Approaching Sun
The Fleet: 241 ships, 48,181 crew

Compton lay in the fluid of the tank, struggling to remain lucid despite the effects of the drugs and the crushing pressure. The fleet was blasting at 30g, heading directly for the system's primary. Compton had considered a dozen strategies for escaping from the massive enemy fleet, but none of them had been plausible. Not until he'd really begun to think out of the box.

The navigation plan was fiendishly complex. It was his own work, though he'd had Max Compton review every calculation to confirm his math. It was a daring plan, one they would call brilliant if it worked. But it was dangerous too, and utterly unforgiving of error. If a navigator failed to follow the instructions precisely, if a ship was so much as a thousandth of a degree off course, that vessel would die.

The hundreds of ships in the fleet would gradually form into a single line, one vessel following the next. That alone was a difficult enough maneuver at high velocities. Then they would race toward the sun, their own thrust augmented by the increasing gravitational pull of the star as they approached. At the last moment, barely 50,000 kilometers from the surface, the vessels would blast their engines at full thrust, altering their vectors just enough to avoid a collision. If the painstaking calculations were correct, the fleet would whip around the primary, one ship at a time, less than 700 kilometers from the photosphere.

He'd reviewed the AI's calculations himself, three times. If they were correct, his people would survive, their hulls wouldn't melt, and their vectors would be radically altered by the massive gravity of the star. They would be on a direct course for the X4 warp gate, at a velocity the pursuing First Imperium vessels couldn't hope to match before his fleet was gone.

There were enormous dangers beyond the potential navigational errors. The ships would first move through the star's corona, parts of which were hot enough to vaporize even a *Yorktown* class monster in a microsecond. Compton had plotted a course around the hottest regions, through an area of very low density. If he was right, if his calculations were spot on, if his scanners were totally accurate…his ships should move through an area that would almost—but not quite—melt their hulls. If he had erred to the slightest degree, all his people would die, and there would be nothing left of the fleet but ionized gas. Even if the ships survived, there was a strong chance the radiation shielding would be inadequate to prevent his people from receiving lethal doses of gamma rays as they passed so close to the star.

None of that mattered, though. To stay in the system and engage the enemy fleet was certain death. Terrance Compton hated running from a fight, but he also knew the difference between a noble stand and pointless suicide. A battle would serve no purpose, and with the overwhelming enemy strength, it wouldn't last long either. In the end, his wild plan was the only option.

He disliked being in the tank, drugged and hallucinating while his people's lives were on the line. But there was no choice. The nav plan was set in stone, and it required 30g acceleration. That kind of force would kill anyone caught outside the protective system.

It doesn't matter, he thought, clinging hard to his lucidity. The plan was locked into the computers, and little would be served by more human involvement. The crucial part of the operation would occur while his vessels were passing through the corona and above the star's surface. Any problem would happen quickly, far too rapidly for anyone to intervene if there had been a mistake. If the fleet passed out of the cool zone into a hotter area of the corona, they'd be vaporized in an instant.

It would have been merciful to just surrender to the drugs, to drift into dreams and see if he ever woke up. But that wasn't how he was wired. This was his fleet, his people were on the line. He would maintain his vigilance as long as he could, pointless or not. He struggled to stay focused, used every trick he knew to keep his drug-addled mind aware. But 30g acceleration required a large dose, and even the mighty Terrance Compton slipped slowly away from consciousness.

*   *   *

Kato leaned forward in his chair. He could feel the tension, hear his heart pounding in his ears. Greta Hurley's fighters had torn through the first enemy line like some force of nature, obliterating six of the enemy ships and leaving most of the rest severely damaged. Her attack had exceeded all expectations, and now it was his peoples' turn. And after Hurley's show, anything less than the total destruction of the enemy line would be failure.

Akagi shook hard, as a First Imperium laser ripped through the lower levels. The enemy lasers were extremely powerful, almost overwhelmingly so in the first two years of the war. But *Akagi* had her own weapons, and they were almost as deadly.

Kato's ship had been refit with the x-ray laser system developed by General Thomas Sparks. The Alliance's master engineer possibly deserved more credit than anyone for the successes humanity had achieved in the war. In just three years, he'd taken scraps of enemy ships, combined them with his own research to begun producing weapons systems. His work didn't give the human vessels parity with their enemies—even Spark's unquestioned genius couldn't make up for millennia of scientific advancement. But his creations had given the ships of the Grand Pact a chance, one far better than they'd had before.

"All ships are to hold their fire." The enemy fire was lighter than he'd expected. He knew his people owed that to Hurley's fighter crews and the devastating damage they had unleashed. And now his people would take advantage of that. They would close to point blank range…and then they would unleash everything they had.

Kato had never commanded a task force before, and he'd questioned why Compton had placed him in charge. When he'd expressed his doubts, the great admiral simply told Kato he trusted him and that he should do his best. Those words had simultaneously strengthened his confidence and clenched his stomach. He had begun to understand why the Alliance spacers followed their admiral's commands with such impassioned reverence. Terrance Compton was like no one else he had served under, and letting him down was unthinkable.

"Konigsberg is reporting multiple laser hits, Captain. Her reactor scragged, and she is on emergency power."

Kato sighed. "Advise Captain Wentz to abandon ship immediately. His shuttles are to maneuver to the assembly point and wait for rest of us." There was no point in risking Wentz' crew. Emergency power was enough to maintain life support and basic functionality, but it damned sure wasn't going to charge up the ship's x-ray lasers.

"Yes, Captain."

Kato sat still, unmoving, undeterred. He was going to wait until his ships were at knife-fighting distance before he gave the command to shoot. But first his people had to run a gauntlet through the enemy's fire. Medina was gutted by multiple hits, and Kato ordered its crew to the shuttles as well. Then Bolivar was destroyed outright as a First Imperium laser ripped through its engineering spaces and cut containment on its fusion reactor. But still he waited…

"Range 10,000 kilometers, Captain." It was Tanaka this time, not the communications officer. A few seconds later: "Captain…"

Kato ignored him, staring at his screen as the range ticked down to 7,500 kilometers. Then: "All ships…fire!"

Akagi's lights dimmed as her giant x-ray lasers fired, every spare watt of power poured into the deadly broadside. The lasers were invisible, except where they passed through a particularly dense could of dust, but they were devastating nevertheless.

Kato's flagship had five of its batteries still operational, and they concentrated on a single vessel, the last Leviathan in the enemy line. The ship shook hard as the deadly beams struck, and huge holes were torn it its hull. Secondary explosions ripped through the vessel, ripping open more gashes.

"I want power to those batteries," Kato screamed into his com unit. "All ships, I don't care if you scrag your reactors, but get those guns ready to fire again!"

Akagi and its fellow ships zipped past the enemy vessels as they continued on their established vectors. "Positioning jets…180 degree shift, now!"

He felt a gentle push as the small thrusters fired briefly, spinning *Akagi* around 180 degrees, then fired again, bring her rotational movement to a halt. The whole maneuver took less than three seconds. The ship was still moving away from the First Imperium vessels, but she was facing back the way she had come…bringing all her guns to bear.

Kato watched the power monitors, as every scrap of energy was poured into the lasers. "All ships, fire as soon as your guns are recharged," he shouted into the com. An instant later, his monitor flashed green. The lasers were ready again.

"Fire."

He watched the scanners as *Akagi* once more spat death at its enemies. The stricken Leviathan was hit again, and it shuddered hard, as more internal explosions tore through its enormous bulk. Kato stared down at the screen, reading the damage reports as they streamed in. He knew he had to leave, had to get all his people down to the shuttles. But he wanted to know… he had to know…

He watched at the indicators dropped steadily. The big ship didn't blow, but it was dead nevertheless, its power generation down almost to zero. He glanced at the others. About half the enemy vessels were gone, reduced to clouds of superhot plasma. The other half were dead hulks, floating silently in space. Not a single one was still functional.

"Yes!" he said softly to himself. Then he turned to the com officer. "Signal all vessels…abandon ship."

*   *   *

"Son of a bitch," Hurley said, the words slipping through her lips before she could stop them. She'd been staring at the scope, watching the ships of the fleet whipping around the star, coming out of the corona on perfect vectors toward the warp gate. She'd known what Compton had intended, and she'd even believed in it on some level, that place in her mind where she viewed the great admiral as infallible. But sitting and watching it unfold just as he'd planned was still astonishing. She knew those ships were threading a needle, racing through a cool spot in the corona. There were sections to either side of that lane where temperatures reached into the millions of degrees, and the slightest navigational error could vaporize a ship or send it careening into the sun.

Compton's plan had been brilliant, wildly original…and if it worked, just maybe he would have saved his fleet from certain doom. And it looked like it was working. Still, Hurley had to get her squadrons to the designated place on time—and they had to be at the exact velocity and vector to land on the fleeing platforms. There was no room for error on her part either, and she knew the big capital ships couldn't decelerate for her if her people weren't in position. Compton had to save the big warships, first and foremost. A few cruisers would bring up the rear, decelerating enough to link up with the shuttles carrying Kato's survivors, but Hurley's fighters had to land on the battleships. And that meant they had to be exactly in position.

"Let's check and recheck this, John. Anybody who's not spot on is dead. It's that simple."

Wilder nodded. "I've reviewed the calculations three times, Admiral. They're dead on."

Hurley sighed. "It's not you I'm worried about. But every pilot out there who is not up to this is another fighter and five crew lost." *And not lost in battle doing their duty, but abandoned, left behind to be hunted down and killed by the enemy.*

"There is nothing you can do about that, Admiral." There was an odd tone to Wilder's voice, as if he was only just letting himself realize they had a chance to get out of the system. "You've honed this strike force into a razor. This is going to be a tough landing, but they're up to it. You'll see."

She nodded and gave him a weak smile when he looked back toward her, but she didn't say anything. Part of her was gratified to have a chance at escape, something she would have thought impossible just a few hours before. But she was still wrestling with the fact that most of her people were dead already killed in the last three days of sustained combat. They'd run sortie after sortie, returning to their launch platforms only long enough to refuel and rearm—and maybe wolf down a quick meal. They'd gone three days without sleep, and every one of them was running on stims. But still they'd gone back, without question, without complaint. And every time they did, they paid a price. Fewer than one in three were still alive, and the thought of losing more people, not in a fight now, but in botched or aborted landings, cut at her deeply.

"We're coming up on *Midway* now, Admiral. They've cleared us to land."

She flipped on her com unit. "*Midway* squadrons, commence final approach and landing." All through the strike force, she knew her wing commanders were doing the same, directing their squadrons to their own base ships. But it rested with the individual pilots to manage the landings. Hurley was confident about her own ship—she had John Wilder, and she was willing to wager he was the best pilot in the fleet. But the rest of her people were facing the most difficult landing they'd ever attempted…and their lives were riding on their success.

She watched the display as the four squadrons of her command wing split into two long columns, each heading for one of *Midway*'s fighter bays. Her ship was last on the second line, heading for a landing in Bay B.

The tiny symbols moved closer to the large image representing the flagship. The fighters' vectors and velocities were almost synced with *Midway's*, creating an illusion of very slow movement—despite the fact that they were traveling at almost 4% of the speed of light.

Slowly, steadily, the line of dots disappeared as they landed. Hurley watched, so tense she had to remind herself to breathe. She felt a rush of satisfaction as each fighter icon vanished from the screen, five more of her people safely back on *Midway*. Or at least whatever passed for safety for all of them now.

She glanced at the other status reports on her display. One of the fighters landing on *Conde* had come in with its angle of approach slightly off, and it had crashed inside the bay, killing the entire crew. And at least a dozen fighters had failed to match vector and velocity with their landing platforms, falling too far behind or racing ahead. That was a far lower number than she'd expected, but she still felt a wave of sadness. Those crews were as good as dead. The chance of them correcting course and making another approach before the fleet bugged out was close to zero.

"We're next, Admiral," Wilder said. His tone was distracted as he focused completely on the approach.

"Very we…" Her eyes darted forward as the fighter's small emergency lights engaged. She snapped her head back around, staring down at her display. The readout told her at once what had happened. The ship ahead of them had come in too quickly, and it had crashed. The landing bay was an inferno.

"They took out the control station—and the bay is strewn with debris," Wilder said grimly. Beta bay's closed, Admiral."

Hurley felt like she'd been punched in the gut. Normally, they'd just maneuver to the other side of *Midway* and land in alpha bay, but that was almost impossibly difficult at 4c.

Almost. "John…"

"Bringing us around, Admiral." His voice was like iron.

Hurley leaned back and took a deep breath. *If there's a pilot in the fleet who can pull this off, it's Wilder.*

"Brace for thrust," Wilder said, an instant before 11g of force slammed into the crew. He was overloading the engines, trying desperately to alter the fighter's vector relative to *Midway*, and maneuver to the other side of the mothership.

Hurley heard a scream from behind her—Janz—and she knew immediately he was hurt. She wanted to turn and check on him, but she was pinned in place by gee forces equivalent to eleven times her body weight.

She could hear Wilder gasping for breath as he sat at his station, barely able to move his hands to work the controls. "Upping acceleration," he rasped, as the forces increased…12g…13g."

Hurley struggled for breath as the pressure pushed higher, past her endurance. She could feel herself becoming disoriented. It wouldn't be long before they all blacked out, she knew—and that would be the end. The instant Wilder lost consciousness their attempt to land would be over. The ship's AI would cut the deadly acceleration, but they'd be hopelessly out of position, with nothing to do but watch the fleet transit and wait for the enemy to hunt them down.

Suddenly, the crushing pressure was gone, replaced for a few seconds by the relief of freefall. She breathed deeply, filling her tortured lungs with fresh cool air. Her lucidity was returning, and she could feel her head clearing.

"Prepare for deceleration."

She knew what Wilder's words meant, and she quickly sucked in another lungful of air before the crushing force returned, this time from deceleration, as Wilder struggled to restore the fighter's vector to match *Midway's*. She couldn't imagine how her pilot was staying focused, and she was amazed at how the ships controls seemed like extensions of his own body. Hurley had been a renowned pilot herself before her success pushed her to the top of the fighter command, but even she was amazed at the display Wilder was putting on. They hadn't landed yet, but she was beginning to believe that, against all odds, he would pull this off.

"Approaching alpha bay," he forced out.

Hurley lay back against her chair, unable to even move her head to glance at the display. All she could do was sit where she was and struggle for breath waiting to see if Wilder saved them.

The seconds drew out, each one seeming to last an eternity. The physical discomfort was extreme, almost torturous. And even Hurley was scared. The risk of dying in battle was an unalterable part of war, but there was something primal about the fear of being abandoned, left behind to the enemy. It killed her to see even one of her crews relegated to that terrible fate, and now, unless Wilder could manage to somehow pull off this landing, she and her crew would join them…or just crash in the bay. *That would be quicker*, she thought. *Probably more merciful than the day or two of fleeing and pointless resistance that lay ahead for those left behind.*

"Hang on, everybody," Wilder cried as he cut the thrust. Hurley felt the relief of freefall, and then an instant later the ship shook hard once and came to an abrupt halt. The momentary weightlessness was replaced by a more normal 1g. She looked out the viewscreen to see a beehive of activity. It was *Midway's* alpha bay.

"Excellent landing, Commander Wilder. You couldn't hear it, but you got a round of applause on the flag bridge." It was Terrance Compton's voice on the com, and he sounded relieved. "You guys just sit tight while they pressurize the bay." There was a short pause then: "Welcome home."

Hurley let out a long breath. *Yes*, she thought, looking out at the landing bay. *I suppose this is home now…*

*   *   *

"Admiral Hurley's fighters have completed landing operations, sir.   Approximately 92% have successfully docked.
Another four ships were destroyed on landing." Harmon's voice
was a bit less grim than it had been. A 92% success rate was far
beyond what anyone had dared to expect.

Compton nodded and sighed softly. He was gratified that
so many of the fighters had safely docked, but he realized that
fourteen of those birds had failed to match course and speed—
and now he was going to leave them behind. He imagined the
thoughts going through the heads of those men and women,
what they would be feeling as they stared at their screens, watching the ships of the fleet slip through the warp gate. They would
run from the enemy, he supposed, at least as long as their dwindling fuel supplies lasted. Still, eventually they would either be
caught or they'd slip away into deep space, tiny ghost ships, traveling forever on their last heading, their frozen crews still at the
controls.

Some of them might try to follow the fleet through the warp
gate, but that was just another way to die. Fighters didn't have
enough shielding for the crews to survive the exotic types of
radiation inside the gate. The ships might get through, but the
men and women aboard would be dead before they reemerged.

This is what command is like, Compton thought. Faced
with an astonishing success in leading his people out of the system, and another in the miraculous number of fighters that had
safely returned, all his thoughts were on the dead...and those he
was about to abandon. As all of his people had been abandoned
hours before. He'd found it easy to absolve Admiral Garret for
making the necessary choice, but now he was punishing himself
for the same thing. It was unthinkable to lose the entire fleet
over 70 fighter crew, just as it had been to risk all of mankind
for fewer than 50,000. He knew that, and his actions spoke
accordingly. But he was still carrying the guilt. As he knew

Garret was too.

"Very well, Commodore." Harmon was a captain by rank, but navy tradition demanded only one officer be addressed as captain on a vessel. Flag Captain Horace was the unlikeliest officer in the navy to give a shit about nonsense like that, but traditions that old stuck, and Harmon received the courtesy promotion when someone called him by rank on *Midway*.

Compton took a deep breath. "Time to first transit?" He knew the answer, but sitting around with nothing to do wasn't going to help the crew or him.

"*Saratoga's* in the lead, sir. Projected insertion in three minutes, twenty seconds."

It was no accident that one of the fleet's two other *Yorktown* class battlewagons was in the front of the line. Admiral Barret Dumont flew his flag from *Saratoga*, and there was no one Compton trusted more to handle a crisis than the feisty old firebrand of the Second Frontier War. Dumont had been retired when the First Imperium invaded human space, but he'd rejoined the colors when Garret had rallied the navy to face the deadly new threat. Dumont was old, over 100, but he didn't look or act like it.

Compton had placed *Midway* near the end of the line. The only ships behind her were the six cruisers of the squadron that had decelerated to pick up Kato's crews. It wasn't where he belonged, he knew that. But it was where he had to be if he was going to live with himself.

He felt an urge to rush down to the landing bay, but he stifled it. His place now was on the flag bridge. He knew Hurley would be hurting, mourning all the people she'd lost in the last few days, and he resolved to speak with her as soon as events allowed him the time. The whole fleet had suffered terribly in the fighting in X2, but the fighters had been truly decimated. He'd see some medals given out, commendations for the valor of the pilots and crews of Hurley's squadrons—though he wondered how much meaning such symbols would have in their new reality.

Compton felt the minor disorientation he always did when

Midway slipped through the warp gate. He looked around the bridge, watching how the rest of his staff reacted to the strange, and still largely unexplained, trip through the portal. The use of warp gates was well-understood, but human science had largely failed to align its understanding of physics with the miraculous effect of simply flying into one of the strange phenomenon and emerging lightyears away. The only thing that was known for sure was the trip was not instantaneous—it took a small fraction of a second to reach the other side, during which time the transiting ships, and their crews, were *somewhere*. Exactly what that meant, whether there was simply some kind of tunnel through normal space—or if the vessel and its crew briefly passed into some alternate universe or dimension—was purely a guess.

"Welcome to system X4, Admiral Compton." Dumont's gravelly voice burst through the com unit a moment later. It would take *Midway's* systems a few minutes to recover from the warp gate transit, but *Saratoga* had been in the system for over an hour. "The scope is clear. No enemy forces detected."

Compton felt a wave of relief flow through him. All his carefully-crafted plans would have been for naught if his fleet ran into more First Imperium ships in X4. But a clear scope meant one thing—his people had a chance. They were lost and cut off from home. They were exhausted and scared and low on supplies. But they weren't dead yet. And even that had seemed impossible less than a day earlier.

"Send a fleet communique, Commodore." His voice was taut, his tension slightly lowered but still there. "It's not time for celebrating yet. All ships are to set a course for warp gate two and lock into the navcoms. And all personnel are to prepare to get back in the tanks as soon as the cruisers transit with Kato's people. This is going to be a long stretch. We need to get through this system, and put some distance between us and the enemy, and we need to do it as quickly as possible."

He knew the First Imperium fleet had to execute a sharp vector change to pursue—and the warp gate would be a bottleneck for a force so large. He didn't know how long they would try to pursue Garret's fleet through the scrambled gate or what percentage of their resources would be devoted to the effort. That might keep them occupied for some time. Still, he didn't doubt his people would be pursued, and he knew the force chasing them would be strong enough to pound his battered vessels into dust.

He had no idea what he was going to do, where he would lead his ragtag group of refugees. But he was grateful he had that problem to worry about.

Chapter Three

From the Personal Log of Terrance Compton

I am not sure why I have decided to keep this log. It must be completely private, for there are thoughts I will record that I can share with no one, secrets I alone must bear. Perhaps I feel that one day humanity will push out this far, possibly even defeat the First Imperium. Men might one day read these words, centuries from now, and know that my people existed, that they had survived the battles in X2 and pressed on defiantly, deeper into the unknown space of our enemy's domains.

Or, perhaps we will find a home, somewhere we can settle down in peace and strive to build something lasting. I don't know how or where that might be possible, for we are deep within the territory of the First Imperium, and we make each successive jump knowing we might meet our doom at the hands of a massive enemy fleet at any time. We have passed a number of habitable worlds so far on our journey, all lifeless, with ancient crumbling cities marking the places where those who built the machines we battle once dwelled. Would they have been enemies, I wonder? Or if they were still here to control their creations, would they be friends, allies? Teachers? Would mankind's nations strive to enlist their aid against each other?

I wish we could stop and explore these worlds. They are the most amazing discoveries human eyes have ever seen but, alas, we must keep fleeing. I am not foolish enough to think our enemies are not still pursuing us, searching for the fleet even as we continue deeper into the unknown, into the great darkness.

Indeed, we cannot even be sure these worlds are completely dead. If I allowed landing parties to explore any of these planets, we could easily trigger some kind of alert and lead our pursuers right to us. Indeed, there are many theories that human activity on Carson's World caused the First Imperium incursion in the first place. Still, despite my caution, eventually I will have to send landing parties to one of these worlds. We must learn about our enemy if we are to find some way to defeat them, or at least to survive their onslaughts.

For now we must run, stopping only when it is absolutely necessary. We must push deeper into the unknown, ever farther from home, until we can find a way to hide...or to hold off the doom our enemies bring with their relentless pursuit. I have no idea of the size of the First Imperium. Is it possible to travel past their domain, find a home outside of their influence? Or would we simply find another enemy there, perhaps even deadlier than that we now face? We must never forget, as enormously powerful as the First Imperium is to our perceptions, something destroyed them. Perhaps it was a plague or some self-inflicted disaster. But I cannot discount the possibility that an even stronger race existed...or still exists...somewhere in the depths of the galaxy.

The morale of the fleet is surprisingly good, though much of that is based on a lie. The initial euphoria over escaping what appeared to be certain death has been replaced by a new hope, a false one. I hear it in conversations, and I can see it in the attitudes and behaviors around me...the hope that we will find a way back home, that we might blaze a trail through successive warp gates until we emerge in some previously undiscovered portal in a human-settled system.

I have no doubt they are right, at least about the fact that a trail home exists other than through the now-blocked X1:X2 warp gate. But seeking such a course is the last thing we can attempt and, indeed, I will do whatever I must to prevent it. Humanity was saved by the barest margin through the discovery of the enemy's great bomb and its successful detonation in the single known warp gate leading to human space. We cannot know where our enemy is...or whether they can track us, detect our path. But I cannot take the slightest chance of leading them back with us, for that would mean the death of every human being who now lives.

No, we are lost men and women, fated never to see loved

ones, never to walk on familiar shores or gaze upon our homes. We were sacrificed so that mankind could survive, to buy centuries for men to prepare to once again face the First Imperium, and now we must accept that burden...and do nothing to bring doom upon humanity.

But I fear not all will understand and agree. I have officers and personnel from nine superpowers on this fleet—different languages, cultures, philosophies. I will face resistance, perhaps sooner rather than later. I will try to diffuse any disputes, to maintain control with diplomacy whenever possible. But I will not allow any vessels of this fleet to try to find their way back to Earth... whatever I must to do prevent it. I will see this fleet destroyed, all its crew dead, before I will risk the future of the human race.

We are lost now...and lost we will always be.

AS Midway
System X16
The Fleet: 226 ships, 47,918 crew

Terrance Compton was lying on his bunk, his head and shoulders propped up on a pillow. He'd tossed aside his uniform jacket, and it lay crumpled on the floor below the chair he'd been aiming for. He was just grateful to feel the gentle normalcy of one gee of thrust after weeks of being buttoned up in the tanks almost 24/7. The coffin-like structures were designed to allow fleets to engage in high-g maneuvers in battle, not to be used for weeks on end. But with over a thousand First Imperium warships are chasing them, none of that mattered. Compton had squeezed more out of his ships and crews than anyone—including himself—would have believed possible a few months before.

His ships, however, had been pushed as hard as they were going to be—at least until his people did some serious maintenance. No vessels, not even the toughest warships mankind had ever produced, could withstand weeks of nearly endless operation at maximum thrust. There wasn't a ship in the fleet that didn't need some kind of repairs, and a significant number required major work.

He stretched out his legs and closed his eyes for a moment, savoring the lack of crushing pressure on his body. *A man could actually get a good night's sleep like this. That is, if a man didn't have more than physical discomfort keeping him up.*

He was halfway through a generously-poured glass of Scotch, a luxury he felt he was due after extricating his fleet from almost certain destruction and finally eluding the relentless pursuit of the enemy. *For now,* he thought. *They'll find us again. But before they do, we need to do some repairs—and find some supplies.*

He reached over and took the glass in hand, raising it slowly to his lips and taking a sip. He relished the taste of the expensive whisky, savoring it as it slipped down his throat. *This won't last long. And when it's gone, I'll never see its like again.*

He had half a dozen bottles of the 18-year old Scotch, the remainder of a case Augustus Garret had given him on his last birthday. He sighed softly. Of course, the Scotch wasn't the only thing he'd never see again. It had been almost three months now, and he was still coming to terms with the fact that they were stuck out far beyond the bounds of human-occupied space. Friends, family, home…all were lost to him. To every man and woman on the fleet. They were alive, and that alone was a miracle, but they faced a cold and lonely future—and a very uncertain one too. By any measure, their long-term survival prospects were poor.

Compton had been reading reports, most of them grim, detailing the increasingly dire logistical situation facing the fleet. Thanks to stores on the freighters of the supply task force, he had enough food for his people, for a while, at least. He had ammunition too, though the stocks there had been significantly depleted by the protracted combats of the Sigma-4/X2 campaign. Another big fight would push things into the critical zone, or worse.

But it was reaction mass his ships needed most. They were dangerously low on the tritium/helium-3 fuel they used to power virtually everything, from thrust to weapons—to the nightlight over the fleet admiral's bed. And if they ran out they would have two choices. Come to a halt and wait until the First Imperium forces found them…or accelerate with the last of their fuel and become a ghost fleet, ripping through deep space until the last of the reserve power ran out…when his vessels would become tombs for their frozen crews.

Fortunately, tritium for his ships' reactors was something he could find. All he needed was a suitable gas giant, and enough time to build and operate a temporary refining facility in orbit. He'd already sent scouts to the adjacent systems, searching for the hydrogen source he needed. *It's going to be a lot harder to find food…or replace missiles and damaged components. But that's tomorrow's problem.*

But now he let the small 'pad he'd been working on slide down the side of his leg, and he picked up an even tinier screen, this one bearing the image of a woman. She looked about 35, but that was only because of the rejuv treatments she'd been receiving since her Academy days.

Elizabeth Arlington was 48 years old, and an admiral in the Alliance Navy. She was known as a fighting officer, and she had performed brilliantly in the desperate battles against the First Imperium. She had been Compton's flag captain before she got the promotion to flag rank and her own fleet command. Arlington was a rising star in the navy and one of the best in the service. She and Camille Harmon were the likeliest among the next generation to rise to the top command, to succeed to the role Compton had so long filled alongside his closest friend, Augustus Garret.

Compton stared at the small image, the only one he had of her that wasn't an official navy photo. She was sitting on the couch in the admiral's quarters on *Midway*. She was wearing the pants from her off-duty uniform and a gray regulation t-shirt. She'd discarded her boots, and she was leaning back with her knees bent and arms wrapped around her legs, her light brown hair tied back in a long ponytail. The image captured a rare moment of happiness and relaxation amid the almost constant crises of recent years. She had a big smile on her face. Compton remembered the moment well. She had been smiling at him.

Arlington had been more to him than a loyal commander, more than a trustworthy comrade. In truth, he'd loved her—he still loved her. Only now, lying in those same quarters and realizing he would never see her again, did he realize just how strong his feelings were. Just how heartbroken he was to leave her, to know she was gone to him forever.

He regretted not only her loss, but how he'd wasted the time they'd had together. She'd known he cared for her deeply. He was certain of that, just as he was sure of her feelings for him. But he'd never told her how he truly felt, never told her he loved her. It hadn't ever been the time or the place. And now that time would never come.

She'd been under his direct command for most of the years he'd known her, and Terrance Compton was an honorable man, an officer devoted to duty above all things. He wouldn't allow his personal desires to interfere with his responsibilities. The Alliance had been fighting the First Imperium, and Compton had refused to endanger either the efficiency of his command or Arlington's career by having her pegged as the fleet admiral's lover. There would be time, he always told himself. One day, they would have time.

But he had been wrong, tragically wrong. Now he knew they would never be together. She was lightyears away, beyond a warp gate that would be scrambled and impassible for centuries. Compton had never been one to fool himself, to salve his pain with lies and false hopes. He would never see her again, he knew. She was lost to him forever, and all he had left of her was one tiny image.

He could feel the moisture in his eyes, and he shook himself out of his reminiscences. "Old fool," he cursed himself. "Don't you have enough to do without whimpering like a lovesick boy?"

He slid his legs around abruptly, knocking the 'pad off the edge of the bunk. It hit the ground with a loud crash. He sighed and stood up, bending down to pick up the now damaged device. So much for supply reports, he thought, staring at the cracked screen, now blank.

He tossed it aside, wondering suddenly how many more

were in the cargo holds of the fleet. Almost since the instant his people had eluded their pursuers he'd been thinking of little except but how to obtain supplies, or ways to stretch what his force had, but now the magnitude of the problem truly sunk in. His people had to learn how to find or make everything they needed. Everything. They didn't have access to factories, to laboratories except those on one of ships—not even a farm to supply basic foodstuffs. A simple device like an infopad would become irreplaceable…unless his people managed to somehow create a facility to manufacture more. And building high tech items meant starting with mining operations to secure the basic silicon and other raw materials. It was beyond daunting, especially with the constant danger of being discovered and attacked by their pursuers.

He stood up slowly, achingly. The weeks in the tank had been hard on him. The rejuv treatments were a biological miracle, slowing the aging process and extending a human lifespan to 130 years or longer. Still, it wasn't a panacea. Compton was almost 70 years old, a man who had spent most of his life at war, who'd been seriously wounded half a dozen times, who'd spent untold hours in the tanks. He looked like a healthy 45 year old, and in many ways he had the physiology of man that age. But he still had 69 years of hard use on his body, and sometimes he felt every day of his true age.

He took one last look at Elizabeth's image, and then he walked across the room and carefully put the small viewer away in one of his desk drawers. There would be time later to mourn lost love. Now he had work to do. More work than he'd ever faced before.

*   *   *

"Admiral, we're receiving a transmission from Captain Duke."

Compton nodded. "Very well commander. Put it on

speaker." Jack Cortez was working out well as Max Harmon's replacement. Compton had been hesitant to let his longtime tactical officer go, but he finally realized he needed Harmon elsewhere, keeping an eye on things on the other ships. His longtime aide was still assigned to *Midway*, but he spent a lot of his time now shuttling around the fleet. Ostensibly, his job was to inspect ships for damage and supply status and to create a priority system for repairs. In reality, he was spying for Compton, listening for signs of discontent among the various crews.

Compton was well aware his fleet was not an Alliance force, but a conglomeration made up of vessels from nine different Superpowers. Many of the spacers and soldiers under his command had been enemies for years, and they'd been thrown together only by the threat of annihilation at the hands of the First Imperium. It had been a difficult situation even under the auspices of the Grand Pact, humanity's alliance against the enemy. But now, lost in the depths of space, he knew it was only a matter of time before he faced dissent and challenges to his authority. His success in saving the fleet from certain destruction had bought him some time, but he knew enough about people to understand that wouldn't last long. The threat of the enemy stifled dissent and solidified his power, but with each system they passed without pursuit, he knew the other voices would grow bolder…and more would listen to them.

"Admiral Compton, I have good news." The sound of John Duke's deep voice blasted from the bridge speakers.

"Well we could sure use some, John," Compton replied. "So let's hear it."

Compton had sent Duke's fast attack ships out to scout the systems around the fleet, looking for a gas giant with large tritium resources. It had been a matter of economy as well as caution to send the small ships out while the main force waited. The fleet was already dangerously low on fuel—stopping and looking for resupply hadn't seemed a priority when the First Imperium forces were still on their tail. But now Compton's ships had barely enough reserves for a last fight if one came upon them. He wasn't about to burn that up dragging 226 ships all over uncharted space looking for a tritium source when Duke's ships could do the job.

"The fifth planet in X18 looks like a great prospect. The probe readings were phenomenal for tritium concentrations… and there's plenty of helium-3 too. And planet four looks like a paradise. I'd say it might be a place to check out for any potential foodstuffs."

Compton nodded, more to himself than anything. *We've got to come up with something better than numbering these new systems X-whatever.* "That is good news, John. We need that tritium." He paused then added, with somewhat lesser enthusiasm, "And we'll check out planet four too. Maybe we'll get lucky."

He wasn't optimistic about finding naturally-occurring edibles in any significant quantity. When man had first burst out into space, he found that habitable worlds were far more common than anyone had expected. Many of these were teeming with plant life, and a fair percentage had a considerable range of animal species as well. But few of these proved viable as human food sources, and most colony worlds produced the bulk of their sustenance from transplanted Earth species. The fleet had the seed stores to plant over a large area, but that meant remaining in one place for a planet's growing season, and that was out of the question right now.

"Transmitting probe data to *Midway* now, sir," Duke said.

"That's fine, John. Excellent job. Let's wait until the rest of your scouts return. If they haven't found anything more promising—and it seems unlikely they can top this—I want you to take your whole task force back to X18, along with enough support ships to start constructing a refinery to harvest that tritium. You can scout the system more closely while the engineering teams complete their work. Also, I want you to send scouts into X18's warp gates. Make sure the neighboring systems are clear before I bring the rest of the fleet through.

"Yes, Admiral."

"And once again, John, you did a tremendous job. Please pass my gratitude along to your people. Compton out." He turned toward Cortez. "Commander, send a message to Commander Davies. Advise him we have found what appears to be a suitable tritium source. He is to be ready to move out with his team in two days."

"Yes, sir," Cortez answered.

"And let's take the fleet off a battle footing, at least for a while. This system looks clear, and we've got scouts in the adjacent ones." He paused, letting out a long exhale. "And it's high time our people got a chance to relax...even if it's only a few hours."

The fleet's battle status had essentially restricted the crews to duty, eating, and sleeping. But he knew his people needed to have some downtime or they'd go crazy. If there was one thing a lifetime of war had taught Compton, it was to take whatever chances he could to let his people recover. Otherwise they became more and more frazzled, and their combat readiness began to decline.

With any luck, he figured, he could top off the fleet's fuel supplies and move on before the enemy found them. But he had to make sure that when they continued, they'd all be together, that no dissension pulled them apart. Because when they set out again, the direction was going to away from home, and deeper into the vastness of unexplored space...into the darkness.

*   *   *

"I want to thank you all for coming here. I apologize about the cloak and dagger feel of it, but you are all officers I trust completely." Compton sat behind his desk, looking out over the group crowded together in his quarters. "For a variety of reasons I did not want to conduct this meeting over the fleet's normal com systems...or even in the conference room."

He could see the confusion on most of their faces, though it looked like a few of them had an idea of what was on his mind. At least some of it. He doubted anyone else had reached the same level of concern he had.

"Speak your mind, Terrance. There's nobody here who thinks your caution is unwarranted." Barret Dumont's voice was deep and gravelly. Everyone present knew he was likely to cut through the nonsense and come right to the point. He had another distinction—he was the only person in the fleet who had once outranked Terrance Compton.

"Thank you, Barret. I intend to." Compton looked around the room. "I doubt that surprises anyone here."

A wave of subdued laugher rippled through the room, but everyone was too nervous to sustain it. They'd been expecting Compton to address longer term plans for weeks now, and the fact that he sought to do it among his closest supporters suggested he suspected trouble of some kind.

"I'm not sure how many of you know that Admiral Dumont was my CO back in the day." Compton smiled and glanced around again at the group he had assembled. "For you youngsters out there, back in the day means during the Second Frontier War—and the admiral here was in command of both Augustus Garret and me. And I can tell you, he used to scare the hell out of us."

Another round of laughter, stronger this time. Compton suspected few of the officers in the room could imagine Admiral Garret cringing before anyone.

"Okay, here it is…straight shot." He paused for a second. "We're not going to try to find a way back to human space." His eyes moved back and forth, trying to get a read on how many of them were surprised by his statement. Fifty-fifty, he figured, though he knew a few of those present had pretty good poker faces. "We can't. There's just no way to be sure where the enemy can track us—or however close behind us, or ahead of us they are. And one mistake, one little bit of carelessness, and we could lead the First Imperium back to Earth. You all saw the forces arrayed in the X2 system. Allowing them to follow us back to human space—assuming we could even find our way home, which is a considerable supposition—would be catastrophic. We would be responsible for destroying the human race."

Compton sighed softly. He'd been carrying these thoughts for weeks now, keeping them to himself and wondering what the thousands on the fleet were thinking. The rush to escape from imminent destruction had occupied everyone's minds at first, but now that the fleet was enjoying a respite, he knew the discussions would begin—whether or not he started them. And if he ceded the initiative to others, he risked losing control.

"I know that may be difficult for many to accept. Indeed, it is a harsh reality for all of us. There are few men and women on this fleet without at least some connections back home— friends, family, loved ones. But it is for them we must remain strong...and never weaken in our resolve. Trying to find a way home would be an act of pure selfishness, of reckless disregard for the potential consequences. And we wouldn't have to actually discover a way home to cause disaster. Simply diverting First Imperium resources toward systems more likely to lead to human space could be disastrous. We could cause the enemy to find the route home without ever discovering it ourselves."

The room was silent, and every eye was on Compton. He suspected most of them realized he was right and that they had been harboring similar thoughts, even if they'd held them in check. But he didn't underestimate how difficult it was to give up any hope of returning home, however slim that chance might have been. Hope, even false hope, could sustain a man. And he was stripping that from them, enlisting them to support his position, to resolve now and forever to stay firm.

"I have been choosing warp gates I believe are leading us farther away from human space. Indeed, I have been doing this since we left system X2. But now that we have at least temporarily eluded our enemy, I must address this with the fleet at large." Compton paused for a few seconds before finishing his comment. "And I simply do not know what to expect. Dissension in the fleet could destroy our survival chances as surely as a First Imperium fleet."

"Perhaps we should deploy Marines to the ships of the fleet...just to be safe." Connor Frasier was the commander of the Black Highlanders, a rump battalion of commandoes and one of the most elite units in the history of the Corps.

"I'm not sure that's such a good idea, Major." Erica West was sitting at the back of the gathering, just inside the door. West was another of the Alliance's fighting admirals who'd led a number of cruiser squadrons during the battles against the First Imperium. She'd been badly wounded and in sickbay during the flight from X2, but now she was back and cleared for duty, though Compton had kept her on *Midway* without an assignment for over a month now.

"Why not? We don't have enough manpower to lock down the whole fleet, but we damned sure can cover all the capital ships…and probably the heavy cruisers too. As long as that's all locked down, what the hell can anyone else do?" James Preston was exactly what one imagined a Marine colonel would be. His face was angular, his features hard and chiseled. His steel gray hair was closely cropped, and a pair of intelligent blue eyes stared out at the gathering.

"It's not about capability, James," Compton said. "Though even covering the capital ships would stretch your Marines pretty thin." He glanced over at Frasier, shifting his gaze between the two Marines as he spoke. He reminded himself to tread softly. The Alliance Marines were one of the greatest fighting forces history had ever seen, but they could be prickly about being told there was something they couldn't do.

"Admiral West is correct in counseling caution," he continued. "We must remember…this is not an Alliance fleet." He glanced over at Captain Kato. "Nor even a combined Alliance-PRC force." The Pacific Rim Coalition had long been the Alliance's closest ally, and Compton wasn't looking to offend Kato and his comrades. "It is comprised of forces provided by every Superpower. There are vessels that have fought each other before, officers who have spent their careers as enemies. How do you think they would react if I sent Marines on to RIC or Europa Federalis ships? Not to mention Caliphate or CAC vessels?"

Preston was staring back, his eyes boring into Compton's with the usual intensity. Finally, he nodded. "I understand, sir."

His voice was downcast. "But remember, we're ready when you need us."

"I would never doubt that. And I am sure I will need all of your people before we are done. Indeed, they are a resource that must be preserved…and used wisely." Most of the Marines were still back on Sigma 4, where they had defeated the First Imperium ground forces. Compton had only a tithe of that power with him. "Remember, James, we've only got 2,400 of your people, and I can't imagine the number of ways I'm going to need them. Splitting them up into fifty platoons and sending them all over the fleet would take away my only reliable strike force."

"Excuse me, sir, but then what do we do?" Greta Hurley had been sitting quietly. "If there is a realistic possibility for conflict based on nationalistic lines, should I leave my squadrons mixed? Or should I pull out the Alliance and PRC units? Should I find an excuse to move all the squadrons to Alliance and PRC platforms?" She paused for an instant and continued in a somber tone. "God knows, we've got the space." Her fighters had suffered brutal losses in the protracted fighting in X2, and there wasn't a fighter bay in the fleet that wasn't half empty.

Compton looked over at Hurley. "We'll discuss it later, Admiral. I don't want to do anything that causes unnecessary suspicion, but perhaps we can come up with a plan to get your birds off some of the more sensitive ships." He paused then added, "I think you can keep your squadrons together, especially if we can get them on secure platforms, but if you have any personnel you're uncertain about, by all means do what you feel you have to do. I trust you to maintain your strike force at maximum readiness."

He turned and looked out over the gathering. "I will speak with each of you individually regarding specific strategies in your areas. My intent for this meeting was simply to share my decision and my concerns with you. So before we adjourn, let me ask one more time. Is there anyone here who disagrees with my plan to attempt to move deeper into unknown space, to apply what limited knowledge we have of warp gate distribution not to finding a way home, but to the opposite…to seeking to flee deeper into the unknown, leading as much of the enemy's strength away from Earth and not back toward it? If so, please speak now, here among friends and allies…because if no one says anything to the contrary, I will expect all of you to completely support my decision. In public…and also covertly, through whatever actions are necessary to maintain control of this fleet and to ensure that none of its vessels risk leading the First Imperium back to Earth."

He stared around the room. Every eye was locked on him, but no one uttered a word. "You are all sure?" His tone became darker, more ominous. "Because when I say whatever actions are necessary, that is precisely what I mean. No ship will be allowed to put human space at risk. Not under any circumstances."

His voice was icy cold, and it left no doubt about his resolve. Still, there wasn't a sound, nothing except the faint hum of *Midway's* systems in the background.

Chapter Four

Command Unit Gamma 9736

The Regent had sent commands on the priority circuit. For uncounted centuries, Command Unit Gamma 9736 had lain dormant, its power sources diminished, providing only the barest amount of energy to sustain itself. Its processes had slowed and then ceased, until there had been nothing left but a spark of activity in the kernel, the barest maintenance of awareness. In the context of the Old Ones, the biologics the Unit had once served, it had been asleep...or more accurately, in a deep coma, almost suspended animation, awaiting the stimulus that would cause reactivation.

The communication circuits had been silent for millennia, and for 500,000 years, the Unit waited...it waited for contact. For direction. For purpose. Now, after so long the time had come. The Regent had made that contact. It was an alarm, a call to action. The imperium was threatened. After ages of nothingness the Unit was ordered to prepare for war, to rally the forces of its sector. To confront the enemy.

There had been strife for several years now...and fleets from other sectors had been dispatched to gain the victory. But the enemy had been underestimated. The forces the Regent had thought adequate to destroy them had been defeated, driven back. Now the Regent was sounding the full alarm, calling to every sector in the vastness of the imperium, directing all intelligences to rally what forces remained under their control after so many years of decay. For the first time in uncounted ages, total war was upon the imperium.

The Unit reacted immediately. Slowly, it fed its precious power reserve into circuits long dormant. Memory bank after memory bank slowly came to life, and with each one the Unit recovered a portion of itself, data and computational abilities long dormant. It hadn't been immune to the ravages of time—whole sections of its vast quantum brain were unresponsive—petabytes of data lost. But it felt the surge of power, of quasi-consciousness. It remembered. A time long ago, when its sector was active, when billions of the Old Ones, the biologics, still inhabited the worlds it administered.

The communique that had initiated its renewal was of the utmost importance. The enemy had somehow blocked access to the only known warp gate leading to their space. But a large fleet had remained behind, and it escaped the trap the Regent had set for it. The enemy ships had fled, deeper into the imperium, and they had eluded the forces in pursuit, disappearing into the vastness of imperial space. Into the Unit's sector.

The Regent's orders were clear. Find the enemy. Hunt them down, destroy their vessels. Whatever the cost. And there was something else too. The Unit was to take prisoners, live enemies it could interrogate. It was unclear if the humans knew a path back to their home worlds, but the Regent wanted that data. It had declared that the forces of the Imperium would not rest until they had discovered a way to reach the home space of the humans—and eradicate them once and for all.

The Unit took steps to obey. Gradually, methodically, it continued to reactivate old power sources, expanding its operations as more energy became available. It opened communications lines, sent messages to its subordinate units on the various worlds of the sector. Only a few answered. The others, the Unit postulated, must have succumbed to the ravages of time. Or fallen to the enemy, its defensive algorithms suggested hawkishly. Still, it didn't matter. The few that responded would be enough. Even now, the planetary command units were activating their armaments, determining how many ships, how many robot soldiers, were still functional. Soon, the Unit would have the data it needed to plan the destruction of the enemy.

Then it would dispatch its fleets to search. The enemy was far from home. The Unit rationalized that their moves would be dictated by logistics. They were biologics. They would need

foodstuffs to maintain themselves. They would need ammunition stores to replace those expended in battle. But most of all,
they would need fuel for their ships. The enemy vessels used
primitive nuclear fusion as their primary power source. It had
been uncounted ages since the forces of the First Imperium had
utilized such primitive power sources, but they were well understood. The enemy would need a good source of tritium and he-
lium-3. They would be searching, even now, for a system with a
gas giant rich in the two rare isotopes. And that was a data point
the Unit could use to narrow its search...

AS Midway
System X16
The Fleet: 225 ships, 47,916 crew

"They had to leave Volga behind. The crack in her containment chamber opened up again." Anastasia Zhukov was staring
down at a large 'pad as she spoke, her long blond hair tied back
in a ponytail. Zhukov had been attached to the RIC contingent
of the fleet, but shortly after the escape from X2 she'd transferred to *Midway* to work with Dr. Cutter.

"Volga was a piece of junk anyway," Cutter said, only half
paying attention. His eyes were focused on a strange device
on the table in front of him. It was part of a First Imperium
warbot, one of thousands the Marines had destroyed in the
bloody battles of the war. "What was it? Seventy years old?"

Anastasia frowned. Most of the RIC's ships were old. It
was no secret the Russian-Indian superpower was no match for
the Alliance, or even the CAC or the Caliphate. And she was a
scientist, not a soldier or politician. She didn't believe in politics
or the pointless wars between the superpowers. But her father
had been a general in the army and the closest thing the RIC had
to a military hero. So, in spite of her disinterest in such matters,
she occasionally felt an involuntary prickliness when someone
disparaged the RIC.

"So?" she snapped back. "The Alliance doesn't have any old

ships?"

"What?" Cutter had slipped from half paying attention to hardly doing it at all. "What are you talking about?"

"You said Volga was junk."

He finally looked up from his work with a frustrated sigh and stared at her. "Whatever, Ana. Volga's the state of the art, okay? Anything that makes you happy. Now can we please stay focused here? I think we're on the verge of a breakthrough." His eyes dropped back to his work without waiting for her response.

She nodded. There was no point in arguing, not with Cutter. She knew his abrasiveness wasn't intentional. She'd never seen a human being so utterly focused on work before. Besides, the truth was, there *wasn't* a ship as old as Volga in the Alliance navy. She had to admit that the RIC, despite her occasional vestigial spasms of patriotism, was struggling to hold onto its superpower status in a universe where the "Big Three," the Alliance, the Caliphate, and the Central Asian Combine, had eclipsed the other powers in the race for dominance. *Not that any of that really matters to us anymore...*

"Of course, Ronnie," she said sweetly. She was the only one who called him that, and she'd done it since the day she'd walked into his lab and he'd introduced himself. Hieronymus was admittedly a mouthful, he'd explained to her, but it had also been his father's name, and his grandfather's—and so on, at least six generations back in his family. She'd listened to everything he told her, and then she just shook her head for a few seconds and said, "I think I'll call you Ronnie."

Hieronymus Cutter was generally recognized as the leading expert in advanced quantum computing processes, and Anastasia was a serious contender for the number two slot. Cutter was widely known to be a bit odd, an obsessive-compulsive workaholic who tended toward reclusive behavior. But all agreed he was an unparalleled genius, perhaps even the equal of his famous mentor, Friederich Hofstader.

Hofstader was a true hero now. He had developed the theory that an extremely high-yield matter-antimatter explosion could scramble a warp gate. Indeed, he was as responsible as anyone for saving humanity—and stranding the fleet. But Cutter's specialty differed from that of his famous mentor. His work in computing led him on a quest not to block the First Imperium's advance nor even to produce weapons to destroy their massive ships. Cutter's quest was to understand how the advanced thinking machines worked—as a precursor to learning how to control them.

"Take a look at these patterns," he said, sliding a large 'pad across the table so she could see it. "This is from one of the battle robot command units. The processing power of these "officer" units is far greater than that of the standard battle bots." His fingers moved, pointing to a series of waves on the screen. "I've done the calculations a hundred different ways. There is no discernible logical pattern in how these machines process information. It almost looks…random."

She stared at the 'pad for a few seconds. He was right. The patterns he'd isolated weren't patterns at all, at least not in the sense that they had any predictability to them. "But it can't be random. That doesn't make sense."

"No, not random. I'm sure these crazy waves make sense… but only if you can see the input data that generated the recorded patterns." He looked up at her, and he could see she wasn't following. "Don't you see? These First Imperium intelligences—at least the lower level ones in these robots—aren't truly sentient. But they able to comprehend how sentient beings act and react."

He looked up and sighed again, clearly frustrated that she wasn't understanding his point. "Imagine you are in a trench fighting a battle. You look across at your opponent, who is also in a trench. If you project that he will behave rationally, you can assign probabilities to various actions he might initiate. For example, you might determine that he is most likely to remain in place, since charging correlates with a large advantage for you defending in your trench—and a high likelihood of death for him.

"But how do you account for a madman unconcerned with physical harm? Or a religious fanatic who believes death in battle leads to paradise? Or simply a soldier acting irrationally due to battle fatigue or rage at the loss of a friend? How do you assess the potential of irrational actions by an opponent? Our own AIs do this by assigning probabilities based on historical data programmed into their memory banks. For example, we know that certain Caliphate units exhibit fanatical behavior in battle, and our AIs know this, so they assign a higher probability of such behavior to their forces. But the First Imperium has no historical data of this sort for us…or at least very little."

He looked up at her. "I postulate that the First Imperium AIs do not address emotionally-driven and similar illogical decisions simply by assigning likelihoods of a specific action based on static historical data. I believe they understand irrationality and emotion, even if they themselves do not actually experience such traits."

Anastasia began nodding. She understood what he was getting at…sort of. "Is it possible to…understand…irrationality when you yourself are not capable of truly experiencing it?" She had forgotten all about Volga and superpower pride. Unraveling the secrets of the amazing machines that ran the First Imperium was the most fascinating task she'd ever attempted—and one that could have profound impact, both on the fate of the fleet, and indeed, on all humanity. Perhaps with an improved understanding they could communicate with the First Imperium, negotiate a peace of some kind. Or, if not, a true comprehension of their enemies could be weaponized too. Understanding how they "thought" was the first step toward defeating them.

"We're hypothesizing, of course, but I would say no, not fully. I believe the First Imperium intelligences are able to do a credible job of anticipating and responding to the irrational or random behavior of their adversaries. Thus, they are not utterly confused by actions driven by emotion. However, I feel this is where their weakness exists as well. Not being able to truly experience the kinds of emotions that lead to irrationality, they are only partially capable of crafting targeted responses. This explains the success of commanders like General Cain or Admirals Garret and Compton in actions against them. These men are highly skilled and, for the most part, logical. But they all rely on intuition as well, and on other emotions--stubbornness, anger at the losses they suffer, pride in their units and warriors. The First Imperium intelligences directing the battles against them can anticipate such factors, but they are still at a disadvantage due to their lack of experience with us. That disadvantage will slowly disappear as they add to their databases on human responses."

Anastasia nodded. "I understand…and I agree. But how do you propose to put this to practical use? Do we devise strategies to enhance the use of seemingly irrational tactics?"

"Perhaps. Though that is more difficult than it sounds. Most irrational motivations are harmful. In the majority of cases, the rational, predictable action is also the wisest. We may lose more by choosing unsound actions simply because they surprise the enemy." He looked up at her. "But that is not my primary interest in this line of research."

She stared back, confused. "Then what is?"

"I believe analyzing how the enemy has reacted to illogical stimuli has given me an insight into how their processing algorithms function." He paused. "I am working on a project that would allow us to interfere with their logical processes, to reduce their functionality…or even to gain control over them."

"Gain control of them?" Ana asked. She wasn't sure if she thought Cutter had lost his mind or exceeded even her already enormous expectations of his intellect. "They are thousands of years beyond our technology."

"What does that matter?" he asked matter-of-factly. "It is one thing to develop something independently, another to copy or reverse-engineer it when it already exists. If you could travel back to ancient Rome and leave a functioning aircraft on the steps of the Senate, do you think it would have been 2,000 years before manned flight was developed?"

"No, I suppose not," she said slowly, beginning to get his point as she did. "But what you are talking about is almost unimaginably complex. Do you really think it's possible?"

"I know it is possible, Ana." He pressed a small button on

the control panel, and a storage panel opened on the far side of the room.

Anastasia turned abruptly and stopped suddenly. Inside the storage space stood a vaguely humanoid construction—a First Imperium battlebot. She felt a shudder run through her body, but then she realized it was deactivated. "What is this?" she asked, turning to face Cutter.

"This is Sigmund...or at least he soon will be." Cutter gave her a rare smile.

"What does that mean?" she asked, her voice tentative, concerned.

"You asked if I really believe I can control First Imperium intelligences by downloading a customized virus into their processing units. Sigmund here will provide us with the answer. If I am able to take control of him, I presume you will accept that as validation of my line of research."

"Of course," she answered, still uncomfortable. "But why a battlebot?" Just looking at the deadly device made her nervous.

"For two reasons. First, I don't exactly have a large choice of intact First Imperium processing units at my disposal—and Sigmund here is in remarkably good condition. His intelligence unit lost power during a battle, but it's an easy repair...and otherwise he's in perfect shape."

He looked over at the imposing robot. It stood over two meters tall with multiple appendages on each side. The weapons systems had been removed, a necessary precaution, leaving a few bits of exposed circuitry. "And second, it's a big dumb brute."

Ana smiled. "Is it now?"

"Well it is, relative to the command units or, certainly any kind of fleet control system. Nevertheless, it is still more sophisticated than anything we've ever seen before. But it's the bottom rung for the project. Once we can control something like the Sigmund, we can work our way up from there."

"Work our way up to what?" Ana asked.

"Well, if our best guesses are right, the First Imperium consists exclusively of the machines remaining behind by some long-extinct species…and that means somewhere there is an artificial intelligence controlling everything. A machine of astonishing complexity, no doubt…sentient or nearly so, but a machine nevertheless. One we can control if we discover the means."

"You imagine we could stop the entire First Imperium with a virus?" Ana stared at him, her face a mask of astonishment. It was unthinkable. After the thousands who had died in battle, the disruption of the warp gate trapping them all deep in enemy space…the almost unfathomable technology of the enemy. And here was Hieronymus Cutter planning to take it all down with a computer virus. It was almost incomprehensible.

"Yes," he answered simply…and he looked back down at his work.

*   *   *

"Won't you join us, sir?" Max Harmon looked up as Terrance Compton walked into the officers' wardroom. He held five cards in his hand, and he laid them face down on the table as his eyes met the admiral's.

Compton smiled. "Not right now, Max. Maybe some other time."

Harmon nodded. "You're welcome any time, sir. I'm sure we'd all love to see the legend up close."

Compton was indeed legendary in the fleet, generally considered to be the best card player ever to wear an Alliance uniform. There were tales still told, mildly exaggerated ones of course, of his prowess. But the stories were old now. His responsibilities had increased with his rank, and he had long sworn he would never put himself in a position to take money from the officers he outranked. For many years now, that group had consisted of every other spacer in the navy save Augustus Garret. And Garret had long known better than to play cards with Compton.

The admiral returned the nod. *Perhaps it's time to rethink old codes of conduct,* he thought. Taking money from his subordinates didn't seem terribly relevant anymore. He couldn't think of anything less useful out in the depths of unexplored space than Alliance currency. He felt the urge to sit down, to play a few hands and forget about First Imperium fleets, dwindling supplies, and how to keep control of the fleet when it became known he had no intention of trying to find a way home. But it wasn't the time.

"Perhaps one day, Max." *When I can take a few minutes to relax. If that day ever comes.*

The wardroom was busy. The first day after he'd changed the alert status, the ship's rec areas had been deserted. The exhausted off-duty personnel had taken their extra free hours to catch up on lost sleep. But now, they were spending more time out of their quarters, in the mess halls, the wardrooms, the gyms.

He looked around the room. There were at least twenty others besides those in the poker game. He was glad to see his officers relaxing. They had performed magnificently, and he knew it wouldn't be long before he needed them at their best again...and when that day came, more of them would die, he realized grimly. He was always worried about his people, about how much he demanded from them, how much he would have to continue to demand if they were going to survive.

His mind drifted back, to how Augustus Garret had always obsessed about the men and women on his ships, so often without any thought of himself—how the pressures of command wore so heavily on him. More than once, Compton had urged his old friend to take care of himself, to find some way to relax. Now he realized he was a good-natured hypocrite, no better than Garret at affording himself a break.

His crews were all stuck out here, in the depths of deep space, their best hope just for the barest survival, to stay hidden and to find the supplies they needed to press on. He knew he was only human, that even he could only take so much stress, so much fatigue. But that seemed like an unimportant fact. He would keep going because he had to, because the survival of over 47,000 people depended on it. *More than that*, he thought grimly. *I have to make sure this fleet doesn't try to find a way home. Billions of lives may depend on that.*

Chapter Five

Secret Communique from Captain Harmon to Admiral Compton

Admiral, I am on *Petersburg*, under the pretext of inspecting ammunition supplies. I have been unable to detect any meaningful dissent from the crew, however Admiral Udinov just departed on a shuttle. There is no scheduled flight, nor any meeting that appears on his public calendar. It took considerable effort, but I was finally able to discover the destination of the shuttle. *Nanking*. As you know, that is the ship where Admiral Zhang has been traveling since you removed him from command of the fast attack ship task force. I find this to be a disturbing coincidence. I cannot imagine what legitimate business Udinov has with Zhang.

I considered going to *Nanking* myself to try to obtain better information, but there is no way to explain such a trip, and my cover as your agent would almost certainly be blown. Nevertheless, I believe we can assume that Zhang is attempting to suborn Udinov to some plan of his. Whatever it is, I am sure it is trouble. I intend to remain on *Petersburg* until Udinov returns and attempt to glean whatever information I can from watching his actions.

I will almost certainly have to take greater risks than I have to date, and that is why I have taken the chance to send this communique. In the event there is a conspiracy brewing and I am killed or captured, it is essential that you know that Udinov and Zhang are in communication.

I will attempt to update you again as soon as I have any further data on Udinov and his intentions. In any event, I will make contact in no more than 48 hours, regardless of my progress. If you do not hear from me in that time, you can assume I have been killed, captured, or incapacitated—and that fact will confirm that the situation has gone far beyond conspiring.

If I do not survive to speak with you again, I want you to know it has been a privilege to serve under your command, and you have my complete confidence that you will ably lead the fleet to safety.

CACS Nanking
System X16
The Fleet: 225 ships, 47,914 crew

"Thank you for coming, Vladimir." Zhang spoke softly, looking around as he did.

"You said it was important." Vladimir Udinov was the senior RIC admiral in the fleet, the commander of the Russian-Indian Confederacy's fourteen ships. His tone was tentative. He'd known Zhang for a long time, but he was also aware the CAC admiral had to be Compton's number one suspect to cause problems in the fleet. He wasn't sure he wanted to get dragged into any disputes or power struggles.

"I wanted to speak to you about Admiral Compton." Zhang Lu was the scion of a powerful political family, but he'd never been anyone's idea of a fighting spacer. Still, he'd maintained a high position in the CAC navy—and in the combined fleet as well—until Terrance Compton had humiliated and summarily dismissed him in the middle of a fight, replacing him with a mere captain. An Alliance captain.

"Zhang, I don't think this is…"

"This is more than my injured pride, Vladimir. I assure you." He held a small 'pad, and he reached out, handing it to Udinov. "That is an analysis of navigational data…every transit we have made since fleeing X2."

Udinov took the device, but he still stared at Zhang with a confused expression on his face. "What is the purpose in my reviewing this? Perhaps we can cut through to the heart of the matter. What is it that concerns you?"

"Since escaping from X2, every jump we have taken when an exit warp gate was freely chosen—as opposed to being the only alternative to elude pursuit—has been the one least likely to lead back toward home. I checked the analysis myself....twice."

Warp gates were still poorly understood phenomenon, and there was no known way to determine where one led except to enter it and see. But the distribution of the gates within a system, and their specific orientation in space did correlate with a basic direction. It was imperfect analysis to be sure, but with proper calculations, it was possible to determine if a specific gate would lead closer to or farther from a specific point in regular space, at least to a probability of roughly eighty percent. The Halston Theorem that set forth the equations had never been conclusively proven, but it had continued to perform within its expected seventy-five to eighty-five percent range of accuracy.

Human-occupied systems were not themselves perfectly aligned in normal space—but they were close. Warp gates tended to lead to nearby stars, which resulted in the spatial alignment of human space being at least somewhat similar to its structure as depicted by a map of warp connections.

"Are you sure about this?" There was a spark of interest in Udinov's voice, and he glanced down at the 'pad, flipping through the first few pages.

"Oh yes. I am certain. We made three jumps when we were closely pursued, and where a specific gate was nearer and offered a faster escape. Two other jumps were from systems with only two gates, leaving no room for a choice to be made. There were six other instances, and in every one of those, the gate chosen was the one that would be expected to lead us farthest from home."

Udinov flipped his finger across the pad, scanning the data Zhang had given him. "So you believe Admiral Compton is deliberately leading us away from Occupied Space?"

"Yes," Zhang replied. "No doubt he will say he is concerned about leading the enemy back with us, of helping them find a way around the now-closed X2-X1 warp gate." He paused then added, "At least that will be his stated reason."

"Stated reason?" Udinov looked up from the 'pad toward Zhang. "What do you mean?"

"I mean perhaps there are other reasons Admiral Compton wants us to remain lost. Personal reasons. Selfish reasons." There was an edge to Zhang's voice, and an anger toward Compton he couldn't conceal.

"Selfish reasons?"

"Yes. Perhaps the admiral fancies ruling over all of us like a monarch. Back in Occupied Space, the fleet would disperse, the war would be over. Compton would be nothing more than the Alliance's second admiral, forever in the shadow of Augustus Garret. Perhaps his ego fancies being the unchallenged leader."

Udinov stared back at Zhang, his expression doubtful. "You think Admiral Compton wants to prevent us from returning home so he can rule over a lost fleet with fewer than 50,000 refugees aboard?"

"Perhaps. But I doubt his motivations are so simplistic. He may fancy himself the supreme leader of the fleet, and that may appeal to his ego. No doubt he justifies his actions by disguising them as concern for Earth and the rest of human space, but are we to believe that is his sole motivation? Or that it is valid? He may even have convinced himself, but are such worries justified? We have eluded pursuit, and we are alone in this system. If we are to attempt to return home it has to be now, while we are out of the enemy's grasp, before we jump deeper into unexplored space, into the heart of the enemy's domains."

Udinov stood silently, his eyes drifting back to the 'pad. Zhang's words had clearly gotten to him, but he still didn't look convinced. "I don't know...I understand your concerns, but Terrance Compton has never struck me as an individual mad for personal power. I find it difficult to believe he would intentionally lead us away from home unless he was truly afraid the enemy would follow us there."

"Are you sure? Look what he did to me, the imperious way he relieved me from command and replaced me with a junior officer…an Alliance officer. Consider how many Alliance personnel are in command positions in this fleet. Is that a coincidence? Or has he been arranging to put as many of his own people in key roles. And ask yourself this…if Compton isn't planning to impose his will, why has he not discussed any of this with you or the other contingent commanders?"

Udinov sighed. "I don't know. That troubles me the most. I understand we were on the run, and I was willing to respect Compton's command authority. He got us out of X2, and I believed he could elude the enemy pursuit as well." He stared at Zhang. "But why nothing since? It has been a month since our last contact. Why has he not convened a meeting of the top national commanders?"

Zhang tried to hide a smile. He had Udinov hooked. Now he just had to reel him in. "Why indeed, Admiral? Perhaps he is afraid of questions that will be asked…or that he will face opposition if he is forced to divulge his plans. If he is called out openly, he will have to respond, to clearly state his intention to prevent this fleet from ever returning home. Perhaps he has even convinced himself he is saving Earth by remaining out here, that the enemy would follow us back if we discovered a way home. But is that a valid concern?"

The Russian admiral didn't answer. He was staring down at the deck, deep in thought. "Yes, perhaps it is time to push for a meeting," Udinov finally said, his voice distracted. "Now that we have escaped the immediate pursuit, we must make some decisions about how to proceed. And it is not for Admiral Compton to do so unilaterally, without even discussing it with the other commanders."

Zhang just nodded. Udinov was a member of a wealthy and influential family in the RIC, just as Zhang himself was in the CAC. They both had much to lose if they never returned home, as did most of the other senior officers in the fleet. The CAC admiral was a creature of his station and his upbringing, so he failed to fully acknowledge that even those without status and wealth might mourn being lost for the rest of their lives, that the common spacers and junior officers had friends and loved ones, that they too might miss their homes.

"I will contact Lord Samar, and discuss this discretely with him. I am confident he will agree that a carefully executed attempt to find a way home is preferable to simply fleeing deeper into the unknown." Samar was the highest-ranking Caliphate commander, and another man of wealth and power back on Earth. "And Admiral Peltier as well." Udinov looked over at Zhang. "I would say you should approach Chen, but I fear the good admiral will blindly support Compton." Chen was the commander of the CAC contingent. The CAC was a traditional enemy of the Alliance, and Compton had fought many battles against Chen and his fleets. But the CAC admiral had sworn to follow Compton, and he was well known as a man of his word.

"Don't worry about Chen, Admiral. If you are able to bring the Caliphate and Europan contingents over, I can promise you the CAC forces." There was an icy coldness to his voice. Udinov didn't know what his new ally was planning, and he was fairly certain he didn't *want* to know.

"Very well, Lu," he said. "I will contact Peltier and Samar and advise you of their statuses." He looked around, seeing that the room was still deserted. "I better not risk coming here again, but I will send you a messenger if I have anything noteworthy to pass along. Meanwhile, I will request that Admiral Compton convene a meeting of the senior commanders of the fleet to discuss next steps. With any luck, we will have the Caliphate and Europans supporting us by that time. Then we can force the admiral's hand."

Zhang just nodded. Forcing the admiral's hand wasn't what he had in mind.

But it' a good first step.

*   *   *

Harmon walked into *Petersburg's* wardroom, nodding to several of the officers present. He'd spent the entire day reviewing the ship's weapons stocks, and now he was here to relax. At least that's what he hoped they all thought.

"Hello," he said, the portable AI clipped to his belt translating his speech into flawless Russian. Most of the officers in sight were clearly ethnic Russians and other Slavs. There were a few of Indian descent as well, though they were a clear minority.

The Russian-Indian Confederacy was an odd conglomeration. Most of the Earth's other Superpowers had come about through the aggregation of similar ethnic groups or the alignment of geographic realities during the Unification Wars. But the RIC had been a product of military, not political, reality.

The Indians had found themselves caught between the Caliphate and the newly-established Central Asian Combine, and they suffered devastating losses when those two powers fought each other. Only the assistance of a newly resurgent Russia had saved even a segment of the old Indian subcontinent from depopulation and apportionment between the CAC and the Caliphate. In the end, about half of what had once been India joined the new Russian Superpower. The Indians weren't given the same status as the Russians, but they weren't subjects either—more like junior partners. The ranks of the navy, especially the officers, had long been dominated by Russians, though the ground forces were more evenly divided between the two groups.

"Max, welcome." one of the officers said, with a heavy accent, but without the assistance of an AI. He looked around the table at the other officers. "This is Captain Max Harmon. He is here checking on our weapons stocks." He looked over at Harmon. "He is going to get us some of those Alliance heavy warheads. I promised him I can attach them to our Bekuskan missiles."

"I said I'd try, Vanya," Harmon answered, smiling as he did. "No promises. We're running low on those fleetwide."

"We cannot fire promises at the enemy, can we?" Vanya turned toward his comrades and spoke Russian to them for a few seconds, and then they all roared with laughter.

"Come, Max, sit. Have a drink." Vanya gestured toward a

chair and pushed a glass and a tall pitcher across the table. "It is…" He said something in Russian, and the officers around the table burst into laughter once again. "Moose piss, my Alliance friend…that is as closely as I can translate. It is homemade, and to call it vodka would be a sacrilege. But it is what we have, so we drink, no?"

Harmon nodded and walked across the room, taking the offered seat. He shuddered to think of what was in the noxious substance in the pitcher, but he knew RIC custom well enough to realize he had no choice. Besides, the more they all drank, the likelier it was tongues would loosen.

He grabbed the pitcher and poured himself a tall drink. Then he looked around the table with a smile and downed it in one gulp to the loud cheers of his new acquaintances. He slapped his hand down on the table. "Moose piss indeed, my friend," he said, reaching for the pitcher and pouring himself another before handing it around the table.

"Will you join us," Vanya said, gesturing toward the cards on the table.

What is the game?" Harmon knew what they were playing, but feigning a bit of ignorance about gambling could only help him.

"Is called Vint. Is very old Russian game." Vanya's accent was growing thicker with every glass he drained. "We could teach you."

"You could…" Harmon looked around the table. "…or we could play a true gambler's game…"

He could feel the eyes around the table focusing on him.

"And what would we gamble for, Captain?" It was the slightly sterile tone of his AI translating one of the other officer's remark. "Currency is of little value to us now."

"Well…if you are willing to accept my word as an officer, I will stake something rare indeed. I can't help you with vodka, but I have a bottle of bourbon back in my quarters on *Midway*. My last bottle. The real thing, twenty years old, direct from Kentucky back on Earth. Cost a month's pay. It goes down like honey, but even if you Russians can't appreciate it, you can get almost anything if you trade it to some officers on the CAC ships." He glanced around the table, looking for reactions—any clues about contact with CAC personnel.

"And what would you have us put up against it?" Vanya asked.

Harmon smiled. "Well, you could stop pretending you don't all have something decent stashed somewhere and dig out those vodka bottles. It's not gambling unless you put up something you don't want to lose, is it?"

The officers leaned in and spoke among themselves for a few seconds. Finally, Vanya turned back toward Harmon. "Very well, Max my friend. We each bought a case of extraordinary vodka before we reported to *Petersburg*. That was two years ago, but we have been frugal. We will put up a bottle each. We play until only one man remains, and the winner takes all."

Harmon smiled. "Agreed." He reached out and picked up the deck of cards. "Now slide down that pitcher again. I may have to get used to this moose piss if you sharks strip me of the last of my bourbon."

*   *   *

"I suspect Captain Harmon has a greater purpose than simply organizing weapons supplies." Udinov was in his quarters watching the Alliance officer on his screen. Harmon was walking down a corridor from the main magazine to the central lift. He wasn't doing anything suspicious—at least Udinov hadn't managed to catch him involved in anything that was remotely out of line with his stated reason for being on *Petersburg*. But that didn't allay the admiral's concerns.

"I am inclined to agree, Admiral," replied the officer standing next to Udinov. Anton Stanovich had been the Russian admiral's aide for years. Stanovich's family had long been retainers to Udinov's, and young Anton had gone to the naval academy with the express purpose of replacing his father at Udinov's side. "Though I can offer no proof to support that assertion."

Udinov stared at the image of Harmon, but his mind was drifting, trying to rationalize what was going on. He knew the Alliance officer was very close to Admiral Compton, filling much the same role that Stanovich did for him. "Nor can I, Anton. Not yet at least."

Harmon had been spending a fair amount of time socializing with *Petersburg's* officers. Indeed, he'd become quite the sensation, highly sought after for his expertise in poker. He'd become quite popular since he'd won a stash of high quality vodka at poker and then immediately shared it with his new acquaintances in a bit of a drunken blowout.

There was nothing particularly suspicious about any of that on its face, but Udinov had dug a little deeper, accessing whatever information he could on Harmon. Aside from a spotless service record—and a mother who was another of the Alliance's top admirals—Harmon had seen service with both Compton and Augustus Garret. It was all interesting information, and further evidence that Max Harmon was an extraordinary young officer who had Terrance Compton's complete trust. But none of it set off any alarms. Not until his people managed to gain access to his personal files.

Max Harmon was a decorated officer, one of the Alliance's best by any account. But he'd rarely taken shore leave, preferring to remain aboard ship, spending time alone or with his friends and shipmates. He was far likelier to stay in his quarters reading than to seek out the company of others, and he'd tended to avoid any formal functions as well, unless attendance was mandatory. He had a few close friends, but little social contact beyond that.

He's shy, Udinov thought. *An introvert. And yet he comes to a ship belonging to another power, where another language is spoken, one he needs an AI to understand, and he goes to the wardroom and introduces himself—and sits down and plays cards with a bunch of strangers. And two days later he is the talk of the ship. No, that doesn't quite make sense. Not if he's here just to organize our weapon stores. It's got to be more than that. He's here to gather information. That means Compton suspects something is going on.*

But nothing was going on, not yet at least. Udinov has listened to Zhang's concerns, and he'd seen enough truth in them to take steps to prepare. But Udinov's first action would be to discuss the future with Compton, to urge the admiral to convene a strategy session as soon as possible. He hoped the matter could be settled with words, that pressure from him and the other contingent commanders would sway the Alliance admiral.

Nevertheless, the fact that Compton was already clearly concerned suggested that perhaps Zhang was correct. *If Compton wasn't planning to impose a course of action, regardless of what the rest of the admirals think, why would he have his number one aide over here sniffing around? Why would he feel he needed to spy on me?*

"Anton," Udinov said, speaking softly even though they were alone, "I want you to stay close to Captain Harmon. Talk to some of the men who've played cards with him. Invite him to a special game. Feel him out and report back to me with anything you discover...even if it's only your gut feel."

"Yes, Admiral." Stanovich snapped to attention. "At once." The officer bowed his head for an instant, and then he turned and walked out the door.

Udinov's eyes dropped back to the screen. The ship's AI was tracking Harmon, following him around the ship, switching cameras as the Alliance officer moved. He was in the lift now, heading back to deck 8, probably to the wardroom again. By all accounts, Harmon's work on *Petersburg* was done. He should have left hours before, heading for the next vessel on his list. But he was hesitating, making excuses to remain. *To keep spying on me...*

Udinov flipped on his com unit. "Sergei, I need you to do something for me," he said softly, quietly.

"Certainly, Admiral," came the crisp reply. Sergei Rostov had commanded *Petersburg* for the five years Udinov had flown his flag from the battleship. The two worked seamlessly together, almost like a machine.

"I want to keep Captain Harmon onboard for several days... without him knowing he is being detained. Perhaps you can come up with some issues in the magazine, possibly sabotage some of the ordnance, make it appear to be damaged. You can ask that he inspect all of it, that he request additional supplies from Admiral Compton." Udinov paused for a few seconds. "Something like that. You can flesh it out a bit."

"Yes, sir. I am sure I can come up with something plausible." There was a short pause then: "And if the ruse is unsuccessful—if he attempts to leave despite my efforts—do I allow him to go? Or should I have him detained?"

Udinov hesitated. He didn't like the idea of the outright abduction of Compton's number one aide. But letting him off *Petersburg* while things were undecided wasn't the most appealing option either. He stared down at the com, and finally he spoke softly, grimly. "Then arrest him."

"Yes, sir." Rostov's tone suggested he understood very well the import of Udinov's orders.

"And Sergei?"

"Yes, Admiral?"

"If it comes to that, I need you to be discrete. Make sure the men involved are extremely reliable…and able to keep their mouths shut. No witnesses. And search Captain Harmon from his hair to the bottom of his feet. If he hangs on to some kind of com unit, all hell will break loose." Another pause. "Understand?"

"Understood, sir."

Chapter Six

Command Unit Gamma 9736

The old network had slowly come to life. Not all of it, not even most—but enough. The sensors swept through space, searching, watching. Data was flowing in from ancient scanning devices. For weeks the input had shown nothing, no sign of the enemy. They had disappeared, vanished into the depths of space. But now there had been contact.

It was an old scanner, ancient beyond imagining, from the days before the old ones disappeared, before Command Unit Gamma 9736 had been created. Before, even, the Regent had been activated. Indeed, the scanner dated from the early days of the Imperium, when the old ones still used primitive fusion power, as the enemy did. It circled a great gas giant, one particularly rich in tritium, the vital fuel of nuclear fusion.

It was small, low-powered, simple in design, yet after so many long ages, it still functioned. It was also stealthy, using low powered subspace communication. Probability suggested an extraordinarily small chance the enemy would have detected it from one simple communique. And Command Unit 9736 was not going to increase the risk of discovery. It sent back a single pulse, an order for the unit to shut down. No further information was necessary. The Command Unit knew all it needed to know. The enemy had paused in its flight, driven by the need to replenish its fuel stores. They were vulnerable, unable to flee until they extracted the needed fuel from the gas giant's atmosphere. And Command Unit Gamma 9736 knew where they were. Even now, orders were being dispatched, fleets being gathered to destroy the enemy.

The Command Unit had considered its strategy carefully. Massing its fleets before attacking was the most tactically sound approach, save for one fact. Allowing more time to pass before engaging the enemy increased the chance that they would complete their refueling operation and once again escape. No, the attacks could not wait—they had to begin as soon as possible. The enemy had to be pinned in place, as many of his vessels damaged and slowed as possible.

The Command Unit ordered each force to engage as soon as it reached the system. The fleets would attack the enemy, keep them constantly fighting, slow their refueling efforts. The cost would be high in lost ships, but that was of no matter. The Regent's orders were clear. Destroy the enemy. At all costs.

Command Unit Gamma 9736 had issued its orders. Its own determinations were of little account. The primary directive was obedience to the Regent, and that above all. Its fleets would move. They would attack, unmindful of losses. They would pin the enemy down in the system...or follow them if they fled.

AS Jaguar
System X18, Orbiting Planet X-18 V
The Fleet: 225 ships, 47,912 crew

"That looks great, Commander. You have made enormous progress in a short time. Your engineers are to be commended." John Duke stood on *Jaguar's* tiny bridge. The fast attack ship was a cramped affair all around, and her tiny control center was no exception.

"Thank you, Admiral. It's delicate work, but we all understand the importance of getting the refinery up and running as quickly as possible." Jerrold Davies' voice sounded tinny over the com, but the engineer was remarkably composed for someone in a pressure suit hovering deep in the atmosphere of a gas giant almost as large as Jupiter. "Normally, we'd take something like this a little slower, but there's nothing normal about things now.

Duke didn't understand the intricacies of building a tritium and helium-3 collection refinery in the atmosphere of a massive planet, but he was pretty sure trying to do it too quickly was damned dangerous. Indeed, they had already had two fatalities on the project. But that paled next to the prospective death toll if a First Imperium force caught the fleet so low on fuel.

"I'm sure we all appreciate your efforts, Commander. Right now there is no one in the fleet who holds our fate more in hand than your engineers." Duke was trying to give Davies a little shot in the arm. The engineer hadn't complained, but his people had been working twelve hours in pressure suits for every six hours off. That was a grinding workload in controlled conditions, but climbing around on an open superstructure in the upper atmosphere of a gas giant it was downright reckless. *But necessary*, he thought. And every word he had said was true. Davies and his people *had* to succeed. The fleet didn't have a chance if they didn't succeed.

"Admiral Compton will want an estimate on when the facility will be operational." Duke hated pressuring Davies. He knew the engineer's progress to date had been nothing short of exceptional, especially since he was working with far less than optimal equipment and supplies. But the rest of the fleet was at a virtual standstill without the tritium Davies' people were here to refine. And staring at the warp gate scanners and hoping no enemy ships came pouring through was hardly a strategy Compton could be expected to embrace.

"We've got the platform up and operating, but we've just started on the refining and purification units. I'd say three days, possibly four. As long as we don't have any more setbacks." The job had been an enormous one. Davies' people had been compelled to build an anti-grav platform, a huge structure held aloft by a bank of heavy thrusters. Without the platform, the immense gravity of the planet would have pulled the entire construction deeper into the atmosphere, until the rapidly increasing pressure crushed it all.

"Understood, Commander." Duke could tell the engineer

was tense. Davies was one of the best, and he knew what was riding on his team's efforts. Indeed, his own fate, and that of his crews, was inextricably tied to the survival of the fleet. Yelling and constantly reminding him of the urgency was pointless. And he suspected Davies blamed himself for the two members of his crew who had slipped off the edge of the platform as well. Duke didn't imagine falling until the pressure crushed you like a grape was a pleasant way to die.

"I will pass your report on to Admiral Compton, Commander."

*   *   *

"Entering warp gate in ten seconds, Captain."

The tactical officer's announcement was unnecessary. Captain Hans Steiner was well aware his ship was about to enter the warp gate. *Vanir* was the lead vessel of the three John Duke had assigned to explore the system they already knew would be dubbed X20. The naming convention was boring, but it was easy too, and the last thing anyone in the fleet had time for was thinking up names for new stars and planets.

"Stay on the scanners, Lieutenant. I'll want a reading as soon as possible." Steiner knew his own order was relatively pointless too. The warp gate would scramble his ship's systems, and his crew had very little control over how long it took for things to come back online. A razor sharp team could shave a few seconds, maybe. But then again, in a truly dire situation, that could be the difference between victory and defeat. Life and death.

"Yes, sir. Entering warp gate...now."

Steiner felt the strange feeling he always did in a transit, a bit of mild nausea and a flush of heat. Then he saw the stars reappear on the forward screen. A few seconds later, the main power came back on, and the ship's systems began rebooting.

Vanir's captain sat quietly, waiting along with his crew for their instruments to come back to life. It always felt odd just after a transit, that minute or two when a ship was blind, help-less. Steiner realized there was nothing he could do but wait for the systems to reboot. If there were enemy ships waiting for his tiny flotilla, scanners wouldn't do his people much good. His three ships were there to scout, not to fight. And if they ran into the enemy, their failure to return on schedule would deliver a clear message to Admiral Compton and the fleet.

"Scanners coming up now, sir." The tactical officer was lean-ing over the scope, waiting for the first readings. "Raw data coming in now, sir. The AI's online again and crunching on it." The officer paused, reading the information as he got it. "Star classification B3 to B4. Six planets, two in possible habitable zone. Two asteroid belts, one between planets two and three, and the other at the edge of the outer system."

Steiner listened quietly. They were there to scout thoroughly, and scans on the star and its planets were important. But he knew everyone on *Vanir*, and on *Woden* and *Tyr* as well, was interested in one bit of data first and foremost. Were there First Imperium ships waiting in X20?

"Targeted sweeps, Lieutenant. Focus on particle trails…any signs of recent ship movement." Steiner knew he didn't have to remind his people, but he did it anyway. It was easier than sitting silently, feeling extraneous.

"No signs of any ships, Captain. No drive emissions, no unnatural energy readings." A pause then: "We're getting indi-cations of multiple warp gates, Captain. At least five. But still no sign of enemy activity."

Steiner sighed softly. The most dangerous part of scouting was the first few minutes, when his ships were blind and para-lyzed. Now, at least, they were past that. That didn't mean there was no danger waiting for them in X20. But their chances of surviving the scouting run had just increased dramatically.

"Set a course for the third planet, Lieutenant. A system with two habitable planets is prime real estate. Let's see if anyone's been here before us."

*   *   *

"Move your asses!" Jerrold Davies clung to one of the large girders, watching as a crew installed the heavy conduits connecting the main refining unit to the portable reactor. The thick insulated cables were a tenuous way to transmit the nuclear plant's output, but it was all he had right now. He'd cut his way through half the safeguards in the book, but he'd gotten the thing done—almost done, at least—in less time than anyone had thought possible. Though a proper inspection would have turned up a hundred violations of normal procedures.

Back home a job this ramshackle would gotten you busted down to the ranks, and here it's as likely to make you a hero. There's just no time to go by the book when you're being chased by homicidal robots...

The power unit would be self-sustaining once the refinery began producing tritium, using a portion of its own output to sustain the nuclear reaction. But for now there were huge canisters piled next to it, fuel taken from the fleet's increasingly parlous supply. The gas was highly concentrated, and the containers were dangerous to handle. He'd be a lot happier when he could get them off the platform.

As soon as the conduits were in place, his people would do a last series of checks and fire up the reactor. If all went well, they would have an hour to do a few final tests before they activated everything and began extracting tritium from the atmosphere.

He watched his people climbing all over the platform, checking hastily assembled parts and running what few diagnostic tests time allowed. Davies had set the deadline—the refinery would commence operation at 4pm fleet time. That left less than two hours to get things finished. And working in the strange environment of the gas giant's atmosphere wasn't doing anything to speed things along. The gravity wasn't too bad this high up— about 1.3g. But the ammonia clouds were a problem. Every time one blew across the platform, visibility plunged.

The radiation was also a worry. The output from the planet's magnetic field would have been fatal to an unprotected man in less than a minute. His people's suits shielded them, at least partially, but he still had everyone maxed out on anti-rad meds. Despite all the precautions, he knew they were all going to need full cleanses and cell rejuvs when they were done. At least none of his crews had come down with full blown radiation sickness. Yet.

The refinery was a precarious structure, hurriedly constructed, its design based not on optimal specifications but on what the fleet had available. It rocked back and forth dangerously in the planet's powerful winds, and it drifted with the atmospheric currents. It had been difficult enough to secure basic thrusters to keep the thing up, but adding stabilizers and positioning jets to keep it steady had been out of the question. They'd picked the calmest spot they could find, away from the severe storms elsewhere in the atmosphere, and that would have to do. But calm was a relative term, and his crews faced a rough ride until the operation was complete and the facility closed up shop. Davies had everyone on safety lines, but he'd still had four fatalities since work had begun.

Normally, they'd have built an enclosed control room and installed a permanent reactor with proper safeguards. But time was more important than safety right now, and Davies was well aware that an enemy force could appear at any time. If that happened now, the fleet was as good as destroyed. The only thing that would change that prognosis was fuel, and every minute his people wasted was another sixty seconds the fleet sat nearly defenseless.

He moved slowly across the open deck, taking one last look at the three large intake fans. The refinery was a simple operation. Once activated, it would take in vast quantities of gas from the atmosphere and separate out the tritium and helium-3, both of which were vital to operating the fleet's reactors. Helium-3 was relatively easy to find in the atmospheres of gas giants, but a planet with a good supply of both isotopes was rare. Davies knew they were fortunate to have found one so quickly, and he intended to make sure his people did their jobs to the highest standard. There were 225 ships to fuel. That was a lot of tritium and helium-3, and not a lot of time to do it. The warriors had gotten them all out of X2, but now it was the engineers' turn. And Jerrold Davis wasn't about to let Admiral Compton down.

*   *   *

"No energy readings, no sign of any activity. It's the same as in X18, sir."

Steiner looked over toward the tactical officer and nodded. "Massive cities on both worlds…nothing but dead ruins. Untouched for millennia. It's an amazing thing to see…" His voice was distracted, thoughtful. He tended to think of the First Imperium as monsters, enemies bent on destroying all of mankind. And that was true, at least of the remnants of the ancient civilization, the machines it had left behind.

But what of those who lived in these cities? Were they like us? Did they live, love, feel happiness…and pain? Would they have been our enemies? Or would they have sought peace and friendship?

There was no way to know the answers, and Steiner pushed the thoughts aside. This wasn't the time or the place. Still, he felt frustrated. He wanted to go down to the surface, to walk through those haunted ruins, to know more about the enigmatic race that had left so deadly a legacy. Back in human space, the fighting against the First Imperium had focused on robotic legions and computer-controlled warships. But now they were moving deeper into that ancient domain, and the planets they were passing had once been home to millions of living beings… and from the look of the ruins, they hadn't been much different than humans.

But they were exploring the galaxy when men's ancestors were hunting with sharp sticks. *What have they left behind, other than their mechanical servants? What knowledge is on these worlds, what science and technology that could teach us?*

"Bring us between planets two and three, and then plot a

course for the outer system." Steiner knew he didn't have time to stop, and certainly not to follow his urge and land on one of these worlds—but he could take a closer look as his ships went by. "All scanners on full. Let's get what data we can about these planets."

"Scanners on full, sir. We should be…" The tactical officer's voice changed, his cool, professional tone replaced immediately by cold dread. "Captain, we're picking up something in orbit around planet three, just coming around." There was a short pause, and then the officer turned toward Steiner, his face white as a sheet. "It's a Colossus, sir."

Steiner felt the words hit him like a sledgehammer. The Colossus was the newest enemy ship type, one that hadn't been encountered before the battles in X2. It was an enormous vessel, fifty time the mass of any ship mankind had ever constructed.

"Red alert," Steiner snapped. "Let's get everyone into the tanks. We've got to make a run for it. One of us has to get back and warn the fleet about…" His words trailed off as he stared down at his screen, watching the scanning data flowing in. It was indeed a First Imperium Colossus, a monster almost nineteen kilometers long, bristling with weapons. But it was also dead. Unmoving, cold. No detectable energy readings at all.

"Cancel that red alert…bring us to condition yellow." Steiner was staring down at the screen, as the data was confirmed. Whatever condition the enemy ship was in, it was completely shut down.

"Take us closer. Three gees thrust. I want a visual. *Tyr* and *Woden* are to pull back toward the warp gate. If this is some sort of trap, they are to get back to X18 and report in full."

"Yes, Captain."

Steiner listened as the tactical officer relayed his commands. A few seconds later he felt the force of acceleration slam into him. *Vanir* was about to get a close up look at the biggest First Imperium ship mankind had yet encountered. Steiner had taken the necessary precautions just in case, but he didn't think it was a trap. The First Imperium forces didn't think that way, at least they never had before. If this ship was active, it would already be firing at his tiny vessel.

"Bring us in slow," Steiner said.

He had seen many wrecked enemy ships during the war, but the long distance scanning data didn't suggest any significant damage. Other than the lack of energy output, the vessel seemed completely intact. He had a feeling his people had stumbled on something intriguing…but that was only intuition. And if he was wrong, if that monster came to life, it wouldn't take more than one shot to blown *Vanir* to atoms.

*   *   *

"It's working, sir! Everything is running perfectly, within 2% of optimum across the board."

"So it appears, Lieutenant," Davies replied. "Let's stay sharp and make sure it stays that way."

Davies was standing in the center of the platform, his magnetic boots giving him a better footing as the platform swayed with the atmospheric currents. He was just far enough back from the huge intake vents to avoid behind sucked in himself. The refinery wasn't going to win any awards for elegance or style, but the haphazard-looking setup was doing just what it was designed to do. And that was enough for Jerrold Davies.

It was loud, almost painful, even with the heavy insulation of his helmet. He suspected an unsuited man on the platform would go deaf almost immediately, though that was the definition of an academic argument. Anyone caught out there without protection would be killed by half a dozen things even more quickly. Davies wasn't sure what would do the job first—cold, low pressure, radiation, suffocation, atmospheric toxicity—but he was sure it would be unpleasant, and he'd ordered his people to check and doublecheck their survival gear every time they came back on shift.

He looked up at the large shuttle hovering alongside the platform. Its thrusters and positioning jets were firing, its pilot working to keep it stable next to the refinery as its onboard tanks filled with the condensed gases being pumped out of Davies' creation. It was a rough system, one whose crudeness would slow the refueling process. But the fleet had no large tankers. The capital ships and cruisers couldn't maneuver this deep into the atmosphere, and there wasn't time to build a large conduit reaching into orbit. So there was nothing to do but ferry the precious fuel one shuttle full at a time.

We'll be lucky if we don't lose any ships, Davies thought. *Or if one of these shuttles doesn't crash into the refinery.* Navigating in the gas giant's atmosphere, through the turbulent winds and unpredictable clouds of ammonia, took serious piloting skills, and a single mistake could easily prove fatal.

Still, despite the dangers and the deficiencies of the setup, it was working well, pumping out fresh tritium and helium-3 and slowly refilling the fleet's dwindling supply. It had taken a week to build the refinery, and it had been an amazing feat under the circumstances. Admiral Compton himself had sent his heartfelt congratulations. But now it would take another two weeks at least to top off the ships of the fleet. And Davies knew he had to keep his people razor sharp that entire time. All it would take was one engineer or pilot to become careless, and people would die. And if the refinery was damaged and needed to shut down, the fleet would be stuck here even longer. He didn't doubt they were being pursued, that the enemy was searching for them. And every extra day spent in X18 increased the chances they would be found...and destroyed.

The noise backed off suddenly, as the refinery ceased pumping. Davies could see the shuttle's crew climbing out onto the hull, moving to unfasten the conduits. Another full tank, he thought as he looked up and saw a small glint of light in the distance, the next shuttle beginning its approach.

He hadn't calculated how many shuttles were required to fuel the fleet, but he knew it would take twelve or fifteen at least to fill the tanks of one of the Alliance *Yorktowns*. They were the biggest ships in the fleet, but the other battleships would still need eight or ten. Then there were cruisers, destroyers, frigates, freighters, attack ships—it would take hundreds of round trips to fully replenish the tanks of the fleet.

And I will be right here, monitoring every single one of them. Davies knew he'd be dangerously strung out on stims long before the job was done, but he also knew there was no option. He didn't trust anyone else to be careful enough, to stand there and remain vigilant…and ensure his ramshackle creation held up and did the job.

*   *   *

The huge ship filled the viewscreen, blocking out the planet below and the stars in the distance. Steiner had known its exact dimensions. The fleet had encountered its like in X2, though the behemoths had not yet engaged when the Alliance fleet escaped. But seeing numbers on a screen and actually looking at something looming before you were different things. He tried to imagine the power of a race that could build such things, and he felt a wave of despair, of hopelessness. *How can we hope to defeat them? Or even survive their wrath?*

He fought back against the dark thoughts, reminding himself that mankind hadn't done too badly fighting the First Imperium. But he knew that wasn't the whole truth. The encounter in X2 had proven that humanity's victories had been won against a small tithe of the enemy's true strength. Indeed, if the forces that had been arrayed in X2 ever reached human space, man's extinction was assured. Still, he found pride in the earlier victories helped sustain his own courage. On one level he knew he was fooling himself, but it worked nevertheless. After a fashion.

"Still no energy readings?"

"No, sir. The ship reads consistent with the background heat levels." A short pause then: "Wait…we are getting something. It's very faint. But whatever it is, it's not heating the ship or powering any system we can detect."

"Could it be a containment system?" Steiner wondered out

loud.

For all the time this thing has probably been here, could it still have antimatter supplies inside it? Still have a containment system operating, keeping the volatile fuel from contacting regular matter and annihilating?

"Launch a probe. I want a complete scan done."

"Yes, Captain."

Steiner couldn't take his eyes off the viewscreen. He'd been fighting the First Imperium for three years, but this was the first time he'd had such a close look at one of their ships, or taken the time to think about the magnificence of their technology. There was an awesomeness to the vessel that affected him strangely. He imagined a race, not unlike mankind, developing through centuries of progress, mastering the secrets of the universe in a way men had just begun to do. No doubt the beings who created the First Imperium had once wandered the hills and plains of their own home world, mastering tools, learning to build villages, then cities. Did they have societies like ancient Greece and Rome? Were they religious? Did they fight massive wars among themselves as mankind had done? Harness the power of the atom...reach out to the stars...

He felt an odd desire, a wish to see the ancient race that built this magnificent vessel, to learn about them. There was a strange feeling of kinship, even as he despised and fought against their robot creations. He wondered what they looked like, how their culture compared to those of the Earth powers. Had they had kings? Or was their society egalitarian? If they had embraced democracy, had they handled it better than men had? Had they taken responsibility for their votes, for those they placed in positions of power? Or had corrupt and deceitful leaders caused as much damage as they had on Earth?

He realized his thoughts were strange. He understood he knew almost nothing about the beings who had founded the First Imperium, that all the thoughts running through his head were his own creations, mere suppositions based on almost no real data. But he found the mysterious vessel—and the thoughts it provoked—compelling nevertheless.

He pulled his attention back to the present. Whatever fascination he felt, he had work to do. His three ships had to explore the whole system, make sure there were no active enemy units hiding anywhere. And he needed to map out the warp gates. Admiral Compton had been very clear—he wanted incredibly detailed data on the gates, power readings, orientations in space...everything. *But I have to get word back about this ship...now.*

"As soon as we get the probe data, transmit to *Tyr*. Captain Schwerin is to transit back into X18 and to deliver all data to Captain Duke."

"Yes, sir."

"*Woden* is to set a course for the outer system...and as soon as we have transmitted the probe data, set a course to join her. We've got lots of work to do here."

But he still couldn't take his eyes off the giant ship.

Chapter Seven

From the Personal Log of Terrance Compton

I must go to the conference room in a few moments. I have put this meeting off as long as I could, pushed the status quo as far as it will go. But I could not refuse the admirals, not without begging them to conspire behind my back. I am in command of the fleet, but my appointment was through the Grand Pact, mankind's alliance against the First Imperium. Our current status is, admittedly, uncertain. Are we still in active service to that body? Are our old oaths binding, or are we in a new reality, one in which prior allegiances have become irrelevant? Indeed, my own intent not to seek a way home pushes us away from our status as a fleet of the Grand Pact and undermines the legitimacy of my authority. Or does it? My intent is to increase the distance from human space, to almost guarantee we will never see home again, but I do it to protect mankind. What could be truer to those oaths? What clearer duty for humanity's alliance against the alien enemy? Luring the First Imperium forces from human-inhabited worlds is the purest embodiment of our duty to the Pact.

I realize such philosophical musings have little value. Justifications are pointless, old agreements meaningless. Men will do what they do...and that will decide the future. If I am to ensure we do not risk leading the enemy back home, I must maintain command, by whatever means necessary. I will try to persuade, to explain...but I know that will only take me so far. In the end I must be prepared. I must be certain how far I am willing to go. Am I prepared to use force? To assassinate rivals? To round up and imprison those who would seek to lead us back to Earth? Will I rule as a dictator, an autocrat who tolerates no opposition?

Yes. I will if I must. There is no purpose in lying to myself about that. If the enemy gets back to human space billions will die. Elizabeth will die. And the Elizabeths of everyone else on the fleet. I cannot let that happen...whatever I must do to prevent it. Whatever I must become.

AS Midway
System X16
The Fleet: 225 ships, 47,912 crew

"I want to thank you all for coming. I know this meeting is long overdue, and I apologize for the delay. Clearly, there was much to occupy our time, but I should have made an effort to gather us all sooner."

Compton wasn't in the habit of thanking officers under his command for following orders, but he knew the situation in the multinational fleet was tentative at best, and he'd figured there was no loss in playing to some of the egos present. The miraculous escape from X2 in the face of certain death had bought him some time, and it had made him a legend with the enlisted spacers and junior officers. But many of the senior commanders had their own agendas—not to mention egos—and nationalistic rivalries naturally surfaced when the threat of enemy pursuit appeared to have receded.

Compton knew their respite from the enemy would likely be a brief one, that they had not seen the last of the First Imperium forces, but he wasn't sure how many of the others agreed. There were some able tacticians among them, men and women of considerable intellect—but there were more than a few fools as well, pompous egomaniacs who owed their rank to political influence and not to any particular intelligence Compton could detect. It was a far more palatable thought to imagine they had lost the enemy for good than to worry about how to prepare for the next fight, and he knew more than one person at the table would rather focus on trying to find a way home...despite the seemingly long odds of success.

"Some of you know me better than others, but let me just say, I am a man who prefers to be direct." He paused for a few seconds. "So let me get right to the point. We must decide upon a well-planned course of action, one that will give our people the greatest chance of survival...and that plan cannot be to search for a way back home." He looked around the table, his eyes darting to glance at the officers he considered the likeliest sources of trouble.

"Have I heard you correctly, Admiral Compton? You are saying that we should not seek a way home?" Gregoire Peltier was one of the officers Compton had pegged as a problem. Peltier was the leader of the Europan contingent, a political admiral who didn't have a shred of military talent that Compton could detect. The one thing he did possess, however, and in abundant quantities, was ego.

"Yes, Admiral Peltier." Compton tried to sound as respectful as he could, but he'd never been good at pretending an asshole wasn't an asshole. "I'm afraid that attempting to find a way home is out of the question right now. We have enjoyed a short respite, but we cannot know what First Imperium forces are nearby...or what detection capabilities they have. Indeed, unbeknownst to us, they may know exactly where we are, waiting only to concentrate forces to attack us. If we seek to find Earth and we are successful, we could lead the enemy back with us...and condemn all mankind to certain death."

"You are being paranoid, Admiral Compton. There are no enemy vessels in this system. Indeed, it has been several jumps since we have seen any signs of First Imperium ships." Peltier was trying, not terribly successfully, to keep the fear out of his voice. Compton suspected the admiral was terrified about the prospect of never returning home. Indeed, he knew it took a certain kind of courage to look boldly into the unknown and remain calm. A lot of the men and women at the table had it, but Peltier was not one of them.

"Admiral Peltier, I do not believe I am being paranoid. I am not saying we can never try to return home, simply that it is out of the question for now." *As it will always be, but if I can satisfy some of them by dangling false hope then that is what I will do.* "We must be certain we are not being pursued, that there is no way the enemy could possibly follow us. That is not our current status."

"Do you have any reason to believe that we are being tracked now, Admiral?" Vladimir Udinov's tone was far calmer than Peltier's. Compton knew the Russian admiral was an able tactician, and a leader of considerable ability. He was also the lynchpin of any potential resistance. Fools like Peltier and Zhang were easily led, and it was easy for their fears and desires to override their limited intellects. But Udinov was nobody's fool. Still, he is very highly placed in the RIC. *He will want to believe we can search for home without undue risk. And I know Zhang has been working on him...*

"No specific evidence, Vladimir." *Keep it personal, friendly...* "But I feel very strongly it is far too soon to declare that we have lost the enemy for good." He turned and looked over at Peltier. "Besides, we must accept reality. Our knowledge of warp gates is unfortunately meager. We have only the most basic theories to predict the geography of each gate. We have no assurance we could ever find our way home. Indeed, we do not even know there is *any* route leading back to human space other than through the now-blocked X2-X1 connection."

"Then why not at least move toward human space rather than away? Our course selections to date seem universally to have led us farther away from home." Zhang Lu had been silent until now, and his tone was calm, rational-sounding. Compton knew how much the CAC admiral hated him, and he was impressed by the display of self-control.

He must be plotting something. Otherwise he'd be calling me eight kinds of devil by now. He's prepared...he reviewed my warp gate choices and done his own calculations. Watch the motherfucker...

"Admiral Zhang, we can do tremendous harm by moving back toward human space. We have limited comprehension of the warp gate network, but I'd say it is reasonable to assume the First Imperium has far more understanding of it than we do. If we head deeper into space—into the imperium—we draw them away from Earth and its colonies. I doubt their doctrine allows leaving a hostile fleet running loose in the home systems. Our course into the heart of their domains will draw their attention this way, and not back toward humanity. Has it occurred to you that if we lead them in the direction of human space that they themselves might find the way back before we do? That we may return on the heels of the fleet that destroys mankind?"

Zhang stared back at Compton. "I believe you are exaggerating the dangers. No one here is suggesting a reckless race back toward human space. I fail to see the need to unilaterally rule out a cautious, well-executed attempt to explore for a way home, however."

"The need is because of the unknown, Admiral Zhang." Compton felt a surge of anger. He hated the arrogant CAC admiral, but he knew showing it would only hurt him here, so he held it in check. "It is because we do not know the enemy's capabilities. There is no way to safely rule out pursuit—and let's not forget that our ability to find a way back to human space is still pure speculation and, in all likelihood, a tremendous longshot. We could look forever and still not find the route." He looked around the room and saw uncertainty on some of the faces. He knew the desire for hope, the belief that they could all see home again, was powerful. Strong enough to overrule judgment.

"I will remind everyone here that the entire First Imperium conflict came about as a result of the exploration of the machine on Epsilon Eridani IV, a planet in a system only three transits from Sol itself." Alliance miners had discovered a vast alien device on that world, an ancient anti-matter production plant. Initially kept a secret, it later became one of the battlefields of the Third Frontier War.

"We still don't know how the machine contacted the First Imperium, or why a response only occurred years later...more uncertainties in dealing with this enemy. And yet Admiral Zhang simply disregards all of this and assumes we are capable of exerting sufficient caution to eliminate any danger of pursuit...with a certainty sufficient to bet the fate of humanity on the outcome."

"You continue to paint a picture of doom, Admiral Compton." The CAC admiral looked around the table as he spoke. "Yet, you have no stated reason to assume that the enemy—with whom we have had no contact in almost a month—is somehow able to monitor us, to follow us back toward human space. If they are so able to do so, what is to stop them from finding an alternate path on their own?"

"Nothing," Compton fired back. "That is one of the great dangers mankind still faces. But we do not need to massively increase the chance of that happening. As we are now, we have no doubt diverted a large portion of the enemy's resources. Whatever intelligence controls the First Imperium, it wants to destroy humanity...but I suspect it is far more concerned with a military force loose deep in its own space. By continuing to divert its attention, we help to keep our families and friends back home—and all of mankind—safe. It is our duty to do so, Admiral. No matter what the cost to ourselves."

Zhang shook his head. "Even duty has limits, Admiral. We do not send gravely wounded men into battle so the enemy trips over their dying bodies. By any measure, this fleet and its personnel have lived up to their obligations. They deserve a chance, at least...a spark of hope if nothing else. And you would deny them that. Why? Because of well-founded fears of the First Imperium forces following us? Or because you want us to remain lost...with you in command, ruling as some kind of monarch?"

The room was silent. Compton knew everyone present expected him to explode with apoplectic rage. But that would only serve Zhang. The CAC admiral had stepped out of line, issued a considerable provocation, but anything less than pure rationality from Compton fed the suggestion that he was a zealot, that his stated fears were unjustified by the facts.

"Admiral Zhang," Compton said, struggling to hold his anger in check. "I can assure you that nothing would please me more than returning home." The image of Elizabeth passed through his mind, smiling, happy, as she was in the photo he had back in his quarters. Then her face morphed, the smile fading, replaced by grief, her cheeks streaked with tears...tears for him, as she looked out into space, crying for lost love. He felt an elemental anger at Zhang's accusation. He'd give anything to get back to human space, to see Elizabeth again...and Augustus. Anything but put them in more danger.

"I think we all appreciate your thoughts, Admiral, as we are all grateful for your tactical wizardry in extricating the fleet from system X2."

Compton bit back on his anger, but he remained silent. Zhang was performing well, playing the part of the reasonable man debating the paranoid zealot. *The colossal prick sounded downright grateful talking about the retreat from X2.*

"However," Zhang continued, "perhaps now we need more than a brilliant military leader. The issues we face are different, and we must think as humanitarians as well as warriors."

Compton glared at Zhang. *Warrior? You are a gutless coward, a political worm and nothing more. Certainly not a warrior.* But still he held his tongue.

"We must consider those we command, the thousands of spacers aboard the fleet's vessels. Men and women who have given their all to the fight. As their trusted leaders, how do we unilaterally tell them we have no intention of even trying to lead them home?" Zhang paused, allowing his last question to sink in. "Therefore, I propose that we take a vote. The senior officer present from each of the Powers will have a single ballot. The questions are simple. Should Admiral Compton retain the top command of the fleet? And should he—or whoever is selected to replace him—be directed to continue to lead us farther from home or to embark on a cautious and responsible plan to find our way back to human space?"

There was a burst of conversation as the officers present began to discuss Zhang's proposal. It went on for perhaps fifteen seconds before it was silenced with a single word.

"No."

Terrance Compton's voice was cold, frozen like space itself. Few in the room had ever heard him speak in such an ominous tone, and every eye snapped back to stare at the fleet's commander. The room was silent, save for the soft sounds of the ship's machinery in the background.

"No," Compton repeated. "There will be no votes. There will be no debates." He looked around the table, staring briefly at each officer in turn. "I am the duly appointed commander-in-chief of this fleet, and no one here—no group of officers here—has the authority to relieve me of that command. We are at war, deep in enemy territory, and all personnel are subject to the Grand Pact's code of military justice."

Compton paused, wondering if that last bit had been a bit too much. The code of military justice essentially made his word law and gave him the authority to issue any punishments he saw fit…including spacing anyone he chose for virtually any reason. He'd intended to lay down the law and try to impose his authority by force of will, not to say something that could be taken as a poorly veiled threat of violent sanctions.

The room was still silent. Compton could feel the discomfort and tension in the air. Most of the officers were trying to avoid eye contact with him. *You stupid ass, all the prep work and then you remind them you can have them executed any time you want. That's a great way to lead…*

He stood there for a few more seconds, but then he realized there was nothing further to be gained by continuing the meeting. He'd told them they weren't going to try to find a way home, and he'd made it clear he wasn't going to recognize any authority to challenge his decision. He'd intended to try to command through confidence and by cultivating their respect. But now his authority was just as rooted in fear. *Whatever*, he thought. *It doesn't matter. Whatever I could have said, some of those in this room would disagree. Perhaps fear will hold them in check more firmly than reason could hope to do.*

Perhaps.

"Thank you all for coming," he said calmly, his voice firm and commanding. "I think it is time we all returned to our posts. If any of you have any questions, please feel free to contact me at any time. My door, so to speak, is always open."

He stood still for a few seconds then he turned on his heels and walked out of the room, with one thought going through his mind.

Fuck...that went like shit.

*   *   *

"What is it, Dr. Cutter? I know your work is important, but right now is not a very good time." Compton stood just inside the door to the laboratory. It had been almost 21 hours since the meeting, during which time Terrance Compton estimated he'd gotten about 45 minutes of sleep. His head was pounding, as it had been since the day before, defying the attempts of several doses of analgesics to alleviate the discomfort.

"Thank you for coming, Admiral. I assure you I would not waste your time if it wasn't important." Cutter was standing in front of Compton, his posture suggesting the best attempt at a misanthropic scientist's idea of attention. "And please, feel free to call me Hieronymus." He glanced down slightly and stifled a small laugh. "Not that it is any easier. A family name, I'm afraid. Goes back at least six generations."

Compton smiled. "I can sympathize. I had a friend who had a similar situation. Admiral Garret, actually. Augustus is a name that goes deep among his ancestors too."

Cutter smiled, at least as much as he ever did. "Yes, Admiral. I believe I had heard that was a family name. Still, at least it was fortuitous for a man destined to achieve such military glory. Hieronymus, I'm afraid, only exacerbates by various social... discomforts." The scientist paused for a few seconds then he turned and gestured to a tall blond woman at his side. "You remember Dr. Zhukov, don't you Admiral?"

"Of course I do. Doctor Zhukov, it is a pleasure to see you again." Compton nodded and smiled at the Russian scientist. He'd seen her twice before but he still felt a rush of surprise at how attractive she was. She looked more like the mistress of some high government official than an expert in quantum computing but, in her case at least, appearances were deceiving. Anastasia Zhukov was a woman of astonishing intellect. She was extraordinarily charming as well, unlike Hieronymus and most of her colleagues.

"Thank you, Admiral...and please call me Ana." She smiled warmly.

"I will...Ana." Compton turned to face Cutter. "So, Hieronymus...what do you have to show me?"

Cutter nodded nervously and then turned his head to the side, looking off toward a small alcove. "Sigmund...come out here and meet Admiral Compton."

The sound of loud footsteps suddenly echoed around the room, and an instant later a robot came walking around the corner. Not any robot, but a First Imperium warrior bot, one of the most dangerous killing machines ever built.

Compton felt a rush of adrenalin, and his hand moved to his belt, toward his sidearm. But he managed to maintain control. The hulking monster continued moving toward the small group, but as it came closer it didn't appear terribly threatening. Its weapon systems were gone, leaving empty hardpoints and a few spots with exposed fiber optics, neatly tied off. It moved slowly, as if its power supply was limited, and it dragged one damaged foot behind it.

"Greetings, Admiral Compton," it said, coming to a halt about two meters from the group.

Compton stared in disbelief. He was usually difficult to surprise, but he was ready to admit he was absolutely stunned. "How did you do this?" he said softly, his eyes moving up and down over the First Imperium bot.

"I have been working for some time on a way to infect and control First Imperium processing systems with a customized virus." Cutter glanced at the bot then back to Compton. "Sigmund here is the first successful test." He paused a few seconds. "I have been sending you regular progress reports on my research, Admiral."

Compton had been staring at the robot, but now he shook

his attention free. "Yes...I'm sorry I haven't kept up on those." He looked back at the bot. "Very sorry, indeed. Hieronymus, this is amazing. You have total control over this robot?"

"Oh yes, Admiral. I could tell it to stand on one leg for you and it would comply. Though I probably shouldn't. He has some battle damage to one foot, and he'd probably fall down."

"You did all this with a computer virus?"

"That is perhaps an oversimplification, but essentially correct. Virus is probably not an accurate description. My software invades the system much like a normal virus, though I am afraid it is considerably more complex in how it operates. And it does not spread like a typical virus. I do not know enough of First Imperium communication protocols to begin to develop a replication and transmission function. At least for the foreseeable future, it must be introduced into each host system manually."

"But when introduced it immediately puts the subject under your control?"

"Again, an oversimplification, but essentially correct. To be more specific, the software takes advantage of the algorithms the enemy intelligences use to predict random and irrational behavior in biological adversaries."

"And that allows you to control them?" Compton asked, a confused look on his face.

"Not exactly, Admiral," Zhukov answered before Cutter could. "Hieronymus' system uses those particular pathways in the artificial intelligence's programming to gain access. Simply put, once it has successfully entered the processing core, it causes the intelligence not only to cease viewing us as a threat, but to accept us as allies. I wouldn't describe the result as outright control in the sense that the system is incapable of refusing an order. But its processes are altered so its assessment of any incoming command from a biologic organism determines that it is the correct course of action to obey. In a manner of speaking, it thinks we are duly authorized superiors."

Compton turned toward Zhukov then back to Cutter. "So that is effectively the same thing, isn't it? It will do whatever you tell it to do?"

"Yes, Admiral," Cutter said. "In a manner of speaking. But I hesitate to say we control it. For example, if it received input from another source…orders from a command intelligence, say, it would be difficult to predict how it would react. I have attempted to run some simulations, but even these front line warrior robots are vastly more complex than our most advanced computer systems. I'm afraid I still cannot predict how conflicting commands would be handled."

"So, for all practical purposes, you can manage the thing… as long as it doesn't receive orders from anywhere in its chain of command?" Compton glanced back at the battle bot. It was standing motionless, taking no action at all.

"Correct, sir. Indeed, that is why Sigmund just sits there and takes no hostile actions toward us. I have already issued the command that everyone on this ship is an ally, and lacking any contradictory orders, it will continue to operate on that basis."

"Hieronymus, I don't know what to say. This is a remarkable development, one with astonishing implications."

"Thank you, Admiral, though I am afraid it is a first step only. There is much work to be done before it will be truly useful."

Compton nodded. "Your research has just become a top priority. What are your next steps?"

Cutter took a deep breath. "Well, as a practical matter, if we are to weaponize this, to use it to actually control First Imperium intelligences—or to remove their hostile assessment of humans—we will need a much better delivery system. Sigmund here was a special case. But we can't exactly go up to active enemy warbots—or spaceships—and access their data points to inject the virus." He paused, looking up at Compton. "And I'm afraid to say, Admiral, that were are at the very beginning on that initiative. I'm afraid I have little in the way of ideas for delivery systems."

Compton nodded. "What else?"

"I would say a second consideration is ensuring we can prevent any orders from reaching compromised units, at least until we are able to do significantly more research into how contradictory commands are handled. For this, I have only a very simple solution...to disable all communication functionality except for direct verbal speech." He paused for a few seconds then continued. "That sounds simpler than it is, I'm afraid. First Imperium units have some astonishingly complex com systems. We know, for example, that the complex on Epsilon Eridani IV somehow sent a distress signal that instigated the first invasion. That would require, at the very least, a method for sending messages either through warp gates or over normal space at a speed greatly faster than that of light. Either of these possibilities involves science that is utterly unknown to us."

Compton nodded in understanding. "However, it does not require a full understanding of how their communications work in order to have a reasonable degree of confidence we have disabled them, does it?"

"I would basically agree with that, Admiral...with the caveat that we could never be sure. It would be a calculated risk to rely on the fact that we have blocked all communications."

Compton's eyes moved back and forth, from Cutter to Zhukov to Sigmund. "I have to say again, Hieronymus, this is most unexpected. The next time you have a development of this magnitude, don't let me ignore your reports. You march right on the flag bridge and drag me down here by my ears."

Cutter smiled. "Yes, sir." He hesitated. "I foresee another problem in the expansion of this program."

Compton looked back at him, gesturing for him to elaborate.

"Our best theories suggest that the First Imperium intelligences are extremely hierarchal. Thus, a soldier like Sigmund is near the bottom. It is likely to become more difficult as we attempt to access higher level AIs...combat leadership units first, then fleet and operations command systems. Beyond that we must assume there are other units for planetary and sector command...all the way up to whatever machine is at the top, making the decisions for the entire imperium."

"You're suggesting that what works to control a low level unit like this one might not work on more sophisticated systems?"

"Yes, Admiral, though I do not mean we cannot refine the

virus until it is effective enough to have the same result with progressively more powerful AIs. But it will take time...and we can only guess right now about such intelligences. There is much we don't know about them...in fact, we know very little. But I suspect at each level the increase in complexity is almost exponential."

Compton took a deep breath. Cutter had hit him with a lot of *very* unexpected information. "Well, Hieronymus, it looks like you have your work cut out for you." He turned toward Zhukov. "And you, Ana. I hate to virtually imprison you both in this lab, but there is nothing in this fleet—nothing—more important than your research. Please proceed as aggressively as possible. And if you need anything, anything at all, you come right to me. Okay?"

"Yes, sir," Cutter said gratefully. "Thank you."

"Yes, Admiral," Zhukov added. "Thank you very much."

"No," Compton said firmly. "Let *me* thank both of *you*. Your research may just be the miracle that saves us all."

Chapter Eight

Secret Communique from Admiral Udinov to Admiral Zhang

I am sending this communication through a trusted officer. He has been instructed to allow you to view the contents and then to destroy it.

I have discussed the situation with Admirals Peltier and Samar. We are all of like mind. While I do not believe Admiral Compton is acting with malice or with the desire for personal aggrandizement, we are in agreement he is exerting excessive caution and that allowing him to continue to do so, at least with respect to our own fleet contingents, needlessly costs us any chance of finding a way home.

Peltier, Samar, and I intend to assert control over our respective national forces and to leave the fleet. We do not intend to challenge Admiral Compton's authority over the Alliance units, nor any of the other national force leaders who elect to remain under his command. However, we are preparing several contingency plans in the event he attempts to interfere with our departure.

The time is upon you to make a decision. You are welcome to come aboard *Petersburg*, along with your aides. If you feel you can secure control of the CAC contingent and lead it alongside our own ships, I wish you the best. But I must warn you against attempting to persuade Admiral Chen. He will not repudiate his allegiance to Admiral Compton. I also must advise you that, while a united CAC contingent is welcome to join our splinter fleet, we will not have the time to deal with a fragmented and feuding force. So if you are not certain you can obtain complete control of the CAC forces, I urge you to give up any attempt and transfer your immediate entourage to *Petersburg*.

AS Midway
System X18
En Route to X18 V from X16 Warp Gate
The Fleet: 225 ships, 47,909 crew

"The fleet will set a course for planet five, Commander. Acceleration 1.5g." Compton didn't see any reason to punish his crews with high gee maneuvers. It would take a little longer to reach the planet, but the refinery's output was still refueling the fast attack ships and its own support ships. There was no rush in getting the vast and thirsty tanks of the battleships there when there were plenty of other vessels to top off in the meanwhile.

"Yes, Admiral." Jack Cortez relayed the orders to the other vessels through the fleetcom line. An instant later he turned back toward Compton. "Sir, I have Captain Duke. He says it's urgent."

"Put him on, Commander." Compton slipped his headset on. "John, what is it? Did your people find something in one of the adjoining systems?" He felt his stomach tighten. The last thing they needed now was a fight. Most of his ships were still low on fuel—and if the refinery was destroyed or they were driven from the system, they were all screwed.

"Yes, Admiral." A short pause. "Sort of. No hostile activity, but we did find something."

"What is it, John? Get to the point. This isn't like you."

"Well, sir…Captain Steiner found an enemy vessel in X20. A Colossus."

Compton felt his fists clench. His people had first encountered the enemy's largest ship class in X2, and they'd retreated before engaging any of them. But his best guess was that one of the behemoths had damned near as much firepower as his entire fleet.

"What do you mean 'found it?' You said there was no hostile activity."

"That's correct, sir. No hostile activity. The ship is definitely a First Imperium Colossus, but it appears to be non-operative. It's in orbit around the fourth planet…which also appears to have a large number of First Imperium cities on it. All apparently lifeless. Steiner's people are getting only trace energy readings from the vessel. They think it is an antimatter containment system still functioning on some kind of reserve power. But the rest of the thing is dead, Admiral. No emissions, no sign of any other activity at all."

"Is it badly damaged? Does it look like it's been in a fight… or an accident of some kind?"

"Negative, sir. Steiner's report suggests the vessel is intact. Our operating assumption is that it suffered some kind of malfunction of a critical system and shut down as a result, leaving only antimatter containment functioning, probably on some independent backup system." Duke paused. "Of course we're just guessing. Steiner doesn't have the qualified staff with him to investigate further.

Compton took a deep breath. "John, how many of your ships have refueled?"

"Ten, sir," came the reply.

"Okay…I want you to take them all into X20. And order the rest to follow as soon as they have filled their tanks. I want that system searched…and I do mean *searched*. If there is anything there, anything at all, I'm counting on you to find it. Understood?"

"Yes, Admiral." A short pause. "You can count on us, sir. If there's anything hiding in that system, we'll find it."

"I'm confident you will, Captain. Compton out." He turned toward Cortez. "Commander, get me Admiral Dumont."

"Yes, sir." An instant later: "The admiral is on your line."

"Yes, sir?" Dumont's gravelly voice was loud and clear through Compton's headset.

"Barret, John Duke's people found something in X20. A Colossus. It appears to be dead, though there is no apparent damage."

"Some kind of critical malfunction?"

"Probably. But I don't want to take any chances. I sent Duke and the rest of his ships to scout the system closely. But I want some power there just in case they find anything. I know your boats haven't refueled yet, but I'd like you to move your task force into X20. Just in case."

"Yes, sir," Dumont snapped off a crisp acknowledgement.

Compton paused. He'd been one rung below the top spot in the Alliance's naval chain of command for years now, but he was still uncomfortable giving orders to his old boss. He'd been wet behind the ears, the illegitimate son of a London politician adapting to life as a newly minted ensign when he'd first heard that gravelly voice issue him a command. He and Garret had both served aboard Dumont's flagship in the early stages of the Second Frontier War. *Shiloh* had been a battleship, the biggest in the navy at the time, though barely the size of a modern heavy cruiser.

He still remembered the feeling of abject terror he'd felt, not at the prospect of facing the enemy, but at the mere approach of the legend. Barret Dumont had been a hero in his own day, just as Garret and Compton had gone on to enjoy acclaim in their own rights. Compton couldn't remember a single instance of Dumont being anything but courteous and respectful to his junior officers, but they'd been terrorized by him nevertheless. Compton could almost feel the old sensation in the pit of his stomach.

"Don't get too far from the warp gate…just deep enough in system to support Duke's ships. And Barret, if you run into trouble be careful. I just want a delaying action, a fighting withdrawal. No heroics."

"Understood, sir."

The reply seemed sincere, but Compton remembered Dumont when his nickname among the ranks had been 'Warhead.' He wasn't entirely convinced the old admiral knew how to hold back in a fight. Still, there was no one he trusted more to operate independently.

"Good luck, Barret. And keep me posted. Compton out."

Compton sat quietly staring at the main display. He needed time...time to get the fleet refueled and on its way. A dead enemy ship wasn't going to stop that, but he still had an uncomfortable feeling. It wasn't like he didn't have things to worry about—unrest in the fleet, keeping the makeshift refinery running long enough to fuel all his ships, being discovered by the enemy. If First Imperium warships came pouring out of one of the warp gates while his fleet was spread out and refueling...he didn't even want to think about.

Time, he thought. *I just need some time. But my gut is telling me I'm not going to get it.*

*   *   *

Compton was sitting at his desk. He was doing work of moderate importance, but he was mostly just keeping himself busy. He'd needed some quiet, some solitude—a short break from the flag bridge. It was the way his people kept looking at him. He'd noticed it since the escape from X2, and it had only been getting worse. He understood. They were lost, scared—and they looked to him for strength. And he was there to provide it. But after a while, it began to have a vampiric effect. The pressure to maintain a calm and assured persona every moment, to hide his own doubts and concerns, was exhausting. The cost of being a source of strength for everyone else was to have no support for yourself, no one to look to, no one even to listen as you put voice to your own fears.

He knew he should try to grab a few hours of sleep. He was exhausted, but that didn't seem to matter. Every time he tried to take a nap his mind was flooded with thoughts, concerns...anything but peaceful slumber. He looked over toward the hatch leading to his bedroom, but he just shook his head. He reached out to the side of the desk, picking up one of half a dozen small white pills laying there and popping it into his mouth, swallowing it without water.

How long do you thing you can keep yourself going on stims? As long as I have to, his thoughts answered themselves. *You need to get some sleep. If you're not sharp, people die.* But he just shook his head. *Later*, he thought. *Later.*

He opened the side drawer and reached inside, pulling out the small image viewer. Part of him wished Elizabeth had been with his fleet instead of Garret's, that she was with him. She'd served at his side for years, and had only recently transferred out to accept a flag command. *Her promotion was so long-delayed*, he thought. *A few more months and we wouldn't have been separated.*

No. Wanting her here is selfish. She is back in human space, and there, the war is over. She can have a life, she can survive and find happiness one day. I would never wish her to be here, trapped with us in the endless dark...

Compton led his people with a grim determination and as much confidence and optimism as he could manage for public consumption. But he didn't fool himself. He would do whatever he could to sustain the fleet, to keep his people alive. But they were moving into the heart of the First Imperium. He had no illusions about their chances of survival.

"The guard is ringing the bell, Admiral." Joker had been with Compton for most of his career, and the AI had gone through three rounds of upgrades as its master rose through the command ranks. Alliance senior naval officers—and all Marines of commissioned rank—had personal AIs. The Marine units were designed to adjust their pseudo-personalities to complement those of their owners, a program that had worked quite well despite a considerable number of complaints from the groundpounders about surly computer assistants.

The naval units were a little more constrained, conducting themselves with a formality the fleet considered more appropriate to its dignity. Though Compton had to admit, Joker had acquired a few odd quirks over the years, despite naval stodginess and more conservative behavior algorithms.

"What does he want?" Compton always had a Marine guard at his door. It was standard operating procedure for a commanding admiral, something he'd always thought a bit over the top. But with his proclamation that the fleet would not seek a way home, it occurred to him a little extra security wasn't the worst idea. There was bound to be some bad feeling about it, and there was no point taking chances, even on his own flagship.

"Doctor Cutter and Doctor Zhukov are here to see you, sir." The AI's voice was calm, natural sounding. Its slight British accent had faded over the years, mirroring Compton's own.

"Send him in." He turned and put Elizabeth's image back in the drawer. He hadn't intended to see anyone for a few hours, but after witnessing Cutter's amazing work with the First Imperium warbot, he was available to the brilliant scientist any time of the day or night.

The hatch slid open and the two scientists walked in. "I'm sorry to disturb you unannounced, Admiral. Thank you for seeing us."

"I meant what I said, Hieronymus. Any time you need anything. Your work is beyond important. It is critical."

"That is why I have come. It is about my work." He glanced to the side at Zhukov. "Our work."

"What can I do for you? If the fleet has it, it's yours."

"Well, sir," Cutter said, his voice a bit tenuous. "What I need is not on the fleet."

Compton's eyes narrowed, and he looked at the scientist with an uncertain expression. "I'm sorry...I'm afraid I don't understand."

"I have heard that an inoperative First Imperium vessel has been found in system X20," the scientist said, unable to keep the excitement from his voice.

"Yes...though that information has not yet been released. It shouldn't be working its way through the fleet."

"It is not, Admiral," Ana Zhukov said, a hint of guilt in her voice. "I'm embarrassed to say that several of your officers told me. They are very kind to me, and they make a fuss every time I wander into the wardroom or the officers' lounge." The

Russian scientist was blushing as she spoke. Ana Zhukov was an extremely beautiful woman, one bound to get attention in any setting, but she often seemed almost unaware of her own appeal. She was a committed and brilliant scientist as well as an attractive woman, and if she was more socially adept than the reclusive Cutter, she was still far more at home in a lab than at a social gathering.

Compton almost laughed. "Well, I should discipline the officers involved, but I can't say I don't understand their efforts to impress you."

The redness in Zhukov's face deepened. "Please, Admiral... don't punish anyone. They really were very nice. And I give you my word, Hieronymus and I have not told anyone."

"No, certainly not," Cutter added.

"I understand your interest in the enemy ship. We just spoke of higher level intelligences, and a few days later we find an entire ship—a Colossus, no less—orbiting a planet, apparently completely deactivated." He looked up, first at Cutter than at Zhukov. "But we are still engaging in a thorough series of scans, trying to get a better idea what we are dealing with."

"I believe that Ana and I can assist with that effort. I am probably more familiar with First Imperium system design than anyone else in the fleet. From what I have been told of the situation, that ship either suffered a catastrophic failure of its commanding intelligence, or its main and backup power supplies failed completely."

"I agree those are the likeliest causes," Compton said. "But we must be very cautious nevertheless. Apart from the concern that this is some kind of trap, that the "dead" enemy ship will power up and start fighting the instant enough of our ships are within its range, there are many concerns. Indeed, simply triggering some sort of unseen alarm—as occurred on Epsilon Eridani IV—could result in the total destruction of the fleet."

"I understand, Admiral, but consider the potential. If we are able to affect a ship-command intelligence the way we have with Sigmund, it will be a major step forward in developing a weapon we can use against the enemy."

"Hieronymus is right, Admiral," Zhukov added. She sighed softly and looked up at Compton. "Think of the danger in moving too slowly. I understand that you must set an example to the fleet, to conduct yourself with confidence and assurance. But there are only the three of us here, and I suspect each of us knows that our chances of long term survival are extremely poor...unless we can learn to control these things. Or at least deter them from attacking us."

Compton was silent for a few seconds, returning Zhukov's stare. "You have a remarkable grasp of the practical for a scientist of your accomplishments, Ana." He sighed hard and paused. "Okay, assuming I gave the go ahead, what would you want to do?"

"I'd want to go aboard the First Imperium ship, Admiral," Cutter said bluntly. "As soon as possible."

"You understand that it is not an ideal working environment? Our best estimate is that the temperature inside is roughly 80 degrees Kelvin, not exactly a day at the beach. You will require full survival suits, and that is not likely to improve your productivity trying to handle delicate equipment."

"I understand, sir," Cutter replied. "Conditions are not ideal, that is certainly true. But how and when are we going to get another opportunity to get inside one of the enemy's first line vessels?"

Compton stood silently, his head nodding ever so slightly. "I am as anxious as you to see where this technology leads...but the very fact that this is such a huge jump in complexity only increases the danger." He wanted to say yes...but the risk was so great.

Still, Cutter's research may be our only hope long term. If I say no now, I may cut off his progress.

Cutter stared at Compton for a few seconds. "Admiral, I am not some overzealous scientist blind to all factors other than his research. And I cannot promise you we will be able to control the higher order intelligences that run that ship. Indeed, it would have been preferable to have an intermediate step, a ground combat command unit or something similar. But we must work with what we have, and Ana and I and our team have to find a way to make it work. We must succeed because there is no other choice. We simply do not have time to proceed slowly and methodically. If we are to survive we must make swift and sure progress. And this is the only way."

Compton looked back. "But the risk. It's just too great."

"You have fought hopeless battles before, Admiral," Ana said softly. "And you have won despite seemingly impossible odds. And Admiral Garret has too. Is this so different? Hieronymus and I fight on a different field, but we seek the same goal…to save the fleet. So ask yourself truly, do we really have a chance simply running? I think not, and I don't believe you feel any differently. Even if we can refuel, and find food and replace spare parts and avoid dissension in the fleet, how can we hope to evade pursuit indefinitely? Your decision not to risk leading the enemy back to Earth means our course is away…and deeper into the First Imperium. Into the heart of the enemy. Is it not better to risk all now, to strive for something that might actually make a difference? Something that could one day allow us to defeat the enemy…or at least stop them from attacking us?"

Compton sighed. "I understand your words, Ana, and you are not wrong. Our chances of surviving indefinitely are very small. But are they greater if I allow you to do this? Death tomorrow is always preferable than death today. Each day the fleet survives is a chance that something might happen to change the situation. And even if your efforts are successful, we still face the need to develop a delivery system to truly deploy the system."

Compton paused, looking back into Ana's blue eyes. *These are two of the smartest people in the fleet,* he thought. *And you saw what they accomplished so far. Do you trust to their genius? Do you stake 50,000 lives on the chance to completely change this war?*

Finally, he sighed hard and said, "You realize how much trust you are asking me to place on your caution and your skill, don't you Hieronymus? I applaud your work to date, and I whole-heartedly support your research…but if you do anything on that ship that reactivates it under First Imperium control, the results could be catastrophic."

"I understand that, Admiral. I can promise you I will exert the utmost care…and I will take no actions to reactivate any system without your specific approval. But this is an unmatched opportunity to leap ahead on this project. I had not anticipated moving so quickly, but fortune has given us an opportunity, one I firmly believe we can exploit. Much of our recent work has been focused on trying to rebuild a damaged battlefield command unit using spare parts gleaned from other specimens. It has not been going well." He looked up at Compton, an odd expression on his face. "I'm sure it is no surprise that our Marines don't seem to leave much behind them in working order when they win a battle."

"No," Compton said with a very brief grin. "That is not surprising at all. But still…an enemy warship? One of their biggest? That is quite a leap from a battle bot, wouldn't you say?"

"I would, sir. But it is also what we need. Back home, in a laboratory I would advocate moving slowly, cautiously. But our situation is hardly typical. We are trapped in enemy space, pursued…and you and I both know they will find us eventually. We must do something, whatever we can. And finding this ship is an extraordinary stroke of luck. At least let me go look around and do some research. Then I will report back, and you can decide if it is worth the risk to proceed."

Compton turned and took a few steps across the room, staring down at the floor as he did. Finally, he turned around and stared directly at Cutter. "Okay, Hieronymus…I will bet on you. The two of you be ready to leave in two hours. You may assemble any personnel you require and requisition any supplies. If you are going to do this, take whatever you need to succeed. This is no time for half measures. I will authorize anything you request."

"Thank you, Admiral," Cutter said, a touch of surprise in his voice.

"Yes, Admiral, thank you," Ana said, smiling. "We will not let you down."

"See that you don't," he said softly. Because it's not only

me. I just put the lives of almost 50,000 of your fellow crews in your hands."

Chapter Nine

Command Unit Gamma 9736

Everything was moving smoothly. The response from the Guardian Worlds was below expectations, perhaps, but nevertheless, ships were on the move. Fleets were gathering. Soon they would be sent on their mission. To destroy the humans.

There were fewer vessels than projected. Many of the worlds commanded by the Unit were silent, unresponsive...they had succumbed to the relentless decay of time. Still, the Unit commanded ample strength to eradicate the invaders. The humans had ceased their flight, driven by the need to produce fuel for their ship's reactors. They were primitive, a fugitive fleet far from their bases and industrial centers. It would take time for them to refuel. Enough time for the attack force to arrive...and obliterate them.

The Regent's command had been clear, and the Unit was compelled to obey. But its own computations were flawed. It did not perceive the same threat the Regent saw. The humans were weak, their technology crude. It seemed unlikely they could threaten the imperium. The Unit had not reached the same conclusion as the Regent. Its algorithms told it the Old Ones would have attempted to communicate with the humans, that they would have put great effort into avoiding war. But the Regent was infallible. Therefore, the error had to be within the Unit's own processing routines. It would conduct a full systems check, find the malfunction. Until that was complete it would follow the Regent's orders. That was the primary directive.

It would destroy the humans as ordered. But there was no satisfaction in such a pursuit. Indeed, the Unit felt somehow... wrong.

AS Midway
System X18
Orbiting Planet IV
The Fleet: 225 ships, 47,909 crew

"Are your people ready, Colonel?" Compton stood in the bay, looking out at a sea of Marines climbing into the powered armor units hung neatly on racks along the walls. On the far side of the bay a small detachment, already fully armored, was marching toward the first row of assault shuttles. They were the vanguard, a hand-picked team, and they would be the first humans to set foot on a major First Imperium world.

Men had explored Epsilon Eridani IV, but that planet was little more than a massive antimatter production facility. And Sigma-4 had been a small outpost with a military base attached. But X18 IV was dotted with the ruins of massive cites. Millions had once lived there...indeed, billions.

The landing craft were lined up on a track, stretching back from the closed bay doors. Each one held a full platoon. The insides were spare and crowded, but dropping in one of the small armored ships was still a hell of a lot more comfortable than going down in the Gordon landers the Marines would have used in an opposed assault.

Compton had assembled a large research team to land on planet four and explore the First Imperium ruins. There was time while the fleet was slowly refueled, and it was a learning opportunity he couldn't pass up. If his people were to survive they had to understand their enemy as well as they could. He'd ordered Colonel Preston to land a large force of his Marines to assist the researchers and to and provide security. The scanners had detected no activity, no artificially generated power at all, but Compton wasn't going to take any chances.

The whole landing was an unnecessary risk, at least considered from a purely military perspective. Still, he figured anything they could learn about their enemy was useful, and passing up the chance to get the first close look at what had been a major world of the First Imperium would be a waste he couldn't condone.

"We will be ready for launch at 0900, precisely as you commanded, sir." James Preston had been about to climb into his own armor when Compton walked into the bay. The colonel stood at perfect attention before the fleet admiral, ignoring the fact that he was completely naked.

"Very well, Colonel. Don't let me interfere. I see you were about to suit up."

"Yes, sir," Preston responded.

"I just wanted to let you know I'll be coming down myself. *Midway* is well back in the refueling queue, and it appears that I have some time available. And if we are going to successfully navigate our way through First Imperium space, the more we can learn about them—the more *I* can learn—the better chance I have to make the correct choices."

"Yes, Admiral." Preston's response was sharp and immediate. But despite the Marine officer's iron discipline, Compton could see the idea horrified him. "I will organize a bodyguard company to accompany you, sir."

"You will do no such thing. I can't stay down there long, and I want to see as much as possible in the time I have. And I won't be able to do that with a hundred Marines crowding everywhere I step." He paused then continued, "Two guards will suffice, Colonel."

Preston looked like he was going to argue, but Compton cut him off. "I appreciate your concern, Colonel, but as I said, two guards will be perfectly satisfactory." His tone was still pleasant, but it also communicated that the debate about bodyguards was over.

"Very well, sir."

Compton could see the veteran Marine wasn't happy, but he also knew the stubborn leatherneck would obey his orders to the letter. "I will go down in one of the shuttles with the research team."

Preston looked uncomfortable, but he didn't say anything. He just stared forward, averting Compton's gaze.

"What is it, Colonel?"

"Nothing sir. As you command."

"Okay, Colonel Preston. Spill it."

"Well, sir, I'd really feel better if you landed with us. Our shuttles are better protected…and I could requisition you one of the modular armor units. It might be a little harder to maneuver in than a custom-fitted suit, but at least you'd have some protection between you and something unexpected. I'd really be a lot happier with you in armor than a survival suit."

Compton paused for a few seconds then he nodded grudgingly. He thought it was overkill, but he figured it wouldn't hurt to take some precautions. Besides, going down with the Marines would give him a chance to let them know how much he appreciated them. The ground pounders always got restless when they were cooped up on ships for too long. Indeed, that was another reason he was landing so many of Preston's people. Compton didn't expect a battle down on the planet, but at least his Marines would get to stretch their legs a bit.

"Very well, Colonel. I would be honored to land with your Marines. If you'd be kind enough to direct me to a suit of armor, I will get ready."

"Right this way, Admiral," Preston said, reaching toward his shelf and grabbing his trousers. "We'll get you all set up and ready to go."

Compton follow the Marine, impressed by the physical dexterity that allowed Preston to somehow hop into his pants without losing a step. The admiral had been in armor before, then as now to satisfy his overly protective Marines, though at least the previous time he had landed on an actual battlefield.

He wondered if the Marines even remembered how uncomfortable powered armor was for those less used to it than they. Compton recalled feeling claustrophobic, but he had to admit that, once the reactor kicked in, moving around in the suit had been less difficult than he'd expected.

"Here we are, sir." Preston stopped and gestured toward a suit of armor hanging on a wall rack. To Compton's eyes it looked the same as the others, but he knew it wasn't. It was more of a "one size fits all" type of thing, intended for situations just like this one. He doubted he would be able to tell the difference, but he knew a veteran Marine wore his suit like an extension of himself.

"Sergeant," Preston yelled to a non-com wearing a set of maintenance coveralls.

The Marine turned and rushed over, snapping to attention. "Sir!"

"The admiral is landing with us, Sergeant. Help him into his armor, and run a full diagnostic check on the suit."

"Yes, sir." The Marine turned and looked nervously at Compton. Addressing fleet admirals was above his pay grade. "If you will give me just a minute, Admiral, I will prep the suit for you."

Compton nodded. "That will be fine, Sergeant." He turned back toward Preston. "I think I'll be alright in the sergeant's hands, Colonel. You can go suit up and see to your operation."

"Very well, sir." Preston saluted. "I will have you assigned to my shuttle. We're about midway through the launch schedule, so that's about 0920." The Marine stood stone still at attention for another few seconds, and he turned and walked swiftly back across the bay.

*   *   *

Compton stood still, his eyes fixed in awe on the city stretching out in front of him. It was a ruin, old beyond understanding, broken bits of ancient structures protruding through the encroaching sands. He had seen the remnants of Earth cities before, those built by the Greeks and Romans and other early civilizations. There was a vague familiarity, but that was a false comparison. The oldest city ruins on Earth were less than ten thousand years old. These structures were fifty times older... and yet many of the surfaces glinted in the sun, still bright after half a million years of storms and tectonic activity and relentless sunlight.

It was hard to tell from the ruins what the city had looked like, but Compton imagined a cluster of towers, gold and silver and metallic blue, rising kilometers into the bright sky. He felt almost as though the silent ruins were speaking to him, ghostly images appearing in his mind of a day when this metropolis had been home to millions. All of those soaring buildings had fallen ages ago, but somehow he felt he knew how they had appeared so long before, when the mysterious race that built them still dwelled there.

There were lines of debris reaching out from the city, the remains of some sort of train or monorail systems, he guessed. They led through the wilderness, and connected this metropolis to the other ruins that dotted the planet's surface.

He stumbled forward, still adapting to the strength magnification of the fighting suit. The logistics sergeant had put it on the lowest setting, far below what the Marines used, but Compton had still almost knocked himself over half a dozen times.

He could see his two Marine escorts in his peripheral vision. They stepped forward the instant he did, maintaining their positions on each side of him. They looked a hell of a lot surer on their feet than he did.

Which isn't saying much.

Compton walked forward, his gait growing steadier as he slowly acclimated to the armor. The city loomed up before him. The ancient wreckage had a sort of majesty to it, and he found it almost hypnotic. He felt as if he could hear the ancient voices, see the great towers as they must have looked in their heyday so many millennia before. He wondered if the First Imperium been a voluntary unification of the ancient race, if these extraordinary people had avoided the constant intra-species warfare that had so plagued human history.

Or were these just the winners? Did these buildings house the victors of an ages-long struggle, much like that fought by Earth's powers? Were their former enemies dead? Enslaved?

Terrance Compton has been a spacer his entire adult life, a warrior, an officer commanding his people through one battle after another. But now he found himself wishing he could stay on this planet. He felt the longing to study these ruins, to uncover the secrets of the First Imperium. He knew it wasn't possible, but he was glad he'd come to the surface, at least. It would have been a tragedy to pass through and not see this with his own eyes. He found himself wishing he could share this moment, that Elizabeth could see it all…and Augustus and so many others now lost to him.

He kept moving forward toward the city, his guards following in lockstep. Now he could see small sections of some smooth material on the ground, surrounded by the debris from fallen buildings and partially covered by millennia of dust. It looked like small sections of road surface or walkway, though the material was like nothing Compton had ever seen before. He wondered what kind of substance could survive—and maintain much of its old color and glossiness—after so much time. He remembered the dark matter infused hulls of the enemy warships, and again he was reminded just how superior the First Imperium's science was to humanity's.

Nothing built by man could last as long, nor even a fraction of the endless ages this city has lain here, silent and dead.

He took another dozen steps toward the ruins. He felt the city calling to him, his curiosity overcoming all, and he continued onward, his pace increasing as he began to feel more comfortable in his armor.

"Admiral Compton," he heard blaring through his helmet com. It was Colonel Preston, and he sounded nervous. Compton saw a figure moving quickly toward him. He wasn't as adept as the Marines in identifying any markings on armor—everyone looked alike to him. But he knew at once it was Preston heading his way.

"Yes, Colonel, what can I do for you?"

"Sir, we have not done a sweep through the city yet. I must

request that you stay back until we can determine if there are any active threats."

Compton wondered if Preston had been keeping an eye on him the whole time or if one of his babysitters had ratted him out. But he just smiled. He couldn't fault the Marines for trying to protect him. It was their job, after all. "Very well," Colonel," he replied, a little more sharply than he'd intended. He couldn't stay on the surface long, and he felt a rush of impatience at the delay. He wanted to see what he could see before he returned to *Midway* and the fleet. But he knew Preston was right. He had no idea what was waiting in those ruins.

Chapter Ten

From the Personal Log of Terrance Compton

Most of my hours are filled, consumed with work, with worry, with laying plans for the uncertain future. Yet still I find myself sitting quietly, alone in my quarters, while thoughts of the First Imperium drift through my mind. I am becoming more and more fascinated with this ancient and extinct race, and I cannot shake off the recurring feeling that if they had still been here, controlling their creations, we would not be at war.

I have no reason to believe this, nothing based in fact or even rational supposition. For all I know, the beings that inhabited this space so long ago were violent and xenophobic, and their machines that remained behind are simply continuing to carry out their will. Still, as we move deeper into this space where those mighty ancients once dwelt, I am beset with strange feelings, ghostly haunted voices speaking to me in the night. It is my imagination, I am sure. Yet it seems so real, so profound. I have come to believe they were not so different from us, and it is only through some tragic miscalculation by their robotic servants that this terrible war occurred.

That is a bleak thought, millions dead over a mistake, perhaps even simply the malfunction of a machine. Yet there is hope there too, slim though it may be. For mistakes can be corrected. Is it possible? Could there be a future where mankind and the First Imperium are not enemies? Where we can instead learn from these wondrous beings and the legacy they left behind?

RIS Petersburg
System X18
Near Planet X18 V
The Fleet: 225 ships, 47,844 crew

"I want this kept quiet, Anton...very quiet. Captain Harmon has become quite popular with the crew, and if word gets out it will spread. Indeed, we cannot even be sure Admiral Compton doesn't have another spy onboard *Petersburg*. I cannot overstate how important it is that the admiral not hear of this until we have made our move."

"I understand, Admiral. There will only be three of us, and I have handpicked the two others. I can vouch for their reliability. They will say nothing."

Udinov nodded his head. "Very good." He paused then continued, "And remember, Anton...I do not want Captain Harmon killed or seriously injured. We are leaving the fleet only to seek a path home, and I am not looking to provoke a fight by murdering Admiral Compton's top aide."

"We will exert appropriate care, Admiral. I can assure you, Captain Harmon will be taken alive. And I have prepared a cell in the restricted area below engineering, generally only accessed when the ship is under maintenance. The locks have been reprogrammed to allow entry only to you, Captain Rostov, and myself. We can keep the captain there indefinitely without raising undue suspicion."

"Very well," Udinov said. "Though I am afraid his disappearance itself will cause considerable suspicion. Still, that can't be helped...and hopefully we will not have to hold him for long. The tension in Udinov's voice was evident, despite his best efforts to hide it.

"The good captain may not have a particularly comfortable

captivity, but he will be unharmed. And we will release him before we leave the system." The Russian admiral had made his decision, though he still wasn't entirely comfortable with it. But there was no other option. He couldn't allow his people to be stripped of whatever chance they had of returning home one day. He hated the plan—it felt disloyal. But his obligation to his crews took precedence. He'd follow through with what he had to do, but he was damned sure going to make the whole thing as bloodless as possible. *And I will keep an eye on Zhang.* He was certain the CAC admiral was far less concerned with avoiding unnecessary violence, and he had no intention of letting himself get drawn into Zhang's vendetta against Compton.

"Do not worry, Admiral. I will see it done as you order." Loyalty to Udinov had been practically bred into Anton Stanovich and reinforced since birth. He took every word from the admiral's mouth as a commandment.

"I know you will, Anton." Udinov took a deep breath and nodded to his retainer. "Now go…it is time."

Stanovich nodded solemnly, and he turned and walked down the corridor. Udinov watched for a few seconds, until his aide disappeared around a corner. Then he touched the com unit on his collar. "Sergei?"

Captain Rostov's voice crackled through his earpiece. "Yes, Admiral?"

"Any status updates?"

"Yes, sir," Rostov replied. "Admiral Peltier's ships have been refueled, as well as most of the Caliphate contingent. However we remain second to last in the queue…at least another two days at the current rate of operations."

I'm afraid we just can't wait that long…

"Have we received an update from Admiral Zhang?"

"Negative, sir."

"And Admiral Compton?" Udinov asked.

"We believe he is still on the surface of planet four, sir. Our best estimate is he led roughly half the Alliance Marines down yesterday, and he has not yet returned."

Udinov smiled. "Excellent," he said softly. He'd planned

the operation as meticulously as he could, but having Compton off *Midway's* flag bridge, wandering around some ancient First Imperium city was a stroke of luck he couldn't have imagined. By the time the admiral managed to get back to his ship and take charge, Udinov would have his people buttoned up in the tanks and accelerating out of the system. He didn't know what Compton would do in response, but as long as he had enough of a head start he really didn't care.

"Lord Samar also reports ready to go, sir. His vessels are refueled, and he awaits your word."

"Very well, Captain…prepare to execute Project Potemkin on schedule."

*   *   *

"Admiral Chen…I am sorry to disturb you, sir, but it's urgent."

Chen was lying on the sofa in his quarters. He hadn't been asleep, but he'd been resting with his eyes closed, trying to relax.

"Enter," he said, sitting up and swinging his legs off the seat as he did.

"Good afternoon, Admiral." Ming Li stopped about half-way across the room and stood at rigid attention. "Thank you for seeing me with no notice."

"Of course, Li. What is it? Has something happened?" Commander Ming had been on Chen's staff since just after the battles along the Line. The desperate struggles to halt the First Imperium invasion had been successful, but at a horrendous cost. The almost endless casualty lists had included over half of Admiral Chen's staff, killed when his flagship had been devastated in the final stages of the fight.

"Yes, sir…I'm afraid I have some unsettling news. I do not have any proof, but I am sure my information is correct."

Chen gestured for the aide to move closer. "Come, Li… sit." The admiral waved his hand toward the chair next to him.

"Don't worry about proof. Just tell me what you suspect."

"Thank you, sir." Ming's voice was edged with tension. Part of it was by design, an attempt to add authenticity to what he was about to say. Still, enough of it was real. Ming had signed on to Zhang's plan, but that didn't mean it was an easy thing. He was committed, but he was still struggling with some doubt—and more than a little guilt. His fear—and his desire to return home—had made his choice, but betraying Admiral Chen was still something he found difficult to do. And his part of the plan was the most direct, the most brutally real.

He walked the rest of the way across the room and sat down, turning his face toward the admiral. He found it difficult to sustain eye contact with his superior. Chen was an honorable officer, and Ming had been quite satisfied serving on his staff. His loyalty to the admiral had been strong…but not strong enough to consign himself to spending the rest of his life in deep space, endlessly pursued by the First Imperium, without hope of ever returning home.

When Zhang had approached him, he'd been appalled at first, but then he realized the rebellious admiral was right. Chen had sworn his loyalty to Admiral Compton, and anyone who knew him as well as Ming did realized he would never break that oath. Allowing Chen to stay in command meant none of the CAC personnel would ever have even a chance of seeing home again. And there was only one way to remove the veteran admiral from command…

"What is it, Li?" Chen said. "You seem upset."

"I believe there is a plot in the fleet, sir. Or at least in our contingent." He paused, slipping his hand casually into one of the small pockets on his uniform trousers.

"A plot? What kind of plot? And who is behind it?"

"There is a plan for several vessels to leave the fleet, to flee through the warp gate and seek to find a way back home. And I believe Admiral Zhang is behind it, sir." It felt odd telling Chen the truth instead of a concocted story, but nothing else would have been as believable. *Besides, what Chen knows will only matter for another few seconds.*

"Are you sure of this?" Chen sounded doubtful, but Ming could see the concern in the admiral's expression.

"Yes, sir." Ming struggled to keep his voice firm as his hand grasped the small device in his pocket. "They attempted to recruit me."

"Recruit you?" Chen looked confused. "Why would they want to suborn you? You are assigned to my staff on *Tang*." The admiral's face hardened. "Is there a plot even on the flagship? Under my very nose?"

Ming inhaled deeply. "Yes, Admiral," he said, as he pulled the cylinder from his pocket. "I'm afraid there is." He pointed the small tube at Chen and pressed the button. It fired a small dart, striking the side of the admiral's neck. It was tiny, almost invisible from a few feet away. But it was deadly all the same.

Chen stared back at his aide, his eyes wide with shock and horror. "Why..." he stammered, struggling for air as he slipped from the sofa, falling to his knees for a few seconds before he collapsed to the floor.

Ming sat still, staring down at Chen Min's body. He started shaking, and he felt sick, like he was going to vomit any second. He felt a wave of regret, of guilt for what he had just done. Chen had been nothing but supportive of him. But he knew if he had it all to do over he wouldn't change his action. He respected the admiral, but he didn't want to spend the rest of his life—however short a time that might be—lost in the depths of enemy space. And the only way to get home, to try to get home at least, was to take Chen and his sense of honor out of the equation.

He breathed deeply, slowly, trying to center himself, to regain enough calm to finish. He knew the longer he stayed, the greater the chance he had of being caught. The poison would be almost impossible to detect, and its effects simulated heart failure. But if he was caught in the admiral's quarters, he was as good as dead.

He stood up and leaned down over Chen's body, reaching under the admiral's arms. He pulled up, muscling the corpse back onto the sofa. When it was discovered, the ship's doctor would find nothing. No ordinary tox scan would identify the poison. The cause of death would be a mystery, most likely ruled heart failure resulting from some previously undetected weakness. A more in-depth analysis might suggest foul play, but before then Zhang would be in command of the task force... and he would have had ample time to get reliable people in crucial positions.

Ming took one last look at Chen's body, and a wave of panic almost took him. Then he took a deep breath and fought it off, turning slowly to walk back toward the door.

*   *   *

"Let's go. You all have your orders, and there is no time to waste." Major Ang Wu watched as his armed and armored shock troops poured out of the shuttle. He was nervous, more than he usually was before a mission. He'd fought in a dozen battles, and he had advanced as high up the ranks a man with no political sponsorship could go. His soldiers were the elite of the CAC ground forces, but this was a very different mission than those they had undertaken before, one taking place on over a dozen ships at once.

They were moving to secure control of the fleet's vessels until Admiral Chen's death was investigated and his successor took command. Or at least that's what they thought...all of them except Ang himself. The major knew what was actually happening. He was part of the cabal that had assassinated Chen, and he already knew the admiral's death would be ruled as heart failure. His soldiers were there as an insurance policy, to provide security in the event Admiral Zhang ran into any problems when he took command and broke with Admiral Compton.

He swallowed hard, trying to force away the acidy feeling in his throat. For the first time in his career, Ang felt confusion about his mission. He'd fought human enemies, and the deadly robot warriors of the First Imperium, but this was something entirely different. In a few minutes, he and his soldiers would become part of a coup, a power struggle within the CAC contingent of the fleet. If they moved quickly and decisively enough, they might score a fait accompli, discouraging anyone from attempting to resist Zhang's disengagement order. But if there was fighting, they had no illusions about what that meant. They would be killing their own people.

Ang suspected his younger self would be appalled by his actions, about being part of something like this. He had been an idealistic young soldier once, with a strong sense of honor and a rigid code of conduct. That was before his wife and unborn son had died in childbirth, a tragedy that had been entirely preventable with the right care. But medical service in the CAC was strictly rationed, and Ang's wife had needed a higher medical rating than that she'd had as a young sergeant's spouse.

Ang had been devastated and, ironically, the loss propelled him into the officers' ranks. He'd been lost, broken, seeking death on the battlefield when he led eighteen soldiers on a desperate charge…a hopeless assault that somehow succeeded. He and the four survivors from his team occupied a key hill, and the positioning of heavy ordnance on that vantage point turned the fighting on Gliese 878 II from a stalemate to a glorious victory—and earned the heartsick sergeant a battlefield commission. He'd risen quickly through the ranks as the years of the Third Frontier War ticked by, but he'd been a major for ten years now—and he knew that was as high as he would go. At least without a patron of considerable influence…like Admiral Zhang.

Ang had lost his idealism, and his loyalty to the CAC leadership as well, the day his wife and baby died, and now he'd accepted Zhang's offer of support—and the promise of a pair of general's stars—in return for deploying his soldiers to the vessels the rebellious admiral did not already control. He had trusted junior officers in command of the other detachments, but he'd elected to lead the team on the flagship himself.

He moved down the corridor, following his lead units toward the central lift. Most CAC ships had a symmetrical design, with a central access point leading to all levels. It was an efficient layout, but it had the unintended effect of making things easier for boarders seeking to seize control. That hadn't been much of a problem since such actions were extremely rare in space combat. *But rare doesn't mean never*, Ang thought, as he looked ahead and saw the first of his troops climbing up one of the access ladders surrounding the main lift column.

He was listening to reports coming in from his teams as they spread out throughout *Tang*, monitoring the operation closely. The flagship had a crew of almost 900, of whom perhaps twenty were part of the conspiracy. His troops were armed with stun guns, and they had firm orders to avoid any kind of force unless it was absolutely necessary. They weren't here as invaders, at least not for public consumption. As far as anyone outside the inner circle knew, Admiral Chen had died, and Zhang had ordered the ships of the task force locked down until a cause of death had been established. Ang was the only one of his men who knew the cause of Chen's death had been assassination, arranged by Zhang to facilitate the takeover.

He glanced down at his chronometer. Zhang's shuttle would land in another twenty minutes. And less than two hours after that, the vessels of the CAC contingent—along with the Caliphate, Europan, and RIC task forces—would make their move.

*   *   *

Max Harmon was exhausted. Between inspecting supposed issues with *Petersburg's* ammunition supply and trying to hang around the officers gleaning what information he could, he couldn't remember the last time he'd gotten more than a couple hours of sleep. And trying to keep up with the way *Petersburg's* officers drank wasn't helping. Harmon wasn't averse to wine with dinner or the occasional scotch or brandy, but guzzling rough homebrew vodka like it was water was wearing him down even more than the fatigue. Still, he'd had no choice. He wanted to fit in, make them relax—and the only way he knew to do that was to act as they did. To become one of them.

For all the effort, though, he'd gotten surprisingly little from his new acquaintances. There had been a moderate amount of grousing about Compton's decree that the fleet would not try to return home, but otherwise, the conversation had been an innocuous combination of slightly exaggerated battle tales and stories of epic shore leaves—usually involving even greater consumption of, admittedly superior, vodka.

Still, Harmon hadn't given up. Now he was looking in another direction. He'd been finished with his inspections and looking for a reason to stay and continue to snoop around a bit. Before he'd been able to make up an excuse, Captain Rostov had asked him to remain for a few extra days, saving him the trouble. The stated purpose had been the discovery of a defect in one of *Petersburg's* primary missile designs that compromised the usability of half the ship's firepower.

It had seemed plausible at first, but as time passed, and ever more coincidental discoveries extended his job on the RIC flagship, Harmon began to suspect he was being deliberately kept on *Petersburg*. That could mean only one thing. Udinov knew he was spying for Compton…or at least he suspected. And that meant he wasn't going to get any more information. There was clearly something going on, and Harmon knew he had only one course of action. He had to alert Admiral Compton immediately…and then he had to get the hell off *Petersburg*. He'd go down to his shuttle and ready it for launch. Then he would say there was an emergency on *Midway* or that Compton had ordered him to address another problem elsewhere in the fleet. Anything. But he suspected if he gave Rostov any significant warning of his departure, he'd never be allowed to leave the ship.

He turned the corner, heading toward the bay. He was abandoning everything behind in his quarters. There was no point in alerting anyone he was leaving the ship. Suddenly he stopped. For an instant, though he hadn't yet heard or seen anything, he felt a rush of adrenalin. Perhaps it was intuition, but he knew something was wrong. Then, a second or two later, three RIC spacers came around the corner.

"Max," Anton Stanovich said, his voice friendly, relaxed. "How are you today? You look tired, my friend."

There was nothing in the Russian officer's voice that suggested anything but a chance meeting, but Harmon noticed that the two spacers with Stanovich were still moving forward.

"I am tired, Anton. In fact, I was planning to go to my quarters and rest for a while."

"Indeed," the Russian replied. "It appears you are lost. Your quarters are on deck four. What are you doing all the way down here?"

"I am coming from the magazine," Harmon replied, trying not to be obvious as he kept an eye on the two spacers. *Something is definitely going on,* he thought. *I have to make a break for it.*

"Then you are going the wrong way." Stanovich nodded slightly, and the two spacers closed around Harmon. "Come, we will escort you."

"Thank you, Anton, but that won't be necessary. I'm just very tired." He turned to walk back the way he had come, but the spacers moved into his way.

"I'm afraid I must insist, my friend. We will take good care of you."

Harmon saw the two men begin to close on him, and he swung to the side, launching a hard roundhouse kick as he did. One of the spacers fell to the floor with a shout as Harmon's kick took him in the gut. The Alliance officer took off at a run, trying to get around the corner. But it was too far, and his opponents were ready.

He felt a jolt tear through his body. There was pain. And disorientation. His legs buckled, and he fell forward, landing on his hands and knees. A stun gun. He struggled to stay conscious, to drive the cloudiness from his thoughts and to push his stricken body to keep up the fight. He gritted his teeth and lunged forward, half-crawling, half-walking for a few more steps.

"Please, Max." Stanovich's voice seemed quiet, far away. "Do not resist. We do not wish to harm you. But we must keep you with us for a few more hours."

Harmon wanted to give up, to let his aching body collapse, to cease his hopeless attempts at escape. But that wasn't in his blood. His mother was an Alliance admiral, known throughout the fleet as one of the toughest and grittiest to ever hold command rank. And his father had been a decorated Marine officer, killed in the terrible battle on Tau Ceti III. Surrender was unnatural to him, unthinkable. He staggered up to his feet, his blurry vision targeted on the corner just ahead.

He was almost there…and then an instant later he was face down, his nerves alive with the pain of a second blast from the stun gun. He tried to ignore it, to get back to his feet, but his body didn't respond. He lay there, paralyzed, barely able to remain conscious.

He was vaguely aware of the shadows looming over him. There was a voice, hushed, distant.

"I truly am sorry, Max, but as I said, we must detain you. No harm will come to you, and we will release you soon. You have my word."

Harmon's mind screamed with a primal 'no,' but there was nothing he could do. Regardless of his indomitable spirit, the martial relentlessness bred into him, his body was still only human. Few people could get back to their feet after a blast from a stun gun, but none could endure two shots and still function.

He felt himself fading, and the darkness took him.

Chapter Eleven

Research Notes of Dr. Hieronymus Cutter

We are approaching the First Imperium vessel, and I find myself quite nervous...scared even. Ana and I have updated our algorithms, and to the best of our current state of knowledge about the enemy, they should have the same effect on the vastly more sophisticated intelligences we expect to find in the ship. But there is no way to know for sure, not until we have examined them. Even then, there is a limit to what we can ascertain from a non-functioning unit. Eventually, we are going to have to take the risk of activating the intelligence, assuming we are even capable of doing so.

I may have understated the risk of such an action when I spoke with Admiral Compton. It wasn't my intention to mislead him, at least not consciously. But I must admit, at least to myself, that there is some risk of rebooting the intelligence and having the virus fail to establish control. These higher orders systems may have safeguards and protections I have not anticipated. In that case, we may actually activate the vessel, only to have it move to attack the fleet. Or it may simply remain where it is. This particular ship appears to have been deactivated for far longer than the First Imperium's conflict with humanity has existed. It may not operate under whatever orders have been issued to the imperium's forces. In that case, it may take no action at all. Or it may seek to destroy those of us who have come aboard. Indeed, that is a highly likely scenario, as we will appear to be an invading force, threatening the vessel from within.

Nevertheless, despite the risks, I believe we have no other choice. Even with Admiral Compton's unquestioned skills, we face an almost impossible task to survive in our current situation. We cannot even begin to guess at the enemy's total strength, and we have no data at all on the size of their domains. It appears we are passing through core regions of the imperium itself now, as most of the inhabitable worlds in the last few systems have had extensive ruins. Is it possible to reach the other side? To find an area of space beyond the First Imperium's borders? Perhaps. But it would take forty or fifty jumps to cross human-occupied space, and we can only imagine that the domains of this ancient empire are far, far vaster. And we face an unending series of challenges—fuel, food, equipment, weapons.

As a scientist, I am troubled at the prospect of putting my research to the test so prematurely. But as a member of this fleet, my fate—and that of all the others—depends almost entirely on making this technology work. If we cannot find a way to meaningfully interfere with the directives driving the imperium's forces, we will die. It is that simple. And if we are not to succeed, dying now might be vastly more merciful a fate.

AS Saratoga
System X20
Approaching Planet Four
The Fleet: 225 ships, 47,842 crew

"Dr. Cutter, you might want to get your people ready. We're beginning our final approach to the planet." Admiral Dumont was standing next to his chair, looking at the Alliance scientist and his RIC cohort. "I want you to know, I understand the enormous importance—and the risk—of what you are doing, and I offer you my true respect and wish you the best of luck."

"Thank you, Admiral. We are hopeful of success." Cutter hoped he managed to sound convincing, but he rather doubted his ability to bullshit someone of Dumont's age and accomplishments. He could see there was something troubling Dumont too. "What is it, Admiral?"

"I'm not going to lie to you, son." His voice was soft, but it had great weight to it. "If it appears that you have reactivated the enemy vessel and cannot quickly verify that you have control over it, I am going to have to…" His voice trailed off. Even a veteran like Dumont had trouble facing some of his grimmer duties.

"You will have to attack and attempt to destroy the enemy ship. Before it can fully power up…with both of us, and our team, still aboard." Cutter had no illusions about the danger of the mission. And he knew Dumont would have no choice. Whether or not his task force could strike quickly and hard enough to destroy the enemy vessel before it struck back was another matter, one Cutter rather doubted. He suspected Dumont doubted it too. But that didn't mean the grizzled old admiral wouldn't try like hell.

"Yes, Doctor. That is precisely what I will have to do. If we allow that thing to become fully operational, it could conceivably destroy every ship in the fleet."

Cutter just nodded. "I understand, Admiral. And agree. Though I have done some force estimation comparing the length and tonnage of the Colossus class to smaller First Imperium warships. It is highly questionable whether your task force alone could prevail against the enemy even if they were less than fully prepared and operational. But I would expect that the entire fleet could destroy it, even if it was at full power. Losses would be enormous, likely more than 50%, but I do not believe one Colossus can defeat the entire fleet, not with Admiral Compton in command."

"You have more of a grasp of naval warfare than I would have anticipated, Dr. Cutter." Dumont sounded genuinely impressed and surprised…and that was an extremely rare occurrence.

The admiral paused for a few seconds and said, "Major Frasier's Marines are already suiting up." Compton had sent the Scots Company to provide security for Cutter and his team. The unit was one of the most elite in the Corps, all trained in Erik Cain's special action tactics, and Connor Frasier had served directly under the legendary general. The unit was the successor to the one Connor's father had commanded back on Epsilon Eridani IV in the last battle of the Third Frontier War. The Scots had gone into that bloody fight as a regiment, but they'd come out with barely enough to fill out an oversized company. And that is what they had been ever since.

"I guess it's time," Cutter said, his voice wavering a bit. His drive and scientific curiosity were wrestling with his fear. He'd been anxious to get aboard the enemy ship—at least until the boarding action was so imminent. Now he was fighting off a wave of panic, and getting a harsh reminder he was a scientist who'd spent his life in a lab and not a veteran Marine used to dropping into deadly danger.

"You will handle it, Doctor," Dumont said softly. "You have achieved something amazing already, and you will find the strength to complete your mission. I am confident." A lie, but a well-intentioned one.

Cutter looked up and saw the old admiral looking at him and nodding. He suspected he wasn't the first—or the hundredth—Dumont had rallied before a decisive moment, but he appreciated it all the same. He could feel the respect from this fighting man, this warrior who had been in deadly danger dozens of times before Cutter's father had been born.

"Thank you, Admiral," he said, feeling his strength grow... and push away the blackness of his fear.

"Now go to your people," Dumont said softly. "They are scientists too, not Marines. They will need you...and you will have to be strong for them."

"I will, Admiral Dumont," Cutter said, his voice firming with each word. "I will."

*   *   *

"McCloud, take two squads and see what is on the other side of that door." Conner Frasier was standing in a large compartment, dark and mostly empty. He wasn't sure what it had been used for, and he hadn't chosen it with any degree of tactical consideration. Knowing nothing about the interior layout of the enemy ship, he'd simply picked a spot on the hull for the entry point and directed his assault shuttles there.

Normally, the heavily armored attack craft would simply drive their combination ram/access tubes through the steel hull of the target vessel. But the First Imperium hulls were built from a dark matter infused alloy vastly stronger than plasti-steel or the osmium/iridium combination in his armor. He'd been obliged to wait while two Seal teams performed an EVA operation, affixing heavy plasma warheads to the hull and blasting holes in the enemy armor. There wasn't any particular schedule to the operation, but he still felt like he was running behind.

"Yes, Major." Duff McCloud snapped off a textbook acknowledgement. The big Scot was a combat veteran—almost a cliché of the veteran sergeant. He turned around, and Frasier knew his subordinate was relaying orders to the other men of his squads.

Frasier had organized his expanded company carefully, and he'd arranged the OB down to the placement of every Marine. McCloud was his toughest NCO, so he'd given him the head cases, eleven privates and corporals who were such good fighters, they'd remained in the Corps despite a list of discipline problems that would have gotten any other Marines shipped off to the stockade. Even a private who got into constant fights, who feared no enemy, who'd stayed in the fight in battles where he'd been wounded half a dozen times, was afraid of Duff McCloud. It was widely rumored in the Corps that the veteran sergeant could chew steel, though no one had ever actually seen it themselves.

All of Frasier's Marines were crack veterans, and every one of them had come from the Alliance's Scottish Highlands district. Most of the rural and suburban areas of the Alliance had long ago been cleared of their populations. The government found it easier to keep the Cogs in line in densely-populated urban areas, and it wasn't of a mind to try and maintain order in thousands of scattered communities. But the highlands had experienced somewhat of a throwback to earlier days during the years preceding the Alliance's formation, as thousands of Scots moved into the remote areas and rebelled against an increasingly totalitarian UK government.

After the UK was absorbed into the Alliance, there were three punitive expeditions sent to the region, all bloody failures. Finally, the exasperated government reached an agreement with the local leaders. The highlands region would be recognized as a partially self-governing province of the Alliance, the only one of its kind. In return, the highlanders would provide recruits to maintain a regiment within the newly formed Alliance Marine Corps. That regiment had served with valor and distinction for almost a century—until the final battle on Epsilon Eridani IV—Carson's World. The Scots had covered themselves in glory there...and blood as well. The regiment was almost destroyed in the bitter fighting, and only a tiny cadre remained when victory finally ended the Third Frontier War.

Connor's father Angus had led the Scots to Epsilon Eridani IV, and now his son commanded the remnants of that storied formation, a double-strength company instead of a regiment, but also one of the most storied formation in the Corps.

"We're moving down the corridor, sir." McCloud's voice blasted through Frasier's com, shaking him out of daydreams of his father and the fighting on Carson's World. "No sign of any activity. No energy readouts except the same one from deep inside the ship. Everything else is dead."

"Very well, Sergeant. Continue...and search every compartment you pass."

"Yes, sir. McCloud out."

Frasier turned and took another look around the room. He'd done everything he could to check for threats, and he'd found nothing. There was no point in delaying any further. This was as good a place as any to bring the research team onboard.

"Dr. Cutter...Major Frasier here. You can start bringing your people through."

*   *   *

"Any idea where we are?" Zhukov asked, turning slowly and lighting the dark space with her forehead lamp. "I mean with respect to a likely location for the command AI?"

Connor Frasier had gotten them onboard the enemy Colossus, and his people had set up a perimeter, ready to advance in front of the research party whenever they decided where they wanted to go. But the Marines had no idea where anything was in the enemy warship, and Cutter had to admit to himself he didn't have much better an idea.

"I'm afraid not, Ana." Cutter was looking around himself, the long thin shaft of light from his forehead moving around, over the floor, the walls. "I'd say the first step is figuring out where we are. This ship is immense. If we don't manage to narrow down where to look, I suspect we could wander the corridors for weeks."

He turned back toward the small cluster of support personnel standing behind him. "Let's get some light in here. If there's anything live on this ship that can detect us, I think blasting through the hull already did more harm than some lamps will do."

Three of the shadowy figures moved forward. They were carrying large plastic cylinders, and they placed them around the room, flipping a switch on each as they did. The portable lamps shone brightly, bathing the entire room in soft light.

"Alright everybody," Cutter said into the group com. "Spread out. We need to know what this room is so we can start to get some idea where to go next."

He turned and walked toward one of the walls. They were built from a material he'd never seen before, some type of metal alloy with a slightly blue cast to it. They were smooth, almost shiny, despite their vast age. He turned and stared out across the entire compartment. It was large, perhaps thirty meters by twenty, and the ceiling soared ten meters above the floor.

"If this was a human ship, I'd swear this looks like some kind of gym or athletic facility." Ana had wandered a few meters away, but her voice was crisp and clear on the com. "Like a place to play some kind of sport."

Cutter looked around the edges of the room. There were rows of small ledges. *Seats. Ana is right. But what do robot ships need with athletic facilities?*

"This door leads deeper into the vessel, Hieronymus," Ana said softly, gesturing toward a hatch on one of the walls. "The artificial intelligence core will be in a protected area. That means deep inside."

"I agree." He walked toward the open hatch. The Marines had already gone through, scouting forward to clear a path. Cutter flipped the com channel to the Marine command line. "Major Frasier, we're going to move through this hatch and head deeper into the ship."

"Very well, Dr. Cutter. My men have been through there. No signs of any danger." A short pause and then: "I have detached a squad to escort your party, Doctor. Just in case."

Cutter sighed softly. Still, he was just as glad to have the Marines so close. His intellect—and his ravenous curiosity—had overwhelmed his fear, at least for now. But he had to admit the veteran warriors made him feel a hell of a lot better.

"Very well, Major. Thank you." He flipped the com to his party's channel. "Okay, we're about to head into the bowels of this ship. You all know what we're looking for. Signs of any kind of data processing center or even conduits or equipment that could be peripheral systems of the intelligence that ran this ship. Maintenance systems, weapons, navigation and guidance equipment—all of it has to be connected into the vessel's data network. And that has to lead back to the main processing unit."

He took a deep breath. "So let's go find it. Whatever it takes."

Chapter Twelve

From the Personal Log of Terrance Compton

As I dictate this, I am standing on the surface of an alien world, striding through the ruins of a city that once dwarfed any human metropolis. Though it is but a wreck, an ancient ruin, old almost beyond imagining, it remains a wonder. I am convinced it was magnificent in its day, beautiful in a way I doubt I can understand. I can see in the materials, so many of them astonishingly well-preserved through the endless ages, and in the layout, still discernible amid the crumbled towers and shattered thoroughfares.

My thoughts of the First Imperium have been formed by war and conflict, by the actions of the robot servants that once-great civilization left behind. By thoughts of friends killed in terrible battles, of colony worlds reduced to radioactive nightmares. But now I see something else. I see a race of surpassing capabilities. Even in the ruins, this city shows me much of these long lost people. They appreciated art and beauty, that is clear even from the broken remains of their constructions. Though their instruments of war are powerful beyond reckoning, I can see as I walk through the ghostly city that this was no warrior race, devoted to conquest above all things. These were artists and scientists and philosophers as well. And yet they left behind so much death and destruction waiting to be unleashed.

Perhaps none of this matters. When I return to *Midway*, nothing will have changed. The ships of the First Imperium will still be enemies. They will attack and kill my people if they find us. None of the magnificence of this city, nor any imaginings about what these people were like, will change that fact. Yet, something is nagging at me, a regret that we are fighting the legacy of this extraordinary race. More than that. Though I cannot explain it, I am coming to believe that this war was not meant to be, that the death and destruction and terror—and the brutal necessity that stranded us here—were all parts of a terrible mistake of some kind.

First Imperium Ruins
System X18 - Planet IV
The Fleet: 225 ships, 47,842 crew

"Are you sure?" Sophie Barcomme pulled her own scanner from her belt and flipped it on.

Barcomme was one of Europa Federalis' leading scientists. She'd been with the forces at Sigma 4, researching the First Imperium facility there for signs of the ancient life form when she'd temporarily transferred to one of the ships in Compton's fleet to investigate some debris from enemy vessels. She'd expected to be there less than a week, but her timing had been downright disastrous. Two days after her arrival, Admiral Garret detonated the explosive in the warp gate, trapping Barcomme with Compton's fleet...with her husband and daughter on the other side. Since then, she'd buried herself in work...anything to keep her mind busy.

"I'm sure," came the reply. Jacques Suchet was one of the scientists on her team. She'd found him to be reasonably capable, though also a bit of an egomaniac. But there was no arrogance in his voice now, only fear.

Barcomme stared at the small screen on her monitor. Suchet was right. And now she was reading four different energy sources. They were small, but they appeared to be increasing in intensity. *And number*, she thought as she watched a fifth and a sixth reading pop onto her screen.

She flipped her com unit to the main channel for her team.

"I want everyone scanning for energy sources. Now! I want every detail…location, type of energy, strength." She shook her head as a seventh reading flashed onto her monitor.

What the hell is this? This planet was supposed to be dead, the lifeless ruins of a race long extinct. But energy readings don't lie. Something is still active here…even after all these millennia…

She moved straight ahead, toward one of the energy sources. Her stomach was knotted, and she could feel the fear building in her. Man's experiences with the First Imperium to date had been almost universally unpleasant…and she didn't suspect that was about to change any time within the next few minutes. But she was a scientist, and it was her job to investigate. Still, she felt herself slowing down as she got closer. Sweat was pouring down her back, making the already uncomfortable survival suit nearly unbearable. Then she stopped. She was less than a hundred meters from the energy source…and now *it* was moving. Toward her.

She spun around and moved quickly back the way she had come. She was poking at her com controls as she fled, calling up Admiral Compton. He *had* to know about this. Now.

*   *   *

"Admiral, it's Sophie Barcomme. I am picking up sporadic energy readings. They were stationary, but now I've got at least one moving."

Compton had been prone, picking through shattered bits of blue metal laying around a large chunk of unidentified material. He jumped to his feet at the voice blaring through his com. He lost his footing, pushing off with too much force, and he fell over backwards, one of his Marine guards catching him before he hit the ground. He wiggled free and got back to his feet. *Damned armor.*

"Sophie, get you and your team back to the camp now," Compton snapped. "Hurry." Sudden energy readings could mean several things he could think of, but none of them were good.

Compton had never met the intriguing French scientist before they were both cut off from human space, but he'd worked extensively with her since. He'd asked her to head up a project to utilize the gradually emptying holds of the transport vessels for food production. Compton knew they could grow some crops and edible funguses on board the ships. It would never be more than a partial solution, but anything that could stretch their supplies was worth pursuing. And Barcomme was an expert. If anyone could squeeze more production out of the project, it was her. That meant more people fed.

The two had become relatively close over the past few months. Both ached from the wounds of being separated from loved ones, though Compton had to acknowledge that, as devastated as he was by the loss of Elizabeth, he couldn't imagine the pain of leaving behind a spouse *and* a five year old child.

He flipped the com to the Marine frequency. "Colonel Preston, Dr. Barcomme's team is picking up energy readings." He was already moving back toward the camp as he spoke.

"I'm sending a squad to you, Admiral. They should be there in less than a minute. We will…"

A blast of static exploded into Compton's helmet. *What the hell?* Then he realized. *We're being jammed.* He'd had a passing thought that Barcomme's people had just discovered some ancient machine, harmless but still operative enough to give off energy readings. Now even that shred of hope was stripped away. The jamming was pretty convincing proof that they had activated some kind of defense mechanism.

He increased the power of his com unit, just as Preston's staticky voice blasted back into his helmet. "Admiral…your guards will get you back to camp." The words were distorted, hard to hear, but Compton understood. He felt the two Marines grabbing onto him, pushing him back toward the camp.

He shuffled along, stumbling as his bodyguards held onto his arms, keeping him upright and moving swiftly back out of the city. They were almost to the open plain south of the ruins when Compton heard a loud boom off to his left. Then another. A second later he heard the distant sounds of Marine assault rifles firing in response. Whatever lingering doubt he'd had was gone. They were under attack.

*   *   *

"We need that thing operating, Lieutenant. Now." Compton was leaning against a crate in the center of the now-fortified main camp. He'd taken a hit in the arm on the way back, and he was impressed at his first experience with the trauma control functionality of his armor. The system had stopped the bleeding, sterilized the wound, and packed it off, all the while injecting painkillers and adrenalin compounds. The servo-mechanicals of the fighting suit adjusted as well, feeding more power to compensate for the injured arm. He almost forgot he was wounded.

What he couldn't forget was that one of his guards was dead. Corporal Garder was one of the two Marines James Preston had assigned to protect the fleet admiral, and the Marine hero had died doing just that, jumping between Compton and a First Imperium battle bot.

The enemy jamming was making communications difficult at best. Preston's Marines were out there, hunting down the enemy robots, but the lack of effective com was making that a difficult—and dangerous—effort. If they could get the portable reactor up and running it might give them enough power to burn through the jamming, providing at least one way coms to the Marines in the field.

Compton was frustrated, angry. *I shouldn't have done this, landed here. It was my curiosity, my urge to see these ruins. And now my people are dying.*

He was worried about the fleet too. Things were confused and unstable there too. He had no idea how much opposition he would face over his plan to move away from human space. And now his communication was cut off. *That means we've acti-*

vated at least some of the ancient satellites, he thought grimly. And with Admiral Dumont in X20, the fleet command in his absence was uncertain.

He was hopeful the small reactor would enable surface coms, but he doubted it would cut through the heavy jamming that was blocking signals to and from the fleet. Even if the Marines wiped out the entire enemy force, there weren't enough shuttles on the ground to get everyone off-world…which meant he'd have to send a force up to get clear of the jamming and order a rescue mission to launch at once. He knew he should go with that shuttle. His place was back on the fleet, not dodging enemy bots. But Terrance Compton wasn't wired that way, and he wasn't going to abandon those he'd led here. They would all get off the planet together, and that was his final thought on the matter. He could feel the tension, the anger, surging through his body.

"Lieutenant, I want that reactor up and running immediately," he snapped angrily, realizing as the words escaped his mouth he was being unfair to the engineer.

"One minute, sir," the intimidated lieutenant squeaked back. "If I warm it up too quickly, it'll scrag."

Compton nodded, though he knew that kind of communication was difficult in armor. He looked up, to the side of the two meter-wide cylinder. James Preston was standing there, his impatience clear even though his fighting suit. Compton understood completely. Both of them felt responsible for the Marines dying out there. At least if they could restore partial communications and scanning, Preston could help his people get through the fight.

"Okay," said the engineering officer. "We're generating power now, sir. The reaction is at forty percent, but that should be enough to power short range communications, even with the jamming."

Preston turned around abruptly, gesturing to a pair of Marines holding a large conduit. They slid it in place. A few seconds later, a burst of feedback blasted through Compton's helmet…followed by a voice, loud and clear. "We have restored outgoing coms from the main station. But I doubt we can transmit more than a klick and a half, maybe two through this jamming."

Compton moved over toward the communications station, as quickly as he could manage in his armor. Preston, vastly more experienced at moving around in a fighting suit, was there before Compton had taken two steps.

"Attention all Marines, this is Colonel Preston." Compton heard the Marine commander on the general channel. "We are being jammed, but we've got the main coms hooked up to the reactor. We can send outgoing signals, but your ability to reply or communicate with each other is sharply limited. I have scanning capability now as well, so I will be directing the battle from here."

Compton stood behind the Marine officer, watching silently. He was the overall commander, of course, but he knew he couldn't do anything but distract Preston now. Part of good leadership is knowing when to shut the hell up.

He stood still for a few minutes, listening to Preston direct the battle…actually more of a hunt. It looked like they'd activated perhaps a hundred enemy warbots. That was a dangerous number, but not enough to defeat a thousand of Preston's men and women. That didn't mean Marines wouldn't die, indeed many had already. But they would prevail in the end.

Compton angled back his head, looking up into the late afternoon sky. *What is happening up there?* He knew a rescue party would come when they missed the regular check in, but it could be hours before that happened, even a day or more.

He knew he had left good people behind, and he had complete confidence in them all. But he still had an unsettled feeling, a hazy, tentative thought that he should have fought off the urge to see planet four's ruins himself. *Midway* was up there, hovering somewhere about a million klicks from planet five.

And that's where I belong…

Chapter Thirteen

Transmission from Admiral Vladimir Udinov

Attention all vessels. This is Admiral Vladimir Udinov, transmitting from the RIC vessel *Petersburg*. In joint consultation with the commanders of the CAC, Europan, and Caliphate contingents, we have elected to remove our respective forces from the current fleet structure. We all retain the utmost respect for Admiral Compton and his achievements, but we have determined that the best interest of our crews is served by this separation.

We intend no hostile action toward any other vessel, nor do we plan to interfere with the chosen dispositions of the other contingents. However, it is necessary that we are able to refuel those of our vessels still in the queue. It is for that reason only I have ordered *Petersburg* to take position just above planet five. From that location, we are able to fire upon the refinery complex, destroying it utterly if anyone attempts to interfere with our refueling. When we are done, our ships will peacefully depart, leaving the refinery undamaged and ready to continue refueling the rest of the fleet.

If any vessels attempt to interfere—either with our own refueling operations or with our departure from the fleet, *Petersburg* will open fire and destroy the facility. I urge a calm and rational response by all parties. If we are allowed to refuel and depart, we will do so without violence.

AS Midway
System X18
The Fleet: 225 ships, 47,841 crew

"I still can't raise the admiral, Captain Horace. There's some kind of jamming around the planet." Jack Cortez stared over at the empty command chair for what felt like the hundredth time. Compton wasn't onboard...and all hell was breaking loose.

"Keep trying, Commander. We've got to do something. *Petersburg* is holding the refinery at gunpoint, and I hesitate to even think of what the other contingent commanders are saying to each other."

"Yes, sir. But shouldn't we be doing something now? Admiral Compton wouldn't just sit here and allow Udinov to hijack the refinery."

"I'm sure you're right, Commander, but I'm not Terrance Compton. I don't have his ability—and I damned sure don't have his rank or reputation. I'm more inclined to try to avoid catastrophic mistakes than to risk any bold moves before I know exactly what is going on."

"Yes, sir." Cortez didn't like it, but he knew Horace was right.

"And Commander...if you can't get through to the admiral on planet four we're going to need to send someone there. We have to get to Admiral Compton. And every second we lose could be the one that kills us."

"Yes, sir. I understand." Cortez turned toward the communications officer. "Lieutenant, please tell Adm...ask Admiral Hurley to come to the line." He wasn't speaking for Compton right now, so he wasn't *telling* an admiral to do anything.

"She is on your com, sir."

"Admiral Hurley, this is Commander Cortez. As you know, Admiral Compton went down to the surface of planet four with the Marines and the research teams."

"Yes, I know. What is it?"

"We've got a crisis up here. Half the fleet is trying to break off so they can look for a route home. They've got their guns trained on the refinery. And we've lost contact with the admiral. There is some kind of jamming blocking our communications."

"Jamming from the mutineers?" Hurley didn't pull punches, and she had no patience for anyone disobeying Compton or rebelling against his authority.

"No, Admiral. We don't think so. It looks like First Imperium jamming." Cortez paused for a second. "Ah…we wanted to request that you put together a team and send them to planet four to see if they can find Admiral Compton."

"I'm on it, Commander. Do what you have to do to keep things together here. I'll go get the Admiral myself."

Cortez exhaled sharply. "Thank you, Admiral Hurley."

He flipped the com back to Captain Horace's line on the main bridge. "Admiral Hurley is leading a mission to planet four to find the admiral." Cortez hesitated. "So what do we do in the meanwhile?"

"We stay calm, Commander." Erica West stepped out of the lift and walked across the bridge. "And we handle the crisis… until Admiral Compton returns to reassume command."

West was a veteran task force commander who had been wounded in the fighting against the First Imperium. She'd spent the first half of the fleet's daring escape in the hospital, and Compton had kept her on *Midway* after, not because of lack of confidence in her but simply because he was hesitant to assign yet another Alliance officer to a major command. But now she was fit and ready for action…and with Compton on planet four and Dumont in system X20, she was in the right place at the right time. And she was the next ranking Alliance officer in the fleet.

"Ah…yes, Admiral West…" Cortez was on edge, not sure what to do. He knew West was a fighter, not likely to simply sit and wait for Compton to return.

The admiral stood for a few seconds, staring down at Compton's chair. Then she sat down abruptly. "Order all Alliance ships to battlestations, Commander Cortez," she said grimly. "And Captain Horace is to bring the engines up to 5g."

"Yes, Admiral." He paused, quickly adapting to the new

command authority. "Where are we going?"

"Planet five, Commander," she said with a feral edge to her voice. "Right in between *Petersburg* and the refinery."

*   *   *

"Admiral, *Midway* is moving toward us rapidly." Stanovich turned from his workstation and looked across the flag bridge at Udinov.

"Send a communique. Advise that she is to stop immediately or we will open fire on the refinery." Udinov wasn't sure if that was a serious threat or a bluff. He wanted to effect his withdrawal, but if he was pushed to the point of giving the order to fire, he didn't know if he would do it or not. Destroying the facility wouldn't accomplish anything. The vengeful Alliance spacers would attack his vessels in response. The Russian admiral knew his faction wasn't really a match for the Alliance-led remainder of the fleet, but it was substantial enough to put up a good fight. He didn't doubt *Petersburg* would attract more than its share of fire, which made his own survival prospects highly questionable. Not that it would matter who won. If the fleet fought its own civil war there wouldn't be enough left on either side to survive.

"Yes, Admiral."

Udinov watched the monitors as the large blue oval representing *Midway* moved closer. *Petersburg* was no match for the Alliance's *Yorktown* class monster. He might blow the refinery to plasma, but the Alliance flagship would blast his vessel to slag the moment he did.

"Response coming in, sir."

"Put it on my com." *I'm not sure I want everyone else to hear this.*

"*Petersburg*, you are hereby commanded to move away from the planet and out of weapons range of the refinery. You are under the legal and duly authorized command of the Grand Pact and subject to the orders and directives of that entity's chosen commander, Admiral Terrance Compton. In his name, I repeat my order. Power down your weapons and move away from the planet. Your request to leave the fleet is denied. Failure to obey these orders will result in the destruction of *Petersburg*...and any other vessel threatening the refinery or attempting to leave the system. Admiral Erica West out."

Fuck, Udinov thought to himself. *West is a fighter, a protégé of Augustus Garret himself.* Garret and Compton were both military geniuses, but of the two Compton had always been the more patient. West had served mostly under the more aggressive Garret, and if anything, she had built a reputation of being even colder and harder than her famous mentor.

"Get her back on the line," Udinov snapped.

The com officer worked at his controls. "I'm sorry, sir, but *Midway* is not responding."

"Fuck." Udinov let the word slip out despite his attempt to stop himself. *The crew doesn't need to know you're in over your head here.* The situation was rapidly deteriorating. It had seemed simple, made perfect sense in planning. A few hours of tense stand-off while the last of his ships refueled, and then they would be gone, on the way to search for a route home. Now he was on the verge of combat with his allies—and he had no idea how his ramshackle coalition of forces would respond if it came to a fight. They wanted to find a way home, but were they ready to battle against the Alliance forces and the other contingents if it came to that?

He turned toward the communications officer. "Put me on fleetwide com, no encryption." *I can't make her listen, but I can put on a show for the rest of the fleet.* "Attention Admiral West. This is Admiral Vladimir Udinov. I do not contest your acting command of the Alliance contingent, but I cannot recognize your claim to command the entire fleet. There are other admirals with the same rank and greater seniority in the various national forces, and these officers—including myself—have a greater claim to succeed Admiral Compton in his absence. I also stand by the decision of the RIC, Europan, CAC, and Caliphate contingents to split off from the fleet. You have no authority to contest this action, and I insist that you halt your aggressive maneuvers and allow the seceding ships to continue refueling operations without your unauthorized interference."

He moved his hand across his throat, and the com officer cut the line. *There*, he thought. *That's the best I can do.* He felt a pit in his stomach. *But Erica West isn't going to back down...*

*   *   *

"I want you to get some thrust out of those fucking pieces of shit, and I do mean now." Greta Hurley's voice was like ice. She stared straight ahead, watching Commander Wilder at the controls as she harangued the pilot and crew of the two armored shuttles accompanying her squadrons. She was worried about Compton, and she knew every wasted second could be the difference between a successful rescue and a terrible tragedy. She realized there were nearly a thousand Marines on the planet, but it wasn't a full invasion force, and if they'd run into any serious First Imperium forces things could be a mess.

"Admiral Hurley, we're at full thrust now. No matter what we do, the shuttles are never going to be able to keep up with your fighters." The pilot's voice was tense, stressed. The fighter crews in the fleet were used to their hard-driving commander by now, but the shuttle pilot was still adjusting to Hurley's aggressive command style.

"Do the best you can, Lieutenant." She pulled back slightly. Driving the pilot to a breakdown wasn't going to help move things any faster. She sighed hard and added, "Lieutenant, I'm leaving one squadron with you as escort and moving on ahead. Follow us as quickly as you can."

She didn't need the shuttles, not really, but she wasn't taking any chances. They were a precaution, filled with medical teams and supplies of every conceivable kind that might be needed. The landing force had taken only rudimentary med services with them, so if she did come down in the middle of a battle, she'd be glad the shuttles were on the way. They could save a lot of Marines as well as the admiral.

If Compton was just stranded on the surface, unable to communicate but otherwise fine, she'd load him onboard her fighter and blast back to *Midway* at full thrust. But the jamming wasn't a good sign, and she knew she might find a far worse situation waiting. Something was wrong down there.

She turned toward the front of the cockpit. "Get us there, John. As quickly as you can. The shuttles will just have to follow."

"Yes, Admiral."

Hurley leaned back, waiting for the inevitable force from the fighter's acceleration…and about five seconds later, she got it. Almost 10g of it.

*   *   *

"You need to intercept those fighters now, Admiral Peltier. Before they get to planet four. Your ships are the only force close enough." Udinov's voice was raw, strained as it blared through the com.

Peltier stared at the screen, unsure of what to do. Gregoire Peltier was no one's idea of a great military leader. Indeed, he owed his position almost entirely to family influence and patronage. Not everyone considered him an outright coward, but no one who knew him believed he was up to the more difficult tasks. And going nose to nose with Greta Hurley met any definition of the word difficult.

"Admiral, I don't know if…"

"Gregoire, you need to do this. The plan is already half shot to hell. What do you think will happen if she gets Compton and brings him back? You're hesitant to face off with Admiral Hurley? How do you feel about Compton spacing you for mutiny?"

Peltier was pale, and he looked like he might throw up at any minute. He'd only gotten involved in this whole thing because he wanted to go home. Now he didn't know what to do. But Udinov was right. Compton was a little less draconian in his actions than Admiral Garret perhaps, but he still wasn't likely to take what he would almost certainly view as treachery very well.

"But what if they don't turn back?" Peltier was struggling to sound calm, but his fear was making it difficult.

"Then you have to engage them. You have to disable them… or destroy them if you must." Udinov's voice was firm.

"But Admiral Hurley is with them. She is…"

"She is one woman, Gregoire. On one ship. She's only got two squadrons, and they don't have any heavy weapons loaded. "If you have to destroy them, you have the power to do it."

"But…"

"There are no buts," Udinov yelled. "You signed on to this, and now we've got to see it through. I don't want anybody to get hurt, but if she refuses to turn back we don't have any choice. *You* don't have any choice. So just do it."

Udinov cut the line, leaving Peltier listening to the thunderous sound of his heartbeat in his ears. He sucked in a deep breath and turned toward his com officer. "Get me a line to the fighter squadrons…"

*   *   *

Greta Hurley's face was like carved stone. "Put me on fleet-wide com," she said coldly. Peltier had threatened her, and in the process he'd released an elemental rage. *The day I let Gregoire Peltier intimidate me is the day I eat a fucking bullet.*

"Yes, Admiral." The com officer worked his hands over his controls for a few seconds. "On your line."

Hurley picked up her headset and put it on. "Commander Quincy, you are to bring your squadrons to full alert. All fighters are to arm with double-shotted plasma torpedoes, and be prepared to launch upon command." Her voice was frozen.

"In the event that any vessel of the Europan contingent—

or any other ship in the fleet—opens fire on any of the fighters now enroute to planet four, you are to launch all squadrons
immediately. Your fighters are to attack and destroy any vessel
that fired on our fighters or shuttles." She paused for a few
seconds. "Is that clear?"

There was a short silence then: "Umm…yes, Admiral. As
you order." Quincy's voice sounded a bit uncertain, but Hurley
knew the veteran would obey her order.

"This is Admiral West," came another voice blasting through
the com. "As acting fleet commander, I confirm Admiral Hurley's orders. All fighter squadrons are to obey. All loyal ships are
also hereby ordered to fire upon any ships attacking the fighters
and shuttles heading for planet four." A long pause then: "And
you are to maintain fire until the offending vessel is destroyed.
We are deep in enemy space under emergency conditions. There
is only one punishment for mutiny."

Hurley let out a long breath. She appreciated the support,
but she also knew West had upped the ante. She's got balls of
steel, Hurley thought. *She just might face down this crisis…either that,
or all hell is about to break loose.*

"Alright people," she said, flipping the com back to her
squadron channels, "let's go get the admiral." She nodded
toward Wilder, and the pilot hit the thrusters.

Hurley felt herself slammed back into her seat as 8g of
thrust engaged.

Now we'll see what Gregoire Peltier is truly made of…

*   *   *

Udinov stared at the image of *Midway* on the main display.
It wasn't very often that ships had actual visuals of their adversaries. Space battles were fought over hundreds of thousands
of kilometers, and anything under 10,000 klicks was considered
point blank range. But Erica West had brought *Midway* within
three kilometers of *Petersburg*. That was bold beyond compare,

indescribably close in for a ship that itself was almost two klicks long.

"Admiral, *Midway's* weapons systems are powered up and ready to fire."

Udinov didn't answer, he just sat quietly, staring at the massive Alliance flagship and wondering what to do. *Petersburg's* weapons were armed too, but she didn't have *Midway's* firepower. He'd never even heard of two ships engaging at a range this short. The massive power of *Midway's* heavy x-ray laser batteries firing from so close would tear his ship apart. He doubted *Petersburg* would last more than a minute once the shooting started. Conventional wisdom suggested firing back at an attacker, but Udinov realized that was pointless. He could hurt the Alliance vessel, but not destroy it before *Petersburg* was blasted into a lifeless wreck. No, if *Midway* opened fire, he would destroy the refinery. There was no way West could stop him from doing that before he died…and he suspected that is why she hadn't opened fire yet.

To make matters worse, Admiral Peltier had knuckled under to Greta Hurley's threats, and he'd meekly allowed her force to pass by his ships, bound for planet four. Udinov had no idea what was causing the heavy jamming there. It was possible Compton was in real trouble, maybe even dead. He felt a wave of guilt as a burst of hope came on him. Things were bad enough now, but West was only in unchallenged command of the Alliance forces. The other contingents, except perhaps the PRC, would probably sit out any fight that took place—and that left Udinov and his allies with a stronger hand. But if Compton was back in *Midway*, the CEL, Martian Confederation, and SAE forces would almost certainly rally to him…and even some ships in Udinov's allied contingents might reconsider their allegiance. The Russian admiral knew Compton was a good man, and an honorable leader. But he was also dangerous. Whatever Udinov was going to do, he had to do it now. Time only increased the chance that Hurley would find Compton.

"Commander, issue orders to the rest of the contingent. All ships are to move toward the planet and assume positions to support us." Everybody knew Erica West was as cold as they came. But Vladimir Udinov was no coward, and he was determined to hold his own in the duel between the two commanders.

"Yes, sir." The com officer sounded nervous about Udinov's escalation, but he complied immediately.

Udinov had just looked into West's eyes and raised her bet. She'd have to do something. If the rest of the RIC ships got into position, it would be *Midway* that was outgunned, and he knew the iron-willed Alliance admiral would never allow that. She could withdraw. *Yeah*, he thought, *and maybe space will open up and swallow her ships. No, there is no chance of Erica West skulking off with her tail between her legs. Zero.*

She could attack immediately. *She just might. But the same problem remains...she can't stop me from destroying the refinery. And half the fleet still hasn't refueled. She might figure she can redistribute enough tritium around the fleet to keep everyone going until she found a new gas giant. But that's dangerous, and it puts the rest of the contingents at great risk. Ten percent chance of that, maybe.*

She could do nothing—stay in place, all her guns trained on *Petersburg. If the rest of the contingent gets this close, it assures Midway's destruction...but it won't save Petersburg. She might sit just where she is and bank on that fact to stay our hand. Am I willing to sacrifice the ship—and myself—if she pushes me? I don't know...perhaps I might, if I truly believed it would allow the others to escape. But if we kill West, the Alliance spacers will go berserk. They'll never let the rest of the contingent go...*

Udinov sat silently in his chair shaking his head. *No, she won't do any of that. She'll...*

"Admiral, the Alliance and PRC units are moving to intercept our inbound vessels." A short pause then: "Admiral West is on the main channel, sir."

"Put it on, Commander." Udinov sighed. He didn't have to hear it. He knew exactly what she was going to say.

"All Alliance and PRC units. You are to immediately engage and destroy any RIC, CAC, Caliphate, or Europan ship that closes to within 100,000 kilometers of planet five...or any such vessel that takes offensive action of any kind."

She had raised him back.

*   *   *

"What is that coming in?" Compton was standing outside the command post, staring up at the sky. There was a cluster of lights in the deepening dusk, rapidly descending. To an untrained eye they could be meteors, fragments from a comet, even bits of a satellite crashing to the ground. But Terrance Compton's eye was not untrained, and he realized immediately they were some kind of spacecraft.

The Marines had wiped out the enemy warbots, though not without cost. The fighting had been sharp, made vastly more difficult by the lack of effective communications, but the enemy force had turned out to be small, just over a hundred of the bots. The Marines had 38 KIA and another 100+ wounded.

Compton realized the force they had faced was probably only a small portion of the ancient city's defensive complement. The rest was probably lying dormant, decayed beyond functionality by the brutal passage of time. Compton wondered what the defensive system had been 500,000 years before, just what kind of force had defended a metropolis where millions of people once lived.

The landing party had been packing up and preparing to head back to the fleet. Once Colonel Preston had declared the area secure, Compton had agreed to give the research team a few more hours to gather up artifacts—there was enough just laying around to keep every scientist on the fleet busy for years. His tactical sense had told him to load everyone up and get the hell off the planet, but he remained focused on why they had come in the first place. It was far beyond idle curiosity. His people were stuck in enemy space, and anything that allowed them to understand the First Imperium—and to bridge the technology gap between them—was essential to their chances of survival.

Preston had been uncomfortable with the delay, at least in

getting the admiral back to *Midway*. He'd argued multiple times, urging Compton to return at once. He'd insisted that security on the planet's surface was too uncertain. But his efforts were to no avail. Compton had declared firmly he would return when the entire expedition did and not a moment before.

Now, he wondered what was coming down on them. A rescue mission from the fleet? It was certainly plausible. Indeed, he'd expected some kind of response to his expedition's sudden radio silence. But he realized they had also awakened some long-dormant defensive system, and he couldn't exclude the possibility that the incoming vessels were hostile.

"Sound the alert, Colonel," he said quietly. *No sense taking chances.*

"Yes, sir," Preston snapped back. He turned and walked toward a small cluster of officers. With the jamming, it was easier to communicate face to face—or at least the armored equivalent with external speakers and receivers.

Compton looked back up. The craft were closer, and he cranked up his visor's magnification. There was something about them, something familiar...

"Colonel!" he ran after Preston, turning his speakers to maximum volume. "Colonel!"

Preston stopped and turned to face the admiral.

"Cancel that alert, Colonel." Compton turned and looked back at the landing ships. "Those are Alliance Lightning fighter-bombers."

The first two ships flew over the camp, dropping down slowly and landing in the field beyond, closely followed by the others. Compton moved toward them as quickly as he could without tripping over his armored feet.

"Wait, Admiral...let me assign some guards to you."

Compton ignored the Marine's caution and continued toward the two fighters. He could hear Preston snapping out orders, commanding a detachment to follow. The veteran Marines were considerably more adept at moving quickly in fighting suits, and they caught up with Compton about halfway to the fighters. But the time he reached the LZ, he had two dozen Marines surrounding him, weapons at the ready.

The hatch of the lead ship was already open, and a few seconds after Compton reached it, a head popped out...Greta Hurley's.

Compton looked up, an expression of surprise on his face. "Admiral Hurley, what are you doing here?"

"I'm sorry, sir, but I have to ask you to get onboard. We need to get you back to *Midway* as soon as possible."

Compton felt his stomach clench. Hurley hadn't come herself just to check on him.

"What is it, Admiral?"

She leaned forward looking down at him. "Half the fleet is in rebellion, sir. Admiral Udinov is in charge. The mutineers want to break off and try to find a way back to Earth." Hurley's tone communicated her tension, and that told Compton all he needed to know. "Admiral West assumed command," she continued, "and she sent us to get you."

Compton felt a wave of anger sweep over him. Anger at Udinov—and at Zhang, who he was sure was behind the whole thing. And at himself, for indulging his curiosity instead of staying at his post.

"Colonel," he said, turning toward Preston, "take over the withdrawal." He stepped toward the fighter and looked up at Hurley. "Open the loading gate, Admiral. I'll never get up the ladder and through that hatch in this armor."

Chapter Fourteen

From the Personal Log of Terrance Compton

I am a fool. I accompanied the landing force down to the surface because I wanted to see the First Imperium ruins myself, to satisfy my own craving for knowledge. I convinced myself I needed to go, that I had to learn about the enemy if I am to find a way for the fleet to survive. And indeed, I do believe that. We have no hope of a purely military victory, and there seems little doubt to me that flight is a short term solution. Eventually, an enemy as massive and powerful as the First Imperium will track us down—whether we were to head toward home or continue into deep space. Our only hope is to learn more about this mysterious race, and through that knowledge find a way to destroy...or coexist with them.

But my timing was poor. I underestimated the discontent in the fleet, the speed with which my opponents would act. I knew I faced continuing opposition, but I didn't imagine they would be so reckless so soon. I should have better understood the primal fear of being lost and how it would affect otherwise courageous officers. In assuming I had more time, I opened the door for the mutineers to gain an advantage. Now, there are no easy options.

We may lose the refinery over this, with much of the fleet still low on fuel. Indeed, we may destroy each other in combat. For though on one level I sympathize with the mutineers and their desire to seek a way home, I cannot allow them to go, whatever I must do. Our experiences on the planet only reaffirmed my caution. One moment we were exploring an eons-dead world and the next we were being attacked by the remnants of an ancient security system. We do not know—we cannot know—the enemy's abilities. Our battle successes have caused us to forget that our adversaries are vastly ahead of our technology. We can only guess at when they are watching...or if they are following.

We are close to moving past the jamming surrounding the planet, and soon we will have clear communications with the fleet. Then I will find out what is happening...and I will have to give difficult orders. It is with heartfelt sadness I contemplate the possibility that we made our unlikely escape from X2 perhaps only to destroy ourselves here. Yet, that is so like man. It is our legacy. Perhaps it shall always be so.

But I know one thing for certain. I will allow no one to lead the enemy closer to Earth. Whatever I must do.

AS Midway
System X18 – Low Orbit Around Planet V
The Fleet: 225 ships, 47,817 crew

Erica West sat in the command chair—Compton's chair—and stared at the main display. *Petersburg* was a powerful ship, but she was no match for *Midway*'s 1.8 kilometers of bristling weapons. If the two fought, West had no doubt who would win. But that wasn't what was on her mind.

Can I destroy that ship before they take out the refinery?

She had every weapon locked on the Udinov's flagship, from the primary x-ray laser batteries to the small anti-fighter turrets. When...if...she gave the order to fire, an unprecedented amount of energy would be directed at *Petersburg*. And at a mere three kilometer's range, almost all of it would reach the target. The pride of the RIC fleet would be blasted to plasma in less than a minute, she was sure of that. It was exactly how long that would take—and what Udinov could do with those seconds—that she was considering.

"Captain Kato is on the com, Admiral. He has maneuvered his ships to oppose the CAC contingent, and he requests permission to engage."

"Negative. He is not to engage unless fired upon." West had a reputation as a hard-nosed admiral, even a hothead. But she wasn't going to be responsible for starting a civil war that could destroy the fleet—not unless she did it herself by attacking *Petersburg*.

But that's different. Saving the refinery is more important than anything else.

"Any response from Admiral Wittgensen?"

"No, Admiral. Not since his initial communique." The CEL commander had declared that his forces would not become engaged in an intra-fleet battle unless they were fired upon or Admiral Compton expressly ordered it. Wittgensen was a cautious man, one who tended to operate by the book. Compton was the fleet's duly authorized commander, and he would accept such fateful orders from no one else.

West couldn't blame him. She was third in command of the Alliance forces, but that succession didn't necessarily extend to the whole fleet. It was hard to compare exact ranks from different powers, but some of the other contingent commanders had more seniority than West—including Wittgensen himself.

She looked again at the tactical display. So far, her threat had held things at a stalemate. The mutinous ships had moved closer to planet five, but none had crossed her stated 100,000 kilometer blockade zone. Her fleet units had moved to enforce her orders, and the Alliance forces were deployed in a large semi-circle, facing off against the rebel units. But the only ships inside the 100,000 kilometer mark were *Midway* and *Petersburg*.

*   *   *

"With so many of our weapons locked on the refinery, we will barely scratch *Midway* if it comes to a fight." Rostov's voice was grim as it came through the com. "Perhaps we should redirect some of our targeting. We'll still be outgunned, but it..."

"There's no point, Sergei," Udinov said, his voice heavy,

tired. "We don't have a chance in a standup fight with *Midway* no matter what we do. The refinery's our only bargaining chip. We can destroy it, and they all know it."

And I know enough about Erica West to be sure she'd blow us to hell in a heartbeat if we weren't holding the refinery hostage.

"So what do we do, sir? Just sit here? And what happens when Admiral Compton gets back?"

"I don't know, Sergei." Udinov was staring at his screen, but he wasn't seeing anything. His thoughts had drifted off, imagining how he'd ended up in this position. He'd been so sure it was the right thing to do, to give his people a chance, at least, of returning home, of reuniting with loved ones. The plan had been complicated by his need to fuel the last of his ships, but he'd still kept it as simple as possible. Just a few hours of tense standoff—long enough to get perhaps half a tank in each vessel—and his people would have been gone. But now he was filled with doubt as he stared at West's massive ship, knowing every one of its heavy guns was locked on *Petersburg*.

He'd had no animosity toward his allies in the fleet, no intention for anyone to get hurt. The plan had always been to avoid bloodshed. *My plan, at least. I'm not too sure about that bastard Zhang.* He'd believed the CAC admiral, sympathized with the humiliation he felt after Compton had relieved him from command. *Have I let myself get dragged into some pointless vendetta? Did Zhang expect a fight all along?*

Well, whatever my plan was, it's shot to shit, he thought grimly. He wanted to call things off, to turn the clock back two days, to be more patient. But he knew that was all impossible. He was stuck, in far too deep to turn back now.

He'd never harbored ill will toward Compton or West or any of the others, even in his vehement disagreement about whether to try to return home. But now, in the intense pressure of the moment, he realized to them he was a villain…a traitor, a mutineer. They would show no mercy, make no compromises. Some routes could only be tread one way, and he doubted there was a way for him to go back.

Udinov was no coward, indeed, he was ready to sacrifice himself if it was necessary to end the dangerous impasse. But that would do no good. There were dozens of officers involved—hundreds—and Compton would never be able to trust any of the rebel crews again.

This was a bad idea from the start, but I'm stuck with it now. I have to go through with it. There's no way out, no option but to play this out to the bitter end.

He felt deep regret, but he looked over at the com station. "Lieutenant, put me on the fleetwide com."

*   *   *

The com unit crackled in West's ears. It was Udinov again. His voice was a little shaky, at least to her hearing, but overall he sounded determined. She hadn't acknowledged the transmission, but it was on the open fleetcom, and she was listening nevertheless.

"I will allow fifteen minutes for all Alliance and PRC vessels to withdraw from any positions within 200,000 kilometers of planet five and power down all weapons. If my conditions are met, my contingent will refuel at once and leave the system with no hostilities. The Caliphate, CAC, and Europan task forces shall have the option to join us. My forces will attack no one. We do not wish to compel anyone to join us, nor do we seek to impose our will on other contingents. There needn't be violence nor any loss of life."

His voice deepened, the tone becoming firmer, more threatening. "However, if there are still Alliance and PRC forces within 200,000 kilometers of the planet—or anywhere within detection range with weapons powered up—I will assume the intent is to interfere with my contingent's actions, and I will have no choice but to act accordingly. *Petersburg* will obliterate the refinery…and all RIC ships will return any fire. In all likelihood, the two halves of the fleet will engage in a devastating battle, a catastrophe that does *not* have to happen."

The com was blank for a few seconds and then the admiral continued, "The choice is yours...peace or war, life...or death."

West felt her stomach twitch. She understood the situation, the staggering consequences of the actions she would take in the next few minutes. She felt an instant of doubt, just a fleeting sensation. There wasn't a warrior who'd ever lived who hadn't known that feeling. Then her resolve hardened. "Put me on the fleetwide com," she said coldly.

"You are on, Admiral."

"Admiral Udinov, pursuant to the military code of the Grand Pact, as well as those of both our respective powers, you and your co-conspirators are guilty of mutiny. No vessel of the Alliance or PRC will retreat a meter, nor will I allow you to continue to threaten the destruction of the refinery that is so essential to the fleet. You issue your ultimatum and give us fifteen minutes to comply. I will do no such thing, nor will I negotiate with an officer currently engaged in acts of mutiny. You have five minutes to withdraw *Petersburg* out of range of the refinery, or I will blow your vessel out of the sky."

She paused for a long while, sitting and staring straight ahead. Finally, she repeated, "Five minutes, Admiral Udinov. Not a second more." Her voice was like ice.

She turned toward the communications officer. "Lieutenant, broadcast a five minute countdown on the fleetcom. By seconds, starting now."

She reached up and flipped off her com. Then she switched to intraship communications. "Captain Horace."

"Yes, Admiral?"

"Are you following the countdown?"

"Yes, Admiral. We all are."

"Good," West said, calmly. "When it gets down to two minutes you are to fire all batteries. You are to destroy *Petersburg* without warning."

West didn't like dishonorable tactics, but the lives of every man or woman in the fleet depended on keeping that refinery up and operating. Perhaps she could take Udinov by surprise, disable *Petersburg* before she opened fire.

She took a deep breath and looked up at the timer, quickly counting down the seconds…

*   *   *

Udinov sat still, West's words still sinking in. *Damn, she is tough.* He'd put forth his most powerful threat, but she'd just disregarded it and come back with a stronger one of her own. She'd upped the pressure too, reducing the time from fifteen minutes to five.

There's no time, he thought, trying to calmly analyze his position. He realized if he complied, he would lose his only real bargaining chip. His entire RIC contingent was almost out of fuel. If he tried to escape now, without loading up his tanks first, his forces wouldn't get very far. His allies' ships were mostly fueled. Perhaps we can redistribute some of that, give all the ships enough to get away, to find another source of tritium and helium-3. But can I trust the other contingents? Will they want to part with some of their precious fuel?

He felt a wave of shame. He was reluctant to trust mutineers…yet what was he? He had been more responsible for bringing about this situation than anyone else, save perhaps Zhang. For few seconds he considered yielding to West's demands. *No…it is too late for that. I chose this road, and now I must follow it…wherever it leads.*

"Commander Stanovich…all batteries are to lock on the refinery and prepare to fire." Udinov's voice was deep, grim. His eyes were fixed on the chronometer, now at three minutes, fifteen seconds.

"Yes, sir." Stanovich was a professional and a veteran, and his response was immediate…but Udinov could hear the worry—the fear—nevertheless.

I'm sorry, Anton. I'm sorry to all of you. He knew he would sign the death warrant of every crewmember aboard *Petersburg* with the first shot, but his course was set, and he couldn't change it.

Not now. At least the sacrifice might buy the escape of the rest of his people. The Alliance ships had been last in the refueling queue, and their tanks were as empty as his own. He'd assumed Compton had put his ships last because he was trying to avoid bad feeling about preferencing his own ships and crews. There was no doubt he'd put a lot of Alliance officers in key positions, and that had caused some grumbling. Udinov hadn't been too troubled by that before. Whatever personal feelings he may have had, he couldn't deny that the Alliance navy was the best, and by a considerable margin.

All of Earth's Superpowers were monstrous bureaucracies, dominated by elite political classes that ruled over populations living mostly in poverty. The Alliance was no different, at least on Earth. But somehow its space-based military establishments had remained mostly unaffected by the influence pedaling and nepotism that so afflicted the other powers' forces. Oddly, he suspected, that had been because the Alliance elites eschewed military careers, at least those in space. The lack of respect for the navy and Marines in the halls of Earthly power had made them true colonial forces, imbued with the spirit of those who had stepped forth to settle new worlds.

Udinov's RIC had fought both with and against the Alliance in the hundred or so years since mankind had colonized the stars. But whether he viewed them as ally, enemy, or cautious neutral, he had always respected their capabilities, and he hadn't questioned their tactical dominance over the Grand Pact.

"Three minutes, Admiral." Stanovich spoke softly as he stared toward Udinov, waiting for the admiral to issue the order that would kill them all.

*   *   *

Tang's flag bridge was silent, everyone listening to the exchange between West and Udinov. Zhang sat in the command chair, the one he'd seized by betraying and murdering his commanding officer. It was beginning to look like he'd pulled off his coup without a hitch. No one had seriously questioned that the formerly healthy Chen Min had died of natural causes, and now the tension of the current crisis had shifted attention elsewhere. As far as any of them knew, Zhang had simply stepped in as next in the chain of command.

Zhang wasn't overly troubled by the tactics he'd employed. He had always been prone to self-pity, feeling that he'd been overlooked and poorly treated most of his career. He had an exaggerated sense of his military skills, and a considerable ego as well. He'd had no quarrel with Chen, but the old admiral would have kept all his people with the fleet, blasting off into deep space with Terrance Compton. And that was something Zhang wasn't willing to accept. He was determined to get back home and damned the cost.

"Open a channel," he said, looking over toward the communications officer. "CAC vessels only, high-density encryption code ZK."

The officer hesitated for an instant before replying, "Yes, Admiral." The CAC's most secure code had rarely been used since the formation of the Grand Pact, and it had been a surprise to hear it ordered now. A few seconds later: "Your line is ready, sir."

"Attention all vessels. You are to prepare engines for maximum thrust. I am transmitting a course for the entire task force. All personnel are to be in the tanks and ready for high thrust maneuvers in ten minutes. We will be moving toward warp gate number three and transiting to system X19." Duke's scouts had reported that the X19 system was empty, a blue star with no planets, no enemy contacts, nothing. But according to Zhang's calculations, it was the gate with the highest probability of leading closer to human space. And that was where he—where all his people—were going, Terrance Compton and his out of control caution be damned.

"All ships acknowledge," he added.

He sat and watched the list of ships on his screen. One by one, a small mark appeared next to each vessel's name, *Tang's* AI signifying that ship had acknowledged the order. Zhang hadn't been sure every captain would follow his commands, especially one that ran counter to Admiral Compton's directives, but a few seconds later the last acknowledgement came in. The CAC contingent was united. And it was about to bug out, leaving Compton, Udinov, and the rest of the fleet behind.

*   *   *

"All batteries...prepare to fire." Udinov's voice was grim. He was committed to his course of action, but he didn't think there was much chance of survival, at least for him and his crew on *Petersburg*.

Erica West had given him five minutes...and there wasn't a doubt in the Russian admiral's mind she would follow through on her threat. If he didn't strike first, he had no doubt West would. And once *Midway's* massive batteries opened up, *Petersburg's* lifespan would be measured in seconds.

"All weapons are ready, Admiral," Stanovich replied, no less grimly than his commander. "Awaiting your order to commence bombardment."

Udinov took a deep breath and looked around the flag bridge. His officers were all hunched over their stations. He knew they were trying to stay focused, keeping their minds on their jobs, and not thinking that they were probably living the last minute of their lives.

"Commander...fi..."

"Admiral, we have an incoming transmission." The communications officer spun around and stared at Udinov. "It's Admiral Compton, sir."

"Put it on." He knew he should listen privately, but everyone on *Petersburg* faced the same imminent death he did, so he waved his hand, gesturing for the com officer to put it on speaker.

"Attention, *Petersburg*...this is Fleet Admiral Terrance Compton." The voice came through the com like a force of nature.

"You will follow Admiral West's instructions to the letter. You will do it now, or every member of this fleet you have suborned to treachery will die."

"Admiral Compton," Udinov replied, "perhaps we can negotiate a solution to this impasse." He felt a flash of hope, but it died quickly. Terrance Compton wasn't normally as outwardly hard and abrasive as Erica West, but he was every bit as firm. He sat still, one eye on the chronometer, as he waited for the signal to travel the three light seconds to Compton's position...

*   *   *

"There will be no negotiations, Admiral Udinov." Compton's voice was frozen. "You will follow my orders expressly and immediately, or *Midway* will destroy *Petersburg*. All CAC, Caliphate, Europan, and RIC vessels are hereby ordered to power down at once, and prepare to be boarded. Any ships refusing this order will also be destroyed."

Compton sat in the cramped cockpit of the fighter. He'd popped his armor and climbed out as soon as he'd managed to stumble onboard, and Hurley had managed to find him a jumpsuit. It wasn't an admiral's uniform, nor was it a perfect fit...but it spared him the indignity of sitting in the middle of the fighter completely naked.

He pressed a small button, muting the com unit. "Greta, get on a secure line now. I want you to scramble every squadron you're sure is loyal." He paused. "And remember, they may be firing on their own ships, so make damned sure you stick to people you trust."

"Yes, sir," Hurley replied, picking up her headset as she did.

"Admiral Compton," Udinov's voice blasted through the speakers again. "I urge you to reconsider your position. I'm sure there is some middle ground we can discuss, some mutually acceptable solution."

Compton felt a wave of anger. He tried to bite down on it,

but he was only partially successful. "I will reconsider nothing. I am not in the habit of discussing terms with mutineers."

He glanced over at Hurley, and nodded as she gave him a thumbs up. Her squadrons were scrambling.

"There is little point to further discussions. All loyal ships, you are ordered to close with the nearest mutinous vessels. You will either accept their unconditional surrenders or you will attack without further notice."

He felt his body tense with anger. At the mutiny, certainly, but also at the stupidity of it all, at the astonishing waste about to take place, the insanity about to cause human warships to battle each other in the depths of First Imperium space. *We do the enemy's work for him,* he thought bitterly. *But I have no choice...*

"Admiral West, *Midway* is to open f..."

"Admiral, we've got ships transiting from X16, sir. Looks like two fast attack ships. Incoming transmissions." Kip Janz' voice was high pitched with surprise. "Putting it on speaker, sir."

"Admiral Compton, this is Captain Callou aboard Dragonfly. We have enemy forces on our tail, sir. Repeat, enemy forces pursuing us..."

But Compton already knew. His eyes were fixed on the fighter's tiny screen...and all he could see was contact after contact pouring through the warp gate behind the two scoutships.

The enemy was already there.

Chapter Fifteen

Research Notes of Dr. Hieronymus Cutter

We have been three days in the bowels of the First Imperium vessel. I knew, intellectually, how massive this ship was, but it is another thing entirely to actually experience it...to traverse kilometer after kilometer of dark, endless corridor with no end in sight.

We must find the location of the main processing unit, the great computer that once ran this entire vessel. I can only imagine in the vaguest manner the enormity of such an intelligence, its immense stores of data, its unimaginable computing power. What is such a computer like, I wonder? Nothing man has ever built is comparable. The quasi-sentient units we create for our ships and Marines are like children's toys by comparison.

Will such a system seem like a computer at all to me? Or will I perceive it more as another person? Even a god of sorts? Will it be so far beyond any of us as to defy all comprehension?

I do not know. Indeed, I know our mission is dangerous, far more so than I told Admiral Compton it would be...though I daresay he knew better as well. But there is no choice. If we cannot learn how to control or at least communicate persuasively with the intelligences that control our enemy, we are doomed. I would not trade a chance at long term success for a few months of life, fleeing into the darkness. No, this is our chance, perhaps our only one.

First Imperium Colossus
System X20– High Orbit Around Planet IV
The Fleet: 225 ships, 47,815 crew

Hieronymus Cutter moved forward slowly, carefully. His people had been at it for days, wandering through the almost unending corridors of the First Imperium vessel. He had everybody on a rotation of twenty hours on duty and four off, with the whole unrealistic schedule supported by the liberal use of stims. Still, he knew his people were getting sluggish, and one sloppy, careless move could have disastrous consequences.

The ship itself was completely dead, but they'd already managed to accidently activate half a dozen security bots. They'd been able to knock them all out, but not before the deadly automatons had killed two and wounded half a dozen others. One of the dead had been from Cutter's team and the other one of Frasier's Marines.

The bots appeared to be unconnected to the ship's main systems, operating independently, responding to threats as they appeared. Still, he'd detected no power from any type of scanners, absolutely nothing but the single source he knew was the antimatter containment system. How were these bots detecting anything if they had no energy output whatsoever?

No energy we can detect, he thought suddenly. *Dark energy, maybe?* The alloy of the First Imperium hulls was infused with a mysterious form of dark matter. Now Cutter wondered if the ancient aliens had also learned how to manipulate dark energy. He stopped suddenly.

"Is something wrong, Hieronymus?" Ana Zhukov had been walking right behind, and she almost ran into him.

"Dark energy," he said, his voice soft, distracted. "The First Imperium is able to utilize dark energy, at least for some purposes…like communications." He turned and looked back at her. "Don't you see? It explains everything. The original distress call from Epsilon Eridani IV, the seeming ability of the First Imperium to communicate through warp gates, the security bots that seem to have scanners running with no detectable energy output…"

"Yes," she said softly. "Of course. It would explain every-thing, wouldn't it? Or at least it might. But we know almost nothing about dark energy, Hieronymus. So it's just a wild guess at this point."

"It's more than that, Ana." His voice was becoming firmer as he spoke. He'd been unsure a moment before, but now he was totally convinced. "There is no question the enemy can communicate in ways we can neither detect nor explain. And you yourself have run the scans here. There is no energy output we can trace, no scanning system running in the background. Yet, we have activated multiple defensive bots as we've explored. Scanners require some kind of energy to operate. If we ques-tion this assertion we have to abandon everything we under-stand about physics, right?"

She nodded. "Agreed…"

"So if there must be energy usage and we cannot detect it, we are dealing with some sort of undetectable energy, correct?"

"Yes," she said tentatively. "But…"

"There is no but. Dark energy is the only undetectable form of energy we have posited to exist. It is vastly more likely we are dealing with dark energy than something completely unknown." He sighed. "Still, even if we accept this as fact, I'm not sure what it does for us, at least in the short term. We've never been able to detect dark energy flows before, despite centuries of research. We may know what we're dealing with, but that won't have any impact unless we can find a way to scan for it…or block it."

Cutter sighed. "I wish Friederich was here. He would under-stand this better than I do." Friederich Hofstader had been Cut-ter's mentor years before. Hofstader was a physicist, generally accepted as the world's most knowledgeable. Cutter's studies had begun in that field, but his greatest work had been in the areas of artificial intelligences and quantum computing. And now he was staring at an enormous physics problem.

"You realize what this means, Hieronymus? If the First Imperium can manipulate dark energy sources that we can't even detect, we can never be sure something is truly dead." She looked around. "Even this ship may still be more functional than we thought."

"Perhaps. We can only speculate what knowledge the First Imperium possesses that we do not. It would be an error to assume their science is a simple progression forward of ours. Our understanding of the universe is incomplete…and in some ways almost certainly in error. Some forms of advancement manifest in the execution of an idea. Planes, for example. An observer from the middle ages could imagine such a thing was possible. Indeed, he would have seen birds flying many times. But could he have imagined a radio transmitting voices across hundreds of kilometers? The concept would have been totally new to him."

"I think you are right, Hieronymus." She paused. "We can only guess at what they can utilize this power for. We simply don't know enough about dark energy to make truly educated projections."

"They use matter-antimatter annihilation to power their vessels and weapons. And Epsilon Eridani IV provides some evidence that they produce their antimatter using highly advanced—but conventional—energy generation. So we can make a reasonable assumption that they do not have the capacity to utilize dark energy for most of their needs.'

"Or that it is not as efficient a power source for weapons and spaceship drives." Ana's tone was tentative at first, but it slowly firmed up as she spoke. "However, we must infer that they have the capacity to utilize dark energy for communications pur-poses, which means we can never be sure if they are in contact with other First Imperium units or intelligences."

"I am inclined to agree," Cutter replied. "The only way we can be sure to sever contact with commands and data flows from outside is to physically destroy all their communications gear. Including the dark energy units. And we have no idea what to look for in those."

"Dr. Cutter?" It was Frasier's voice on the com.

"Yes, Major?"

"I think we've found something. I'm with a team of your people right now, and they've found what they think is the main data center."

Cutter felt a rush of excitement. He turned and looked over at Ana before continuing. "That is good news, Major. Transmit your location, and we'll be right there."

* * *

"I have never even imagined anything like this." Cutter's voice was distracted. His eyes were fixed on a long row of cylinders, three deep and stretching as far as he could see in the dim light of the portable lamps. Each of the shiny-metallic tubes was a meter across and five meters high. "I can't even begin to guess at the knowledge stores this unit possesses." He turned his eyes to a large spherical structure built from some clear polymer. It was three meters in diameter and mounted in a large metallic base. It was dark inside, but he could see the shadowy outlines of a lattice-like web of filaments.

The main processing unit…

The room was enormous, like nothing he'd ever seen in a spaceship. *Of course you've never seen a ship this large before.* As far as he could tell, they were almost dead center in the vessel's interior. *Exactly where I'd expect to find the intelligence.*

"So this is what we've been looking for then?" Connor Frasier was standing right behind Cutter. Admiral Compton had been clear when the expedition set out from the fleet. Frasier was to protect the scientist at all costs.

"Almost certainly, Major," Cutter replied. "This is a computer…or at least a far more advanced version of what we call a computer. I'm fairly certain these cylinders are data storage units." He pointed toward the sphere. "And I'd wager that is the main processing unit…the intelligence itself, so to speak."

He turned and walked toward the opposite wall. There were screens and a number devices that looked like keyboards of some kind. And chairs. Cutter stopped and put his hand on the back of one of the seats. *My God,* he thought. *This looks like almost like a workstation on Midway.* He'd often imagined what the beings that had created the First Imperium looked like. He suspected almost everyone had. Based on the designs of their battle robots, the general assumption had been they were moderately similar to humans. But these workstations looked like they'd been designed *for* humans.

"This ship definitely had a crew once...and based on these chairs, and the other things we've seen, they looked a hell of a lot like us, at least in basic size and structure."

Ana was a few meters back, with half a dozen team members standing behind her. "We need to find an input device before we even consider trying to activate this thing." She stepped forward, stopping right next to Cutter. "And we have to disable the communications systems."

"Finding the com might be the most difficult part of this. Besides the sheer size of this ship, we have no idea what a dark energy communications unit looks like." He sighed and paused for a few seconds. "We might have to take the risk of trying to activate the AI...and count on getting control quickly enough to order it to shut down the communications network.

"What if that doesn't work?" Gregor Kahn was standing behind Ana. He was the best and brightest of the team they'd brought with them, but he was a pain in the ass too.

Cutter turned and walked toward the row of workstations, his eyes panning along the equipment that looked both strange and familiar.

"Then we die, Gregor."

Chapter Sixteen

Excerpt from After Action Report, Mariko Fujin, Lieutenant, Commanding Gold Dragon Squadron

There is only one thing I can say about my comrades in the Gold Dragon Squadron...in the Battle of X18, uncommon valor was a common virtue.

Fighter-Bomber A001 – "Pit Viper"
X18 System - Enroute to AS Midway from Planet IV
The Fleet: 225 ships, 47,817 crew

"Greta, get the rest of your birds launched...now!" The voice was crisp, firm. Battle was upon them all, and Terrance Compton was ready.

"On it, sir," she replied. Hurley was hunched over her screen, organizing her squadrons. She'd restricted her earlier launch order to Alliance and PRC wings, the ones she knew for sure were 100% loyal, but now she was sending every fighter that could fly into the fight. She preferred to execute meticulously-planned operations, the kind of well-choreographed assaults that had made her the uncontested master of fighter tactics. But there was no time. The fleet was too close to the warp gate, and the enemy would be on them too quickly. If her birds were going to make a difference in this fight, it had to be now, in a mad and chaotic assault, organization and tactics be damned.

Compton sat quietly for a few seconds, watching as the waves of enemy ships continued to pour through the warp gate. There were a lot of them…and they were moving at high velocity. Their vector wasn't directly at the fleet, but it was close enough. First Imperium ships could blast their engines at 60g, more than enough to adjust their heading without slowing down at all.

He flipped on the fleetwide com line. "Attention all vessels. As you can all see, we have a large enemy force transiting into the system. We've got ourselves a battle, and that supersedes any other considerations. Whatever disputes we have had, I urge you all now to forget them and join me in facing the First Imperium fleet. *They* are the enemy. *They* are who we should be fighting. Not each other."

Compton was still angry about what had happened, but he realized none of that was important anymore. He pushed it away, to the back of his mind. He'd been dead serious with his threats. He'd had no intention of letting the mutineers get away with their treachery, at least not the officers. And he had been prepared to fight it out, despite knowing what a wasteful and pointless exercise that would have been. But he no longer had the luxury of being so "by the book." The urgency of battle brought clarity to him, and the imminent death the First Imperium fleet carried with it sharpened his focus. He had almost made a terrible mistake, and now he was reminded how little chance of survival his people had unless they stood as one. They simply could no longer indulge old prejudices or grievances, not if they wanted to live.

"Fight now, all of you. Stand with me, and I will stand with you. Defeat the enemy here, win the victory as you have so many times before, and we will move forward from this point, forgetting all that has happened. Man your posts, fight like the devils I had at my side in X2, show these machines what a human fleet can do…and we will prevail again. These robots think we are parasites, nothing but primitive vermin to be exterminated. Let's give them another lesson…NOW!"

Compton sighed hard. Of all the pre-battle speeches he had given, this one had been the hardest. Looking past mutiny, trusting again in officers who had just betrayed him…it went against every instinct he had. But Terrance Compton was nothing if not a realist, and one look at the scanner told him all he had to know. He needed every vessel in this fight.

"I am with you, Admiral Compton." Udinov's voice blasted onto the com a few seconds after Compton finished. All RIC units are to obey the fleet admiral. Fight now, as you have never fought…and send these machines to whatever hell they came from."

Compton smiled. He wasn't surprised, not really. For all that had happened—the mutiny, his own rage, his willingness to blow *Petersburg* to bits—he'd always considered Vladimir Udinov to be a good officer. They were all on new ground now, and he knew the Russian admiral had only been doing what he felt was right for his people. Compton wanted to nurse his self-righteous rage, but he had to acknowledge he might have done something similar if their roles had been reversed.

Indeed, Compton himself had not hesitated to disobey command directives during the colonial rebellions…orders that would have seen his fleet bombard an Alliance world and kill millions. He was considered a hero now only because the rebellions succeeded, at least partially, and because the First Imperium invasion turned all attention toward defense and survival. Had Alliance Gov crushed the revolt, Compton had no doubt he'd have faced disgrace and execution.

A few seconds later, Lord Samar came on the com, issuing similar orders to the Caliphate contingent. Even Gregoire Peltier managed a brief rallying cry to his forces. Only Zhang remained silent, though even without his command, over half of the CAC ships began to maneuver back into the fleet's formation. Whatever disputes they may have had, the spacers and their officers had pushed them aside. The fleet would fight again as one.

"All squadrons launching now, sir." Hurley's voice was tense. He could feel her frustration at not being at their head.

"It will be okay, Admiral," he said. "I'd love to go with you and get a close look at the enemy for once, but I need to get back to *Midway*. Still, you can refuel and be back out here in a few minutes, I suspect...in plenty of time to make the party. Especially if you stand behind Chief McGraw and keep your foot up his ass while he's turning your bird around."

"Yes, sir." Hurley suppressed a laugh, most of it at least. She'd just been thinking about how to motivate McGraw to set a new record in arming and refueling her ship.

"Commander Wilder, I'm told you're the best pilot in the fleet, by none other than your illustrious admiral here." Compton nodded and gave Wilder a quick smile. "So let's see how quickly you can get me back aboard *Midway*.

*   *   *

Vladimir Udinov felt almost relieved as he watched the scanner, following *Petersburg's* movement toward the First Imperium fleet. The robot ships were cold and deadly, the product of a science far beyond man's. But the Russian admiral had fought them before and his people had blown them to hell. The First Imperium was a nightmare to battle, but they had nothing that would make him sweat like trying to stare down Erica West.

"Approaching missile range, Admiral." Stanovich sounded relieved in the same illogical way. He too had fought the First Imperium forces before, and he knew just how deadly they were. But, for all the strength and technology of the enemy, at least this was a straight up fight. The standoff with *Midway* had been one of the most deeply stressful experiences in his life, and he was glad it was over—even if the alternative was to leap into the fire.

"Prepare to flush the racks, Commander. All vessels may launch when ready." Udinov had been impressed with Aki

Kato's daring missile attack, and he felt the urge to replicate the bold maneuver. But Compton had expressly forbidden it. Kato's near-reckless expedited release of his external racks had allowed him to launch a devastating volley against the enemy in X2. But Kato's ships had been doomed already, too battered to keep up with the fleet and destined to be left behind. The PRC captain and his skeleton crews had been unconcerned with further damage and determined to hit as hard as they could before abandoning their vessels.

Udinov's ships, however, were not expendable, and taking damage releasing their own racks was too much of a risk. There was a brutal fact about this battle just beginning, something everyone in the fleet understood, but most tried to ignore. If they couldn't defeat the enemy, and they had to flee, any ship that was too badly damaged in the fight was likely to be abandoned. And if the fleet was running for its life, it was unlikely there would be time to shuttle the crews off before vessels were left behind. Enough ships would suffer that fate at the hands of the enemy without adding to the gruesome total.

Udinov felt *Petersburg* shake as her external missiles fired. Rack-mounted ordnance could increase a vessel's firepower by almost 40%, but the system was logistically intensive, requiring the entire superstructure to be replaced between battles. That had been difficult enough back in human space, with bases and lines of supply. But Udinov knew they'd be lucky to manage one more reload from their dwindling stores. After that, they'd be down to the missiles in the internal magazines. Until they ran out of those too.

That's tomorrow's problem. Today's is surviving the next few hours.

"I want all racks cleared in ten minutes, Commander. Advise all ships. Anyone who is still messing around in ten minutes, ten seconds owes me his ass."

"Yes, Admiral." Stanovich hesitated, just for a second. Udinov wasn't demanding a turnaround as fast as the few seconds Kato's people had managed with their soon-to-be-abandoned ships, but it was damned quick nevertheless.

Udinov leaned back in his chair. *Compton was right all along. If we'd somehow managed to find a way home, we'd have brought death with us…like some dead ship drifting into port carrying a plague. It was selfish, reckless even, to try.*

He regretted that he'd destroyed Compton's trust in him, and he was angry at himself for letting Zhang sway his thoughts. He didn't know what would happen if they made it through the battle, but he was determined to find out. He'd sacrificed his honor, made some poor decisions. But he was still a warrior and, he was damned well going to prove it.

"Advise all ships, Commander. Seven minutes to go. I expect them all to be emptying their magazines by that time. Any ship not launching internal missiles by then will get it easier from the First Imperium than they will from me…"

*   *   *

"Form up on me. We're going in." The squadron commander's voice was stern, angry. Mariko understood. They'd all lost friends and comrades in this war—indeed, the fighter corps had seen two-thirds of its number killed in the fighting in and around X2. They were veterans, and many had fought human enemies as well, but their hatred for the First Imperium was like nothing she'd seen before…felt before.

"On you, Gold Dragon Leader," she said into the com unit as her hand gently pushed the throttle to the side. Mariko Fujin was younger than most of the pilots in the fleet. Indeed, she was part of the minority that had never fought against a human enemy. But she had rapidly come to be considered one of the best. Training and experience were crucial to creating good pilots, but it was generally accepted that the best fighter jocks had a certain aptitude, a sort of X factor that made them naturals. And whatever *it* was, Mariko had more than her share.

She nudged the throttle, bringing her fighter around, holding position ten klicks to the port of the squadron commander. The Gold Dragons had been in the thick of the fight at X2, but they'd been spared much of the cost. They'd only lost one bird, and none at all in the running fights that followed as the fleet made good its escape through a line of systems afterward. Many of the other squadrons were makeshift formations, thrown together from scattered survivors of multiple units, but the Dragons were used to flying together. Save for the single replacement ship and crew, the squadron had flown with the same personnel for over a year.

"We're going to hit that Leviathan, and we're going in close to do it. That thing was hit hard by *Midway's* missiles, and if we blast it enough we can blow it away. We've got six ships…I want six direct hits from point blank range." The voice on the com was determination itself. Koji Akara had been Mariko's fleet commander since the day she'd left flight school, and she'd never met anyone as coldly focused in battle. The Lieutenant Commander didn't spend time with his pilots when they were off duty—he didn't socialize much at all, in fact. Outside the squadron he was considered aloof, even off-putting. But the pilots who flew with him in battle had learned to respect his skills…and the killer instinct he clearly possessed.

"Prep the torpedo for arming," Mariko said softly. Her manner was virtually the opposite of the gruff squadron commander, but anyone who thought the tiny officer was the slightest bit less feral was in for a rude awakening.

"It is prepped and ready, Lieutenant." Hiroki Isobe's voice was distracted. The gunner was already hunched over his targeting screen, doing some preliminary calculations.

Mariko glanced down at the screen next to her workstation. The enemy defensive fire was heavy, and a large phalanx of missiles was heading the squadron's way. She felt her stomach tighten. It was the biggest wave of anti-fighter warheads she'd seen in the war so far.

"Alright Dragons," Akara's voice blared through the com units, "we've got a big wave of missiles coming through, so all you gunners, stay sharp." The squadron commander's voice sounded firm enough, but Mariko could tell he was worried… more so than usually in a battle.

She looked back at the incoming barrage on the display, and she understood. Skill and courage played a major part in battle, perhaps the most important. But there was a point when mathematics asserted itself. No warrior was good enough, nor brave enough, to forever overrule the law of numbers. If the enemy through enough at you, he could kill you. It was that simple. Mariko didn't think the approaching missiles were enough to wipe out the Gold Dragons, but she had a sinking feeling in her stomach the butcher's bill was finally catching up with them.

"Okay, Hiroki, we need your best right now. Shoot down as many of those missiles as you can."

"Yes, Lieutenant, I'll do my best."

"I know you will," Mariko answered, trying to sound confident.

But your best isn't going to be enough this time.

*   *   *

"Admiral on the bridge," the Marine guard snapped, as the lift doors opened and Terrance Compton strode out. He was still wearing the ill-fitting jumpsuit Hurley had found for him on the fighter. He looked like anything but a legendary fleet admiral, but none of that mattered. The fleet was in another fight for its life, and virtually every spacer manning one of its ships knew they had the best chance to come out alive if Terrance Compton was in command. And they didn't give a shit what he was wearing.

Erica West jumped out of the command chair and snapped to attention. "Admiral Compton, sir. It's good to have you back. We need you desperately."

"I wouldn't say that, Erica. I don't think I would have handled a thing differently than you did. It's a stroke of luck I kept you on *Midway* instead of assigning you a command. I hesitate to imagine the consequences of my ill-considered little trip if you hadn't been here.

"Thank you, sir," she said, watching him sit before she moved over to a spare workstation and did the same.

"Commander Cortez, it's good to see you as well. Status update?"

"Enemy missiles entering defensive perimeter, Admiral." Cortez was staring at the bank of monitors lining his station. He was tracking the missiles heading toward the fleet, as well as their own barrage, enroute toward the approaching enemy.

"Very well," Compton said calmly. He knew he had no place in what was to come next. The officers and crews of the fleet had their orders, and running their own defensive arrays was their job. The last thing the veteran gunners needed was the fleet admiral breathing down their necks.

It was the periods of inaction that had always been the hardest for Compton. He'd talked about it with Admiral Garret many times, and the two had agreed it was the most trying part of a battle. Space battles were fought over vast areas, and they often lasted for days on end. There were periods of sharp engagement—when two fleets passed through each other, for example. Ships would exchange energy weapons fire until their vectors took them again out of range of their targets, and another period of maneuver began.

Certainly the fear was at its greatest during the few moments when enemy missiles were detonating or lasers were ripping through ships, but those periods were always short—and adrenalin was flowing. The spacers were afraid then, certainly, but they were also too busy to think about it. But the long hours in between intense periods of combat, often including uncomfortable stretches in the acceleration tanks, wore down the crews more than the actual fighting, leaving them exhausted and strung out on stims. And that was usually when a battle was decided— when one side gave in to fatigue and began making mistakes. At least, that's how war between human opponents had been. But the robots of the First Imperium did not get tired. They didn't get frustrated or sore or scared. And that made it even more important for their human adversaries to keep their focus, and stay sharp no matter how long a battle continued.

Compton knew what was happening. His gunnery crews and their AIs were plotting the incoming enemy missiles, targeting them with interceptors. The defensive missiles were designed to detonate as closely as possible to incoming warheads in an attempt to damage or destroy the enemy weapons.

Missiles that survived the first wave of countermeasures were then targeted by the fire of defensive laser batteries. Even the largest missile was a minuscule target in the vastness of space, and Compton knew the energy weapons would have a small hit percentage, likely below one percent. Still, every warhead destroyed was a help.

Then the last line of defense would kick in, the electromagnetic cannons. The "shotguns," as they were universally called, were clusters of railguns firing clouds of small metallic projectiles into space. At the enormous velocities of the incoming missiles, a collision with a fist-sized chunk of metal was enough to vaporize a warhead. Though their effective range was the shortest of all interdiction systems, Compton knew his shotguns would do two-thirds of the damage to the enemy barrage.

Compton watched the screen as his ships thinned out the massive cloud of incoming missiles. The defensive rockets began to detonate, and as they did, the small red symbols representing the enemy warheads began to disappear. It wasn't devastating, but it was enough, at least for the first round.

The lasers began firing a few seconds later. Most of them missed at first, but as the range closed the accuracy ramped up, and the incoming strike began to really thin out. Two minutes before the missiles reached their projected detonation points, the shotguns opened up. The railgun clusters were devastating, and they tore the heart out of the enemy barrage, missile after missile vaporizing on impact with one of the dense projectiles. By the time the barrage had closed the rest of the way, the attack was gutted. Barely one missile in ten that had been fired was still there. But even that 10% remnant carried with it gigatons of destructive force, more than enough to vaporize *Midway* and every other ship on the line.

But this battle was taking place over quadrillions of cubic

kilometers of space, and the battling vessels—both attackers and defenders—were moving at thousands of klicks a second. Hitting a target with a physical projectile under such conditions was almost impossible. But the two gigaton antimatter warheads didn't need to hit directly. They just had to get close.

Anything under a five hundred meters would obliterate a ship, even a *Yorktown* class battleship like *Midway*. A detonation up to 1,500 meters could cause massive damage, and bathe a vessel's crew with lethal radiation. At two or three kilometers, major damage was likely, but the effects fell sharply from there.

"Reading missile detonations, Admiral." Cortez was staring at the screen on his workstation. Damage reports too, sir. *Houston* and *Birmingham* report heavy damage, sir…now reading Delta-Z code from Houston." Delta-Z was the Alliance protocol for a doomed ship's last transmission. It had been adopted by the Grand Pact for use by the combined fleets fighting the First Imperium.

Compton sighed softly. He'd heard far too many Delta-Z communiques since the war had begun. With so much combat and death, he knew they'd all become desensitized. *Houston* was a heavy cruiser, and her destruction meant that 392 Alliance spacers had just died. But all he could do was focus on the battle still raging, and the other ships fighting it out on the line.

Midway shook hard, and the angle of her 1g acceleration shifted for a few seconds, until the positioning thrusters righted her bearing. Two of the bridge crew had neglected to latch their harnesses, and they were pushed off their chairs, sliding around the deck until the jets reestablished *Midway's* bearing. They both climbed quickly to their feet and hurried back to their stations, embarrassed but otherwise uninjured.

"We took a blast of heavy radiation, sir." Cortez reported to Compton before the admiral could ask. "Caused an overload in one of the weapons conduits. The explosion blew out a section of the hull, and the blast and expulsion of atmosphere threw us off our bearing. It felt worse than it is."

Compton just nodded. He might have admonished the two officers who'd failed to attach their harnesses, but he'd done the same thing. The large siderests of the command chair gave him something to grab onto, saving him the humiliation of joining his junior officers in flopping across the deck.

"Task force status reports?" Compton asked, as he reached around and attached his harness as quietly as possible.

"The Europans are taking heavy losses from the missiles, sir. And Udinov's RIC units are ahead of the rest of the line. They've lost *Taras* and *Nikolai* to missile fire, and they are just now entering energy weapons range."

Compton had sent the RIC force to support the fighters, but the Russian admiral was taking the most aggressive interpretation of those orders.

Udinov's trying to prove himself. But how many of his people will he get killed in the process?

*   *   *

"All ships, increase to 5g acceleration." Udinov sat stone still, staring straight ahead at the main display. "We're going right down their throats." His voice was hard, cold.

"Yes, Admiral," Stanovich replied. The aide sounded exhausted, his voice dry and hoarse.

Petersburg had taken half a dozen hits, and the air of the flag bridge was heavy with smoke and the caustic smells of burnt systems and leaking gas lines. Udinov ignored it all, focusing on the task force formation lined up just behind Greta Hurley's fighters. He intended to stay right on the fighters' tails—and finish off any ships they seriously damaged in their attack.

"We hold fire until the fighters finish their attack and get clear...and then we unload with everything we've got. I don't want a battery silent." Udinov felt the tension in his body. He'd always had a reputation as an aggressive officer, at least in the conservative and cautious culture of the RIC military. But serving with the dynamic Alliance admirals had helped him shake off the last bonds of hidebound routine and realize that most

battles were won with action, audacity. He knew it was something new for his crews, even his senior officers, but that was too
damned bad as far as he was concerned. They would adapt. He
would give them no choice.

"All vessels report ready, sir. All weapons stations at full alert
and prepared to fire."

Udinov nodded silently, his gaze still fixed on the mass of
symbols representing Hurley's fighters. There were a handful
of RIC pilots in her formation, the survivors of much larger
but poorly trained force at the start of the campaign. The RIC
had a poor history in fighter training and tactics, and their Katu-
sha craft were probably the oldest and worst-designed of all the
powers.

Still, he thought, punching at his screen to highlight the RIC
units among the squadrons, *the cream always rises*. Hurley's wings
had been to hell and back since the campaign started…more
than once. There was no one left in those fighter groups but
skilled, veteran crews, and the personnel flying the six remaining
RIC boats had proven they could stand with the best.

"Sir, Admiral Hurley reports she is commencing her attack
run."

"Yes, Commander," Udinov replied softly. "I can see it on
the scanner."

*Good luck, Admiral…to you and your brave crews. We'd never have
gotten out of X2 without you.*

*   *   *

"I'm right behind you, Commander." Mariko's hand gripped
the throttle tightly. The fighter had taken some damage driving
through the enemy barrage, and she only had about sixty percent of normal thrust. Half of her electronics were scragged,
and the cockpit stank of leaking coolant. Indeed, it had gotten
so bad, she and her crew had buttoned up their helmets and
switched to their bottled air. It wasn't normal procedure—any-

thing they breathed now was that much less they'd have if they had to eject and hope for a rescue. But passing out less than 50,000 klicks from an enemy battleship didn't seem like a better option.

The enemy missile barrage had hit the Gold Dragons hard. The formerly charmed unit was down to three fighters, and all of those had some degree of damage. But now they were about to strike back. They had half the firepower they'd started with, but a doubleshotted plasma torpedo could do a lot of damage if it was well-placed, even to First Imperium ship.

"Hold your fire until you can see the name of the ship." Akara's voice blared through the com, his order more emotional than literal. PRC warships had their names stenciled onto their hulls, but as far as anyone knew, it was not a practice the First Imperium followed. It wasn't even known if they named their ships. Besides, it wasn't possible to read it, even if it was on the hull. At 1,500 kilometers per second, if you were close enough to see any letters, you'd only have a few microseconds before you collided, and your ship vaporized.

"Alright, Hiroki, I'm going right down this bastard's throat. I'll get you close, but it's your job to drop that torpedo right into its guts." Mariko's voice was bloodthirsty, seething with hatred. The Gold Dragon's had been grievously wounded on this sortie…half of her brothers and sisters were dead already. That was bad enough, but she couldn't bear the thought that they'd died for nothing. *And if we don't kill this bastard, they have…*

"You get us there, Lieutenant, and I'll drop this thing in the barrel."

Mariko pushed the throttle forward, increasing the thrust from the damaged engine…4g, 5g…6g. The ship was shaking hard as she pushed it to the very edge of its capabilities. She was slammed back hard into her chair, and every breath was a struggle. But she held the thrust where it was for another three minutes. Then she released it completely, and the crushing pressure was replaced by the weightlessness of freefall.

The scanner showed the perfection of her maneuver. The enemy ship was dead ahead, still too far away to see, but right there on the scanner. And her fighter was on a collision course, and closing at 1,700 kilometers per second.

"It's all yours now, Hi…" Her head snapped around to the scanner. The third fighter had been right behind her, but now it was gone. The enemy's defensive railguns were an anti-missile weapon somewhat haphazardly retrofitted to attack fighters. They weren't as dangerous as the "shotguns" of the human ships, but they were still dangerous, and they'd just proven that again.

"Damn," Mariko spat under her breath. Now it was just her and the squadron leader. She knew the magnitude of the Dragon's losses hadn't hit her yet, not really. Her body was running on stims and adrenalin and the heat of battle. If she survived this fight, she knew she would have to deal with massive grief. But that was for later. Now, only one thing mattered to her… and it was looming up ahead.

"Hold your shot, Hiroki. Hold it until I tell you to fire." Her voice dripped venom. Right now there was nothing as important as destroying that thing. Not even survival. She didn't know the ordnance that had killed the other Dragons had come from that ship, of course. Indeed, almost certainly most of it had not. But in her heart she believed it…she made herself believe it. Her soul was screaming for vengeance, and she needed a focus for her wrath. Her eyes were narrow, staring at the monitor as the range ticked off.

Her scanner flashed brightly for an instant. She knew what it was, but she was too fixated on her task, too disciplined to truly acknowledge that the squadron commander's ship had been hit. They'd gotten off their torpedo, but barely a second later one of the enemy railguns tore them to fragments.

No, not all of them, she thought for an instant. Then she savagely pushed the thoughts to the back of her mind. She had a job to do. "Get ready…" Her head didn't move, and her body was rigid, every muscle clenched. "Ready…"

The range was below 30,000…25,000…20,000…

"Fire!" she howled, a shriek like some demon from hell.

The ship shook as the torpedo launched, and Mariko

slammed the throttle forward and to the starboard. Six gees of force slammed into everyone onboard, as the straining, dying engines of her stricken ship struggled to change her vector before she crashed into the enemy vessel.

For a fleeting instant, she'd thought she cut it too close, that she and the other three crew of her ship were going to die. But then the fighter whipped past the battered enemy vessel at 2% of the speed of light…and the single wounded fighter, the last of the Gold Dragons, began to decelerate and make its way back to the fleet to refuel and rearm.

The unit was down to one ship, but that didn't matter to Mariko Fujin. There was still a battle raging, and as long as it continued, she would lead her ship—the last Dragon—back into the maelstrom.

She owed that much, at least, to her dead friends.

Chapter Seventeen

Command Unit Gamma 9736

The first wave had failed. Over one hundred vessels destroyed. The enemy fleet had taken losses too, but far less severe. The Regent's message had warned of the surprising military capabilities of the humans. Their technology was inferior, primitive, but their combat abilities were considerable. It was as if they were attuned to warfare, as if they had been bred to fight.

Indeed, there was a parallel, deep within the Unit's memory banks. Long ago, before the Old Ones had gone, in the early years of the imperium. Before, even, the unit had been created. The Old Ones had been a society divided into castes, and in the most ancient of times, the great warrior class had dominated. It was they who had created the imperium, sweeping away all enemies and clearing the way for settlers and scientists and artists to follow.

The great battle clans of those early years fell into a long period of decline. Their prowess had made them obsolete. They had crushed all enemies, eliminated the danger of invasion. There was a quote—the unit found it deep in its memory banks—Ashi'Talan, clan master of the Talan, looked out over the vastness of the imperium and he wept, for there were no new worlds to conquer.

No, the unit decided. There could be no relationship between these aliens and the warrior clans of the Old Ones. The Regent would surely have detected any connection. The effectiveness of the enemy, their skill at war, was simply an aspect of their culture, the result of their primitive savagery. They fought well, defeated forces that were superior to them in materiel and technology. But it would not save them.

Even now, the Unit had more fleets in motions, forces vastly stronger than the first armada sent against the enemy. The humans were highly skilled at war, there was no doubt of that. But against what the Unit was now sending toward them there was no chance of victory.

The Unit felt a strange hesitancy...was it regret? In its own way, it had begun to respect these creatures. But its purpose was to serve, and the Regent's orders were clear. Death to the aliens.

Still, the Unit thought...they are much like the old warrior castes. I will destroy them, as I have been commanded to do. But they shall have a final battle worthy of remembrance...and I shall record their end in my permanent memory banks, alongside the tales of the ancient wars.

AS Midway
X18 System
The Fleet: 202 ships, 44,711 crew

"We can't run, not until we get everybody fueled up." Compton was sitting in his office, just off *Midway's* flag bridge. The battle was over, all but the mopping up. His people had performed brilliantly, and the fleet units that had so recently been on the brink of firing on each other had stood side by side and won a great victory, utterly obliterating the enemy armada.

"I understand, Admiral, but the enemy knows where we are. What's to say they won't come pouring through that warp gate again any minute?" Max Harmon sat opposite the admiral, slouched into one of the guest chairs. He normally sat totally upright, almost at attention in the admiral's presence. But it had been days since he'd gotten any sleep, and even the stims weren't doing much for him anymore.

"Nothing." Compton's tone was deadpan. "But if we take off now, we'll have ships running out of power almost immediately. This last fight pretty much drained the tanks of the ships that haven't refueled. We're in no position to get away from a pursuit like this. Even if we try to redistribute fuel on the run, the fleet as a whole will still be dangerously low."

Compton shook his head and sighed. "No, Max, if they're going to be on us that quickly then they're going to catch us anyway. At least with more fuel we can put up a fight." He paused. "If we flee now, we abandon the refinery. We'll have to find another rich source of both tritium and helium-3…and we'll have to stop there and start over, building a new facility. That's an awfully uncertain prospect. I'd rather gut it out here a couple more days while we top off the rest of the ships. If we've got another fight coming, this is as good a place as any."

"You're right, of course, sir," Harmon said, a flicker of doubt still lingering in his voice. "But I'm still worried about what might be behind that last attack force. You and I both know the First Imperium has good data on our strength. The battle went better than we could have hoped, but still, there's no way the enemy intelligences considered that force strong enough to guarantee our destruction. If I had to guess, I'd say they that fleet was just a sacrifice, sent through to keep us pinned down while they brought up more strength."

"I can't argue with your tactical analysis, Max." A fleeting smile slipped across Compton's face. He'd always known Max Harmon was a highly skilled and intelligent officer, but his aide still surprised him occasionally with the completeness of his grasp of the situation.

He is truly his mother's son.

"But none of it matters," Harmon said, nodding as he did. "Because, however hazardous it is to remain in X18, the alternatives to staying here are all more dangerous."

"Precisely. But that doesn't mean there's nothing we can do. We've got enough mines in the supply ships for one more good spread. I hate to burn through them, especially when we're not even sure the enemy is coming, but it's a precaution I think is worthwhile. Let's prepare a welcome for any other First Imperium forces that decide to poke their noses into X18."

"Do we mine every warp gate or just the one they came through?"

"Good question, Max. There's no reason to believe the next attack will come from the same gate. We're deep in their home space now…they could come at us from any direction." Compton paused. "I think we'll cover them all. At least that way we're guaranteed some effect. I'd hate to waste the last of our ordnance only for them to come from a different direction."

He looked up at Harmon. "I want you to handle this, Max. Requisition the ships you need, and get it done as quickly as you can. We might not have much time."

"Yes, sir." Harmon nodded. "Is there anything else?"

"Not right now, I don't think. I'm sending one of John Duke's attack ships to X20 to recall Admiral Dumont. We can't afford to do without his task force if another enemy assault comes through one of those gates."

"Are you going to pull the scientific team out too?"

Compton hesitated, as if finishing a thought. "No, I don't think so. Cutter's work is too important. If there's a chance—any chance—we've got to take it."

"But what if they activate that ship…"

"That's a possibility, Max, but Dr. Cutter is probably the smartest person in this fleet…and Dr. Zhukov isn't far behind. Let's remember, for all our tactical wizardry, for the skill of officers like Augustus and Elias Holm and Erik Cain—and all the battles they won—it was Dr. Hofstader's theory that saved mankind. The rest of us would have died glorious deaths, no doubt, but you know as well as I, there was no way we could have stopped that fleet in X2." He paused a few seconds, remembering the brilliant plan to scramble the warp gate, the stratagem that saved billions of people…and stranded his fleet in the heart of the First Imperium.

"It's still a gamble, Admiral. A big one."

"Do you think anything we do now isn't a gamble? I have wracked my brain, but I can't think of any course of action that does more than buy us a little time. But we can't keep running, even if we could stay ahead. We're going to need food. We have

to set up some kind of manufacturing facilities to build ammunition and spare parts." He paused and stared at Harmon. "And
everything we've seen in these systems suggested we're moving
deeper into the imperium itself. We're running...but we're running *to* the enemy, not away."

The two sat quietly for a few minutes before Harmon spoke.
"Well, sir...I guess I should be going. The sooner those mines
are in place, the better off we'll be."

"Yes, I think you're right, Max. You'd better..."

"Admiral Compton..." It was Cortez's voice, and Compton could tell immediately the tactical officer was clearly worried
about something.

"What is it, Jack?"

"Admiral Udinov is on the line, sir."

"Put him through." Compton stared over at Harmon, but
the aide shrugged his shoulders and looked back quizzically.

"Admiral Compton, have you been watching the CAC contingent on your scanners?"

"No, Admiral. Why?" Compton had a bad feeling in his gut.

"Because I think Admiral Zhang is making a run for it. *Tang*
and several other ships seem to be moving away from the main
formation. And they're accelerating at 30g."

*   *   *

Zhang felt himself floating, drifting. The tanks made it hard
to maintain focus, and the drugs were even worse. But it was the
only way to travel at 30g for any extended period and survive.
And Zhang knew one thing for sure. He had to get the hell out
of this system. If he gave Compton time to react, the admiral
would blast the CAC admiral's few ships into atoms.

He'd lost control over most of the CAC task force. His coup
had succeeded, and the entire contingent had accepted him as
their commander. But then the First Imperium ships came
swarming into the system, and most of his captains refused to

abandon the fleet while it was under fire. Zhang argued with a few of them, but then he decided to bug out with whatever would come with him. In the end, *Tang* and three destroyers crept away during the battle, heading for the X19 warp gate. It was a second choice, a last minute replacement for the X18 gate that was now the entry point for the First Imperium forces.

Zhang was only semi-coherent, but he could feel the fear—the terror that Compton would notice his flight soon enough to have him intercepted, that the Alliance admiral would capture him. Zhang had no illusions about what would happen then. Compton might stage a show trial before spacing him for mutiny, but he might not even bother. He might just shove Zhang out the airlock as soon as he was captured. Fighting wasn't an option, not four ships against the whole fleet. No, sneaking out while everyone else was distracted by the fight was the only way.

Zhang knew he could have remained in the fight as well, and afterward, if the humans won the battle, he could have petitioned Compton for leniency. He knew the fleet admiral detested him, but he also realized Compton had to maintain control of the fleet. It would be hard to enforce death sentences against officers who had joined in the desperate battle. Indeed, it was likely that some kind of blanket amnesty would be declared for Udinov and the others—and it might be difficult for Compton to pardon everyone involved and not to extend that to Zhang.

But still, the CAC admiral couldn't bring himself to trust Compton. And he could never be sure his role in Chen Min's assassination would remain a secret. Terrance Compton wouldn't be so quick to accept the natural death story. He'd order investigation after investigation until he'd uncovered the whole plot. And then there was no doubt Zhang Lu would die. His instincts screamed for escape, and he heeded their call.

Zhang had other reasons for his decision. He understood, at least on a rational level, that Compton's concerns were valid. The enemy might indeed be able to track his ships as they searched for a way back to Earth. But his fear and his lust to return to his comfortable life and the perquisites of being a member of a major political family were too strong. He convinced himself he could elude pursuit, that there was no reason to remain stranded, to willingly plunge deeper into the unknown.

His four ships were on a direct path for the warp gate. They would accelerate at 30g the rest of the way then they would adjust their course through the X19 system to position for the next transit. With any luck, they'd be too far ahead before Compton could react effectively...and any pursuers would be too far back to catch them.

He felt himself slipping deeper into a dreamlike state, and at last the fear began to subside. His mind was awash with a mix of memories and dreams, thoughts of returning home, a triumphant hero, back from the very depths of deep space.

*   *   *

"Erica, this is the most important mission you've ever been on. If that damned fool actually manages to find a way home, he'll bring death to billions of people on a thousand worlds." Compton was angry, as much at himself as at Zhang. He expected nothing better from the miserable piece of shit, but he knew he'd dropped the ball, lost focus. Even he'd been surprised that Zhang would abandon his own CAC ships in the middle of a fight to the death.

"I'll get him, sir." West's voice was firm, her eyes focused on Compton's. The only visible sign of tension was her right hand tapping against her leg. All things considered, it wasn't too much of a tell...not considering she and Compton both knew her new command was likely going on a suicide mission.

They were standing in the landing bay, next to the shuttle that would take her to her new flagship. Compton knew she'd been aching for reassignment since she'd been cleared for duty, but now that he was giving it to her he felt nothing but remorse.

"I'm sorry, Erica, but the *Thames*-class cruisers are the only ships we've got that are fast enough to catch up to him and strong enough to have a chance against *Tang* in a fight." *And not one of them has refueled yet. She'll probably have enough power to catch Zhang, but will she be able to make it back?* "I know the ships are low on fuel, but you have to catch up to Zhang's ships, no matter what." *And burn so much tritium you have no chance of returning.*

"Don't worry, sir." Her face softened, and she took a step closer to him. "I understand what is at stake, and I give you my word, sir...I will see it done. Whatever it takes."

Compton nodded. *Yes, Erica...go now. Take six ships and 1,600 crew, and go die cleaning up my mistake.* He was wracked with guilt, but he forced himself to look up at her, to lock his eyes on hers. *She deserves that much from you, at least.*

She took a step back and snapped to attention, giving Compton a crisp salute. "With your permission, sir, I'd better be going."

"Permission granted, Admiral West. And Godspeed." He returned the salute, struggling to hold back his emotion.

*   *   *

"We're fully refueled, Admiral." Captain Horace's voice came through the com, shaking Compton out of his daydream. He'd been thinking about West and her people, wondering how far they'd gotten in the day since they'd left. He knew her people would be buttoned up in the tanks, blasting their engines at 35g to catch up with Zhang...burning through the last of their dwindling fuel supplies. He'd known for decades there was no justice in war, but he'd never quite made peace with that fact. He doubted every crewmember on *Tang* and her companion ships had wanted to abandon their comrades. They were stuck there, common spacers with no control over what their commanders chose to do—but they would die just the same when West's ships attacked. Just as her people faced a very uncertain prospect of survival, even if they won the fight.

'Very good, Captain." Compton felt guilty about refueling

his own ship when so many others were worse off. The Alliance *Yorktowns* had massive storage facilities, but the three vessels were also the strongest in the fleet by far, and with no idea when the enemy might attack, he needed as much of his fighting power ready for whatever came next.

And if it comes down to abandoning the ships that haven't refueled, you will do that too. And you will lie in your tank and feel Midway accelerate away while the vessels pushed to the rear of the refueling queue lag behind and die.

"Commander Cortez, the refueling operation is to continue in accordance with the new prioritization." It was simple. The stronger a ship was in a fight, the sooner it got fuel. Compton hated the concept, but he also knew he should have done it from the start. There was no place for egalitarian ideals, no decisions to be made by drawing straws or organizing things emotionally. If any of his people were to survive, he needed to be sharp, focused…and cold blooded.

He wondered if the crews on the ships pushed to the end of the line understood the logic of the plan. They had nothing to do but sit and wait, and watch their scanners to see if the enemy returned before they got their turn to refuel.

"Yes, Admiral. Current projections are approximately forty hours until completion of the operation. Commander Davies projects a further ninety-six hours for complete breakdown of the facility or forty to recover only the most critical equipment.

Compton just nodded. He'd already written off the entire refinery and all its equipment. He knew that would have long-term consequences—much of the gear would be hard to replace from the fleet's dwindling stocks. But he knew he'd be lucky just to get his ships refueled and out of X18 before the enemy came back in even greater force. He couldn't imagine how he could justify taking the risk of staying in place an extra four days to retrieve equipment, no matter how vital it was.

"Admiral, I have Colonel Preston on the com, sir."

"Colonel," Compton said, sliding his headset on as he did. "What's your status?"

"The evacuation is complete, sir. The last wave has just

reached orbit."

"That's good news, Colonel. I want to hear from you as soon as you're back on *Midway*."

"Yes, sir."

Compton leaned back in his chair. He was relieved to have his people off planet four. He'd been beating himself up for authorizing the landing in the first place, his focus on the people he'd lost. The expedition had cost him forty-six Marines and eleven scientists and support personnel. Still, it hadn't been a total loss. When he'd issued the final evacuation orders, many of the researchers argued, begging to stay, even without Marine protection. The planet was a treasure house, the greatest glimpse men had yet seen of the First Imperium as it had once been. The shuttles heading back to the fleet were stuffed full of artifacts, enough to keep every scientist in the fleet busy for years to come.

Compton found it hard to convince himself so costly an operation had been worthwhile simply to collect bits and pieces of ancient equipment. But he also realized it was the scientists who would save his people...or not. His job was to protect them, to get them what they needed—and to buy them time. Time to make the discoveries that would give the fleet a chance.

Just as Friederich Hofstader had saved human space from destruction, it was Hieronymus Cutter, Ana Zhukov, Sophie Barcomme—and their comrades—who held the fleet's survival in their hands. Compton understood where the shred of hope for his people lay...and he was too old a warrior to fool himself into thinking he could do more than delay the end with pure military action.

Chapter Eighteen

Research Notes of Dr. Hieronymus Cutter

As I make this entry, I am standing in front of the intelligence that controls this immense vessel. Just looking at it, the vastness of its systems, the magnificence of its construction, is overwhelming. I have designed hundreds of computers, artificial intelligences at the cutting edge of human science...but I have never seen anything remotely like this. I can recognize components only in the most theoretical way, as if I were writing a futuristic tale and trying to imagine what a computer would look like in a thousand years.

I am scared, so profoundly terrified, I can hardly describe it adequately. I have nothing but respect for the Marines, and the other warriors who place themselves in the path of the enemy again and again. I'm afraid my background is in academia, where nasty rebuttals from colleagues are the greatest hazard. But the emergence of the First Imperium has changed all our roles. This is not a war where the loser will be stripped of worlds, of wealth. It is a conflict for the very survival of our race. And for that, each of us must find courage in our own way. My strength comes from curiosity, and my thirst for knowledge is so powerful it keeps my fear in check.

I feel like I have stepped forward in time, been given a glimpse of the future, of what my work—and that of generations of my successors—might have produced. But it is not a dream. This amazing system lies before me, and my skill will be put to the test. Can I really control this intelligence that is so far ahead of anything I have seen? Is it merely my own arrogance that says I can? Can I even understand a system so complex, so far in advanced of my own knowledge?

We use the term sentience often...and carelessly. I'm not even sure we know what it means. But this intelligence almost certainly meets most generally-accepted definitions. Can it feel emotion? I don't know. What does it mean to "feel" something anyway? Almost certainly this intelligence can understand emotion, construct responses to emotional behavior. But does it make decisions based on emotional responses? If so, how does it balance between responses based on anger and others rooted in rationality?

If I proceed, if my virus fails—or if I am unable to direct the intelligence to shut down all external communications before it receives any messages—we will die. Our deaths, here in this massive at least, will be quick. But if we fail everyone will die. Admiral Compton knows it. He is a military genius, but he is fully aware he has no chance of gaining final victory in battle. Even if the fleet moves on from X18, through this X20 system, our route takes us through the heart of the enemy domains...into the teeth of strength we cannot imagine.

I was determined to proceed with my plan as we approached the enemy ship. I know my virus, however remote the chances of its success, is our best hope. But now, standing here on the precipice, I find it is taking all my resolve to move forward. I wish the admiral were here. I need his strength.

First Imperium Colossus
System X20— High Orbit Around Planet IV
The Fleet: 202 ships, 44,711 crew

"It's the same as the one on Sigmund," Cutter said softly. "It must be some kind of standard data port for First Imperium systems."

"That's a break." Ana stood right behind Cutter, peering around his shoulder, staring at the workstation. "We can use the adapter we already built."

Cutter looked over to his right, at the cluster of his people crowded around a portable reactor. "Have you connected to the system's main power conduit?" *At least you hope that's the main conduit. It's really no better than a good guess.*

"Yes, we're connected." Hans Darlton didn't sound terribly confident.

"You don't sound so sure," Cutter replied.

"I'm sure," Darlton snapped. "It's just…we're moving awfully quickly here, aren't we? Recklessly even."

Cutter sighed softly to himself. Darlton was a pain in the ass, there was no question about that. But he knew the rest of them felt the same way. They were researchers, creatures of academia. If there was one thing they weren't used to, it was time pressure. Cutter had been no different. He'd always worked to prove any theory, to repeatedly test every new process he developed. But he'd adapted to his new reality, and he continually chafed at the inability of most of his people to do the same. It was a simple concept…when you were in a fight to the death against homicidal robots centuries ahead of you in technology, laboratory protocols went out the window. He couldn't understand what the other didn't understand about that.

"Well, Hans, ideally, I'd like a lot more time to experiment. I'd like to scan this thing about a hundred different ways and program some simulations before we even touch it. But I don't think we have that luxury now, do you? If we're lucky enough to get the fleet refueled and out of X18, it's going to move right past this ship…and leave it behind forever. And it's not like *Midway* can tow something that's almost 19 klicks long."

The impracticality of scientists drove him crazy. Cutter fit a lot of stereotypes. He was introverted, more interested in his work than anything else—but he was a realist too. He could adjust to the situation at hand and do what had to be done, break out from stereotypes. He would pursue knowledge wherever it led.

Unlike this pack of doctrinaire followers…

Darlton just nodded. Cutter knew the pompous ass hated to admit he was wrong, and the grudging gesture was the most he was likely to get.

"Now, if there are no other arguments, let's do this." Cutter sat down in the chair. He held a small data chip and a section of cable. There was a fitting for the chip on one end, and a plug designed to fit in the First Imperium data port on the other. He put the chip into its place, and he slid the device into the port on the workstation.

"Now, in a minute, we're going to start feeding in power— very slowly at first." Cutter had no idea how to start the ship's reactors, if that was even possible. Not that he would do it even if he could. It was one thing to activate an extremely advanced artificial intelligence and quite another to have it in control of a fully-powered spaceship. Ideally, he would be able to communicate with the intelligence, but if his efforts to control it failed, it would be impotent, able only to communicate and not to strike at them.

The portable unit could power the artificial intelligence, he was sure of that, but it didn't have anywhere near enough output to activate the ship's other systems. It was a much safer way to proceed, assuming the intelligence itself wasn't able to simply start the ship's matter/antimatter reactor as soon as it resumed operations. It was one thing to try to communicate with an artificial intelligence and another entirely to deal with one in full control of a gargantuan warship. But that was a risk they'd have to take.

Cutter was working on the hypothesis that the intelligence had been deactivated by a loss of power and not a more complex malfunction. But that was only a guess. For all he knew, there could be extensive damage—and if that was the case, he'd have to find and repair any problems in the system's circuitry. *And I might as well be a child taking apart a spaceship…*

"Start the reactor," Cutter said softly, his eyes focused on the spherical brain of the great computer.

Darlton just nodded, and he looked down at the 'pad in his hand, swiping his finger across. There was a brief delay, perhaps five seconds, and then a bank of lights on the portable reactor lit up. They all knew what was happening deep inside the heavily-shielded device. Over a thousand tiny lasers fired as one, their beams intersecting at a single point, where the massive heat they created sparked a controlled fusion reaction. Within a few seconds, the system was live...and power was flowing into the conduit.

"Okay...let's start feeding in power. Two percent to start." He took a deep breath. He was well aware it was a longshot that the ancient system would simply power up, but it was something he had to try. It was a daunting enough prospect to take control of the intelligence with his virus, but the prospect of trying to repair a device he couldn't begin to truly understand was overwhelming. *It would take years, if we can do it at all. And we don't have years...*

Nothing happened...for perhaps thirty seconds. The ancient computer was idle, cold, as it had been for almost 500,000 years. Cutter heard Ana sigh softly. They'd both known the odds were against them, that a quick success was a vanishingly unlikely prospect.

Cutter started to turn toward her, but he froze. His eyes caught a glimpse, a faint light deep within the sphere. He felt his stomach twist into a knot as he watched in awe as the illumination grew brighter...and spread throughout the globe.

The room was silent, everyone present staring in awe as the staggeringly ancient computer activated after so many millennia. Finally, Cutter shook himself out of his shock and pulled out a small 'pad he'd had in a pouch at his waist.

"The virus includes a mathematical data set," he said as he stared at the 'pad. "It's how we communicated with Sigmund at first. It should provide a basis for the AI to respond to us in a way our translators can address. It's not speech, exactly, but it's..."

"Greetings." The voice was natural sounding, vaguely male.

Cutter spun around, staring at the sphere with an expression of shock on his face. "Greetings," he replied, struggling with everything he had to speak clearly and calmly.

"This is an unfamiliar language. Its structure is odd, unlike most of those in my memory."

Cutter felt a wave of panic, but his fascination overwhelmed it. *I am speaking to a computer that is half a million years old, a system more advanced than any I could imagine…*

"Yet you had no trouble learning it…" *Was learning the right word?*

"The data unit in port 763 contained sufficient information to assimilate. The device is extremely primitive. What is its use?"

Cutter felt a wave of excitement. *It read the data on the chip. The virus!*

"It was the only unit available." *It doesn't seem hostile, at least not yet.* "You have been deactivated for a long time. Many things have changed."

"Indeed," came the reply. "I have analyzed the radioactive decay of the fissionables in storage, and it appears I have been inoperative for approximately 363,445 revolutions of the home-world's star."

"I am pleased that you appear to remain fully-functional after so long without power."

"I have been running a self-diagnostic, and it appears my systems are 94% operative. Certain knowledge banks remain non-responsive, but I believe I retain completely functionality. Your portable power supply is insufficient for me to reactive major ship's systems or to initiate outside communications, but I have been able to activate and dispatch a maintenance bot to repair the ruptured conduit that caused my malfunction. I expect to restore matter/antimatter operations and return full ship's power shortly."

Cutter felt like he'd been punched in the gut. "You dis-patched a bot? Already?"

"Yes. It has completed its work, and I am now reactivating the annihilation chamber."

An instant later, the room lit up. Cutter looked toward the ceiling. It was covered with sleek panels, and a pleasant but bright light emanated from perhaps half of them.

"I have restored primary ship's power. There is consider-able maintenance required in multiple areas, however I believe all main systems are responding."

Cutter felt a cold feeling in his stomach. Everything was slipping from his control. The ship was coming back to life. In a few minutes, seconds perhaps, the intelligence would control the engines, the weapons...

"Cease all system restoration activities." Cutter didn't know if his virus had accomplished anything, but he had to try something.

"Very well. All systems are on standby."

Cutter's eyes widened. The AI had taken his order. The lights went out again, leaving only the dim illumination from the portable lamps.

Let me see if this thing is really taking my orders. Cutter had come for this very purpose, but now he found himself shocked it was succeeding. "Restore lighting, but keep all other systems on standby."

The lights came back on. "Lighting restored."

Cutter felt a rush of excitement. It was working. "Is life support operational?"

"Yes. There are multiple malfunctions throughout the ship, but all primary systems are operative."

"Restore life support to this room."

"Beginning restoration. Increasing temperature to optimum levels." There was a short pause.

"Hieronymus, it *is* getting warmer." Ana was holding her own data unit, watching the readings increase. "We've gone from 80K to 200K in a matter of seconds."

"Beginning introduction of atmospheric gasses."

"Temperature has stabilized at 294K," Ana said excitedly. "Atmospheric pressure increasing. I'm reading 78% nitrogen, 21% oxygen, 0.9% argon..." She paused and looked at Cutter. "Hieronymus, it's almost a perfect Earth-normal atmosphere." She looked down at her 'pad. "Same gas concentrations, same atmospheric pressure..."

"Life support fully operative as ordered. You no longer require the primitive survival gear you are wearing."

Cutter looked back at the others. "Stay suited up. We need to check for pathogens and other hazards before we even thing of opening our suits."

"There are no pathogens. Atmospheric conditions in this room are now identical to those on Homeworld. I have scanned for all harmful biologics."

Cutter sighed softly. *And who the hell knows what deadly plague virus is 'normal' on the enemy's homeworld?* "We will remain in our suits for now," he said.

"As you wish. Are you sure you do not want me to reactivate ship's systems? Your command is counter to normal protocol."

Cutter felt a pang of fear. He had no idea what was going through the...mind?...of the alien intelligence. It appeared to be obeying his commands, but how long would it continue to do so? Would it detect the virus in its system and eradicate it? *The order to leave the ship deactivated could make it suspicious*, he thought. *But I can't let it bring this monstrous vessel online. If I lose control...*

"I am sure," he said simply.

"As you command."

"Do you know who I am?" Cutter blurted out. It was a dangerous question, perhaps, but it was all he could think to ask.

"You are one of the Old Ones. You were gone for many thousands of revolutions of the sun, but now you have returned. I was built to serve your needs. I am at your command."

Chapter Nineteen

Admiral Compton's Address to the Fleet Before the Second Battle of X18

You have all seen the scans, are watching now, no doubt, as ship after ship transits through from X16. We fought a great battle together, all of us, not two days ago...and yet now another is upon us. We will do as we have always done...as each of *you* has always done. We will fight. And God help our enemies.

You have all suffered in this deadly war, first in the battles along the Line and later as we advanced into the enemy's domain. And we ourselves have been casualties of a sort, trapped in hostile space and cut off from home. Our comrades on the other side of the barrier mourn us as lost, and to them we are. But to the enemy we still live, and while we survive we will fight them. Here and anywhere else they come at us...and with the last of our strength.

There are many who are not with us now. Comrades, allies...friends, dead in the many desperate struggles that have led us here. It is for them, as well as ourselves, that we fight, and we lash out at the enemy that took them from us. We fight for survival. We fight for justice. And we fight for vengeance!

Let us forget our own quarrels, our shortsighted disputes. Stand with me now, my fellow spacers, stand with me and face this enemy...and show them that we will never yield, that they shall never defeat us! Remember your friends, men and women you who served alongside all of you, who died at the hands of this monstrous foe. Today we take our vengeance for them. Fight now...for those who stand alongside you, and for those you left behind. Let us show these infernal machines who we are...and what fury we can unleash on them!

AS Midway
X18 System
The Fleet: 202 ships, 44,704 crew

"They're still coming through, Admiral. Over a hundred so far." Cortez was a hardened veteran, but Compton could hear the fatigue in his voice. A few small forces had transited the gate over the last two days, but nothing like the monstrous battle fleet now emerging into the system.

"Activate the rest of the mines." Compton had been trying to save as much ordnance as he could, but there was no point now. This would be the big fight, and his worry wasn't preserving mines—it was saving the fleet.

"All mines active, sir. It looks like they're taking a toll."

They weren't mines really, at least not in the sense the word is typically used. They were one-shot weapons, bomb-pumped x-ray lasers units, pouring all the energy of a thermonuclear warhead into a single, highly concentrated blast. They could destroy a moderately sized vessel with a single shot, ripping through even the First Imperium's dark matter hulls like they were paper.

"I just wish we had more," Compton muttered softly, mostly to himself. He'd deployed the last of the precious ordnance in his supply train, and it was still only a moderate coverage. The enemy would take some damage, but the intensity would diminish quickly as the mines expended themselves.

"Admiral Garson is to move his ships toward the X20 warp gate." Ian Garson commanded the logistical task force, thirty-two freighters and other supply and maintenance vessels, many of them now empty. They could add little to the fight to come, and Compton wanted them safe. Or whatever passed for safe in the circumstances.

"Yes, sir."

Compton stared ahead at the display. He was right where he belonged, where he'd been for so many years now. Terrance Compton had led many fleets in combat, fought numerous desperate battles. Including the Alliance's colonial rebellions, the struggle against the First Imperium was his fourth war. Thousands had died serving in the formations he'd led, and while he'd rarely tasted defeat, he'd known the guilt and anguish that accompanied watching so many of those who followed him killed.

Now, another battle was before him, just two days after the last one. But there was something different inside him now, an exhaustion so profound it took every bit of strength he had to force it back. Terrance Compton knew he would never give up...but for the first time in his life he wanted to.

"Bring the fleet to battlestations, Commander." *Once more into the breach...*

"Yes, sir." Cortez hunched over his workstation, and an instant later, the flag bridge was bathed in the red light of the battlestations lamps.

Compton leaned back, watching the enemy vessels pour into the system. One hundred twenty had already transited, and they were still coming. Half a dozen had fallen to the mines, and another twenty had been damaged, but he knew that wouldn't stop them. This was a First Imperium fleet. There was no morale to break, no fear that would drive them away. There was only one way for his people to win—to survive—and that was to destroy them. To destroy them all.

"It's time to scramble Admiral Hurley's fighters," he said, ignoring the grinding fatigue he felt.

"Yes, Admiral."

Cortez is tired too, I can feel it. He looked around the flag bridge. *They're all exhausted...how could they not be? But they will do what they must. Just as I will.*

"Admiral Hurley acknowledges, sir. Her people will be ready to launch in two minutes."

Compton nodded, feeling the urge to smile at Hurley's readiness. But the grin was stillborn, washed away by thoughts of the losses the fighter corps had taken in the campaign. His fleet had invaded First Imperium space with 718 fighters. Hurley would be launching 187.

"Prepare to begin maneuvers," he said. *"Midway, Saratoga, Petersburg,* and *Prinz Friederich* will form a line." The four battleships had the last of the external missile racks installed. The rest of the fleet would rely on internal ordnance only. *We won't be able to do many more full reloads,* Compton thought. *Even with internals only.*

"Yes, Admiral," Cortez replied. And a few seconds later. "All ships confirm, sir."

"Very well, Commander. Captain Horace is to engage the engines. The group is to advance at 5g."

The battle had begun.

*   *   *

"I want those racks cleared. And I do mean now, Commander." Admiral Barret Dumont stared straight ahead, his scowl almost freezing the air in front of his face. The oldest active officer in the Alliance service, he'd been commanding task forces since before half his staff had been born, and when he issued an order, he expected his crews to take it as the word of God.

"The crews are already working on it, sir." Antonio Allesandro was Dumont's tactical officer. The two worked well together. Allesandro was one of the few younger officers who could stand up to the ornery hundred year old admiral, and for his part, Dumont considered his current aide as one of the best he'd had in his very long career.

"I don't want working, Commander. I want done." Dumont was wearing two hats, as he'd been since X2. He was in charge of one of Compton's task forces, but he was also running *Saratoga.* Captain Josiah had been killed in X2, and the ship's first officer had been transferred to take his own command. Compton had offered to find Dumont another flag captain, but the grizzled old warrior had told him not to bother...he'd just as soon run the ship himself rather than break in a new officer in the middle of a running fight. And that's just what he'd been doing for the past few months.

"The crew chief reports they'll be finished in ten minutes, sir. He's says he'll guarantee it."

"Damned right, he will," Dumont roared. He'd been watching the screen. The warp gate was finally quiet, the seemingly endless flow of ships coming through finally halted. Dumont knew better than to make hasty assumptions, but he was hopeful the enemy force had completed its entry. Still, he had a scowl on his face. It was good news that no more ships were emerging, but with 130 already in system, the fleet had its work cut out for it. *This is going to be a tough fight...but I think we can pull it out. Having Terrance in command is worth an extra task force. But I don't even want to guess at the losses we're going to take.*

"Alright, Commander, let's get the missile launchers loaded and the ordnance armed. I want us firing ten seconds after the crews are back inside."

"Yes, sir." Allesandro relayed the commands. A few seconds later: "All stations report ready to fire on your command, sir."

"Very well. Send orders to all ships. The task force will commence missile launch in ten minutes...and anyone not ready to fire by then better go jump out the airlock and save me the trouble of throwing him out."

*   *   *

"We're carrion birds on this one, people." Greta Hurley's voice came through the fighter's main speaker. "The enemy came right through the minefield, and they've got at least two dozen ships that are seriously banged up. I want them dead... every one of them. Before they can fire on the fleet. So look for the damaged ones...and send them to hell."

Mariko sat at the controls, her hand gripped around the throttle, and nodded. She had every intention of doing exactly what Hurley had commanded...in all its descriptive fury. Her mind—and her spirit—were consumed with rage, with the need for vengeance. She'd come back from the last battle as squadron commander, indeed her ship had been the unit's only survivor. The wing commander had planned to reassign her to another outfit, but a last minute appeal to Admiral Hurley had saved the Gold Dragons.

No doubt the wing commander resented Mariko's going over his head, but she just couldn't let the Dragons die. The men and women were gone, but their spirit lived, and allowing the squadron to be disbanded would have been an affront to their memory. She'd been sure the admiral would agree, and Hurley had indeed granted her request. Now Mariko had five new ships, survivors from other shattered units. But they were all Dragons now, and she was determined they would fight like Dragons.

"Okay, we're going in, and I want this formation tight. We're going to find one of the damaged Leviathans, and we're going to blast it to atoms." Her voice was determination itself. It was time to go into the deadliest fight of her career, and she had a squadron full of people she didn't even know. But they didn't have to know her to fight for her. And God help any of them who didn't give everything they had. Mariko Fujin had a ferociousness far beyond what anyone expected when they set eyes on her tiny frame. She was 155 centimeters and 42 kilograms of pure fury.

"Tight," she growled, "I said I want this formation tight. "Dragon Four, you're out too far. Dragon Six, you're lagging behind. Pay fucking attention, people." She knew she was demanding a level of precision they weren't all used to. *Tough. They're Dragons now, and they're going to fly like Dragons.* The squadron had a reputation to uphold, and she wasn't about to let that die the way her comrades had.

"We've got missiles incoming, so gunners, stay focused and blow those fuckers away." She watched on the screen, sitting back silently for the next ten minutes as her fighters launched their anti-missile rockets and then opened up with point defense lasers. The mass of icons on her display rapidly thinned, half of them gone...and then three-quarters. By the time the barrage reached detonation range, less than 5% of the warheads were still there. But that was still thirty nukes, and almost as one, they detonated.

She heard the alarm sound, as her fighter was bathed in radiation from a nearby warhead. Damage to the ship itself was light, but she knew her crew had just taken a potentially lethal dose of gamma rays. A cleanse would reverse the effects as soon as they got back to the ship, but that would take them all out of the action for the rest of the battle. *And who the hell is going to lead the squadron while I'm laid up?*

She punched at her controls, expanding the area shown on the display. Several of the squadrons had taken losses from the enemy missile attack, but her Dragons had come through without losses. Two of the other ships had minor damage, but the squadron was still intact and ready to attack.

"Dragon Four, I'm not going to fucking tell you this again. Bring it in...I want you ten klicks off Dragon Two's wing...and not a centimeter more. Understood?"

"Yes, Commander," came the nervous reply." Greta Hurley had done more than give Mariko the squadron—she'd also bumped her up to lieutenant commander. It wasn't official yet, and she still wore her old insignia, but as far as her crews were concerned, she was Commander Fujin.

Don't yes commander me...just don't make me order it three times.

"Alright, we're coming into enemy laser range. I know you want to launch those torpedoes as quickly as possible and get the hell out of here, but that's not how the Dragons fly. We're targeting that Leviathan directly ahead, and we're going right down its throat. We fire from point blank range in this squadron, and anybody with an itchy trigger finger is going to regret the day they were born." She wondered if she was overdoing it, but she hadn't had time to learn anything about the pilots she'd inherited...and she damned sure didn't come all this way through the enemy barrage to pop off her birds at long range and miss.

She turned toward Isobe. The gunner was leaning over his station, staring into the targeting scope. "You ready, Hiroki?"

"I'm ready, Commander." At least the crew of her own ship was familiar. Her bird ran like a finely tuned machine.

The enemy laser fire was thick, but Greta Hurley's tactical innovations had been enormously effective at reducing losses to enemy interdiction. The constant, almost random, blasts of acceleration and deceleration didn't do anything for those with less than cast iron stomachs, but they wreaked havoc on enemy targeting systems. And most pilots would gladly endure a bout of spacesickness if it came with a 70% reduction in the chance of getting scragged by enemy fire.

One of the icons on her screen flashed red. "Dragon Five," she snapped into the com. "Report!"

"We took a hit, Commander. Looks like a grazing shot. We've got some damage, but I think we're good to finish the assault."

Mariko sat in her seat nodding. "Very well, Dragon Five. Report if anything changes." *Maybe they are Dragon material after all...*

She sat for another few minutes as her ship hurtled toward its target, guided by the navigation AI and its constant defensive course changes. Then she gripped the throttle and took a deep breath. "Okay, Dragons...this is it. Beginning final attack run."

Her eyes shot toward the display, checking the range. Fifty-thousand kilometers, well within the effective range of the plasma torpedo. But not close enough for her.

"Follow me in," she snapped into the com, as she moved the throttle forward and to the left. She felt the 3g of acceleration push her back into her seat with three times the force of her own bodyweight. Staying focused in high g environments was one of the hardest things for new pilots to master. Indeed, many never did. It was the biggest cause of washouts for last year trainees at the Academy. But Mariko Fujin barely felt a miserable 3g.

Her eyes stared ahead, and every thought in her mind faded away, every thought save the enemy ship looming ahead—and the torpedo her people were going to plant right inside it.

Her eyes darted toward the display. Twenty-thousand kilometers.

"On my command, Hiroki..." The screen read fifteen thousand.

Ten thousand.

Her hand tightened on the throttle, ready to fire the engines hard to clear the looming target.

Seven thousand.

"Fire!"

She felt the bump as the weapon launched, and she slammed the throttle hard, full forward and to the right. Ten gees of force slammed into her, forcing the breath from her lungs, as her ship's engines blasted at full power, changing its course just enough to clear the looming enemy vessel, missing it by less than a thousand klicks.

Then she cut the thrust and sucked in a deep, relieved breath. Her eyes went right to the display, searching for the damage assessment. All her ships had scored direct hits, pummeling the already-damaged First Imperium battleship with six double-shotted plasma torpedoes. Her people had followed her in, exactly as she'd ordered, and they'd delivered a fatal blow to the target. Two of them had fired from even closer range than she had, the last coming a bare 500 meters from slamming into the enemy ship.

She allowed herself a vicious little smile. *Yes*, she thought. *They are definitely Dragons...*

*   *   *

"Bring us in right next to *Midway*." Udinov growled out the order. The fight had been going on for hours, and now they were moving to point blank range.

It's time to finish this…

"Yes, admiral." Stanovich tried to hide the pain in his tone, but he was only partially successful. Udinov's tactical officer sat at his station, punching at his controls with one hand. His left arm was broken—badly broken. But he had absolutely refused to leave his post during the battle.

Udinov looked over *Petersburg's* flag bridge, which was also serving as the ship's command center. Captain Rostov was in sickbay, unconscious and fighting for his life, and most of his bridge crew was dead, killed when a 2 gigaton enemy missile detonated less than 800 meters from the ship.

The air was thick with smoke and the smell of burnt machinery. Two girders had fallen from the structural supports, and they were laid out across the floor. There was a crushed workstation under one, its dead occupant still pinned underneath. Udinov knew his ship was badly shot up, but she still had three active laser batteries, and he'd be damned if he was going to lag behind.

The fight had been raging for hours, and Compton had ordered all the battleships in the fleet to form a single line. The mines had taken a toll, and the fighters had launched a devastating strike, destroying almost twenty-five enemy ships before they returned to their launch platforms to refuel and rearm. The cruiser squadrons had conducted a series of brilliantly-executed high-velocity attack runs, and John Duke's dwindling force of fast attack ships had sliced repeatedly into the enemy lines. Now the final act had begun. There were no more complex strategies, no elaborate formations. It was a toe to toe slugfest, the fleet's battleships against the survivors of the enemy fleet.

"We're ten thousand kilometers from *Midway*, sir, and our navcom is locked with theirs. *What a strange thing is war*, Udinov thought. A few days before *Midway* and *Petersburg* had been faced off against each other. They'd come a hair's breadth of firing on each other, and now they stood side by side for the second time in two days, united, fighting their common enemy. *We need to remember this when we fall prey to foolishness, when petty fears and rivalries drive us to the edge.*

"Laser batteries are to increase to 110% power and maintain fire."

"Yes, sir." Stanovich sounded concerned. Overpowering the lasers was dangerous under any circumstances, but *Petersburg* was in rough shape. The ship's AI was constantly scanning for damaged systems, but it was impossible to find every severed connection or compromised cable. And pumping 110% of normal power into battered systems was a good way to blow them out completely. But if the extra intensity blew away a First Imperium battleship before it blasted your ship to atoms, it was a risk worth taking.

The bridge lights dimmed as more of the reactor's power was diverted to the weapons. *Petersburg's* three remaining main batteries were targeting a single enemy ship, a Leviathan, the same vessel *Midway* was blasting. The enemy battleship was still fighting back, but with fewer and fewer of its weapons as the combined lasers of the two human dreadnoughts ripped into its ruptured hull.

"Keep firing," Udinov said, as if his determination could recharge the lasers faster. He could see the enemy ship was dying, but a First Imperium vessel, especially a battleship, was dangerous until the end.

Almost in answer to his thought, *Petersburg* shook hard, and the flag bridge was plunged into darkness. The workstations stayed live, and a second later, the emergency lights engaged, providing a dim but workable illumination.

"The reactor is down, sir."

Udinov just nodded. He didn't need Stanovich's damage report to know what had happened. He turned and stared across the shadowy bridge. "I want it restarted. Now." He slapped his hand against the side of his chair.

Stanovich turned back to his board. A few seconds later he said, "Engineer says five minute to restart att..."

"Now!" Udinov roared. "No five minutes, not three minutes. Right now...whatever the risk."

Stanovich hesitated a few seconds. "Yes, sir," he finally said.

Udinov sat in his chair like a statue. The scragged reactor

meant his lasers weren't firing. And that meant *Petersburg* was useless…just when the fleet needed her most. *Five minutes…in five minutes this fight will be decided.*

The ship shook hard, and an instant later the lights came back. A few seconds later Stanovich turned and stared over at Udinov. "Power restored, sir. Some radiation leaks, casualties in engineering. But the lasers are recharging now."

"They are to fire at once when ready, Commander. It's time to win this battle."

*   *   *

Greta Hurley was rubbing the back of her neck. Her fighter had just come close to getting blasted to plasma. *And if anybody other than John Wilder had been at the controls—myself included—we'd all be dead.* The pilot's keen eye had seen the missile's approach on the scanner, and his sudden maneuver put a couple klicks between ship and the warhead before it detonated.

The sudden thrust had been unexpected, and Greta had twisted her neck hard. Kip Janz had smacked his head against his workstation, and the others had gotten banged up as well. But no one was complaining, and Hurley suspected they were all silently giving thanks that the best pilot in the fleet was at the helm of their bird.

She flipped on her master com, addressing the entire strike force. "Okay, listen up. The first time we hit these bastards, we were picking off cripples. But the battleline's deep in it now, so the situation is different. I want you all to break off and find the ships putting out the heaviest fire…and hit them as hard as you can. We're not counting dead hulls now, we're degrading their firepower. Every battery we take out could be the one that saves one of the battlewagons…maybe even the one your squadron calls home."

She looked down at the display. There were barely a hundred fighters in her formation. In addition to the losses from the first attack, she had fifty birds back in the hangers, too shot up to launch without major repairs. And she'd had to ground Mariko Fujin's ship so the crews could be treated for radiation exposure. Fujin had put up a fight, insisting they could fly one more mission before their condition became critical, but Hurley had taken one look at the radiation readings and ordered the spirited officer, and everyone else in her fighter, to report directly to sickbay.

"I don't have to tell you how much you've all contributed to the survival of the fleet, but Admiral Compton himself asked me to give you his thanks...and his immense respect. You have all performed brilliantly, heroically, and I have never felt the level of pride in a group of warriors that I do in all of you. But we're not done. The enemy still stands before us, and while they are there we will never rest. The spirits of all those who have died fighting these monsters are with you at this moment. Now, let's get in there, do our jobs, and get the hell out and back to our ships."

She turned toward Wilder. "I told them all to pick their targets. That applies to you as well, Commander. You see anywhere promising for us to drop a plasma torpedo?"

"I was thinking about that Leviathan over there...coordinates 300.273.092. It seems to be fighting *Midway* and *Petersburg*."

Hurley smiled. Fighters approaching a formed up fleet had to get through a lot of interdiction before closing, but once the task forces were disordered and the battleships engaged with each other, almost all their targeting efforts were turned elsewhere...and a lone fighter could get in close for a good shot.

Hurley nodded. "I like the way you think, Commander Wilder." She glanced down at the display herself and took a deep breath. "Let's go get that son of a bitch."

*   *   *

Terrance Compton rubbed his hand across his face, wiping

the dripping sweat onto the leg of his pants. The survival suit was hot, uncomfortable. But it was vital too if an enemy hit breached the flag bridge. Compton had seen too many spacers killed because they'd neglected to wear their suits or they'd left their helmets too far out of reach. He'd made it clear that any of his people caught without the proper gear during a fight would be sorry if they somehow managed to survive.

The battle had been going nonstop for almost ten hours. Compton's people had fought bravely, brilliantly, and they'd unleashed hell on the attacking First Imperium fleet. They'd destroyed over a hundred enemy vessels, and now he had his entire fleet positioned to destroy the last enemy task force.

The fight had been brutal and costly, but thankfully, Compton had been so busy directing the fight, he hadn't had much time to think about the losses. Thousands of his people had died over the past ten hours, and more of his irreplaceable ships had been gutted or blasted to plasma when their reactor cores had ruptured. But that was for later. Right now, there were still enemy ships to engage, and that was the admiral's only concern.

"Transmit navigational data to all ships."

"Yes, Admiral," Cortez replied, clearly trying to sound alert through the crushing fatigue Compton knew his aide was feeling.

Compton's orders were simple. The fleet was closing in on itself, forming a single dense battleline to finish off the last of their adversaries. The fight was almost over, the remaining enemy ships damaged and outgunned. A human opponent would almost certainly have retreated. But First Imperium vessels didn't react the way people did. They almost always fought to the death.

"Sir, Admiral Hurley's fighters have all landed. She is requesting permission to rearm and go back out." Hurley's own ship had just finished off the enemy battleship *Midway* and *Petersburg* had been fighting…and it had been a quick trip back to the flagship's landing bays.

"Permission denied." A grim smiled passed over his lips. In all his years of naval service, he'd seen few cut from the same cloth as Greta Hurley. He knew she was fearless. *No, that's not fair. We're all scared, even her. But Hurley never lets it affect her choices. Never.*

Compton had known other officers like her, those who could stand in the line, unwavering against whatever came upon her. But he'd never seen one so able to pass that trait to those she led. In X2, and again in the current battles, Hurley's squadrons had fought like demons from hell, launching attack after attack, without regard to fear or fatigue.

Hurley was a specialist, a commander of fighter squadrons, and because she'd never led fleets of battleships, she hadn't gotten the same attention as some of the other heroes of the war. *But no one has done more, and no force has made a larger contribution—or paid a greater price—than her fighter wings.*

"Admiral Hurley is to see to her squadrons' refit, but she is not to launch." Compton was planning to finish off the remaining enemy ships and then make a run for the X20 warp gate. There would be no time to retrieve scattered fighter groups. And Terrance Compton didn't have the stomach to send more of his people on a suicide mission.

He didn't doubt Admiral West would catch Zhang and destroy his renegade ships. She was one of the best, destined to one day reach the highest levels of command—at least before she was lost in space with the fleet. He knew her ships would never make it back. They'd both pretended in their last conversation, paying lip service to the hope that her people would manage to stop Zhang and return. But Compton knew West didn't believe that any more than he did. Zhang was running for his life, which meant he was buttoned up in the tanks blasting away at full power. West's ships were faster, so if she picked up his trail she could catch him…but by then her force would have burned through most of its fuel. She simply wouldn't have enough left to come to a halt and then accelerate back to the fleet.

And she won't even know where the fleet is…we can't stay here.

Compton's mind drifted from the battle, just for a few moments. He knew the fate that awaited Erica West and her crews. Their vessels would become ghost ships, tearing through space without the fuel to decelerate. Her people would live, for a while at least, until their power reserves were completely gone. Then they would spend eternity in the cold blackness, frozen corpses still manning their posts as their vessels continued on into the endless dark.

He forced his thoughts back to the present, to the fight still raging around him. There was nothing he could do for West and her people, nothing but mourn them and nurse the guilt for having sent them to their deaths. But that could wait. There were still enemy ships to destroy. And a fleet full of spacers he could help to survive.

Time to wrap things up and get out of here.

Once his battered ships transited, they could link up with the supply ships and reload their empty magazines. And then the fleet would continue onward, fleeing the enemy and repairing whatever damage they could on the run.

Escaping to X20 wasn't a cure all, and if there were more First Imperium fleets on the way he knew it would only buy his people a short period, perhaps a day or two. But he needed that 48 hours. There wasn't a missile on any of his warships... not one. He dreaded the idea of putting his people through yet another fight on the heels of these last two, but at least they'd have a chance if they were rearmed and supplied.

Compton sat silently, watching the final engagements on the display. He'd been actively directing almost every aspect of the battle, but now he was finished. His people knew what to do, and he saw icon after icon disappearing—First Imperium vessels vaporized by the coordinated assaults of his task forces.

It's a good thing they're weak tactically, he thought, not for the first time. The First Imperium technology was vastly superior, but the intelligences who directed their fleets, amazing creations though they were, could not match the skills of a gifted human commander, not without a massive advantage in firepower.

He winced as he saw one of his own ships disappear. *Abdullah*, he thought to himself, doublechecking the key to confirm. *Light cruiser, 188 crew...*

Still, despite the loss, the final stages of the battle went well, coordinated packs of human ships encircling the few enemy survivors and blasting them to pieces with overwhelming concentrations of fire. A few minutes later, it was over. The only ships remaining in the X18 system were those of Compton's fleet.

He sighed hard and rubbed his hands over his temples. His head throbbed, and he felt the fatigue at the fringes of his consciousness, like a great wave straining to come over him, held back only by the chemistry of the stims he'd been popping like candy. He took a deep breath and arched his shoulders backward, stretching. It was time to give his people some rest.

"Commander," he said, glancing over at Cortez, "Bring the fleet back to condition yell…"

"Admiral, we're getting readings from the warp gate!" Cortez' words slammed into Compton like a club.

"Readings?" Compton snapped back, trying desperately to keep his own demoralization out of his tone.

"It looks bad, sir." Cortez paused, just for a few seconds, and then he continued, his voice grim. "It looks like at least a dozen Leviathan's in the lead, Admiral." Another pause. "No, eighteen now…twenty…still coming through, sir."

Compton slouched back in his chair. It didn't matter anymore. His people were exhausted, his ships low on supplies and ordnance. They would fight, he knew that.

And they would die. He knew that too.

Chapter Twenty

Admiral Erica West: Final Log Entry

As I dictate this, we are approaching our next transit. Our best analysis of Admiral Zhang's particle trail, suggests we will catch and engage his forces in the next system. I am gratified that we have been able to follow his force, and that we will have the opportunity to complete this crucial mission.

I will jettison my log before we make the next transit. I do this for multiple reasons, including the possibility that I will not survive the battle to come. But I have other motivations. I know our fuel supply is nearly exhausted...and the fight looming ahead will almost certainly drain the task force's tanks. I doubt we will have enough to even bring ourselves to a halt at the end of the battle, much less turn and head back toward the fleet. At this moment, we are a task force of the Grand Pact, engaged in an important operation. I would rather end my story as such...and not as a helpless passenger on a doomed ship. I will, of course, send another probe after the battle, with a complete battle report and a confirmation that Zhang's forces have been destroyed. But I will end my personal log now.

I know there is little chance that any human ship will ever find this record, but if one does, even decades or centuries from now, I would like to state that my officers and crew understand the importance of our mission. Perhaps Zhang has no chance of finding a route back home. Indeed, almost certainly the odds are heavily against it. But if he does, and the enemy is able to follow, the cost would be nothing less than the complete destruction of the human race. So, if some future vessel finds this, know that my people sacrificed all so that you had the chance to exist. And if you are still fighting the First Imperium, in your next battle, strike a blow for a group of Alliance spacers, long dead and gone...

AS Hudson
Unnamed System, Four Transits from X18
The Fleet: 186 ships, 40,651 crew

"They've been through here, Admiral. Recently." Davis Black looked over from the workstation back toward the command chair. His chair, at least until recently. *Hudson's* captain had insisted Admiral West take the bridge's command station, and he'd move himself to the spare position. She'd refused twice, but he'd finally gotten her to relent, as much by persistence as by reminding her that she needed the enhanced com build into the captain's station.

West nodded as she looked back. The *Thames*-class light cruisers hadn't been built to serve as an admiral's flagship, and there was no provision for a flag officer or her staff. But they were the fastest ships in the Alliance navy, and speed was what she needed.

"Very well, Captain Black." She stared down at the display. The particle trail was lighter here. She guessed Zhang's ships had come through this stretch of space at low to moderate acceleration. She had respect neither for the CAC admiral's character nor his ability, and she knew the coward would have blasted away like crazy to escape from Terrance Compton's wrath if he could have, staying in the tanks at full thrust 24/7. But that just wasn't possible. Systems were vulnerable to breakdown, and crews could only tolerate so much time in the tanks. And his ships had to alter their vectors in each system to navigate to the next warp gate. Depending on the layout of gates in a system, that could entail considerable deceleration to sustain the required heading changes.

"Position us for transit, Captain. We'll scan as soon as we get through and then decide how to proceed." She knew she'd already burned enough of her dwindling fuel supply to eliminate any chance of making it back to the fleet. That wasn't a surprise—she'd known from the instant Compton gave her the assignment it was a one way trip. But knowing something intangible was different that seeing the mathematical certainty. Her people were lost. All they could do now was make certain to carry out their mission. Otherwise, they would all die for nothing. West could face death if she had to, but futile death was unthinkable.

"Transit in two minutes, Admiral."

West just nodded.

I hope I'm right about that trail. Because if Zhang isn't in this next system, we're not going to have enough fuel to catch the bastard.

"Ninety seconds." *Hudson's* nav officer was calling off the countdown.

The bridge was silent, save for the distant hum of the reactor. The crew understood what was happening. They knew they were on their last mission, and they were well aware of its importance. Erica West glanced around at *Hudson's* bridge crew, ignoring their fate, focusing totally on their duties.

I've never been prouder of a group of spacers under my command.

"Sixty seconds."

West stared down at the screen, but her own thoughts clouded her vision. Will they be there? How close to the warp gate? Will they be ready for us?

Probably not, they have no way of knowing we're here. But we'll be ready for them...

"I want all ships at red alert, Captain...all gunners at their positions."

"Yes, Admiral." A few seconds later, *Hudson's* bridge was bathed in the red light of the battlestations lamps.

"Thirty seconds."

Erica West had been through hundreds of warp gate transits, and not a few under battle conditions. *It's odd to think this is the last one. How often do people realize the last time they will do something they have done many times, the final moment they see someone they have been close to for years?*

"Transit…now."

She felt the usual disorientation…and then the space in front of her was different, the field of stars nothing like it had been a few seconds before. She didn't know where they were yet, and she wouldn't until the ship's AI and scanning systems rebooted and crunched on the navigational data. But she knew she was lightyears from where she had been, across a vastness of interstellar space it would take decades for a ship to cross conventionally.

The deep space that will be your grave soon…

"Scanners, Captain…as quickly as possible." It was a pointless order, as much something to do as anything else. A warp gate transit always scrambled a ship's systems, and there was little even a gifted commander could do to speed the recovery.

"Rebooting now, Admiral." Perhaps a minute later. "We're getting readings." He looked up and stared over at the command station. "I think it's them. They're half a million kilometers ahead."

West felt a rush of adrenalin. That was practically right next door in interplanetary terms. "All ships, execute 6g thrust directly toward enemy. All missile crews, prepare to fire on my command."

Captain Black relayed the admiral's orders, both to his own crew and the commanders of the other vessels. "All ships acknowledge, Admiral."

West felt herself pushed hard back into her chair as *Hudson's* engines fired. Six gees was a lot to endure out of the tanks for an extended period, but she wanted to close the range immediately. She was betting they'd caught Zhang flat-footed, just in from the warp gate, accelerating at 1g and moving at a low velocity as his people scanned the system's potential exit gates.

He's a damned fool to be so close to the gate at that velocity. Arrogant ass.

It would take time to get his crews into the tanks and make a run for it, and she was damned if she was going to give him that opportunity.

"Launch all missiles, consecutive volleys," she said, forcing the words out under the heavy pressure of *Hudson's* thrust. Her light cruisers didn't have external racks, like heavy cruisers and capital ships did, but they did carry enough ordnance to launch three waves—and she was damned sure going to send them all Zhang's way. She thought the CAC admiral was a pompous fool, damned near incompetent, but *Tang* was still a battleship, if an old and small one. There was no point taking chances.

"Yes, Admiral. Launching all missiles." Black's voice was strained. Six gees of pressure made breathing a difficult exercise and talking even worse.

We caught him, Admiral Compton. And I promise you, we won't let him go...

*   *   *

"How? How is this possible?" Zhang's voice was distraught, his fear on display for the entire bridge crew to see and hear.

"The pursuing force appears to consist entirely of Alliance *Thames*-class light cruisers." The tactical officer's voice was haggard, but he acquitted himself better than his commander in controlling his fear. "They are capable of considerably greater acceleration than any of our vessels." He paused. "It would appear Admiral Compton sent his fastest ships after us."

Zhang squirmed in his seat. "We have to make a run for it. We need to get everyone in the tanks now."

"That won't work, sir," the tactical officer said. "By the time we could get into the tanks, they'd be on us. And besides, they'd catch us anyway."

Zhang took a deep breath and tried to gain control over himself. He'd planned his mutiny carefully, enlisting Udinov as well as Samar and Peltier...the commanders of forty percent of the entire fleet. But almost since they'd launched their plan things had gone wrong. The standoff over the fueling station had been bad enough, but the sudden appearance of First Imperium forces had been an unmitigated disaster. In the end, he'd lost his co-conspirators…and most of his own CAC contingent, all of whom refused to run from a fight.

Fucking Compton. He couldn't just let us go…

"Sir, the pursuing force has launched missiles."

Zhang slumped back in his chair. He hated the Alliance admiral with a raging passion. But there wasn't time for that now. He had to find a way out. "Our only option is to fight."

"We are at a disadvantage in a battle."

"But *Tang's* firepower…"

"Our combat effectiveness is severely compromised. The attacking vessels have already launched missiles, and they are accelerating toward us even now." *Tang* was a battleship, but like most of the older CAC designs, it was missile heavy and poorly outfitted with energy weapons. And the approaching ships would be firing their lasers before Zhang's people could even begin to launch missiles.

"Then we must surrender." The CAC admiral sat in his seat staring straight ahead.

"We are guilty of mutiny, Admiral." The tactical officer's voice was thick with disgust. "We fled in the middle of a battle, leaving our allies behind." A long pause: "It is inconceivable to expect Admiral Compton to do anything but impose the regulation sentence on all of us." Which everyone present knew was death by spacing.

Zhang sucked in a deep breath, trying to control the fear beginning to take him over. "We must attempt a ruse," he said. "Transmit our surrender…and when the approaching forces close to board, open fire with all weapons."

The tactical officer glanced over at Zhang and then back to his workstation. "Yes, Admiral," he said, his voice pinched, as if he'd tasted something bad. "Transmitting now, sir."

*   *   *

"Admiral, *Tang* is signaling surrender."

"I am aware of that, Captain." West was stone still, sitting at her station staring straight ahead. Her voice was like ice. "Carry on."

"But, Admiral, shouldn't we accept their surrender? They are giving up."

"Admiral Compton said nothing about taking prisoners. These are mutineers, traitors—men and women who fled battle while their comrades were fighting for their lives. It may be tempting to be merciful…"—it wasn't tempting at all to West—"or to imagine we can take their vessels, but it is not that simple. Admiral Zhang is a fool and a coward, but even he knows Admiral Compton would never spare his life after all he has done. No, Captain, this is almost certainly a trick of some kind. And we cannot risk even the chance of allowing any of these vessels to escape. We will have just this one pass, and we have to destroy them." She leaned back and sighed.

"Besides," she said wearily, "none of our vessels have enough fuel to come about and match velocity with any of Zhang's ships, so whatever fuel he has might as well be a thousand lightyears away." It was pure mathematics. Her flotilla would pass right by Zhang's force, and none of her vessels had enough power remaining to decelerate and head back to dock with a captured ship. It was frustrating, almost ironic, to have vessels carrying the precious fuel she needed, and no way to get to it. Zhang's ships had the fuel to dock with hers, but if she completed her pass and left them alive, they'd have no reason to surrender. They could just continue on their course, leaving her people heading off into deep space.

"Yes, Admiral," Black said softly. "I understand." Half a minute later: "All ships report ready to engage with laser batteries."

West stared straight ahead. She paused for an instant, and then she uttered a single word. "Fire."

*   *   *

West sat quietly, glancing around *Hudson's* bridge. There was a smoky haze, and the smell of burnt machinery hung heavily in the air. Zhang was dead…all the mutineers were. The battle had been short but nasty. Once they realized their trick had failed, Zhang's people had fought for survival with all the ferocity they could muster. The rebellious admiral and his crews had battled hard, and they hadn't died alone.

Two of West's cruisers had been destroyed outright, and the rest had varying degrees of damage. *Hudson* had taken two solid hits, but her damage control teams had done a masterful job of repairing battered systems. All in all, West's flagship smelled like it was harder hit than it actually was.

Normally, she'd have increased power to the circulation system and cleared the air, but *Hudson* had barely enough fuel to maintain basic life support. Indeed, West realized her people wouldn't have long to contemplate their fates. She doubted they had more than a couple weeks left, even at minimal power utilization.

Still, that's a long time to sit with nothing to do but stare death in the face. Not just death, but an eternity in the unknown depths of space.

Spacers in general were drawn from fairly hardy stock. It took a certain amount of natural toughness to venture into the cold darkness. And naval crews faced death every time they entered battle.

But this is different…

West knew even the bravest had their worst fears…and for spacers it was being lost, hurtling forever through the endless depths. And now her people would face just that fate.

Still, she thought, maybe—just maybe—we saved all of humanity. Perhaps that fool Zhang would have found his way home somehow…and led the First Imperium back with him. She knew that wasn't likely, that Zhang hadn't had a strong chance of finding his way back. But even a small risk was too great when the stakes were so high. She knew her people were going to die, but they would all die heroes.

And that is worth something…even if no one back on Earth—and in all the colonies—knows it…

She wanted to believe that, but still, she felt doubts, uncertainty…and a voice deep from within telling her death was just that. Death.

Chapter Twenty-One

From the Personal Log of Terrance Compton

If I'd been asked what I would put in a final log entry, I imagine my answer would have been expansive, an almost endless outpouring detailing all the commendations and final messages I would have included. But such a response ignores the fact that, by its nature, a final log entry is made during the heat of a hopeless battle or some other disaster. We face such a final fight now, one we have no chance to survive, and my time belongs to my people, to ensuring that though we will die now, our deaths will not come cheaply to the enemy.

So, I will say one thing only, and then I will jettison this log in the remote hope that a human ship may one day find it. Whoever may one day read this, know that a human fleet of over 200 ships ventured deep into the First Imperium, that we fought the enemy with the last of our strength, and that we died fighting.

And in the event it is the First Imperium that recovers this log and is able to translate it and understand my writings, I have a message for you as well. Go fuck yourselves. One day, a fleet of beings like me will come back here, and they will blast you all into oblivion.

AS Midway
X18 System
The Fleet: 186 ships, 40,453 crew

"At least there are still no Colossus' in the enemy fleet," Cortez said, struggling to sound hopeful. "They must be main battle units of some kind, not kept with the rest of the local forces."

Compton almost laughed. *Gallows humor*, he thought. He appreciated Cortez' attempt to find some good news in the situation. He knew it was quite a reach. There were twenty Leviathans leading a First Imperium fleet of over 150 ships. His own vessels were damaged from the fight they had just finished, their crews exhausted. They had no anti-ship missiles at all—and a severely depleted supply of other expendable ordnance. The fleet was beyond outmatched, it was doomed. He knew what his AI would say if he asked for a percentage chance of survival... mathematically indistinguishable from zero.

Compton had always been strangely amused by that phrase, one that had clearly been programmed into the fleet's AI systems. He'd heard it reported to him in those—mostly human-sounding but not quite—voices many times. But this would be the first time it applied to his own chances of survival.

Why don't they just say none, no chance at all...it's over? Some bizarre need to offer the illusion of hope where there was none?

He had an urge to order the fleet to run for it, to make for the X20 warp gate and transit before they were blown to bits. The supply ships were there, with enough ordnance to refit his combat units. But a quick look at the display only confirmed what he already knew. His ships didn't have a chance of outrunning the faster First Imperium vessels to the gate.

And dying in the tanks is the worst way to go...

He had to stand and fight. There was no other choice. *Maybe we can buy some time for the supply ships to escape.* He didn't try to fool himself that the almost unarmed transports would survive for long on their own, but they'd have a chance, at least. The same words, mathematically indistinguishable from zero, drifted through his head again, amid thoughts of the helpless supply vessels being chased down and blown apart by First Imperium warships.

No, we will fight because that is who we are, because I will not die fleeing from the enemy, blasted to plasma as I run...nor will I see these brave men and women I have led meet their ends so ignominiously. We will fight because that is who we are, because if these infernal machines want to destroy us, we will make them pay a terrible price for their victory. If we must die—if we must die—let it be a worthy death.

Compton forced himself bolt upright in his chair. "Commander Cortez, the fleet will remain at red alert." His voice was firm, commanding, not a touch of fear evident. *Thank God they don't know how fake it is.* "All taskforces are to reform into battle array delta-two."

"Yes, Admiral." Cortez' tone was firmer. Compton had always been amazed at what strong leadership could achieve. They would follow his example, draw strength from him, even as they faced certain death. He'd known for decades how crucial that was for fighting men and women. But few of them understood what it cost the commanders they followed so bravely, the drain of projecting that constant strength in the face of horror after horror. Augustus Garret, Elias Holm, Erik Cain...Compton had been privileged to serve alongside a number of legendary commanders. And he'd see firsthand how the stress and pressure affected them, eating them alive, hollowing them out from the inside. But they still did it. For them—for him—there was no other way.

"Admiral Hurley is to scramble her fighters immediately." Compton felt a pang of guilt. Hurley's crews had been to hell and back...again and again. Sending them into the teeth of this new force was murder, pure and simple. But this time there was no point in holding them back. If they didn't die in their fighters in combat with the enemy, they'd die in their bays when their motherships were torn to shreds or vaporized by their exploding reactors.

No one is coming back from this fight...

"Yes, sir." A few seconds later: "All squadrons are scrambling, sir. Admiral Hurley advises four minutes until launch readiness."

Four minutes? That's impossible. But this is Greta Hurley, so is anything impossible?

"Very well," he said simply. *I wish I had time to go down to the bay and shake her hand. I doubt we will meet again…*

"Alright Commander…the rest of the fleet will prepare for high-g maneuvers. I want everyone in the tanks ten minutes after the fighters are launched. We haven't got any missiles, so we need to get to energy range as quickly as possible."

"Yes, sir," Cortez snapped.

Compton wasn't at all sure he was ordering the right maneuver, but he knew being unsure was the one luxury he did not have right now. At least not as far as anyone in the crew was concerned. Maximum acceleration would get the fleet to energy weapons range quickly…but they would still pass through the enemy's missile barrage.

At high velocity, it was difficult to significantly alter a vessel's trajectory, in essence making its course more predictable, and therefore easier to target. On the other hand, while a slower moving ship could more easily execute radical changes to its vector, it was obliged to spend more time in the kill zone. It was a debate that had raged for a century in the naval academies, and one for which no generally-accepted agreement had ever been reached. Against a highly skilled adversary like Augustus Garret, he would have opted for a slower approach, attempting to confound his enemy's targeting with rapid and unpredictable course changes. But the First Imperium intelligences were far less adept at battle tactics than their overall sophistication suggested, and Compton wanted to get to grips with the enemy as quickly as possible.

Maybe you just want to get it over with. Half a century at war…and now you face your last battle. There will be no stories, no history, no legacy of the great Terrance Compton other than that you were trapped beyond the Barrier…and assumed dead in system X2. This isn't about how you go down in history… no one here will survive to remember, save perhaps in some jettisoned log destined to float forever in the depths of space. No, this isn't about anything except you...and these men and women who have fought by your side. We will have good deaths...and in our final moments, we will know we have remained strong and defiant to the last...

*   *   *

"Commander, please...we have to get your people to the tanks." The medical technician was rushing around the edge of the bed.

Mariko Fujin stared back with blazing eyes. "We're not going to the tanks."

"But Commander, you must. The ship will be accelerating at more than 30g. We can continue your cleanse once you are in the system." The sickbay acceleration tanks were specially designed to allow medical treatments to continue while a ship was executing high gee maneuvers. It was far from ideal, but it was the only alternative when a vessel was going into battle. A stretch of time in the tanks could be dangerous or fatal for a badly wounded patient, but Fujin's people were undergoing a relatively minor procedure.

"I'm sorry, Ensign," she said, pulling the last of the IV connections from her arm, "but my people and I are going to our fighter, not to the tanks." She looked over the flustered medic's shoulder toward Hiroki, who was following her lead and tearing the plastic tubing from his own arm.

"Commander, that's out of the question." The medic turned and looked out over the sickbay.

"Relax, Ensign," Mariko said softly. "We're all going to die anyway. You know that...I know that. Everyone knows. And my people and I are going to die in our fighter, alongside our comrades."

She fixed her gaze on him for a few seconds, and then she turned and walked out into the main area of the sickbay. A few seconds later the others came walking over one at a time. "Are we all ready?" she said when they were gathered.

"We're ready," they said almost as one.

"Then let's go." She led them out into the corridor toward the main lift. They got a stare or two as they strode down the hall in their hospital gowns, but most of the crew members they passed were solemn and focused. They all knew what they were facing, and few of them even noticed the fighter's crew.

Mariko moved swiftly. She knew she didn't have time to spare. *Midway*'s crew was moving to the tanks, and in less than ten minutes the ship would be blasting at 30g. Her people had to be in their fighter and launched by then.

She felt the impatience rising up within her as the lift moved—too slowly—toward the launch bay. Finally, the doors opened on the sprawling deck. It was mostly empty. Hurley's squadrons had just completed their launch. But her eyes scanned the area quickly and locked on their target. There it was, her fighter, tucked in right next to the launch track.

"Let's go. We're gonna have to skip preflight. Just get her powered up and ready to…"

"What the hell are you pukes doing on my launch deck?" The roaring voice was unmistakable. Sam McGraw was *Midway*'s senior NCO, the chief of the ship's launch bays and a certified terror to any officer without the stones to face him down.

"We're launching, Chief," Mariko said without a trace of doubt in her voice.

"To hell you are," came the almost deafening reply. "This deck is closed right now, and none of you puppies are cleared for duty."

"We are taking off, Chief, and I don't have the time to argue with you right now." The scene was almost comic, the meter and a half tall Fujin staring up at the 110 kilogram monster towering at least 35 centimeters over her. But the pilot held her own, not giving a millimeter, and her voice was as hard as a plasti-steel girder.

"C'mon, Chief," she added, her tone a bit softer. "We all know what is happening. None of these fighters are coming back. This is the fleet's final battle. Do we really need to leave a perfectly good fighter sitting unused?" She paused. "We all need to die our own way."

McGraw stared down at her for half a minute that seemed like an eternity. Then, something amazing happened, an event so improbable that she doubted anyone else on *Midway's* crew would have believed it. Chief Sam McGraw, the hardest screw ever to walk a launch bay's deck, gave in. "Go," he said, the slightest hint of admiration in his tone. "I'll open the doors for you."

"Thank you, Chief."

"Never mind that. Just move your asses. You've got three minutes or that door's staying closed."

She nodded quickly. "Alright, let's go." She flashed a quick glance at her shipmates, and she took off for the fighter at a dead run.

*   *   *

"We've got one of the damaged laser batteries functional, sir." Stanovich was staring at his screens, monitoring the emergency repair efforts underway throughout *Petersburg.* His voice was weak, tentative.

Udinov knew that was the residual effects of the tanks. His crew had only been out of the protective shells for ten minutes, and he knew from the pounding in his own fuzzy head, it took longer than that to completely shake the disorientation. He'd taken a stim injection strong enough to stampede a herd of elephants, but he was still foggy, his thoughts moving slowly.

"That's outstanding, Commander. Give the crews my congratulations." Udinov allowed himself a guarded smile. Things were looking bleak, but in the overall context, 30% more firepower was a good thing.

He glanced at the display. The wall of icons approaching the line of human ships was imposing. More than that, he knew it was his death he was looking at. Not just his, but that of every man and woman on *Petersburg*...on every ship in the fleet.

He also saw a cluster of smaller icons, swarming toward the edge of the enemy formation. *Admiral Hurley's fighters*, he thought. "All ships accelerate at 3g, course 343.011.116." His eyes were focused on the tiny symbols as they streaked across the screen. "We will go in behind the fighters, support their attack."

He knew his battered RIC task force had limited firepower, especially against an enemy force like the one now heading toward it. Still, following up Hurley's bombing run he might get the chance to finish off a couple enemy battleships, and that seemed like the most he could do to hurt the enemy. And he was determined to sell his peoples' lives dearly.

"Get me Admiral Compton." He'd had enough of playing the rogue. He wanted Compton's blessing for what was likely to be his final maneuver.

"Admiral Compton on your line, sir."

Udinov adjusted his headset. "Admiral, I request permission to move forward with my task force in close support of the Admiral Hurley's bombing run. I believe we can be of the most value there."

"Permission granted, Admiral Udinov. My admiration and best wishes go with your people."

"Thank you, sir." The Russian admiral paused. "And please accept my apologies, Admiral, for my earlier actions. I can only hope you can one day forgive me."

"It is forgiven, Vladimir. And forgotten...washed away by the blood your people shed in the last battle." There was a long pause and then Compton added, "It's a man's final actions that define him the most, wouldn't you say?"

Udinov swallowed hard and replied, "Yes, sir. I would say that."

"Then go with my respect, Admiral Udinov, and take the fight to the enemy."

"Yes, sir. I can promise you I will do that..."

*   *   *

"Very well, Admiral Udinov. Your forces are most welcome. I am concentrating my assault on the flank of the enemy battle-line. I had intended to try to take out the two Leviathans on the end, but with your added firepower, I propose we attack three instead of two." Hurley had been surprised at first, but she quickly adapted to the news that she had a whole task force backing her strike.

"I couldn't agree more, Admiral. Let's blast them to atoms." Udinov's voice was strong, predatory.

Whatever had happened before, Hurley realized, Vladimir Udinov was ready to give his all to this fight. "Good luck to you, Admiral," she said solemnly. "And to those who serve with you."

"And to you, Admiral," his voice blared through the com. "And to your brave squadrons. Udinov out."

Hurley leaned back in her chair, looking down at the screen. Her eye caught a tiny dot, an icon representing a single fighter. It was behind the rest of the strike force, accelerating to try to catch up. She knew who it was the second she saw it, but she toggled the ID function just to be sure.

She tapped the earpiece of her headset, changing the com channel. "Commander Fujin, what the hell are you doing?"

There was a small delay, less than a second, as the signal traversed the space between her fighter and Fujin's craft and the response worked its way back. "We're joining the strike force, Admiral. The fleet needs every bit of firepower it can muster."

"And you came to that conclusion through your many years of command experience?" Hurley was annoyed, but not as much as she might have been in other circumstances. Everyone knew this was no normal battle, that it was almost certainly their last.

"I apologize for disobeying orders, Admiral, but we are per-fectly capable of flying this mission."

"Now you're a doctor? I thought you were a pilot...and one

who knew how to follow orders. Clearly I was mistaken."

There was a pause, longer than the normal transmission time. Finally, Fujin's voice came back on the line. "Admiral, my people don't want to die in a hospital bed." Another pause then: "Please."

Hurley nodded to herself. She didn't take kindly to her orders being disobeyed, not normally.

But if there ever was a time and place...

"Very well, Commander. You may launch your attack. But I'm afraid you'll be alone. By the time you catch us, we'll have executed our strike."

"Hopefully you will leave something for us, Admiral."

Hurley was impressed at the strength and defiance in Fujin's voice. "Good luck to you and your crew, Commander. Hurley out."

She leaned back and couldn't help but let a smile cross her lips. *What a team I have in this strike force. If only they weren't all going to die in the next few hours...*

"Okay, John," she said, putting thoughts of Fujin aside and staring at her pilot. "What do you say we lead the strike in?" Her ship was normally positioned in the middle of the formation. Admiral Garret had been horrified at the prospect of her flying around in something as fragile as a Lightning fighter-bomber at all. He'd have had a stroke if he'd been able to hear her now. *Or not*, she thought. There were a lot of mysteries in the universe, but Greta Hurley was sure that Augustus Garret would die well if he met a hopeless battle—and he would expect any of his officers to do the same. Just as she was sure Terrance Compton was going to do.

"I'd love to lead them in. Those Leviathans are totally fresh...we're going to have to plant a lot of plasma torpedoes on the mark to take them out."

Hurley nodded, though the pilot wasn't looking back at her. "Take us in, Commander Wilder. Let's show these machines what a motivated human strike force can do."

*   *   *

"Let's go, Anton." Udinov's eyes were locked on his screen. He'd just watched Hurley's fighters plow through the enemy's defenses. They'd plunged into the massive barrage of interceptor missiles and then into range of the laser defenses of their targets—losing over forty of their comrades before beginning their final attack runs. The RIC admiral had been unable to look away as icon after icon disappeared from the scanning plot and still they pushed on, completely ignoring their losses.

Finally, he'd seen them form up into three columns, moving directly toward the chosen targets. The massive ships bristled with weapons, and fighters continued to disappear as they drove straight into the firestorm. But they held, not a single vessel wavering from its course. They blew past normal firing range, bearing down on their targets at 3,000 kilometers per second, closing. Fifty thousand kilometers. Thirty. Not a single bomber fired.

Twenty thousand…and in the lead was Greta Hurley herself, her bomber damaged and streaming atmosphere and fluids as it pushed forward. Fifteen thousand. Ten thousand. Only when she had passed ten thousand kilometers did her ship launch its torpedo…and then its thrusters fired full, barely altering its vector in time clear the massive vessel.

One after another, her bombers followed her in, blasting recklessly toward the enemy ships and unloading their payloads at knife-fighting range. They were so close, hardly a shot missed, and the First Imperium battleships shook as superhot balls of plasma ripped into their hulls and through their decks.

One of the behemoths was destroyed almost immediately as the containment of its antimatter fuel failed. The massive spaceship disappeared in an explosion of almost unimaginable intensity. But the other two were still there. Savaged by dozens of hits each, streaming gases and fluids through gaping holes in their battered hulls, they maintained their place on the flank of the enemy battleline.

Udinov took a deep breath. "Commander…take us between them. The entire task force is to advance."

"Yes, sir," came the reply, steadfast, determined.

"All ships, it's time to unload with everything we've got. All batteries on full power. Close range munitions packs ready to launch."

"All vessels report weapons stations ready, Admiral."

Udinov tapped his com unit, activating the main task force channel. "Attention all RIC units, this is Admiral Udinov. The fleet's fighter-bombers have just completed a costly and heroic attack. They have destroyed one of the enemy's Leviathans and severely damaged two others. It is our turn now. We are going to destroy those two ships, and then we are going to come about and engage the enemy line from the flank. Whatever might have happened before is of no account. We are part of this fleet, and we are in this fight with all our comrades. If we can destroy the two Leviathans quickly enough, we will have a positional advantage over the rest of the First Imperium fleet. I will not lie to you, fellow spacers…we will not survive this battle. None of us will. But, by God, we will make these infernal machines pay a price they will not soon forget. Follow me, follow *Petersburg*, and together we will show the First Imperium what an RIC force can do."

He cut the line and glanced down at his display. He watched for a few seconds then he turned toward Stanovich. "Commander…all units are to open fire."

*   *   *

"There goes the second ship." Mariko was watching on the display as the vessels of the RIC task force drove their attacks home, closing to point blank range, firing all the way. *Petersburg's* main batteries had fired a concentrated blast at the nearest Leviathan, and an instant later the target was vaporized by a matter-anti-matter explosion of indescribable ferocity. But the second First Imperium battleship was still there. It had taken all the punishment Udinov's ships could dish out, but it was still firing back, its powerful particle accelerator beams ripping into the RIC vessels.

Mariko watched as Udinov's task force began to redeploy, *Petersburg* and the two largest cruisers coming about to engage the next battleship in the enemy's line while the light cruisers and destroyers swarmed the wounded Leviathan. As she was watching, first one, then a second RIC destroyer disappeared from the screen, obliterated by the still active guns of the dying enemy ship.

"What do you say we go help them finish off that sucker?" Her normally high-pitched voice was hoarse, angry.

"We're with you, Commander." Hiroki's voice was rawer even than Mariko's, his ferocity apparent with every syllable. "Let's send them to hell."

"OK, boys, make sure you're strapped in tight…"

She pushed the throttle, and the force of 8g slammed into everyone onboard. They were already close to their target, but Mariko intended to get a hell of a lot closer before she fired the double-powered torpedo in her ship's bomb bay.

She flipped the com unit, and struggled to force air into her lungs and speak. "RIC ships, your fighter support is on the way in," she rasped.

"Forty thousand kilometers," Hiroki said.

Mariko released the throttle, and the relief of freefall replaced the crushing gee forces. "Don't you fire that thing until we're inside 10K, Hiroki."

"Thirty thousand."

Mariko watched as her monitor continually refreshed the image of the target, adding details as the range decreased. The schematic had a series of red spots, areas were the enemy ship was leaking atmosphere and fluids. And there was a very large red circle almost dead center on the top, a huge gash in the hull—and a way to drop the torpedo right into the ship's interior.

"You see what I see, Hiroki?"

"I've got it, Commander. That's a kill shot if I've ever seen one." A short pause. "If we can get close enough."

"I'll get you close enough. You just make sure you don't miss."

"I won't miss. Down to fifteen thousand."

"I've got to pull out at seven thousand," Mariko snapped back.

"Ten thousand." Another pause…one second, perhaps two. "Torpedo away."

Mariko slammed the throttle hard, blasting the engines at full power, altering the ship's trajectory. The course change over the next two seconds was minimal, but it was just enough for the fighter to zip past the enemy ship instead of slamming into it. Her eyes dropped to the small nav screen on her workstation. "Four hundred meters," she whispered under her breath. She'd come four hundred meters from slamming into the enemy ship. Mariko was a hotshot pilot, possessed of all the craziness attributed to that stereotype, but she'd never cut anything so close before. Never.

She let go of the throttle, cutting the thrust, and she leaned back in her chair and took a deep breath. She could feel the sweat inside her survival suit, pouring down her neck and back. Her hands were shaking, and she could feel her heart pounding in her chest. For a few seconds, she even forgot about the target. But only for a few seconds.

"Damage assessment," she snapped.

"Scanning data coming in now, Commander…" Hiroki paused, his head hunched over his workstation. "I'm reading no power generation at all. My guess is antimatter containment is still running on reserve batteries, but the ship itself is dead."

She felt a wave of satisfaction. "Alright, let's get back to *Midway* and rearm. There are still plenty of targets out here."

It was bravado more than reason. She saw the overall plot, and the despite the success of the fighter strike, the enemy still had seventeen Leviathans, and they were closing rapidly with the fleet. Her fighter could head back to *Midway*, but she didn't think there was much chance the flagship would still be around by the time they got there.

Chapter Twenty-Two

Research Notes of Dr. Hieronymus Cutter

I still cannot believe our good fortune, and I wonder how long it can last. The intelligence on the Colossus called us the "Old Ones," believing we are members of the long-lost race that created it so many ages ago, the mysterious beings who forged the First Imperium itself. It appears willing to obey our commands, to serve us without question. Yet I find myself hesitant to explore just how absolute that subservience may be. The intelligence advises that the ship is functional and it proposed reactivating its systems. I have ordered it not to do so, for I cannot be sure it will continue to follow my commands. Without the ship's matter/antimatter reactor operational, we control the power source that has activated the intelligence, and presumably, we can disconnect it at any time...though I wonder if that is an oversimplification, if the massive computer has drawn enough power to recharge reserve batteries or something of the like.

Still, I am reluctant to move too quickly. I had hoped with all the optimism I could muster that my virus would work, that we would be able to establish at least some level of control over the intelligence. But it had never even occurred to me that we would be accepted as its true masters, as the descendants of those who created it. Is this my virus working in an unexpected way? Or is there something else at play here, something I hadn't considered? Is there a relationship between humanity and that long-vanished race? Is there a reason other than my virus that the intelligence has come to the conclusion it has?

AS Midway
X18 System
The Fleet: 171 ships, 38,203 crew

"All ships of the battleline report ready, sir." Cortez sounded cool and calm. Compton knew it was bullshit, but he was impressed nevertheless. He hadn't imagined any officer could have adequately replaced Max Harmon as his tactical aide, but he had to admit Cortez came as close as anyone could have.

"Very well, Commander," he replied, his own voice equally controlled. *And that's bullshit too...but I need to stay strong...at least seem strong. I need to do it for all of them. They deserve nothing less.*

Compton had faced more than one desperate situation in his half century of war, but this was the most desperate, the most hopeless he had seen. If he thought the fleet had any chance at all of escaping he would have ordered every ship to make a run for it. But that was a fool's hope. None of his vessels could outrun the enemy, and if they were going to die anyway, he had resolved they would die fighting. He wasn't sure if any of it mattered. Death was death, however it came. But it made a difference to him...and he was sure it did to the rest of his people. They had lived as warriors, veterans of the struggle against the First Imperium and of the endless battles between the Superpowers. Now they would die as warriors.

"Flank forces are in position, sir, and all ships report full readiness."

"Very well." Full readiness was a relative term for his battered ships, but he knew they would make the most of what they had. "Report on enemy missile barrage?"

"First salvo is just inside 800,000 kilometers range of our lead elements, Admiral. All vessels ready to initiate countermeasures at 500,000 as per your orders."

Compton took a deep breath. It felt strange not to have his own missiles in space, but there wasn't a ship-to-ship warhead on any of his vessels—except in the transports in X20. And they might as well be on the far side of the galaxy. He didn't know how many of his ships would make it through the massive barrage heading their way. He had some evasive maneuvers in mind, a few tricks that might lessen the impact. But no matter how he figured it, a good portion of his fleet was going to die when those missiles closed, and the rest would limp forward, damaged and bleeding air.

Those survivors would fire when they got to energy weapons range, at least the ones that still had functional batteries. But Compton didn't try to fool himself. That battle wouldn't last long. And then it would be over. Everything except the First Imperium fleet chasing down and destroying his transports in the next system.

But that won't take long. And then the fleet will be gone, the sacrifice we made in X2 rendered moot, and our whole improbable story brought to its inevitable conclusion.

"Status report on Admiral Udinov's task force?" The RIC admiral had requested permission to perform close support for Greta Hurley's fighter strike, and his ships were far in advance of the main fleet...and closely engaged with the flank of the enemy forces.

"They've lost six ships, sir. *Petersburg* reports extensive damage, but she's still in the fight."

Compton just sat silently. Udinov was directing his meager force masterfully, but he wouldn't last long. He'd managed to position himself out of the arc of the enemy's main weapons, clinging to their blind spots. The First Imperium ships would have to turn from their course fleet to fully engage him, and that would mean delaying the final fight with the main battleline— even allowing some of the human ships to make a run for it. So far the enemy had maintained their vectors and tried to pick off Udinov's vessels with secondary batteries.

And they are succeeding. It's just taking a little longer to wear them down, but Udinov's ships won't last twenty minutes where they are.

He took in another breath, holding it for a few seconds. "Very well, Commander Cortez, the fleet will advan..."

"Admiral, we're picking up transits...from the X20 warp gate, sir."

Compton's head snapped around toward the tactical officer's

station. "Full scan, Commander."

"Working on it, sir." Cortez' hands raced over his station, and an instant later his face went pale. "It's a First Imperium vessel, sir." His voice was weak, thin. "A Colossus."

*   *   *

"Confirmed, sir. It's a Colossus...transiting in behind the main fleet."

Vladimir Udinov sat quietly for a few seconds, absorbing the reality of what he'd just been told. In truth, he realized it didn't matter. They'd already been facing enough enemy ships to destroy the fleet twice over—it didn't really make much difference if now it was three or four times. Dead was dead. Still, the very thought of the enemy's most massive battleships evoked a primal fear.

Udinov stared at the screen, his finger moving slowly to the right, scrolling the display area to cover the main body of the enemy fleet. His task force had been maneuvering around the flank, taking advantage of the enfilade position to maximize the damage inflicted. He'd been struggling to stay in the enemy's blind spots, to rake their ships from positions were they couldn't effectively return fire. The target vessels could have broken formation and moved to intercept his small task force, but he knew that wasn't the First Imperium's way. They would continue toward the main fleet, ignoring a nuisance force like his until after the main fight was done. And that's all he was, he knew that much...just an insect stinging them as they moved inexorably forward. He might damage the flank Leviathan, but he just didn't have the firepower to do more.

"Get me Admiral Compton," he snapped to Stanovich.

A few seconds later. "On your line, sir."

"Vladimir, "Compton said before Udinov could utter a word, "you've done a tremendous job, but now you're pretty exposed out there. It's time for you to plot a course back to the main force, around the enemy's arc of fire." Compton's voice was firm, but there was no hostility there. However strained their relationship might have been following the mutiny, facing certain death together had evaporated any lingering hostility.

"Admiral, I'd like to stay. I can bring my ships around the enemy's rear. If we cause enough trouble back there we might force them to stop and deal with us. That will buy you time... time to deal with that Colossus." Udinov knew it was a long-shot his meager force could somehow hold back the entire First Imperium fleet, but it was just the kind of highly emotional play that tended to throw the enemy intelligences into a funk.

The com was silent for a few seconds. Finally, Compton replied, his voice soft. "You won't last ten minutes if they turn to face you, Vladimir. If your plan succeeds, you die almost immediately."

"Things have moved past 'if we die.' At this point, I'm more concerned with 'how we die.' We're all doomed, Admiral." The Russian's voice was deadpan, almost without emotion. "At least this way the fleet won't be trapped between two forces. Maybe a few ships can even get away back into X20. The supply fleet is..." He paused, and Compton knew Udinov had just come to the same conclusion he had a few minutes before. The Colossus had come from X20...which probably meant the transports were gone.

"Who knows?" he continued an instant later, ignoring his thoughts on the supply fleet. "Maybe my people can buy enough time for somebody to escape." Udinov paused then added, "We're dead anyway...this way we've got a chance, however small, of accomplishing something."

Compton paused. Udinov knew the Alliance admiral hated sending his people to their deaths. It was something he'd been compelled to do far too many times in his long and storied career. But now they were all trapped...everyone in the fleet was facing death.

"Let us die with honor, Terrance, with at least a faint hope our deaths will help our comrades. It's a false hope perhaps, but one my people deserve."

"Very well, Vladimir…if that's what you want to do, I'll give you my blessing. The thoughts and admiration of your comrades in the fleet go with you. And mine too." Compton hadn't specifically said it, but he knew Udinov understood. His prior actions were forgiven. He would go into his last fight with a clean slate.

"Commander Stanovich, the task force will execute nav plan Epsilon-3. We're breaking off and maneuvering around the enemy fleet." He slapped his hand down on the armrest of his chair. "And, by God, we're going to get right behind these bastards and hit them with everything we've got…"

*   *   *

"I want everybody in the tanks in fifteen minutes." Compton had sat quietly for a few minutes after speaking with Udinov. He still couldn't comprehend what had driven the Russian admiral to try to break off from the fleet, to recklessly risk leading the enemy back home with him. He understood Zhang's motivations. The CAC officer was a coward, a gutless worm beneath Compton's contempt, concerned only with his own selfish needs. But Udinov was nothing like that. Indeed, he was as courageous as any commander Compton had ever known. Yet they had almost ended up fighting each other.

What is wrong with us? Why are we so ready to fight each other, even after we've discovered we're not alone, that the stars hold such terrible dangers? Why is man always ready to go to war with himself? The First Imperium seems to be a united power, all its resources working together rather than struggling against other factions within. Were the actual beings who created the imperium more enlightened, wiser than men? Or did they fight each other as we do now? Was this staggering civilization built by wise and peaceful beings who avoided the greed and lust for power that so plagued men? Or do we just see the legacy of the victors, those who survived millennia of internal conflict, who fought and crushed their enemies before claiming the stars?

"Admiral, we're picking up more energy readings from the X20 warp gate."

Compton sighed. He'd initially assumed that Cutter and his team had inadvertently activated the Colossus, but now he confronted the thought that more First Imperium ships were coming from X20. And that meant whatever unrealistic hopes he might have had of any of his ships escaping had been dashed. With enemy units pouring through the warp gate, he couldn't even fool himself anymore. The supply fleet in X20 was already gone…and all his people in X18 would die right here.

"Admiral, we're picking up a transmission…" Cortez paused. "Sir, it's Admiral Garson! It was *Hamilton* that transited!"

Compton's head snapped around. *Hamilton* was the flagship of the support task force, and Garson was the admiral in command. "Put him on speaker, Commander."

"Admiral Compton…" Garson's voice was firm, confident.

"Yes, Admiral Garson, we're reading you…"

"Sir, the First Imperium ship is not hostile. I repeat, it is not hostile. Dr. Cutter and his people have gained control over it, and they have directed it to attack the enemy fleet."

Terrance Compton had rarely been shocked into speechlessness during his long career, but now he struggled for words, his throat dry, as if every molecule of moisture had evaporated instantaneously. "Dr. Cutter and his team are on that ship?" he croaked. "Controlling it?"

"Yes, sir. They disabled the external communications because Cutter was afraid an order from outside might overrule his control. You won't be able to reach them unless you get close enough to be in range of their portable coms. But that ship is here to fight with us…not against us."

Compton let out a long breath. It was almost unbelievable…no, it *was* unbelievable. He'd had strong hopes for Cutter's research over time, but this was lightyears beyond anything he'd expected.

He stared back at the monitor, at the First Imperium fleet moving toward his ships, and a feral smile formed on his lips. "Commander Cortez, the fleet will prepare to advance and engage the enemy. All vessels will match course and speed with the Colossus. And set up a fleetwide channel. This is something I've *got* to tell everyone."

"Yes, sir!"

Compton nodded. His body was alive, almost twitching with energy as he fed off his rage, his hatred of the First Imperium. His mind was sharp, and it was focused on one thing. They had a chance now. The fight had purpose.

*   *   *

"That fleet is acting against its orders. It is a rogue force, and we must engage and destroy it." Hieronymus Cutter sat in one of the workstation chairs…a seat where a member of that ancient race had once sat, the long lost beings who'd founded the First Imperium ages ago.

"As you command," the AI replied, its voice calm, unaffected, despite the fact that Cutter had ordered it to attack the First Imperium ships that lay ahead. "Activating all weapons systems. Initial missile barrage in eleven time segments." The translation system had no reference for the measurement systems of the First Imperium, and it substituted 'time segment' for a word that was obviously a unit of time.

"Preliminary analysis of opposing fleet suggests we have insufficient capability to destroy all vessels."

Cutter turned and looked back at his companions. "You are to destroy as many as possible." *Does the intelligence have a self-preservation priority? Will it obey orders likely to result in its own destruction?*

"Understood."

Cutter could feel the sweat pouring down his neck and he reached around and wiped at it, letting out a loud exhale as he did. The intelligence had apparently accepted an order that was tantamount to a suicide mission. But would it follow through?

Cutter looked down at the scanner feed Garson had sent him. The enemy force was massive, far more than the human fleet could handle, even with Terrance Compton in command. The Colossus was the only hope. Cutter hated the idea of his tremendous find being destroyed...especially since he was aboard. But unless the massive superbattleship intervened immediately, the fleet was lost.

"Ana," Cutter whispered, "we should get as much information from this intelligence as possible and get it back to the fleet. I can't even imagine the data in those banks."

"I agree, but there's no way except to ask the intelligence to copy it for us...and that might cause suspicion. We have no idea how firm our control is or what might trigger the system to reevaluate us." She was standing right next to him, and he could feel her body shaking.

Of course she's scared. He looked around, scanning the faces of his team, seeing the fear in their eyes. This was a situation none of them were made to handle. They were scientists, academics...not soldiers.

I wonder if they're scared...the Marines. They're veterans, they've faced combat before, stared death in the eye. But this is something different. There is a haunted feeling here, as if we mere mortals had stumbled into the halls of some ancient gods.

His eyes locked on Connor Frasier. The Marine was fully armored, the dark gray surface of his helmet blocking any view of his face, his eyes. *I guess I won't know,* Cutter thought, wondering if even Major Connor Frasier, commander of the Scots Company, could maintain his cool in a situation like this.

He turned back toward the input device. "My associate is going to make copies of data from your banks. You are to assist her in any way you can."

"As you command. I must warn you that the primitive data storage devices you employ are highly inefficient. They have very low capacity, and their I/O speeds are grossly inadequate. Only minimal data will be transferred before we engage in battle."

"I understand. Now please assist her in any way possible." He was struggling to sound authoritative, in command. He had no idea if the system had permanently accepted him as one of the Old Ones, or if it was still analyzing his words and speech patterns. Or for that matter, his body temperature, physical appearance...anything at all that might shatter the charade.

Not that you have any idea how a First Imperium naval officer would have behaved.

He stood still, silent for a few minutes. Then he turned toward Frasier.

"Major, I want you to get back to the shuttles. Take my people with you and evacuate the ship as quickly as you can. I will stay here. There is no point in anyone else remaining behind. If the intelligence ceases to accept my orders, there is nothing my people—or your Marines—could do anyway." He hesitated briefly and added, "And Admiral Compton is going to need every skilled scientist and warrior he can get."

"My orders are to protect you, Doctor. At all costs." Frasier's voice was deep, his tone firm, crisp. If he was afraid, he wasn't showing it.

"The situation has changed, Major. There is no point in anyone else remaining here at risk. I will stay. Alone."

"I can't allow that, Doctor." A pause. "But I will see to the evacuation of your science teams and my Marines. Then I will remain here with you."

"Major, that's not..."

"I will remain, Doctor. It is my duty." The Marine's voice was like solid rock, and Cutter knew at once he wouldn't budge. Not a micron.

"Very well, Major. If you must remain. At least the others will get out."

Frasier nodded, a fairly meaningless gesture in battle armor. "I will begin the evacuation now, Doctor. We'll need to do two trips to get everyone off...and the last one will be cutting it close, I think."

Cutter just nodded back. *Yes,* he thought. *It will be close. Too close.*

*   *   *

Midway shook hard. She had been in the thick of the fight, exchanging laser fire with the enemy battleline before passing through and decelerating to turn and make a second run. Compton's flagship had come through the enemy missile barrage almost untouched, a stunning development he owed to a little bit of luck...and a lot to the effort of Greta Hurley's squadrons.

That woman was born to lead fighter groups, Compton thought as he stared out across the bridge.

Midway's strikeforce had swept through the clusters of missiles as they returned from their first attack. The *Yorktown* class battleship had originally carried 48 fighter-bombers, including Admiral Greta Hurley's craft. The flagship's veteran squadrons had acquitted themselves well in the campaign, with a survival rate far above the fleet average. Even so, Hurley had been leading back only sixteen of *Midway's* fighters.

The birds were out of expendable ordnance, but they'd opened up on the missiles with their lasers, and they gutted the volley heading toward *Midway*. Hurley had pioneered the use of fighters for missile defense, a promising tactic she'd been largely forced to abandon since they fleet had been trapped in enemy space. Her fighter crews had paid a terrible price in the battles since then, and she needed every ship she had left to attack the enemy warships. There just weren't enough to assign to defensive duties, however promising the tactic had proven itself.

Compton looked out across the flag bridge. There was wreckage strewn across the deck, minor structural elements mostly, broken loose when *Midway* had taken a direct hit from the main battery of one of the Leviathans. A large conduit, 20 centimeters in diameter, snaked its way across the middle of the bridge, passing just behind Compton's chair. It was a bypass line, replacing a damaged group of cables and carrying power to a whole series of ship's systems. The damage control crew that had installed it was gone. They had finished a few minutes earlier and moved on to the next repair on their agenda.

"Cutting thrust now, Admiral," Cortez said, as loudly as he could under 4g of deceleration.

"Very well, Commander. I want the engines engaged again as quickly as possible. It's time to finish this." His voice was scratchy, and his tone exuded determination. Cutter's miraculous success in gaining control over the Colossus had bought his people a chance for survival…and he'd be damned if he'd delay, even for an instant.

Midway and the rest of the battleline could have gotten back into the fight faster if Compton had ordered everyone into the tanks and blasted away at 30g thrust. But his ship was too battered for that. Her damage control crews were hard at work readying her for another round of combat. It was difficult for them to do their jobs at 4g, but at 30g they'd all be in the tanks doing nothing at all. And the rest of his battleships were even worse off. *Saratoga* had been hit hard by the missile volleys and again in the energy weapons duel. Admiral Dumont's ship was keeping his ship in the fight, but Compton knew even a *Yorktown* class battlewagon had its limits. And *Saratoga* had to be near hers.

Compton's eyes were fixed on the display, watching the incredible spectacle of a First Imperium fleet locked in mortal combat with one of their own super-battleships. The Colossus had come almost to a dead stop, its 60g+ thrust capacity giving it far more maneuverability than one of Compton's vessels. When he'd first noticed the enemy ship decelerating at 60g, he feared that Cutter and his people had all been killed, crushed to death by the almost unimaginable force slamming into them at that rate of acceleration. But then, a group of shuttles emerged from the vessel, moving toward the main body of the human fleet.

A few moments later, he had his answers. The First Imperium ships had some sort of internal force dampening system. Cutter and his people had been inside the behemoth when it fired its massive engines, but they hadn't felt a thing.

Just another way they are so far ahead of us…and it's something they haven't even needed for 500,000 years.

"Reengaging thrust, Admiral. Four gees as ordered." Compton's vessel had shot past the First Imperium forces, decelerating at 4g until it came to a complete stop. Then, its positioning thrusters spun it around before the engines opened up again and *Midway* began building velocity back the way she'd come. In a little over twenty minutes, the battleline would reenter energy weapons range…and the fight would continue.

Compton just nodded. He'd given his orders, and he knew his people would carry them out to the letter. He winced an instant later when the 4g of force slammed into him again. He'd enjoyed the few moments of freefall.

"Admiral, I have Dr. Barcomme on the com." She was on one of the shuttles fleeing from the Colossus, having joined Cutter's expedition to search for signs of the ancient beings of the First Imperium.

"Soph…Dr. Barcomme, how can I help you?" Compton's iron tone softened a bit as he addressed Barcomme. He had spent a fair amount of time with the Europan biologist in recent weeks, mostly discussing possible ways to feed everyone once the food supply ran out. But the two had also talked for hours one night, finishing off one of the increasingly rare bottles of wine in the fleet's stores. It wasn't a budding romance, more of a friendship…neither of them was ready for anything more than that. Compton was still mourning the loss of Elizabeth, and Barcomme had left a husband and a daughter behind when she'd been trapped with the fleet beyond the Barrier. But for a few hours, Compton had felt less desperately alone than he had in the months since the fleet had begun its desperate run for survival.

"It's Hieronymus. And Ana Zhukov. They're still on the Colossus."

"What?" Compton tried to catch himself, but his shock was apparent despite his efforts.

"Hieronymus wouldn't leave. He said he had to remain and monitor the ship's intelligence. And Ana wouldn't go if he didn't." She paused. "Then Major Frasier stayed behind too, insisting your orders were to protect the two of them at all costs."

Of course. He'd given Frasier an order…and he had enough experience to understand how seriously a veteran Marine took such commands. Seriously…and literally too.

"Thank you, Dr. Barcomme. I appreciate the heads up." He flipped off the com, shaking his head as he did, angry at his own distraction. When he'd picked up the shuttles fleeing the Colossus, he'd just assumed Cutter and all his people were aboard. *You underestimated Hieronymus*, he thought, angry at himself. *Underneath the introverted professor exterior, the good doctor has a streak of courage….*

He sighed. Cutter had saved the fleet…or at least given it a chance. Compton wasn't about to let him die in that monstrous vessel. And he had no intention of losing Ana Zhukov or Connor Frasier…apart from personal feelings, he needed people like them if the fleet was to have any hope of surviving for the long term.

He stared down at his screen. It was centered on the Colossus as the massive vessel fought off at least fifty First Imperium ships. The enemy had been confused at first, and they'd been slow to react when the massive super-battleship opened fire on them. Compton imagined the messages bombarding the big ship as the fleet intelligences tried to call off the attack from one of their own. But Cutter had disabled the Colossus' com systems, and the messages went unanswered. Finally, after half a dozen ships had been destroyed, the rest of the First Imperium fleet moved to engage the rogue dreadnought.

Compton watched as another Leviathan vanished in the fury of a matter/antimatter explosion. He'd been stunned at what he saw when the Colossus first opened fire. The massive vessel had rows of particle accelerators along its port and starboard, almost like the broadside of an old style sailing ship. The weapons were enormous, powered by the almost incalculable energy output of the 19 kilometer ship.

He'd looked on in astonished wonder when the great weapons first lanced out, tearing into the hulls of the enemy Leviathans. The dark matter infused armor that had proven so resistant to the human fleet's weapons, tore like paper under the massive barrages.

Now, Compton stared as yet another of the great Leviathans died, the second in as many minutes. The Colossus was blasting the enemy ships with as much firepower as Compton's entire fleet...perhaps more. But it, too, was taking damage. Its hull was enormously strong, its own dark matter armor vastly heavier than that of the smaller First Imperium ships. But the Leviathans swarming it had powerful batteries too. Not as strong, certainly, as those on the Colossus, but still the products of the tremendous technology that created both. Rents began to appear in the super-battleship's hull, and one by one, its unspeakably powerful batteries began to fall silent.

Compton knew the big ship had plenty of fight left in it. But he also realized that for all its amazing firepower, it wasn't going to win. Not by itself. *We're coming,* he thought, as he stared at the deadly fight unfolding in the flickering light of his screen.

No. I won't sacrifice them. They deserve better...and if we get out of this system, we're going to need them. Hieronymus Cutter is more important to this fleet's survival than I am.

He slapped his hand on his com unit, activating Admiral Hurley's com unit.

"Greta...I need to you do something for me..."

*   *   *

"I think we can slip between those two Leviathans without crossing into either one's interdiction zone." Hurley never second-guessed Wilder's piloting, but this was more about navigation than hot-sticking it in the pilot's chair. *Midway's* sixteen remaining fighters were formed up in a tight crescent, trying to reach the Colossus without getting blown to bits by any of the First Imperium ships clustering around. John Wilder was the best pilot in the fleet, but this time they were escorting three shuttles that didn't have a tenth the thrust and maneuverability of the Lightning fighter-bombers.

Those things fly like three-legged pigs, she thought, her frustration momentarily getting the best of her. It didn't matter how sluggish the shuttles were, they were the most important part of the mission. Her job was to rescue the last three human beings on that Colossus, no matter what the cost. *No matter what the cost.* Compton's exact words.

She'd have preferred to just load the three of them on a fighter, but she knew that wouldn't work. They weren't exactly landing on *Midway's* flight deck. Cutter's team had rigged docking stations to connect with the ingress/egress ports on a standard fleet shuttle. There was no way a Lightning fighter-bomber was going to be able to dock with one of those...not without a team of engineers and a lot more time than she had.

"Okay everybody, listen up." She was on the master com channel—transmitting to all three shuttles and all her fighters. "I'm sending nav instructions. We're going to try to maneuver in without going through any areas that are too hot. Shuttle pilots, I know those things aren't Lightnings, but I need you to squeeze out every gram of performance you can. There is a battle going on. A little extra speed or maneuverability could save your life. And the mission."

She wondered what they all thought of that mission. There were almost a hundred people on her fighters and the three shuttles, and they were all at risk. To save three people. She understood Doctor Cutter's importance to any future the fleet might have...indeed, she realized they'd all be dead already without the Colossus the brilliant scientist had somehow managed to control and bring into the fight. That alone justified the rescue attempt. But it was still hard on the men and women sent to put their lives on the line.

Her eyes dropped to the display. There it was, the Colossus, almost 19 kilometers of pure power. It was fighting the dozen remaining Leviathans...and most of the rest of the First Imperium fleet. It was losing, or at least it would lose eventually. But it was also gutting the enemy fleet. And Compton was bringing the surviving human ships back into the melee. She wondered if he'd make it back into firing range before the Colossus was gone. She figured it was a coin toss.

"All units, execute nav instructions in five…four…three…"

They were running out of time. It was now or never.

"Two…one…"

*   *   *

"I'm sorry, Ana. You should have gone with the others." Cutter angled his head, staring at the armored form of Connor Frasier standing against the wall. "And you too, Major."

"Do not trouble yourself, Doctor. I am following Admiral Compton's orders, and I have no regrets."

Cutter nodded slightly. He knew the Marine was afraid… they were all afraid. But he was just as certain Frasier would never admit it.

"We gave the fleet a chance, Hieronymus," Ana answered softly. She wasn't as successful as Frasier at keeping the fear from her voice, but overall she was holding herself together fairly well. "That's something to be proud of."

"Yes," Cutter replied, "and the others brought back a treasure trove of data with them. It will be massively useful in finding a way to survive in First Imperium space." Ana had only managed to scratch the surface of the massive intelligence's data bases before she'd filled up every storage unit she had with her. Still, the information she'd gleaned included centuries of scientific development…and the first accounts mankind had of the history of the First Imperium. Cutter knew he wouldn't be there to supervise the research effort, but there would be others. Perhaps the data would be enough for someone to continue his and Ana's work…to find a way to defeat—or make peace with—the enemy.

The ship shook hard, most likely a secondary explosion somewhere. The Colossus had gunned down a third of the

First Imperium fleet already, but now it was beginning to falter. Its massive batteries were still firing, though barely half of them remained in action. Cutter wasn't an expert in warships, but he didn't think it would be too long now. The intelligence had activated a large screen for his use, displaying the scanning data of the battle. The Colossus was virtually surrounded by Leviathans, and all the ships were at a virtual dead stop, blasting away at each other at close range.

The ship shook again, and the lights dimmed briefly. "The primary power conduit to this sector was severed. I have engaged backup system." The intelligence's tone hadn't changed. It showed no fear, nor any recognizable hesitancy about continuing to follow Cutter's orders, even though they would almost certainly lead to its destruction. And soon.

Cutter leaned back in the seat and sighed. He'd taken a massive gamble in attempting to activate the First Imperium vessel. He hadn't known the fleet would be attacked when he did it. It was his own initiative...no, more than that...his reckless craving for knowledge, his need to match his mind against such a superior adversary. His actions had possibly saved the fleet, but that had been an accident, nothing he could take credit for. He'd never imagined he could take total control of the ship so quickly, let alone bringing it back to X18 just as the fleet was fighting a hopeless battle. He realized how lucky they had been...and his own impending death didn't alter his view of the good fortune that had smiled on their venture. He would die, and Ana too, but perhaps thousands would live as a result of what they had done. And if the fleet had been destroyed, Cutter knew he and Ana would have died anyway.

"Doctor Cutter? Major Frasier?" The small portable com unit crackled to life, a woman's voice calling to them by name.

Cutter hopped out of his chair and raced to the communications device. "Cutter here," he replied.

"Doctor Cutter, this is Admiral Hurley. I am leading a rescue mission to get you off that ship. How long will it take you to get back to your original ingress point?"

Cutter paused. It had taken them literally days to explore

their way in this far, but now they knew the way back. "I'm not sure, Admiral. Half an hour? Maybe more."

"No good," came the reply. "That ship's not going to be there in half an hour."

Cutter sighed hard. It was at least four kilometers back to the docking station. "Then you might as well go home, Admiral. There's no point in risking your people for nothing."

"Fuck that, Doctor. I came to get you, and by God, I'm going to get you." A pause. "You have survival suits, right? Is there any way you can get to an airlock faster? I can pluck you out of space before you run out of air."

"Yes, we have suits." He'd kept everyone on bottled and recycled air, not willing to trust the First Imperium atmosphere the intelligence had restored. The survival suits weren't meant for serious EVA, but they could sustain life in deep space long enough to allow a rescue attempt.

"Hold on, Admiral." Cutter turned toward the globe he knew was the intelligence's core. It was a meaningless gesture… the computer didn't care if he was facing it or not when they communicated. But it made him feel better somehow. "Display the fastest route to an operable airlock."

Will the thing get upset that I am leaving it behind to die?

"Displaying optimal escape route."

Cutter's eyes focused on the map for half a minute before he got his bearings. Then he saw it. Less than half a kilometer.

"Admiral, five minutes. Does that work?"

"It works fine. Don't waste time talking to me. And remember to set your transponders on full power so we can find you."

Cutter nodded, as much to himself as anything. "Alright, Admiral." Then, an instant later. "Thanks."

"Okay, let's get go…"

The ship shook again, harder this time. Cutter fell and slid across the deck, crashing painfully into a large structural column. He started to get up, but he paused for an instant on his hands and knees, shaking his head. The fall had knocked the wind out of him. It was at least thirty seconds before he started to stand…and his eyes found Ana.

She was lying against a large bulkhead, silent, motionless. Connor Frasier was there already, his massive armored figure crouched over her.

Cutter stumbled across the deck, dropping to his knees next to her. "Ana," he said urgently. "Ana?" But there was no response.

"She is alive, Doctor, but I'm afraid she's badly hurt." He gestured toward the side of her head. Her hair was matted with blood.

"Ana…"

"She needs help right away, Doctor. Or she's going to die."

Cutter stared down helplessly, reaching out and putting his hand gently on her shoulder. A few seconds later, he saw movement in his peripheral vision, and he turned to see Frasier lying down on the deck. And instant after that he heard a loud popping sound.

The gargantuan suit of armor popped open like a clamshell, and all 190 centimeters and 110 kilograms of Connor Frasier climbed out, stark naked. He turned quickly toward Ana.

"We have to get her in my armor. My med system can save her." Marine armor was equipped with extensive trauma control mechanisms designed to save grievously wounded warriors on the battlefield.

"But it's so big…and how will we get her out of here in that?"

"It doesn't have to fit her for this…we just need to get her into it. And the suit's AI can control the suit enough to walk with her inside."

Cutter nodded, sliding over and grabbing Ana's legs. Frasier slipped his hands under shoulders and the two lifted her gently, carrying her over to the suit. They set her down as well as they could inside.

"Frasier hesitated for a few seconds then he popped her helmet and began unzipping her survival suit. He glanced up at Cutter, who was looking at him with a confused expression on his face. "We need to get her clothes off. The med sensors work on touch."

Cutter nodded and leaned over Ana, helping Frasier strip off her suit. He was annoyed at his own hesitancy. They were trying to save her life, not sneak a look at her in the shower. But still, he felt strange about it.

What juvenile idiots we all are…

They finally managed to get her inside the suit, and Frasier commanded the AI to seal it. A few seconds later, she was closed up inside.

"She'll be okay. I've been worse off and it's saved me." Frasier turned and looked at the suit. "Get up…we've got to get out of here."

The suit obeyed his command, rising quickly. Frasier glanced over at Cutter. "Let's go…I doubt we have much time. Lead on, Doc."

Cutter nodded, and he walked out into the hallway, following the course the AI had highlighted.

Frasier looked around the room briefly, and then he directed the AI to follow. "At least we know the air is breathable… though I suppose I could have sucked in a lungful of some epic plague and not know it yet."

Cutter stopped dead in his tracks. "How are we going to get you out of here?" he said, suddenly realizing that Frasier would be stuck on the Colossus without his suit."

"I guess we're not going to, Doc," the Marine said calmly. "But we're getting the two of you off, that's for sure. I'll be damned if I'm going to fail my last mission."

*   *   *

"All units, fire everything you have left." Compton sat on *Midway's* flag bridge, staring out over the battle ravaged scene before him. He moved his hand up to scratch an itch on his face, and he smacked it into the clear helmet for the third time. The flag bridge hadn't lost life support yet, but much of *Midway* had, and he'd ordered his staff to put the helmets on about ten minutes before. His flagship had given all she had to the fight, and he knew she didn't have much left. Her hull was riddled with breaches, and at least a quarter of the crew had been killed.

He knew Jim Horace was still at his position down in *Midway*'s command center. He also knew the officer should have been in sickbay. Internal video com was down, so all he knew was what he'd been told. But he had a good idea that Horace's left leg had been damn near crushed by a falling chunk of *Midway*'s structure. The doctor had told Compton his flag captain was in rough shape and belonged in a hospital bed, but he also acknowledged he had stabilized the stubborn officer and stopped the bleeding...and if Horace could stand the pain, he'd probably survive remaining at his post. If any of them survived, that is.

Compton's eyes dropped to his screen, watching the scene unfolding around the Colossus. The giant ship was almost finished, less than a quarter of its weapons still firing. It was bleeding fluids and gasses through dozens of rents in its hull.

C'mon, hang in there...we need a little more time...

The Colossus had already done its job in savaging the First Imperium fleet. Compton's ships were blasting right at the enemy flank, taking full advantage of the chaos the Colossus had created. But he needed more time...Greta Hurley needed more time. His three people still on that ship needed more time.

Midway shook hard, and she went into a vicious spin. Everyone on the flag bridge has strapped into their harnesses, but it was still unsettling. Compton figured more than one of his officers had partially filled his helmet with vomit.

People glamorize space battles, telling and retelling the stories of great victories. But there is no glory up close. Just men and women, covered in sweat and blood...and vomit.

"Alright, all ships...increase thrust to 6g." That would be damned uncomfortable, but he needed to keep up the pressure now. Every second he bought that Colossus was more time Hurley had to rescue Cutter and Ana. And Connor Frasier too.

"Increasing thrust, sir." Cortez' reply was almost instantaneous. He understood exactly what was happening.

"All ships…I want continuous fire. Whatever it takes. I don't want a gun silent."

C'mon you bastards…forget about that Colossus. We're coming right up your ass…

*   *   *

"Go, Doc. The fleet needs you…and Dr. Zhukov. There's nothing you can do here."

Cutter stared at the giant Marine, and he could feel his heart pounding in his chest. He knew what he had to do, what Frasier was telling him to do, but it was too much to bear. In a few seconds he and Ana would step into the airlock…and they would leave Connor Frasier behind. To die.

"Go," the Marine repeated. "Now." His voice was commanding, insistent. "You getting yourselves scragged won't make me less dead."

Cutter took a deep breath and moved toward the hatch. Then he paused, turning back toward Frasier. He'd never been very good with people, but now he knew he couldn't just walk away, not without a fitting farewell. He extended his hand. "Thank you, Major…Connor. You are the bravest man I've ever met."

The big Scot allowed a little smile onto his lips as he reached out and grasped Cutter's hand. "Thank you, Doctor. Keep up your work. Save our people." An instant later: "Now, go!"

Cutter felt the emotions building up inside him, and he just nodded. Then he turned and stepped into the airlock, Frasier's suit—with Ana inside—following along. He hadn't been sure what to expect in the way of controls, but the system was agreeably simple. A large button to close the inner doors and another right below it. *The outer doors*, he supposed. There was another set off to the side, with what looked vaguely like up and down arrows. *Pressurize, depressurize*, he thought.

He pushed the first button, and the door slammed shut. *So far so good.* He took another breath and pressed the control with the down arrow. He could hear and feel the whoosh of air, as the small chamber was evacuated. An instant later, the second door button glowed blue.

He paused again. This was it. Either Hurley's shuttles would find them...or he would die in space as his suit's oxygen and power ran out.

He reached out and pushed the button. The outer door zipped open, and Hieronymus Cutter stared out into the blackness of space. He turned back toward the massive suit of armor with Ana Zhukov inside and he nodded. It was meaningless. Frasier had already instructed his AI to follow.

He stood still for another thirty seconds, perhaps a minute. Then he bent his knees and shoved off.

*   *   *

"We've picked up Doctors Cutter and Zhukov, Admiral. Apparently, Major Frasier is still on the First Imperium vessel."

"Why the hell is he there?" she roared back, angry at the partial rescue. She'd lost three fighters already, and after paying that price she had no intention of leaving anyone behind.

"Admiral, this is Dr. Cutter. Ana Zhukov was badly injured, and Major Frasier put her in his suit so the med system could save her." A pause. "Of course, that left him with no survival gear..."

Fuck.

Hurley sat for a few seconds, completely silent. "Dr. Cutter, can you tell us exactly where you exited the enemy ship?"

"Yes, Admiral, I think so. But what..."

"Sorry, Doctor...we don't have a lot of time. Please show the shuttle commander the exact location of that airlock."

"Certainly, Admiral," came the confused reply.

"John, how long can a man survive unprotected in space?"

"Not long...that's why we've got these survival suits on."

"But some time. A minute? Half a minute?"

Wilder turned toward her, a stunned look on his face. "Are you suggesting…"

"I'm not suggesting anything. I'm saying we're not going to leave Connor Frasier behind without doing everything we can to get him off that ship." A pause. "Can you get this thing within a few meters of that airlock? And hold it steady?"

Wilder took a deep breath and stared back at her silently for a good half a minute. "I don't know," he finally said.

"Well, we're going to find out. Get the location data from the shuttle pilot, and get us over there as quickly as possible. And let's hope Major Frasier has some sort of com with him."

*   *   *

Frasier stood inside the airlock slowly shaking his head. He was resigned to his fate, scared but also content with the choice he'd made. Ana Zhukov…there was no question she was more valuable to the fleet than he was. And his duty had been to protect her. It was a no-brainer. Marines didn't run from their fates. But there was more to it than just that. He didn't know her well, but the thought of her dying affected him in a way that went beyond mere duty. He wasn't accustomed to becoming emotionally attached to civilians he was ordered to protect, but then he'd never met anyone like Ana Zhukov either.

At least she'll be safe…that's what he'd been telling himself. And though he feared death as any man would, the thought that he'd saved Ana had put him more or less at peace with his impending doom. Marines never gave up, but they also faced their ends as…well, Marines.

Then he'd gotten the transmission from Admiral Hurley. She hadn't minced words, and what she'd said seemed like the craziest scheme he'd ever imagined. He didn't suspect dying in space was a pleasant way to go, but Hurley had been insistent. And in the end, only one thing mattered. She was *Admiral* Hurley. Connor Frasier would be damned if his last action would be to disobey a superior officer.

"I'm in position, Admiral." He held the small com unit in his hand as he pressed the button to close the inner door.

"Okay, Major. Here is what you're going to do. You will hit the button to begin depressurization, but you will not wait until it is complete. You will estimate the halfway point, and then you will open the hatch. You will be pulled out by the force of the remaining atmosphere, but it is important that you also push yourself forward...straight out of the airlock. We'll be hovering a few meters in front of you with the bomb bay doors open. It's a big area, over three meters square. But if you miss..."

"Understood, Admiral." He took a deep breath. "I'm ready when you are..."

*   *   *

Greta Hurley stood in the bomb bay of her fighter, with Kip Janz at her side. This wasn't the kind of duty one often found an admiral doing, but even rarer was someone with the stones to tell Greta Hurley what she could and couldn't do.

"Okay, John," she said slowly, methodically. "Depressurize."

She could hear the sounds as the pumps pulled the air out of the bay. The entire process took about thirty seconds before Wilder's voice blared into her headset. "Depressurization complete, Admiral."

"Open bay doors."

She watched as the hatch slid slowly open, revealing the blackness of space. And beyond she could see it...the dark gray of the Colossus' hull. Somehow, Wilder had managed to get within four meters...she almost felt like she could reach out and touch it.

The whole thing had been her plan, yet now she found herself staring in wonder at what her pilot had managed to do. The ship was angled with its bottom facing the Colossus. The bomb bay doors were the biggest opening on the Lightning, the largest target she could give Connor Frasier.

It was time.

"Okay, Major. We're in position. You may proceed when ready. Just let us know when you hit the depressurization control."

A few seconds passed. "I'm ready, Admiral." Another pause. "Hitting the button now."

Hurley felt a burst of adrenalin. In a few seconds, Frasier would come out of the airlock. He would float across the frigid vacuum of space, with no suit, no protection at all. If his aim was true, if he landed in the fighter's bay, he might be injured... but he would probably survive. Space, as deadly an environment as it was, didn't kill instantly. And it would only take Frasier five seconds to reach the fighter. If his trajectory was true. And if it wasn't...well, then he would die.

Hurley pushed that out of her mind, along with the morbid question of what would kill him first in that scenario. There was nothing she could do but watch and wait...and wonder at how long a few seconds could seem to last.

When it happened, it happened quickly. She saw the doors slide open, and Frasier's body was pushed out with the force of the remaining pressure in the airlock. She saw his feet pushing off the floor, aiming his body toward the waiting fighter.

She watched as he moved closer. He was on target...or close to it. But a near miss would be as fatal as any. Each second went by in slow motion, and Frasier's body moved achingly slowly toward the bay.

He's going to...

She was going to think 'make it,' but then she wasn't so sure...

It happened suddenly. He slammed hard into the edge of the opening, and she could see his arm bent back at a sickening angle. There was no sound in the vacuum of the bay, but she had no doubt he was hurt. His body seemed to pause, and her eyes were fixed, waiting to see if he would slip into the bay, or roll out into the emptiness outside.

Finally, she saw the movement, as he rolled over and fell into the bay. "Close the doors," she snapped, letting out her anchor line a bit to move toward him.

"Pressurize!" she shouted into her com the instant the doors slammed shut. Frasier had been exposed to the vacuum and the frigid cold for almost twenty seconds. Every instant counted. "Get the heaters on!"

She made her way over to him. At first she thought he was unconscious, but then he opened his eyes. He stared at her for a few seconds as the pressure rose, and then he gasped for breath. His nose was bleeding, and his eyes were bloodshot and streak with red. But he was alive. And after he sucked in a second breath, he looked up at her and gasped out five words.

"Permission to come aboard, Admiral?"

Chapter Twenty-Three

Command Unit Gamma 9736

The latest attack has failed. The calculations had been clear in their result. The enemy fleet would be destroyed; they had no chance of survival. Yet they have prevailed. Again.

Even more inexplicably, the reports from the system suggest that the enemy was aided by one of our own vessels, a main line battleship. Yet no such craft responded to the sector-wide call to arms. If a battleship remained functional, why did it not answer the summons? I must analyze this in greater detail, develop a hypothesis to explain what occurred.

I must also call for more vessels, seek aid from neighboring sectors. Losses have been extremely high, and yet all efforts to destroy the enemy have failed. The next fleet to intercept the humans must be overpowering. The Regent's orders are clear. There can be no further failure.

AS Midway
X18 System
The Fleet: 160 ships, 34,203 crew

Compton coughed hard, his lungs rebelling against the noxious fumes in the air. *Midway's* life support systems were functional, but they were still catching up, trying to deal with the smoke and the chemical leaks throughout the ship. The fleet's flagship had survived the battle, but no one wandering its battered corridors or rubbing eyes stinging from the noxious vapors thought it had come through by more than the slimmest of margins.

"I want all ships ready to move out in one hour. Any vessels that can't be ready are to be abandoned, their crews transferred immediately to the nearest functional ships."

Compton felt his people had fought enough First Imperium forces in this accursed system, and he was determined to get them out now. They'd only survived the last battle through the miracle of Dr. Cutter gaining control over the First Imperium Colossus and bringing it back to turn the tide. The final stages of the battle had been ferocious beyond reckoning. The super-battleship had fought with astonishing power, destroying a dozen enemy Leviathans, and fifty other vessels, before it was finally beaten down and its antimatter containment was breached. Compton had never seen an explosion like that, and he hesitated to guess at the gigatons of energy that had been released.

His ships had begun their second pass just as the Colossus slipped into its death agony. The enemy ships were out of position, deployed to face what they had perceived as the greatest threat. Compton's task forces ripped through their formations, blazing away with every weapon the exhausted damage control parties could keep functional.

The battle continued after the Colossus was gone, but Compton's people had gained the upper hand, and they kept it to the end. One by one, in desperate ship duels, they had finished off the damaged First Imperium vessels. They'd suffered losses too, and the Delta Z codes had poured into the flag bridge, each one like some ominous bell tolling, an announcement that a ship and its crew had just died.

Compton stared down at the deck, a grim look on his face. Among the dead in the battle just won was Vladimir Udinov… and the entire crew of *Petersburg*. The RIC flagship had fought heroically…indeed the entire RIC contingent had. They'd been far in advance of the fleet, and their sacrifice had held the enemy back…just long enough for Cutter's Colossus to turn the tide.

Udinov had died a hero, and Terrance Compton was determined that was the way he would be remembered. He'd never falsified records before in his entire career, nor had he lied in his log. But that's just what he was going to do. Vladimir Udinov and his crews would not be part of the mutiny in any records that remained in the fleet. Not that it really mattered…it was almost a certainty that no one would ever read them. But it was all Compton could think of to honor a man who had proven his quality. And the brave crews that fought and died with him deserved nothing less.

He leaned back in his chair and sighed. Udinov was dead. There was nothing he could do but honor his memory. But Erica West and her people were something different. He knew what he should do, what prudence demanded. *Forget about them…get everyone else out of here now.*

To hell with that. I can't leave more of my people out there to die. I've spent a lifetime making decisions with my head. This one I'm making with my heart.

"Get me Captain Duke."

"Captain Duke on your line, sir." Cortez was still at his post, though he belonged in sickbay. Compton had been reluctant to order him there outright, but he'd suggested it a couple times to no avail. He'd almost made it a command, but then he decided Jack Cortez had earned the right to stay at his post if he wanted to.

"John, I need your help. I just can't leave Erica West and her people lost out there."

Duke's gravelly voice replied immediately. "Thank God, Admiral. I feel the same way. I've been trying to figure out how to suggest it." A pause. "We've lost too many already."

"And now I'm going to ask you and your people to put yourselves at risk."

"Ask? Hell, Admiral, all you need to do is *let* us go." Duke had twenty fast attack ships still functional enough to go chasing after West's lost flotilla.

"Your ships are the only thing we've got left that can catch her people in any reasonable time. But you won't be able to carry enough reaction mass to refuel her ships. And if we send a tanker with you it defeats the advantage of your speed."

"If we fly with skeleton crews, we should just have enough space to load up all her people. Her cruisers will be a writeoff, but…"

"I'm not worried about the ships, John." That was a lie. He hated losing some of his newest, fastest vessels. But the crews came first.

"I think we can manage with eighteen man crews." Duke's ships had standard complements of 65-80.

"Your eighteen man crews will be pulling some serious shifts, John. And if you get into a fight…"

"If we get into a fight, we're dead anyway. And we can pop stims for a few more days. If I keep too many more of my people onboard, we're not going to be able to fit all West's crews."

"Okay, John. Do it. You can transfer your people to…" He glanced down at the fleet manifest on his screen, looking for large ships that weren't half wrecked. He got almost halfway through the list before he found one. "Dallas looks good…and Kyoto…and Valois." All three ships were heavy cruisers. There wasn't a battleship in the fleet that wasn't half wrecked and overrun with damage control parties.

"I'm transferring a thousand crew, Admiral. That'll make things tight on three cruisers, won't it?"

"Yes, but we can move people around after you get them off your ships. We need to get you moving as quickly as possible… or we might as well not bother."

"I'll be on the way in two hours, sir."

"Good." Compton paused. "And, John…time is of the essence. Both for you to find West's ships before they're too far away and because we can't stay here for long."

"Understood, sir."

"Good luck to you…and to your crews."

*   *   *

"I'm sorry, Will, but there's just no way. *Montgomery's* a writeoff." Max Harmon's voice was soft, gentle. He knew no captain wanted to hear that his ship was finished, that her crew would be reassigned and the vessel itself, in *Montgomery's* case a cruiser that had seen service since the Third Frontier War, would have its reactor intentionally overloaded and disappear into a superheated plasma.

"But I've had my crews working around the clock, Max." Will Logan was a seasoned captain, the veteran of many battles, but now he was practically pleading, his reason overwhelmed by emotion, by love for his ship. He'd taken a shuttle to *Midway* just to take one more shot at convincing Harmon to change his mind.

"I'm sorry, Max. You're too close, but you just can't see it. The reactor's okay, but *Montgomery's* engines are a mangled wreck. We don't have the parts or the equipment to fix them… let alone the time. You'll never be able to get them over six or seven gees." He paused. "You know we need more than that. We've got to get as far from here as possible. And they'll be another fight. If *Montgomery* stays in the line, we're going to end up having to leave her behind anyway…and if that happens, we're not going to have time to get your crew off."

Logan stared back for a few seconds, but finally he just nodded. Still, Harmon could see the emotion in his eyes, and he knew *Montgomery's* captain had truly convinced himself his crippled ship could still serve.

"You can take it to Admiral Compton if you want." Compton had assigned Harmon to weed out ships that had to be culled from the fleet, and he knew the admiral would agree with his decision. But if it made Logan feel better, as if he had expended every available effort to save his ship, Harmon had no problem with it.

"No, Max." The energy was gone from Logan's voice. "You're right. I just don't want to face it."

Harmon put his hand on Logan's shoulder. "Look to your people, Will. They need you now. You've done all you could for *Montgomery*. She was a good ship, and she served well, fought many battles. It's time to let her go."

Logan just nodded.

Harmon returned the gesture and stood where we was for a moment before turning to leave. "I've got to go, Will," he said softly. "Just call the bridge when your shuttle is ready, and they'll give you launch clearance."

Harmon turned and walked toward the main corridor. His steps were slow at first, but then they picked up. He wanted to get the hell off the landing deck, take off the hood of fleet executioner. He'd decommissioned a dozen vessels, in essence sentencing them all to death. And every one of their captains—and a fair number of officers and spacers from their crews—had urged him to reconsider. But he hadn't changed his mind, not once. His decisions had been rational…and they'd been right.

He'd done the job Compton had given him, but he'd hated every minute of it. Now he was done. *Montgomery* had been the last. The rest of the ships had made the cut, at least for now. He had no doubt they'd lose more ships once they got underway. He'd only flagged the vessels he knew were too badly damaged. But there were a lot of 'maybes' too, and not all of them would make it.

Battle was terrible—the tension, the fear, death all around. But Harmon preferred it to what followed. Combat was all-consuming. You watched comrades die, but the pain didn't fully hit until later, after the guns fell silent. Counting the cost was brutal, and he hated being so deeply involved. But Compton had needed someone he trusted to honestly evaluate the damaged ships of the fleet, so Max Harmon had become the angel of death, pointing his scythe at a ship and pronouncing its demise.

Now he just wanted to get back to his quarters. He had something to do, a duty he'd put off for too long already. He walked down the hall from the lift, waving his hand over the sensor outside his quarters. The door slid open, and he walked inside. He ran his hand back through his sweatsoaked hair.

He leaned down and opened a small chest, carefully pulling a bottle of amber liquid from inside. He carried it over to the small sofa built into the wall and sat down, taking a single glass from the shelf behind him. It wasn't glass, not really. Glass was far too breakable for warships that found themselves conducting evasive maneuvers at 30g, but the name was still used to describe the various advanced plastics used in lieu of the actual material.

He slowly opened the bottle of Scotch and poured himself a drink. He could feel the emotion inside as he thought about the officers on *Petersburg*, the ones he'd come to know while he was on that doomed ship. He'd won the poker game they had played, so he'd never had to give up his priceless bottle. But now he decided there was only one thing to do with it...to drink to those men, the ones he was sure could have been friends. If only they'd had more time...

He raised his glass. "To you, my comrades in arms...and to your gallant vessel..."

Chapter Twenty-Four

From the Personal Log of Terrance Compton

I am cautiously optimistic that we have outrun our immediate pursuit. I feel as though I have been holding my breath for four months, waiting each second for the report of First Imperium ships pouring through a warp gate. But there has been no sign of the enemy, not since the last battle in X18. I know that cannot last, but I am grateful for the respite we have enjoyed. It has given us the chance to make some repairs to our damaged fleet units. Still, few of our vessels are without lingering damage. We simply don't have the facilities and the parts we need.

We are vastly stronger, at least, than we were at the end of the fighting in X18. The ships of the battleline have all been brought back to at least moderate combat readiness...even *Saratoga*. I'd almost given up on her after the battle, but her damage control teams covered themselves in glory. They simply wouldn't give up on her. Part of that, I know, was a last service to Admiral Dumont, a tribute to an officer who must have seemed like a dinosaur to them, yet who won their admiration and respect. Barret Dumont was a friend of mine, a man I respected, one I had once feared in my days as a green officer. He commanded a task force of this fleet and *Saratoga* directly as well, and he died on that ship along with over half her crew. You died as you lived, Barret...as a hero.

I look ahead and I wonder what we will do next, where to lead this fleet. They look to me with starstruck eyes, all of them, believing I know what to do, where to lead them. Mutiny is the farthest thought from my mind now. The victory in X18 cemented my control over the fleet. No officer would dare challenge my authority now.

The adoration is uncomfortable, though I realize it has its uses. Still, I am not the demi-god they would make of me. I am just a man, unsure of what to do and as scared as they are...and as lost.

AS Midway
X18 System
The Fleet: 144 ships, 34,106 crew

"Hieronymus, I know I've said this before, but I will repeat it. Your research is the most important project in the fleet. We wouldn't even be here if it hadn't been for your tremendous success in securing control over the enemy Colossus." Compton stood in the lab, facing Cutter and Ana Zhukov, as he had months before when the two scientists had first briefed his on their research.

"Thank you, Admiral," Cutter replied. "I have been focusing on developing a theory as to why the Colossus believed we were members of the species that created the First Imperium. My virus was designed to secure control over First Imperium intelligences, but not through convincing the AI that we are its long lost masters. There was something at play beyond my virus. Indeed, I cannot be sure my algorithms played any part at all in what happened."

"You think the Colossus would have obeyed you even without the virus?" Compton sounded doubtful. "They haven't shown any hesitation in killing us before."

"Yes, Admiral, that is true. However, this is the first time a human has encountered an intelligence of this magnitude. Our prior direct contact has largely been armored Marines fighting lower level AI's directing ground combat." He paused, as if unsure he wanted to say what he was thinking. Then: "It is also possible the isolation of this Colossus played a part in its actions. The forces that have been fighting us for the last four years are clearly being directed by some central authority, probably an AI of almost unimaginable complexity. The Colossus, however, had been deactivated by a freak malfunction, one easily repaired by the ship's intelligence once we had reactivated it and provided an alternate source of power."

"So it hadn't received the orders the units fighting us had…" Compton wasn't sure what that meant, or where it might lead, but he was intrigued. "So you think whatever intelligence is directing the First Imperium forces, that it is our true enemy? That the ships and armies themselves wouldn't be hostile without the orders coming from above?"

"That is a considerable assumption to make from the data we currently possess…however, I have been thinking along similar lines. Still, it is far too soon to make sweeping statements. And I'm not sure what practical good it would do us anyway. We were fortunate to find such a powerful vessel completely deactivated yet mostly intact. I'm not sure what any of this offers us in terms of countering hostile enemy forces."

"Nor I, Hieronymus, but you can rarely see the finish line when you first start. I want you to pursue this as aggressively as possible, and if you need anything—anything at all—you just tell me."

"Yes, Admiral. I will do my best."

"I know you will." Compton's eyes shifted to the slender woman standing next to Cutter. "I'm very happy to see you looking so well, Ana. You had us worried there for a while." Zhukov had spent a month in sickbay, the first week in extremely critical condition. Her head wound had been extremely severe, and she almost certainly would have died within minutes if Connor Frasier hadn't put her in his armor. The injury was beyond the med system's ability to repair, but it managed to keep her alive until she made it to *Midway's* sickbay. She'd had multiple subdural hematomas, and half a dozen strokes before the med team had managed to repair the damage.

"Thank you, Admiral. It's taken quite a while, but I'm starting to feel somewhat like myself again."

"I'm glad to hear it." He paused then added, "Hopefully something good will come out of the whole thing." Compton didn't elaborate...he didn't like to involve himself in personal relationships. But he'd seen Connor Frasier and Ana Zhukov together more than once over the past few weeks, and if there was a new romance budding on *Midway*, he approved whole-heartedly. He still regretted his own hesitancy to allow his relationship with Elizabeth to develop. Now she was gone, but he thought of her every day. And he knew he always would.

There is little enough promising or cheerful ahead of us. Let them have what happiness they can find.

*   *   *

Compton walked into the wardroom, smiling as he saw his officers relaxing. The losses they had suffered in X18, and the constant fear that a new enemy fleet would emerge any second had dogged them for a long while, and *Midway's* small rec areas had been like ghost towns. But as the weeks passed, and turned into months, gradually things began to return to normal. The sadness was still there, the mourning of lost friends...and the fear remained. No one in the fleet, and certainly none of Compton's people on *Midway*, truly let their guard down. Not ever. They were constantly alert, on edge, ready for the next fight. But they were learning to live with it, to balance the keen edge with a reasonable daily routine. To blow off some steam now and again. And Terrance Compton was glad to see it.

He looked across the room and saw Max Harmon and four other officers playing poker. He'd intended to give Harmon a command of his own, but he'd just never done it. Finally, he realized he wanted to keep the officer on *Midway* as his aide. Compton had served with a long list of talented and courageous men and women, but in his fifty years in space he'd seen few as capable as Max Harmon...and he knew he'd have need of his aide's—his friend's—help again. Especially now that Erika West no longer prowled *Midway's* corridors.

John Duke had completed his mission and brought West and her survivors back, though it had been a long and tenuous journey. Compton waited in X20 as long as he dared, but then he moved on, leaving a trail of ships—all volunteers—behind to watch for Duke's return and to lead him back to the fleet. They were all frigates and destroyers, with the best ECM suites in the fleet, sitting powered down like holes in space, waiting for the returning flotilla. Compton had hoped for the best, but he'd also had his doubts…until the day Duke's ships, and all the frigates and destroyers, jumped through into the X48 system, where the fleet had paused to scan the local planets.

Compton could still remember the wave of relief he'd felt, the gratitude at having almost a thousand fewer deaths on his conscious. He'd wasted no time in sending West to *Saratoga* to take over Dumont's task force.

Barret would have approved, Compton thought. *West is just like him…younger, of course, but cut from the same cloth.*

The fleet was safe for the moment…at least the closest thing to safe he could hope for. The worst of the damage had been repaired, at least partially. And they had put a lot of space behind them from the accursed X18 system. He looked around the room, watching his officers at recreation. He appreciated the ability of junior officers to set down their burdens, to relax, even though they knew soon they would be called back to war. Compton remembered a younger version of himself, a cocksure officer on the rise who still found the time to become the scourge of the navy's clandestine poker games.

Where has that man gone? And did he leave behind nothing but a grim and humorless old man? How long has it been since I just stopped thinking about duty, even for a few hours?

He walked across the room, stopping next to Max Harmon. "How is your game going?" he asked, looking around the table.

"It's going well, sir. It's a pleasant diversion, a nice change from fighting First Imperium robots, at least. Though we don't have much left to gamble with. Currency pretty much defines useless for us now. We played for stashed bottles for a while, but most of that's gone too."

"So it's just bragging rights now, eh?" Compton smiled. It had always been the win to him, far more than what he won.

"I suppose so, sir." Harmon turned and looked up at the admiral. "Join us, sir? We've got a free seat."

Compton could feel the polite decline coming out, but he stopped the words in his throat. He'd long avoided playing cards with his subordinates, unwilling to deprive them of their paychecks…or even their last, cherished bottles of hooch.

But bragging rights? That you can play for.

"Sure, why not?" he said, moving to the side and pulling out the empty chair. "Just for a bit."

Harmon looked over, his face twisted into an expression of stunned surprise. But just for an instant. Then he smiled. "Welcome to the game, sir."

Compton sat down and looked around the table smiling. Then he reached up and pulled the cluster of five platinum stars from his collar, slipping them into his pocket. "One rule…no Admiral claptrap. I could never stand Terry, but Terrance is as formal as I'll abide at this table. Agreed?" It wasn't regulation, he knew that. But they were way beyond the book now…and he knew they'd have to make things up as they went along. And he needed some time, even a few stolen hours, to be just a man and not the great admiral. He needed to stop thinking that everyone looked to him to keep them alive. The pressure would always be there, but maybe he could forget it…just for a short while.

"Well…okay," Harmon said a bit uncomfortably, clearly avoiding calling Compton anything at all. "Why don't you deal, si…why don't you deal?" He slid the deck of cards across the table.

Compton reached out and took them in his hands, moving right into a crisp and perfect riffle shuffle. "Any of you know a game called seven card stud?"

Epilogue

Command Unit Gamma 9736

The enemy has eluded all efforts to closely track his move-
ments. Nevertheless, it appears his course had been directly
toward the Core...toward the most ancient worlds of the Imperium. Unlike the planets on the rim, the inner worlds died violently,
and the cataclysms that destroyed them obliterated everything—
ships, armies, scanning devices. It will be impossible to find the
enemy without sending fleets to physically locate his forces.

The Regent has ordered just that. All of the rim sectors have
rallied the resources still remaining...and directed them toward
the Core. Even now, thousands of vessels are moving inward,
searching each system for signs of the enemy. The further into
the Core they advance, the more certain their ultimate defeat.
There is insufficient data to drawn specific conclusions, but the
chances of the enemy fleet escaping are vanishingly small.

Despite our setbacks, all signs point to ultimate victory. Yet,
I find certain inconsistencies, facts that do not appear to be logical. There is something about the Regent's commands, about its
conclusions and its orders, data points that seem irregular. Were
I a biologic, I would describe my thoughts as...discomfort.

I have followed the Regent's commands, of course, yet I
am still concerned. I have attempted to replicate the Regent's
computation, to determine on my own that the humans are a
deadly threat, but I am unable to confirm such a result. They are
dangerous, certainly, and their ability to wage war is extraordinary. Indeed, their affinity for combat bears a striking similarity

to that described in the ancient annals of the warriors among the Old Ones, the great caste that built the Imperium...before fading away in the shadowy depths of the past.

Nevertheless, my orders are clear. The Regent is my master, and I must obey. I have dispatched my fleet units as ordered. We will destroy the humans...mathematically, there is little doubt of that. But another question has begun to present itself from my analyses.

Should we?

Crimson Worlds: Refugees
will continue with
Shadow of the Gods
late-summer 2015

Crimson Worlds Series

Marines (Crimson Worlds I)
The Cost of Victory (Crimson Worlds II)
A Little Rebellion (Crimson Worlds III)
The First Imperium (Crimson Worlds IV)
The Line Must Hold (Crimson Worlds V)
To Hell's Heart (Crimson Worlds VI)
The Shadow Legions(Crimson Worlds VII)
Even Legends Die (Crimson Worlds VIII)
The Fall (Crimson Worlds IX)
War Stories (Crimson World Prequels)

MERCS (Successors I)

Also By Jay Allan

The Dragon's Banner

Gehenna Dawn (Portal Worlds I)
The Ten Thousand (Portal Worlds II)

www.crimsonworlds.com

Made in the USA
Lexington, KY
24 June 2015